Good Friends Are Hard to Come By

First Published in Great Britain 2021 by Mirador Publishing

First edition: 2021

Any reference to real names and places are purely fictional and are constructs of the author. Any offence the references produce is unintentional and in no way reflects the reality of any locations or people involved.

A copy of this work is available through the British Library.

ISBN: 978-1-914965-08-1

Mirador Publishing
10 Greenbrook Terrace
Taunton
Somerset
TA1 1UT
UK

GOOD FRIENDS ARE HARD TO COME BY

A NOVEL BY

DOUGLAS BUCKLAND

CHAPTER 1

I WOKE UP TO SOMEONE pounding on my front door, which was annoying. I live out of town, off the beaten track, so this was an unusual occurrence. It was around eight thirty, the sun was shining, and the birds were chirping, so I figured I may as well get out of bed and see what the problem was. After tugging on an old pair of Levi 505's and a clean t-shirt, I went downstairs, opened the front door, and found a guy leaning against one of the porch posts waiting for me to answer the door. He was just over 6-foot-tall I reckoned, rangy as opposed to muscular, clean-shaven with his long black hair in a ponytail. His complexion was swarthy, but his features were not Latino or Native American. I didn't recognize either him, or the horse he had rode in on, which was standing in my courtyard dropping road apples.

"Can I help you?" I asked.

"That depends on if you're Jebell Rose or not?"

"That would be me, and now that we have sorted that out, who are you?"

"Peio sent me, he's in a bind."

Peio is an old Basque 'sheepherder', somewhere between 50 and 100 years old, who has been squatting on my land since I inherited the place years ago. He is also about the closest thing I have had to adult supervision since I moved back to the States.

"What's wrong with the old coot now?" I asked.

"Well, he fell off his horse yesterday," he replied. "As the horse happened to be standing on the edge of a deep gully at the time, once he hit the ground he just kept rolling to the bottom. By the time I finally found him, after his horse walked back to camp without him, he was in pretty bad shape with a broken arm, an assortment of bruises and dehydrated. I've sorted him out the best I can, but he needs to be checked out properly. He doesn't want to go to town."

"Sounds like Peio. You can sort your horse out beside the barn while I get my first aid kit, then we'll take my truck to fetch Peio. Why didn't you just drive his old Suburban?" I asked.

"Damn thing wouldn't start. The horse didn't need starting and I know how to ride one."

"Makes sense."

We took off heading north. As my house sits on the southeastern corner of my property, I reasoned that Peio would be camped out in his trailer somewhere to the north.

"Where exactly is Peio hiding out these days?" I asked.

"Take the road up to the Bland Reservoir turnoff. Stay on the turnoff until you hit the Butler Mine Road. Go north on Butler Mine Road, and he's about 2 miles up the road."

This also made sense as the meadows up there would be full of grass this late in the spring. Also, there were a few good springs for fresh water, and plenty of deer for Peio to shoot and eat. Eating mutton gets old after a while, say about 2 days.

When we arrived at Peio's trailer, sure enough, Peio was black and blue from top to bottom. His left forearm was broken but splinted. Although he had to be in pain, he was playing the stoic.

"How you doing, you old bastard?" I inquired in my best bedside manner.

"Fine, and you?" was all I got in reply.

"You're lying again. You're black and blue, got a busted arm, and you're so dried out you look even more like old leather than you usually do."

I fed him some Advil, as it was all I had for the pain, while I explained that we were going to take him back to the hospital in town. He argued that he could not go to the hospital since he had no insurance, no identification, and was probably an illegal alien. This I did not doubt. The past five generations of his 'family' of sheepherders had probably been illegal aliens as well, since they really didn't care about rules and regulations and just ran sheep. I had no idea as to who owned the sheep, or who he sold them to, but this set up had been going on for years. I told him not to worry about it, but he had to get checked out. I explained to him that old guys like him were fragile and needed to be looked after. To which he made some gesture with his undamaged hand that I am sure was Basque for the middle finger wave.

I'd thrown an old mattress and a few blankets into the bed of my truck before we left my place. After getting Peio settled in the bed of the pickup, the guy who had been beating on my door, whose name turned out to be TJ, got in the back with him while I slowly drove back to the county road, and then to the hospital in Cadillac Springs.

Once Peio was in the examination room, and I had assured the staff that I would take care of everything, TJ and I drove to the Double Z Bar and Grill and had lunch. The hospital was going to call me once Peio was ready to be collected, so I took the opportunity to find out a bit more about TJ. I really didn't get too far down that road. He was from somewhere in Louisiana, was 32 years old, and that was as far as I got. When I asked how he knew Peio, he said they were family. I refrained from commenting that he didn't look a bit like Peio, and that I didn't know that there were that many Basque residing in Louisiana.

Perhaps a little background is in order. My name is Jebell Rose. I live on an old ranch, comprised of five sections of land, on the Western Slope of the Colorado Rockies. My folks had passed away when I was still in college, courtesy of a drunk driver on I70 several years ago, and the ranch was willed to me at that time. The inheritance also came with several oil leases in the Texas Panhandle around Borger, which keeps me financially independent.

I work as an oil and gas drilling consultant to keep my mind active and to get me out of the house. I'm almost 39 years old, 5-foot-11 inches tall and 175 pounds. I am also a graduate of the Colorado School of Mines in Golden, which is a penal colony cleverly disguised as a university. Shooting, and restoring, or hot-rodding old cars are my hobbies. I stay in shape simply by working on old cars, keeping my place up, and chasing after Rachel. More on that later. I refuse to go to a gym and waste my time and money, so that I can look like a steroid addicted gym rat.

Furthermore, I am going bald on top which does absolutely nothing for my self-image. It is not the 'male pattern' type of baldness where you start thinning at the crown, it is the type of baldness where it looks like you grew through your hair and the middle part of your head, from forehead to crown, is naked. I didn't like it, I felt I was much too young for it, but short of wearing a toupee, getting a 'plug and play' transplant, or spray painting my head, there wasn't much I could do about it.

My place is a few miles outside the town of Cadillac Springs, north and west of

Glenwood Springs. It's an old ranch which was somehow included in the old Mexican land grants in the 1830's. It's a rustic sort of place consisting of the ranch house, the bunkhouse and a barn arranged around a big courtyard. The driveway comes in from the east through a cut in a hill, the ranch house is on the west side opposite the cut, the bunkhouse is on the north side and the barn on the south side. Over the years, since I returned from living overseas, I have renovated the ranch house and the bunkhouse and have rebuilt the barn to use as a workshop. It is a nice little set-up which sits in a bowl, with a rock ridge behind the barn and small hills, with aspen and lodgepole pine, behind the houses.

AROUND TWO O'CLOCK I GOT the call that Peio had been pumped full of fluids, had his arm in a proper cast, had ingested some pain killers, and was ready to go home. TJ and I drove to the hospital and were briefed by the staff on how to handle the patient. We carefully packed Peio into the truck, the cab this time, and drove back to my place. TJ saddled up his horse and rode back to the sheep camp to take care of things there, while I got the spare room set up for my ill-natured guest. Peio was either bitching about being babied or pouting because I wasn't listening to him, but I could tell he was looking forward to a few days and nights of civilization.

While Peio got comfortable on the couch and got the TV fired up, I went to the pantry freezer and got out a couple of sirloins. I also got a couple of potatoes off the shelf to bake. I knew Peio liked a dram or two with his dinner, so I went out to the barn to get a bottle of Laphroaig. I keep a case out there for when Peio visits, or for the rare guest who doesn't like beer.

While I was headed to the barn, I saw something odd. Just on the left-hand side of the barn, where I have a lean-to garage, was the well chewed leg of a deer. Not a piece of leg, the whole damn thing. Judging by the marks on the bone, whatever had drug it up here had a good set of teeth on it. There was a slight depression behind the leg, where the animal had scratched out a place so it could get down on its stomach while it gnawed away. I felt the ground and it was still warm. Whatever it was had taken off when I came out of the house. Note to self: keep eyes open when wandering around the place.

Peio, as you'll remember, was propped up on the couch watching TV. I fixed him a Laphroaig, no water or ice, and grabbed a Coors out of the refrigerator for me. After handing him his drink, I plopped down on one of the two over-stuffed recliners which flank the fireplace and began interrogating him.

"I don't mean to intrude on your CNN, Peio, but who the heck is TJ, and why haven't you ever mentioned him before?"

"It's really none of your business, Jeb. Some people, yourself included, like their privacy," I was told.

"Well, as he is apparently staying at your camp, which is on my property I might add, and showed up on my porch unannounced, I feel that it would only be common courtesy to let me know something about him. He could be a serial axe murderer for all I know."

Now Peio and I have both been around the horn a few times, and although I didn't know his whole story, we both respected each other's privacy and neither of us is much in the way of a conversationalist. I let him run sheep on my land basically because I was doing nothing else with it and I liked his company. I was not asking about TJ to invade his privacy, but I really needed to know something about him in the event that somebody else showed up asking about him.

Peio thought about this for a while, then said, "He was sent to me for safekeeping."

"And why would a grown, healthy man, need to be sent to you for safekeeping?" I asked.

"Have you ever heard of The Crime Family down in New Orleans?"

I admitted that this subject had somehow escaped my classical education. He then gave me the Cliff Notes version, which went something like this; the New Orleans Crime Family was the Mafia based in New Orleans going as far back as people can remember. Carlos Marcello ran the family since the 1950's and made it one of the most powerful crime families in the States. During the 1980's they had some setbacks. After the death of Carlos in 1993, the Feds simply put them out of business.

"I am sure that is an interesting subject, but what does that have to do with TJ and the reason he was sent to you for safekeeping?" I asked.

"Be careful when you ask for information, once you have it you cannot return it, and you are responsible for it."

I pondered his reply, then said, "Peio, I am already responsible for the knowledge that he is staying with you and have now learned that he is somehow involved with an old crime family out of New Orleans. I really think that you should let me know as much as I need to know about him."

Peio twisted around on the couch until he was looking me in the eye and said, "TJ was a button man, a shooter, for the Marcello crime family. He was very, very good at it and never came to the attention of the authorities. When Carlos passed on, TJ lost his 'roof' as the Russians say. That is, he was no longer protected. Although law enforcement is practically ignorant of his existence, some of the crime families who fell on New Orleans after Carlos died may, or may not, be aware of him. I am not one to make judgements, and he was a younger man when he was 'active', for lack of a better word. He is respectful, is a hard worker and has caused me no grief at all. There are not many Basques in Louisiana, but those there tend to get along quite well with the Cajuns. TJ is Cajun. The Cajun community asked the Basque in the area if they knew of a safe place to store TJ and my name came up. We are a tight knit community across the country and I cannot refuse my people. I picked TJ up at the Steamboat Springs bus terminal a month ago. We avoided any CCTV cameras, and he was in a rough disguise, he knows how to do these things. I am keeping him until I am instructed what to do with him or he moves along on his own."

He was still looking at me when he added, "Now you know as much as I do and are responsible for that knowledge."

"Fair enough," I replied. "Why don't you hang on to him for a while, see how he behaves, and let me think about all this. Is he getting in the way of your sheep operation or causing a problem with the other Basque in the area?"

Grinning, he said, "It is hard to inject a non-Basque heathen into our community without causing some friction. That said, he is a hard worker, a quick learner and very quiet. He cannot stay forever without a problem arising, so I could use a plan if you can think of one."

"Let's give it some thought. If you believe he would be someone to keep around, I'll get him sorted out. It would be handy if he has a good cover identity so that I do not have to worry about social security numbers, driver's licenses, background checks and so forth."

"You're not very familiar with this sort of thing, are you? TJ *is* his cover identity; it is solid, and it has been backstopped as required."

And that is how we left it. After a few days of Peio hanging around my house, eating my food and drinking my Scotch, I drove him back to his trailer near the old Butler Mine. When I stopped the truck, TJ came over from the trailer to see how Peio was getting along and thanked me for the help. I really couldn't picture him as a successful button man, but then again, I've been fooled before.

Getting back to my house, I cleaned up the place and was getting back into my truck to drive into Cadillac Springs for groceries, when a Marimba red 1964 GTO pulled into my courtyard. I grinned. This GTO had obviously been restored as a 'numbers matching' car and, to my eyes, was about as close to perfection as an old muscle car could get. The driver had climbed out by the time I got to the front of the car and opened the hood. Sure enough, it had the 389 motor with the Tri-Power setup. This 'Goat' was the real deal, and I was sure that it was one of the original 8,250 produced which came with the six-pack carburation setup as stock. Many considered this vehicle to be the first true 'muscle car'.

"I think I'm in love," I said while drooling under the hood.

The driver by this time had come around and said, "With me or the car?"

To which I replied, "This old girl has the looks and curves of an Aphrodite and the muscle to go with then. You, not so much…"

At this point I took a short jab to the ribs. I banged my head on the hood as I straightened up gasping for breath. I turned and took a good look at the driver. She rents my shop and runs her own restoration business in Cadillac Springs out of it. I used to run my own shop, but she talked me out of it. I originally tried to keep a professional, platonic relationship with her, but as a fit, red-blooded male, with a higher level of testosterone than is considered healthy, I failed miserably.

Rachel Chen is getting close to 30 years old, physically, not mentally. She's 5-foot- 8 inches tall, and 120 pounds of well packaged female, if you like them built for speed, not comfort. She has jet black, glossy hair that falls halfway down her back, black almond shaped eyes, and an olive complexion due to her half-Chinese, half-Israeli heritage. The hair, eyes and complexion are complemented by long, shapely legs topped by a glorious basketball-sized butt which is, in my mind, the perfect size and shape for a female backside. Upstairs, pert and proper-sized breasts, not those disgusting oversized melons which some guys find attractive, detract one's attention from a teasing sense of humor, which hides a volcanic temper.

She is incredibly fit due to her addiction to Bikram yoga, her regular boxing workouts, her weekly Krav Maga session, and her job. Simply put, she is so hot that she could make a preacher kick out a stained-glass window. Today she was wearing an old, faded pair of Levi 501's, my missing 1986 REO Speedwagon Miami River Tour t-shirt, and Nikes. On her it looked incredibly sexy.

"When did you finish her?" I asked.

"Late last night."

"Got a buyer for it yet?" I queried.

"$114,000 from a collector in Nevada. Thought I'd bring it by before I detail it and get it ready to ship."

"Do you really have to sell it?"

"Only if I want to stay in business," which I took as a 'yes'.

"What's next on the agenda?" I asked.

"A 1969 GT500 Mustang, numbers matching."

"Do we have to sell it as well?" I asked.

"I refer you to my previous reply," she replied.

I could see this conversation was getting into a rut, which was eventually going to have me in tears, so I asked Rachel if she would like to go to lunch, or would she prefer to see me naked? She chose lunch.

"Let me get a clean shirt on and I'll follow you back to town."

I went in the house, got a clean t-shirt on, and cleaned up some. Rachel has seen me at my worst, so it wasn't worth the effort to clean up too much, plus I was getting hungry.

The restoration shop sits on the west side of town and is built out of a defunct Sinclair gas station. Once she had the GTO back in the shop and locked up, we took my truck down main street, Roosevelt Avenue, to the diner. I had the usual cheeseburger and fries while she had a chilidog and onion rings. The girl eats like a horse. How she does it I have no idea, but it all ends up in the right places. It must be that yoga nonsense. While she was mopping up the ketchup with her onion rings, I sensed that she had something on her mind.

"What's up?" I asked.

"I can show you better than I can tell you."

We got back in the truck, and she told me to drive to her house. I thought that this might be my lucky day, and that maybe she really did want to see me naked, but it was not to be. When we pulled in front of the house she rents in town, her problem was obvious. One of the main branches, of what was probably a 100-year-old cottonwood tree, had broken off and crashed straight through the roof and into the attic.

"I can see where that would put a crimp in your lifestyle, unless you can work around it," I observed.

I got another jab, in the shoulder this time.

"I need a place to stay while they rebuild this place."

"I've got just the place for you!" I exclaimed. "You can have the guest room at my place, and we can run around scantily clad whenever we feel like it! I think this is an omen, Rachel."

"As enticing as that sounds, I was thinking that I could rent the bunkhouse out at your place until this place is repaired. As frisky as you are, I think it is best that we try to act responsibly and try to maintain a reasonably professional relationship."

I was looking at her as if she was speaking Swahili, so she quickly added, "Okay, perhaps a little friskiness, but I still want my own place, to do my own thing."

In the back of my mind, I knew that I may have a Coonass button man staying in the bunkhouse at some point in the near future, so her staying there wouldn't work. Furthermore, I knew I couldn't turn either her or Peio down. At some point I'd need to explain the situation to her.

"What are you doing for dinner?" I asked.

After she packed up a few bags and threw them in the bed of the truck, we did some chores around town before driving back to my place. She tossed her stuff on the couch in the living room before coming back to the kitchen. I'd already taken two pork chops out, wrapped two potatoes in foil and was starting on a salad. Rachel hopped up on a bar stool on the other side of the kitchen island and watched what was going on.

"Got any cheese to go on that salad?" she asked.

"Cheese makes you fat."

"I believe that earlier, while you were salivating over the GTO, you were of the opinion that I needed more curves, isn't that correct?"

That is considered a loaded question, and as such, should be avoided at all costs. That said, I have been told that I like to live dangerously.

"Well, you could move some of that spongy butt up to your chest I suppose, but other than that, you're looking fine."

She hiked one hip off the stool and took a minute to study her 'spongy butt'. She then got off of the stool and came around on my side of the island, took my hand and placed it on her backside.

"Best give this a test thump, like a watermelon," she said. I gave it a test thump; it was as hard as a soft rock.

"Test thumps are okay, but sometimes I prefer to peel the fruit and check the meat."

"Perhaps later," she replied while returning to her stool. "Right now, I'm hungry and may need my energy later."

“Yeah, why would you require energy later?”

With a mischievous look in her eye she said, “For the guy I plan to pick up in town later, who wants me just like I am.”

“Do I get to watch?” Two can play that game.

CHAPTER 2

RACHEL CHEN AND I GO back a few years, but only became an item in the past year or so. She blew into town like a whirlwind. Girls like her are extremely rare in little towns on the Western Slope of Colorado, well anywhere actually. As I said earlier, she is of mixed Israeli and Chinese descent, a mixture which is as exotic as it is rare. Having a shape that could kill waist high corn only adds to the overall effect. While every unattached guy for miles around was hitting on her, and some attached gentlemen as well, she fended off the advances and made it known she was waiting for me to get back in town. I suppose I should have felt flattered, but I see myself in the mirror every day and am well aware that my GQ days are behind me, assuming I ever had any to start with. You can't lie to yourself. She was all about business.

I had made sort of a name for myself in the auto restoration community, after having entered a few restored vehicles in shows around the region prior to auctioning them off. She, on the other hand, was an artist when it came to restoring muscle cars.

Apparently, she had gotten involved with restorations while in high school back in Washington D.C., where her father was somehow associated with the Israeli embassy. Her mother was a second-generation American Chinese lady working for an IT firm. After high school she attended various trade schools, anything involved with working metal, building engines, hydraulics, auto body repair and so forth. Her folks were fairly well off, and although not too happy about her career choice, set her up with a shop in Maryland for her twenty-second birthday, and off she went. She did well for about 5 years, built up the reputation of the shop, and then for some reason sold it suddenly, came out west, and ended up in Cadillac Springs looking for me.

At the time I was working a contract in Angola on a 28 days on, 28 days off rotation, which is common in the international drilling business. Rachel had to take a room at a local motel for a couple of weeks until I got back into town. Now Rachel is an outgoing kind of girl who draws a lot of attention to herself, much of it unwanted. She is also an only child, and the apple of her father's eye. In an effort to prepare her for the real world, and him being Israeli, he had the guys at the embassy teach her that Krav Maga stuff. For those that do not know what this is, suffice it to say that it is the Kung Fu of Israel. It combines boxing, wrestling, Aikido, judo, karate and whatever else they could throw in the mix. It is an exceptionally effective way to fight. Anyhow, during the 2 weeks she was waiting for me to get back into town, she was accosted in a local bar by a couple of dickheads who felt that she should get off her barstool and dance with them. They ended up in the hospital with a collection of broken bones, and she spent a night in jail. After several witnesses came to her defense, they let her go. Now all the guys, except me, give her a wide berth. As mentioned earlier, it has been said that I like to live dangerously.

I had gotten back from the job in Angola, relaxed for a couple of days, and then went to my shop in town expecting to get some quality time in with a 1954 Buick Super 8 that I was restoring. Much to my surprise, there was a stunningly attractive girl napping in the rocking chair I keep under the old metal awning where the gas pumps used to be. I had not been informed about the woman who had kicked the crap out of two guys at the bar a couple of days ago, so thankfully, I was acting like a gentleman that morning.

"Can I help you?" I asked as I walked around the left side of the building to open the bay doors to the workshop.

While I was pulling the first door up by the chain, she had walked around the shop behind me and said, "Is that a 1954 Super 8, with the 322 nailhead motor?" This got my attention as not many women in their late twenties would have any idea of what the car was, or what motor it had originally.

"Yes, it is," I said. "And how would a young thing like you happen to know that?"

"It's what I do," she said.

"That's an odd statement. What is it that you do?"

"Without putting too fine an edge on it, I restore cars to collector standards. Better than you I might add."

It is not every day that some incredibly good-looking young woman tells you that she can restore a car better than you can. I was getting annoyed at this young tart.

"Do you now? In that case, shouldn't I have heard of you?" I replied trying to get the upper hand in the conversation.

"Have you ever heard of Rachel's Restorations out of Severna Park, Maryland?"

Anybody in the restoration community has heard of Rachel's Restorations, they are one of the top three shops in the country involved in the period correct restoration and sale of muscle cars.

So, I replied, "Who hasn't?"

To which she replied, "I'm Rachel."

You could have knocked me over with a feather. Rachel's Restorations had never posted a photo of the owner on the internet, or on any of their catalogs. Rachel was a ghost. Most people just assumed that it was a name, not a person. To find out that 'Rachel' was a hot young thing in faded jeans was…interesting.

"Okay, I assume that you realize that Rachel's Restorations has never published a photo of the mysterious Rachel, and that most car guys either fantasize about her, or simply believe it is just a name for a shop. Do you have some way to prove that you are 'that' Rachel?"

"Let's go into your office, I bet that you have one of our old catalogs laying around as you seem to be at least somewhat serious about your business." She obviously wasn't going to let up on me.

We scooted past the Buick and into my office, which would have been the front of the old Sinclair station. The glass windows at the front of the building, running from about knee height to the ceiling, had been tinted so that you could watch the traffic on Roosevelt Avenue, while still staying cool with the help of the air conditioner. I had a large desk toward the back door leading to the shop bays, with a couple of filing cabinets behind it. Underneath the front windows, beside the front door, was a leather couch. In front of the desk were two overstuffed chairs. This was more of a meeting place for car guys to hang out in than an office, but it did fair double duty. I noticed that she didn't seem to mind the various 'vintage' tool calendars on the walls. They were really an art form sent to oblivion by the politically correct crowd. I never saw anything wrong with tool catalogs and calendars highlighting the female form, it is simply art appreciation in my book.

I plopped down in the chair behind my desk and Rachel took one of the overstuffed chairs in front of it. I wheeled around in my chair to the proper filing cabinet and pulled out the most recent catalog from Rachel's Restorations, and flipped it onto the desk in front of her.

"Okay, now what?"

She shoved the catalog back in front of me.

"Open it to the inside of the back cover." I did.

"There is a number there for the shop. Call it and ask for Henry, he's the new owner."

I dialed, got a receptionist, and then asked for Henry. A few minutes later Henry got on the line. I put my phone in speaker mode and laid it on the desk.

"Henry, you are on a speaker phone. This is a bit awkward, but I'm Jebell Rose from Rose Creations in Colorado. I have a young lady sitting in front of me who claims to be Rachel of Rachel's Restorations, who I believe you have recently bought out. Is there any way that you could possibly confirm her identity?"

This brought a deep, booming chuckle from Henry.

"Is she a really hot, somewhat oriental looking young thing, that makes you wish you were a few years younger?"

"That's a definite," I said.

"Is she busting your chops?"

"Two out of two, Henry."

"Okay, I'll bet that she's wearing old 501 Levi's. Ask her to show you her tattoo. I'll remain on the phone."

I looked over at Rachel and said, "You heard the man, show me your tattoo."

Unsmiling, Rachel slowly rose from her seat keeping her eyes on mine while she leaned over the desk and addressed Henry.

"Henry, you asshole!" she said. "Couldn't you have asked him to check my scar on my shin? No, you had to pick the tattoo! I am going to kick your butt into next week when I see you again!"

You could hear Henry chuckling over the phone before he replied, "Your scar is pretty common, Rachel, but your tattoo is a definitive piece of artwork. Show him your tat, let him read the menu, but don't let him order!"

Rachel slowly leaned back until she was standing up straight, and unbuttoned her jeans to show a portion of what appeared to be a really nice black lace panty. She then began to slowly roll down the edge of the black lace. At this point she had my full attention. As she continued to roll the edge of her panties down to a level just above the interesting bits, and a little to one side, a nicely inked tattoo of a wasp with either hand wraps, or possibly MMA gloves, appeared. I was studying the artwork intently when the panties rolled back up, the buttons were buttoned up, and the show was over.

"Perhaps you can quit staring at my crotch and tell Henry what you saw," the Ice Maiden said.

To be honest, I had been staring at her crotch. "Henry, there is a well-executed tat of a wasp with gloves on in a very interesting location."

"Well then, that's Rachel. Sad to say, but that is likely the only time you will ever see that wasp. Rachel, I'll call you later tonight to rub it in." With that, Henry hung up.

With credentials like that, it must have been 'the Rachel'. She was now sitting back in her chair. I think she may have been blushing, but hard to tell with that complexion.

"Well, according to the boxing wasp tattoo, you are who you say you are," I said with a grin.

"If you ever, ever tell anyone about this tat, or that I showed it to you, I will beat you senseless. Is that understood?"

"No problem, I've had my fun. What did you want to see me about?"

"I have a business proposition for you. I want to buy out your shop and get back into the game."

I thought about that for a minute, then said, "First, I am not sure that I want to sell the shop as I kind of want to stay in the game myself. Second, if you wanted to stay in the game, why did you sell a perfectly respectable, well known business back East?"

"Jeb, you are gone half the time drilling oil wells. You do this for a hobby, not a business. To answer your second question, I ended up being a business manager and not a restorer. I want to be back where the art and craftsmanship is practiced and appreciated. Plus, I wanted to get away from the East coast, it's too crowded."

I hated to admit it, but she was correct. I wasn't really a big name in the game and treated it like a hobby. True, I had some successes at a few shows and auctions, but it was not something that was going to get me my own TV show or a place at Pebble Beach Car Week. Also, I was still working the drilling arena internationally, which took up a lot of my time.

"Okay, what are you offering?" I asked.

"I'll buy you out straight for a quarter million dollars, lock, stock and barrel. You can keep the 1954 Buick."

Now a quarter of a million bucks may not sound like much to some folks, but you have to remember that this was a defunct gas station in a small town on the Western Slope in Colorado. I counter offered.

"I'll take two thousand a month in rent and fifteen percent of what you make in profit. You pay the bills."

She countered, "Twelve percent and we split the bills."

"Two thousand a month, you pay the bills and I get ten percent of the profit." I countered the counter offer.

"I'll take it," she said while she reached over to shake my hand.

I know, I was not being logical, and that my thinking was somewhat clouded as the girl really turned my crank. The fact is that I didn't really need the money and I wanted to keep her around.

"Who is Henry?" I asked.

"Henry is my uncle. He's a huge Chinese guy who runs a security firm in D.C., who also wants to run a restoration shop as a hobby. Kind of like you. I'm hungry, I'll let you take me to lunch in celebration of our deal." Cheeky little minx.

Over lunch, Rachel let it be known that she was tired of living in the hotel and was waiting for her rental house to be rewired and painted, so needed a place to stay until it was finished. She asked if she could use my bunkhouse until her place was finished. The girl had done her homework that was for sure. She stayed in the bunkhouse for a couple of weeks at this point while waiting for her rental house to be ready. That is also how she knew that the bunkhouse was an option when she stopped by with the 1964 GTO and needed another place to stay.

Getting back to the housing situation caused by the tree branch pile-driving her rented place, Rachel hemmed and hawed all the time I was grilling the steaks and fixing the spuds, but finally came out with it.

"Can I move in to the bunkhouse until my house gets fixed?" she asked.

"The spare bedroom is not an option I suppose?"

"Correct, we both need to act like responsible adults here."

"That would be a first. Can I charge the same rates as the motel?" I enquired.

"Only if I can charge you 'visitation rates' to the bunkhouse."

"You drive a hard bargain, Ms. Chen. Let me think about it. Now eat, you'll be needing your strength," I said with a smile.

During dinner that evening, I explained the situation concerning Peio and TJ. She knew about Peio, and had met him many times over the past couple of years. She was the daughter he never had, and he spoiled her rotten every time he saw her. Rachel knew that I liked my privacy, knew that I wasn't one hundred percent sure about TJ, and knew that I wouldn't let Peio down. She simply accepted the facts. She also graciously accepted the guest room as opposed to rooming in the bunkhouse with TJ. I already owed TJ and didn't really know the guy.

I told her that I would be going back to Kurdistan in 3 weeks or so, and that if she was still here waiting for her place to be repaired that she would have to watch herself. Generally, she is more than up to the task, a retired shooter from New Orleans living next door was another matter. The fact is, if TJ took a wrong step, Peio would be all over him like the white on rice. I do not know Peio's history, but I do know that people tend to treat him with a healthy dose of respect. He is not someone you want to intentionally annoy, for reasons which still eluded me.

The next morning, I woke up early, around seven, got the coffee and scrambled eggs going while waiting for Ms. Chen to get up and running. Taking my coffee out on the porch I saw a streak of black go down the driveway. Whatever it was, it was the size of a small bear, of which there are many about, but it wasn't moving like a bear. This brought back memories of the gnawed-on deer leg beside the barn earlier.

Around eight o'clock Rachel came down the stairs looking ravishing in a pair of Dickies coveralls. Not many girls can look ravishing in work coveralls, but she pulled it off with ease.

"Coffee is hot in the pot, and the scrambled eggs are warm in the oven," I informed her. There was no sign of recognition since she is in zombie mode until that first cup of coffee is down her neck. She grabbed a mug and a plate, filled the mug with coffee, filled the plate with eggs, grabbed the Tabasco, and after liberally dousing the eggs, began eating. After she had a chance to shovel a few forkfuls of egg in her mouth and drink half a mug of coffee, I asked her what the game plan was for the day. She was booked solid getting the GTO ready to ship and getting it on its way. I told her I'd give her a ride to work, do some shopping then come back and do some work around the house. I'd see her later as she could take her own vehicle to her Bikram yoga session after work. This yielded a nod and a full, double overarm stretch, which, even in coveralls, had my full attention, and was a great way to start the day.

"Do you have anything on under those Dickies?" I inquired.

"A real man would take it upon himself to find out," she said.

I came up behind her and ran my hands down her sides. "Did you know that

Dickie coveralls have a slit pocket on each side so that you could reach the pockets of whatever you are wearing underneath?" I asked as I put a hand into the slit pockets on each side.

"Any luck?" she asked.

Well, not as lucky as I wanted to be as she had a pair of cut-off jeans on under the coveralls.

"Not really, your cut-offs are getting in the way."

"Christmas is all about unwrapping the presents, Mr. Rose, keep that in mind. Now unhand me and take me to work, I've got a lot to do."

I brought my 1981 Ford F-150 pickup from in front of the barn, to the front door, and collected Ms. Chen. Chen is actually a Jewish name, although it sounds Chinese, which is funny considering her genetic make-up. I got Rachel to work on time, and for the trouble all I got was a peck on the cheek and a little finger wave as she walked toward the front door of the shop. I take what I can get, and took my time watching her walk away. She does have an exceptional posterior.

After hitting Ace Hardware for some odds and ends I needed around the place, I stopped off at the Safeway to top up on groceries to replenish the larder. On the way home I swung by Al's Gun Shop for a few hundred rounds of cheap 9mm ammo for my practice sessions. Getting back to the house I put things away, made a peanut and banana sandwich, grabbed a bottle of water and headed out to the barn.

The barn, as mentioned earlier, sits on the south side of the courtyard formed by the house, the bunkhouse and the barn. In reality the barn is my workshop. I had to essentially rebuild the barn and pour a reinforced concrete floor. The shop is immaculate and has a large workbench overlooked by windows along the west wall. An open work bay with a hydraulic lift is in the middle and large tool cabinets line the east wall. Along the south wall, on the ground floor, are a variety of tools such as an industrial air compressor, a shot blasting cabinet, a drill press, and a lathe. There is a mezzanine level along the south wall where I keep spare parts, cans of nuts and bolts, gaskets and a gun safe.

Presently the work bay in the middle is occupied by a 1956 Ford pickup that I am hot rodding, not restoring, to my personal specifications. Since I had rented out the shop in town to Rachel, I no longer felt the pressure to go out and find numbers matching vehicles to restore for profit. So, like a kid in a candy store, I now went out to find rolling chassis that I could hot rod to my heart's desire. Less profitable, more fun. I was still making ten percent off of the fruits of Rachel's labor anyhow.

The engine stand now held a 429 Ford Super Cobra Jet engine, which I was overhauling to put in the truck. The engine came out of a 1971 Torino and would be a huge improvement over the original 292 cubic inch motor. Stock, the Torino motor would give me 370 horsepower as opposed to the original motor's 167 horsepower.

I worked on the motor for a few hours before cleaning up and starting dinner. Rachel loves chicken Kiev, and I am trying to learn to prepare it correctly. I prepped the chicken for the oven and was fixing a salad when I heard Rachel drive up in her classic 1976 Whale Tail Porsche 911. The girl does have good taste in cars. I had left my F-150 pickup in front of the barn so she could pull into the lean-to garage on the left-hand side. I heard her Nikes slapping on the porch steps, so I came out of the kitchen to watch her come in the door. This is an event. Previously, after her Bikram yoga workouts in the spring and summer, she would just towel off, hop in the Whale Tail and go to her rented house, which was only a few blocks from the yoga studio. In this case, as she was homeless, she had to come to my place. Fit women in yoga shorts and sport bras are truly a work of art, Rachel was an order of magnitude above that. She gave me a peck on the cheek again, dumped her kit on the couch and asked me what was for dinner. I told her the chicken Kiev was ready for the oven and would take about 30 minutes.

"Just enough time for a shower," she said.

"Depends on if you have help or not," I said.

"If you help, the Kiev will never get finished and we'll end up eating frozen pizza," she said.

"I don't mind sacrificing for the team," I replied, while wondering if I even had any frozen pizza.

"Not this time, cowboy, I want to clean up, eat, and get on your computer to organize getting that GT500 shipped. The GTO is gone, and I need to get work lined up."

"Once again my nefarious plans are foiled," I told her as I retreated back to the kitchen to put the chicken in the oven. I was hoping for better luck later in the evening.

After we had eaten dinner, and while I was washing the dishes, Rachel had retired to the dining room, which I used as an office since I always eat in the kitchen, and began making calls and working the internet to get the GT500 delivered to her shop. After tidying up the kitchen, I went out to the barn, turned on the lights and climbed the stairs to the mezzanine level. Opening my gun safe, I took out my Czech made

CZ75 9mm pistol, the old pre-B model, and carried it down to the workbench. I cleaned and oiled the pistol then set it aside along with two hundred rounds, ready for a practice session tomorrow. Walking back to the house I closed the front door for the night and headed toward the living room, where I could hear the 60" flat screen TV making noise. Getting to the living room I spied Rachel lying on the couch with a glass of wine, wearing one of my old rock and roll t-shirts, and apparently not much else. Sometimes good things come to those who wait.

CHAPTER 3

RACHEL LEFT FOR WORK ABOUT eight the next morning, in a fresh set of Dickies. I was not allowed to check what was underneath, a bad start to the day. I finished my coffee before heading out to the barn to get my pistol and ammo. Climbing into my F-150, I headed north to my personal shooting range. Where the road to Bland Reservoir goes to the left toward Peio's place is a mailbox set on a post. There is not a house within miles, but this is how I pass messages to Peio, as cellular reception is dodgy in this part of the country. I placed a note inside the mailbox asking if Peio and TJ could meet at the ranch for a barbeque next Friday. I wanted Rachel and TJ to meet before I handed over any keys prior to heading back to Kurdistan. Peio and I would provide adult supervision while we watched how the kids got along. Hopefully, they got along fine, and TJ would stay in the bunkhouse, forcing Rachel to remain in the guest room.

That done, I continued north on the county road for a few more miles before coming to a dirt road heading off into the trees to the left. Getting out I unlocked the gate, drove the truck through, then relocked the gate. Getting back into the truck, I drove a quarter of a mile through the trees until I came out in a long meadow. Years ago, I had rented a Bobcat and leveled out the meadow and made berms for a shooting range. I had a pistol range out to 50 yards on the left, a rifle range at 100, 200 and 300 yards in the middle, and a place set up on the right where you can make a 1000-yard shot, if you think that you are capable of it. The shooting stations had a concrete floor with a single, shingled roof extending over the entire firing line. Each range had a proper shooting bench set into the concrete floor. It was a fairly professional set up.

Moving to the pistol range on the left, I set the CZ75, in its carrying case, on the bench along with the four boxes of ammo. Walking down range, I set out three targets at 7 yards then headed back to the bench. I loaded three magazines with five rounds each. Loading a magazine into the CZ, I got into a comfortable stance, adopted the 'thumbs forward' grip and fired five rounds at the left target, changed magazines, fired five rounds at the middle target, changed magazines and fired five rounds at the right-hand target. Ejecting the final magazine and locking the slide open, I set the pistol down on the bench and walked out to check the targets. The left-hand target had four rounds in the black, all within about a 3-inch circle centered in the middle of the target, with one 'flyer' off to the right. The middle target had all five in the black, in the center, in a 3-inch circle. The right-hand target was the same. Not good enough. I kept this routine up until I'd fired sixty rounds and had consistently grouped, in the center of the black, in two-and-a-half-inch circles. I did the same at 10 yards, then at 15 yards. The final twenty rounds I fired left-handed at 7 yards. I kept them all in the black, but it wasn't pretty. I try to get up to my range every week that I am home just to keep my skill level honed. I may never need to use my skill with a pistol, but it is a perishable skill, and you never know when it will come in handy.

Getting back to the ranch, I went into the barn to clean and lubricate the CZ75 before locking it in the gun safe. After that, I got back to work on the 429 motor. Rachel does the Bikram thing 2 days a week, Tuesday and Thursday. She goes to Gold's Gym 3 days a week and does boxing classes with a guy from Philly named Bret Crosby, on Mondays and Wednesdays. Fridays she practices her Krav Maga and beats the crap out of the local MMA wannabees. Bret runs the Gold's Gym in town and is a boxing guru. He's a nice guy, but he has the fastest hands I have ever seen. He's about my size, but several years younger, leaner and meaner. Some Fridays I'll go watch Rachel work out and drink a beer with Bret while she showers up afterwards. It was a yoga night so I knew Rachel would be home late. After working on the engine for a while, I cleaned up the house, did some vacuuming, set out new air fresheners, and was busy cleaning the surface of the stove when Rachel walked in.

"What's for dinner?" she asked.

"Frozen pizza," I replied with a grin. Frozen pizza for dinner was code for 'let's get frisky and forget cooking'. Getting serious I asked, "Have you seen some strange black animal, about the size of a small bear, hanging around the house?"

"Yeah, it's a big dog, I think. I put an old wok with water in it outside the back door to the pantry, in case it gets thirsty."

"You've actually seen it standing still?" Before she could answer I continued, "What do you mean you think it's a dog, it either is or it isn't?"

"What I mean is, if it is a dog, it is a huge dog. It kind of looks like a Belgian Shepherd on steroids. He's cute in a *Hound of the Baskervilles* sort of way," she said.

"How close have you gotten to this thing?"

"He lets me scratch his ears now," was the reply. "But it's taken awhile to get there."

"Does it have a name?" I asked, wondering how far along their relationship had progressed.

"I call him Dog."

"That's an original name for a dog. Didn't put a lot of thought into it did you?"

"Actually, I did," she explained. "In the John Wayne movie 'Big Jake', Big Jake McCandles' dog was named Dog. Any real John Wayne fan would know this. Furthermore, with your age induced short-term memory loss, even you should be able to remember that name."

"Good point. Want to work up an appetite for that frozen pizza?" I asked.

Friday rolled around, so once I got Rachel out the door with a slap on that amazing butt, I got into my truck and rolled down to the Safeway to get the barbeque supplies. I don't really barbeque, which takes skill, so much as grill. So, stocking up wasn't that difficult: steaks, hamburgers, bratwurst, buns, cheese, ketchup, mustard, beer, and mesquite wood briquettes for the grill. On the way out of town I stopped at Gold's Gym and asked Bret if he would like to come out for dinner as well.

Once back at the house, I drug out my grill, which is made from a fifty-five-gallon drum split lengthwise, with expanded metal for the grilling surface. After scrubbing it out with a wire brush, I put it by the left-hand side of the front porch and loaded it with briquettes and mesquite chips. I marinated the steaks, made the burger patties, and ensured that I had enough paper plates and plastic utensils to go around.

About six thirty a beat-up Chevy Suburban drove into the courtyard, and Peio and TJ jumped out. I had a beer ready for TJ, and a Laphroaig ready for Peio. Thinking that it was a good time to do so, I fired up the grill. A little after seven I heard the growl of the Whale Tail out on the county road, and I knew Rachel had arrived. She had freshened up at the gym before coming home and looked stunning in my 1977 .38 Special at Soldier's Field t-shirt, cutoffs and flip-flops. As soon as she had the Porsche safely tucked away in the lean-to garage beside the barn, she came flying straight at Peio. She wrapped her arms around his neck and gave him a big kiss on the cheek. Peio acted like he was embarrassed by this show of affection, but actually he eats it up. He adores Rachel and she has him wrapped around her little finger. Rachel just loves the old guy and treats him like a king. It's disgusting behavior from an almost grown woman, if you ask me. Peio was in the process of introducing Rachel to TJ, when Bret showed up in his 1966 Impala SS low rider. It had been tricked out by Rachel and was a sweet ride. Bret is black, so he has rhythm, style, dresses properly, and acts the clown when he is rolling in his Impala.

"Hey," I yelled at him over the cammed up idle of his 427 motor, "are you lost? There aren't any pool halls or gyp joints around this neck of the woods."

"Heard you white folks were having a barbeque, no way you know what you are doing with barbeque, so the brothers sent me to rescue you from a culinary disaster."

"Us white folks don't barbeque, we grill," I told him while I handed him a beer as he got out of his car.

"Let me introduce you around. The homely lass in the shorts you know." Rachel punched me in the shoulder again.

"The rangy long-haired dude is TJ, he's new around these parts. I think you may have heard about Peio there, the octogenarian who is drinking my Scotch."

Bret gave Rachel a big hug, told TJ he was pleased to meet him, then said to Peio, "It is a pleasure to finally meet you, sir."

Now this surprised me. I had no idea that Bret had any idea as to who Peio was, nor did I expect the formality from Bret. He never acted formal to anyone as far as I knew. Running a gym, he probably ran into some who skated along the edge of the law. TJ, I knew was a skater. I began to realize that Peio might be a skater as well. Interesting.

Regardless, there were steaks, burgers, and brats to grill. Since it was my place, I needed to get busy. There were a couple of old couches on the porch along with a couple of old upholstered chairs, so everyone got comfortable, with a beverage of their choice, while I slaved over a hot fire.

After everyone was fed, they all helped with the clean up before finding a comfortable spot to relax on the front porch to let the food digest, facilitated by beer and conversation. That is everyone except Peio, who had another few fingers of Laphroaig to assist digestion.

Getting down to business, I told everyone that Rachel would be staying at my place until her house was repaired. This caused the rolling of eyes and some "cradle robber" comments, which I ignored. I then told everyone that TJ would be staying in the old bunkhouse until he got settled into the area. Bret raised his beer to TJ and told him if he needed a gym, to come see him.

"Does anyone foresee a problem with this arrangement?" I asked.

TJ brought up the point that the neighbors may start talking about a newcomer to the area that is suddenly staying at the home of a 'local', along with a semi-attractive local woman. He took a shot to the shoulder at this point, although not as hard as the ones I seemed to receive.

"I've taken care of the neighbors," Peio responded.

I had known Peio for a few years now, and although I knew he had better connections in the area than what you would normally expect from an old Basque sheepherder, I was starting to get the idea that there was a lot more to him than met the eye. He came and went all over my property like he owned it, which was fine as I was not using it for anything. He rarely went into town, so I did his monthly grocery and miscellaneous shopping in town. I thought he just didn't like crowds. I was getting the impression that there may be another reason.

"Peio, I think we need to talk before you retire for the evening."

CHAPTER 4

AROUND NINE O'CLOCK THE PARTY broke up. TJ went to the bunkhouse to check it out before heading home, Rachel went upstairs, Bret got in his pimpmobile and headed back to town leaving just Peio and I on the porch.

"Peio, I don't mean to pry again, and I know you'll either tell me or you won't, but I get the feeling from a few things which have been said, that you may be a little more than an elderly Basque sheepherder that camps out on my place. Don't get me wrong, you are more than welcome to stay where you are as long as you like, I'm just trying to get a feel for what is going on around here."

This drew a stern look from Peio, which eventually mellowed.

"I guess I do owe you some sort of an explanation, but again, be very careful when you ask for information. Once you have it, you are responsible for it."

I nodded that I understood the implications of receiving whatever information he was about to give me. I felt that I really needed to know who I was surrounding myself with as it seemed my place was becoming the center of a unique group of people, and I needed to know as much about them as I could find out.

"You will need some background first. I was born in the Basque region of Northern Spain in 1948. I was raised until I was 15 in a village outside of Onati. At that time my parents, like yours, were involved in a fatal traffic accident. I, again like you, was an only child. My father's brother came to the funeral and suggested that I should go live with him in Bilboa. I did not realize at the time that my uncle was involved with the Cosa Nostra, and I would not have cared in the least. There were good schools, abundant food, plenty of girls to chase, and opportunity. I attended what you would call high school in Bilboa, graduated, then attended university in Spain. I found that I had a gift for languages and took a degree in civil engineering."

Peio reached for his drink while considering how to proceed.

"While I was attending university in Spain, my uncle would visit often and we would take in the cinema, visit the tourist attractions in Spain, and sample the various local cuisines. On each visit he would introduce me to certain people. I was told that these people would be important to me later. Suffice it to say that I was being groomed for the Cosa Nostra. Do you know much about the Cosa Nostra?" he asked.

"Just the general Hollywood version. I have never really looked into them."

"There is much information about this organization, which is incorrect, and further tarnished by what you see on TV. The Sicilian Mafia was a well-organized crime syndicate built around the 'family' or clan, which is called a cosca. Each family was given sovereignty over a territory, or perhaps a certain racket within that territory. Needless to say, as a non-Sicilian, I could never have attained any real rank within the organization, and I really did not want to become a criminal. I became an arbitrator, which is one who would oversee business deals and arbitrates disputes between the various coscas. I was ideal for the role as I was not associated with any 'family', was well educated, and spoke fluent English, Spanish, French and Italian."

After another sip of Scotch for lubrication, he continued. "I traveled extensively around Europe and America settling disputes and organizing deals between various crime syndicates and the Cosa Nostra. I became fairly well known within the criminal community without ever committing a crime. But that did not last."

He continued, "There are some crimes which are forbidden within the Cosa Nostra, people are generally not aware of this. Theft, including burglary, muggings and kidnapping are forbidden. I do not know why this is, but it is so."

At this point Peio seemed to hesitate before continuing.

"While I was organizing a deal between an Irish American gang in New York City and the local cosca, a disaffected Irish group decided to enter the negotiations by kidnapping the wife of one of our lieutenants. This was a foolish act not only because the husband was not in a decision-making capacity, but it also terminated the enterprise and required a response. Remember, kidnapping is forbidden. I happened to know both the husband and the wife and had been to dinner with them several times. She was young and pretty, and with the enterprise now a failure, I expected the worst from the kidnappers."

Taking another drink of Laphroaig while organizing his thoughts, Peio continued, "Keep in mind that I was not a vicious criminal. Most people knew that I was more of a businessman than an active participant. That said, I had taught myself weapons, shooting and how to pass myself off as something that I was not. I had many tutors. I went into the Irish part of town posing as something other than what I was. I kept in touch with our people and kept my ears open. Eventually I discovered where they were keeping the woman. After staking the place out overnight, without sanction from my organization, I went to the warehouse early the next morning, and simply rang the bell. When the door was opened, I shot the man in the door with a suppressed pistol. I entered, kept walking forward, and shot four other hoodlums before I found the woman chained to a bed in a storage room. She had been abused. I cleaned her up as best I could. I told her that we had to go quickly, but I needed to find a vehicle first. As she was naked, I gave her my overcoat, then we walked back through the carnage. I checked each body for keys and ended up with three sets. Going back into the warehouse I saw that there were several cars parked inside. I keyed each fob, when I saw the lights flash on a car near the bay door, I placed her in the back seat laying down. I then pressed the button to open the bay door and simply drove her to her home, where I explained the situation to her husband."

Another sip of Scotch.

"You realize that by taking this action on my own, I could no longer go back to the Cosa Nostra. I had taken action without approval, I had killed five people, and I had upset the balance in New York. Under the circumstances, the organization allowed me to walk away peacefully. I had cultivated friends within the Basque community in New York and utilized them to get out of the city and set up a new identity within the Basque community in Nevada. Organized crime is still entrenched in that state, so I could not remain indefinitely. I came here, found your ranch vacant, and moved onto your property in the guise of a sheepherder."

Peio took a healthy hit of Scotch, raised the glass and studied it before turning to me.

"Now you know the highlights of my story. I would fully understand if you would like me to vacate your property."

I thought about this for a minute while I digested his story.

"Peio, this really doesn't change a thing as far as I'm concerned. Everyone has a back story, although I must say that yours is far more interesting than most. Feel free to stay as long as your heart desires, and as long as it holds out," I said with a grin.

"That's good, young man as I really do not have anywhere else to go, and making you disappear would only cause problems," he said somewhat seriously before grinning as well.

"Okay, since that's out of the way, how are you getting home?"

"I am staying in your guest room tonight and TJ can come back and fetch me in the morning."

"Well, we may have a problem with that. Rachel is staying in the guest room at the moment."

"Even more reason to stay the night," he said with a grin.

"Don't push your luck, old man. I had better go re-arrange the arrangements. Finish your Scotch and I'll come fetch you when your accommodation is ready."

CHAPTER 5

THE NEXT MORNING, I WAS up earlier than my two houseguests, so I made the coffee, mixed the batter for buttermilk pancakes, chopped up enough bananas to keep everyone happy, got out the butter and syrup, and began the pancake assembly line. Once the first cakes were in the skillet, I went up to my room to roust Rachel and told her to get ready for breakfast, then went across the hall and beat on Peio's door. At about pancake number twenty-two, Peio came down the stairs, heading for the coffee machine. We are a coffee addicted bunch. I placed five cakes on a plate and set it down on the island for him. While he was adding butter, syrup and bananas to the pile, Rachel decided to grace us with her presence. As I said earlier, she is mobile, but comatose, until she gets that first cup of coffee down her neck. While Rachel was reviving and Peio was going onto round two of the cakes, I made myself a plate and sat down.

"Peio, I've thought about it and there is no reason that TJ can't move into the bunkhouse whenever he wants, so I'll leave that up to you. I'll be heading back to work in a little over a week, so just get in touch with Rachel when you decide to move him on down the road. This will give Rachel time to air the place out and to practice her housekeeping skills."

Rachel was at the other end of the island, which ensured that I did not receive either a shot to the shoulder or the ribs, although I did get 'The Look'.

The bunkhouse is really a misnomer these days as I had rebuilt and remodeled it at the same time that I did the old ranch house. It was now about a 1,500 square foot apartment, although it still retained the wide and narrow dimensions of the original bunkhouse. It really is not a good idea to have a place like that sitting empty, so I had no problem with TJ moving in as soon as possible, as long as he took care of the place. Plus, the longer he stayed there, the longer Rachel was stuck in the main house.

Peio replied around a mouthful of pancake, "If that's the case, he can move in tomorrow. He's cramping my style at the camp, just not enough room."

I found this amusing. When you think of a Basque shepherd roughing it in a camp, you think of one of those 7-foot by 12-foot shepherd's wagons you see on the History Channel. Peio's 'wagon' was actually a double wide trailer that he somehow hauled up the Butler Mine Road. He had also hauled in an industrial-sized diesel-powered generator, and had internet access. The double wide was decked out with every modern convenience you can imagine, and I am sure that this is where Peio held court. I just didn't know who the other courtiers were.

But Peio had a point. At his age, which I now knew to be 70 years of age after our talk on the porch last night, and being on his own his entire life, anybody within a mile or two would be cramping his style.

"Okay, I'll switch on the power and open the water line to the bunkhouse this morning and have a talk when TJ comes to collect you."

At this point, Rachel pipes up and says with a smile, "I guess my habit of sunbathing in the nude won't cause any problems then?"

At this, Peio coughed up some pancake and turned beet red. Rachel apologized profusely and said she was joking. As I collected the dishes and started to clean up, I kept forming a mental image of the nude sunbathing as, to be honest, I had never witnessed such a thing. Something to look forward to.

TJ showed up in the Suburban about ten thirty while the three of us were having coffee on the porch enjoying the Saturday morning sun. I fetched him a cup of coffee and told him that Peio was kicking him out and he could move in tomorrow. After they left, I tried to talk Rachel into sunbathing in the nude but was told that she was heading into town to do some shopping, clean out the shop, get ready for the arrival of the GT500, and maybe have a boxing workout with Bret.

I said, "What about a wrestling workout here on the living room floor? I could teach you a few moves."

"You must be joking," she said. "Every time we wrestle, I win."

"What happens every time after we wrestle?" I asked.

She thought about it for a minute, until it dawned on her what I meant, then blushed beet red.

"That's right, Sweet Cheeks, if the ends justify the means, then I would have to say that I win, every time!"

Rachel got ready and drove to town, and I got back on breaking down that old Torino 429 motor. I had it totally apart by noon and loaded the engine block into the back of my truck by using the chain hoist in the barn. I needed to get the block and the heads acid soaked so that it would be ready to put back together when I returned from Kurdistan. I had ordered the rebuild kit from Barnett, and it should arrive while I was away.

I drove over to The Foundry Machine Shop and dropped off the block. I explained what I wanted done and asked them to give me a call when it was finished. I then went to the K-Mart to stock up on the usual toiletries required for a month at work, then drove over to the restoration shop. Rachel wasn't there so I drove over to Gold's Gym to make sure Bret wasn't horning in on my action. Sure enough, Rachel was in the ring with Bret. She had that boxing body armor on, but Bret was not going easy on her. She hates it when people treat her like a girl. What Bret has learned over the years is that if you keep pummeling her with the boxing, she gets annoyed and reverts to that Krav Maga stuff, which boxing was never intended to deal with. Bret pushes her right to the edge, then tells her to cool down. I think that he is the only one she ever listens to.

Anyhow, I stole a beer out of the refrigerator in Bret's office, pulled up a folding chair by the ring, and sat down to watch. After a while, they had pummeled each other sufficiently to call it quits. Rachel went off to shower up while Bret grabbed a beer and pulled a folding chair over by mine.

"You do realize that the woman you live with is an extremely dangerous piece of work, and that if you do not behave yourself, she'll likely put you in traction?" Bret informed me as he drained half his beer.

"I revel in living dangerously, Bret, it just adds spice to the romance."

"Can I get on your life insurance policy?"

"Let me think about it. You'll have to take a number and get in line."

Rachel appeared in her uniform of faded jeans, only 501's allowed, flip-flops and my vintage, mint condition, 1995 Lynyrd Skynyrd '*The Last Rebel Tour*' t-shirt.

"Hey! That shirt has been missing for months now. You should take it off immediately and give it back to its rightful owner," I demanded.

"Well, I could, but I'm not wearing a bra."

"If it's not your shirt, proper etiquette suggests that you should really give it back," Bret said with a lascivious look on his face.

I was sure he had an ulterior motive and I needed to revise my demands at this point.

"Okay, as a scholar and a gentleman, I will allow you to retain your modesty, and my t-shirt, until we are safely back at the house and away from this lecherous gym rat."

Bret looked at me as if I had stolen his birthday present. "You gutless wonder! This is a matter of principle. Tell her to take it off now, while I watch!"

Bret received 'The Look', and decided it was time to go do some paperwork in the office.

Rachel had some tidying up remaining at the shop, so I went home and got some leftover burgers out of the refrigerator. While waiting for Rachel to show up I grabbed a beer and parked on the couch to watch 'Forged in Fire' on the History Channel. This is a manly show which I find interesting. I am sure I could forge a sword or a battle axe but needed more tutelage. Eventually I heard the Whale Tail approaching, then Rachel walking up the porch steps and in the front door. She dumped her kit in the foyer and came over by me and sat on the couch.

"What's for dinner?" she asked.

"Leftover hamburgers. I didn't feel like cooking."

"A lazy bastard, aren't you? Although leftover burgers happen to be a favorite of mine, so you're safe."

"Bret was beating you like a drum this afternoon. You were hitting like a girl." I had a plan.

I got 'The Look', followed by an annoyed half-Chinese, half-Israeli supermodel launching herself at me and knocking me off the couch onto the floor. When all was said and done, although I was fairly pinned at one point, I had once again won the wrestling match, if the final round justified the means. This match depleted our energy reserves, so we replenished them with the previously mentioned leftover burgers and beer, as opposed to the usual frozen pizza post-wrestling feast.

CHAPTER 6

TJ, PEIO AND THE OLD Suburban showed up around ten o'clock Sunday morning. While Peio went in to say hello to Rachel and drink coffee, I helped TJ unload his personal belongings from the Suburban and take them into the bunkhouse. TJ didn't really have a lot of stuff, a large hard sided suitcase on wheels, a couple of old military duffle bags, a briefcase-sized Pelican waterproof case, and a couple of rifle cases. I was curious about the contents of the last three items.

After stowing his kit, I showed TJ where the fuse box and the water supply valve were located. I also made sure that he had a full set of keys, showed him how to work the security system and gave him the codes. We then trooped over to the house where I poured a cup of coffee for myself and TJ before sitting down at the kitchen island to chat with Rachel and Peio. Rachel was telling Peio that he really needed to upgrade his accommodation as an old double wide trailer simply was not appropriate for a man of his position and station in the community. I had no idea what his position was except that it mandated drinking my Scotch.

Peio was saying, "You are correct, but where would I put down roots at my age? Where would I build a house, and where would I get the money?"

"Well, first off you can't move too far away from us. Secondly, I am sure that the old bald guy across the table would be more than willing to let you build somewhere on his property, most of which he doesn't use in any case. Isn't that right?" she said. The last part combined with an insincere smile and a narrowed gaze that could freeze water.

"I'll need to think about this, if you don't mind. Giving away my inheritance is not something to take lightly," I said in an effort to avoid the issue.

The minx was giving away my land! How did this happen? On the other hand, if I did not sort out a place for her old 'Uncle' Peio, I might find my social calendar, and my bed, strangely unfilled for days, weeks, or months to come.

Peio, sensing the direction the conversation was taking, and being the gentleman that he is, stood up to take his leave.

"Rachel, I appreciate your concern, but I am fine where I am at for the moment."

I noticed that he qualified his statement to keep the option open. Crafty old bastard. I knew there would be further plotting between them while I was away in Kurdistan.

After we walked Peio out to the Suburban, and he headed home to his unsuitable trailer, I asked TJ if he needed any help getting settled in? He said he had it under control.

"What are you going to do about a vehicle?" I said. "I expect you'll need to get in and around town."

"You've already done enough, but if you had something laying around that you are not using, I'd be happy to rent it."

"Come with me."

Just to the side of the lean-to garage where Rachel was presently parking her Porsche, I had a vehicle under a tarp. It was what I had used when I first took over the place years ago. Grabbing the corner of the tarp I yanked it off and asked TJ what he thought about it.

"What is it?" he asked.

"What you see is a mint condition 1950 Chevy five window pickup with a rebuilt 235 straight six, four-speed with granny low, and a state-of-the-art sound system," I proclaimed. "A veritable chick magnet. You'll need to re-tag it and get insurance, but it is reliable. That said, I reckon you'll need to find a job to go to first."

He looked a bit sheepish, then said, "Actually, Rachel offered to let me help her around the shop until something else comes along."

"Fair enough I suppose, as long as you are actually doing some work, and don't get too friendly with the boss. I might get jealous or something, you know, the usual," I said, half joking, but not really full-on joking. You've got to set parameters for these button men or else they'll run all over you.

The next week and a half went by fairly normally. Rachel got the 1969 GT500 bedded down in her shop, and her and TJ got busy stripping it down to the frame. Bret was running his gym, and Peio was doing whatever Peio did when we weren't around. I'd driven up by our mailbox a few times, but the flag wasn't up so I knew that there were no new messages. I'd gotten the call that my block was ready, so I went over to The Foundry Machine Shop and picked it up. After driving home, I got the block out of the bed of the truck and installed it on the engine stand in the barn. Since I was leaving shortly for work, I didn't want to get into the actual rebuild yet, not to mention the rebuild kit had not arrived yet. Once you get into the actual rebuild, it becomes a Zen thing and you really want to get it done in a single blast of energy, stopping only for food, drink, bathroom breaks, and perhaps a wrestling match with Rachel as time permits. Engine rebuilding, like cleaning guns, and sharpening knives is a stress relieving activity for me.

Rachel's rental house was not ready, and would not be for a few months, so I had her as a captive audience for a while. I'd be gone for a month or two during that period while I was working abroad. She had nominally settled in to the guestroom once Peio had left, which is a bit weird for a non-platonic relationship, but it worked out fairly well as she had her own schedule to follow and she still exercised her 'visitation rights', without the threatened rate hikes, often enough to keep the edge off.

TJ was more or less just keeping to himself at the bunkhouse, but he had a standing invitation for dinner each night, and usually took us up on it. Afterwards he and I would down a beer on the porch as it got dark and got to know one another a bit better.

One night I finally worked up the courage and asked, "What was in those cases you had when you moved in? They looked like long and short gun cases."

He thought for a minute, then replied, "Peio let me know what he told you regarding my background, and that is all that you really need to know at this point. So, without going into detail, those are my old tools of the trade. Needless to say, I don't use them much anymore, but I like to keep in practice and keep the muscle memory in shape. I am fairly handy with the pistols and carbines, but I am trying to work on my long gun skills."

This was right up my alley and I felt this would be a good male bonding opportunity.

"I don't suppose that Peio told you that I shoot quite a bit and, like yourself, still practice to keep the muscle memory intact. I further don't suppose that Peio told you about my shooting range, did he?"

"Must have slipped his mind. You realize he's getting to that age."

"I've got to start tightening things up around here so that I can get away for my next hitch in Kurdistan, but if you can get the morning off from the tyrant you work for, we can do some shooting tomorrow morning."

The next morning, bright and early, I knocked on the bunkhouse door and stood back to watch the sun rise while I waited for TJ. Eventually he came out carrying the briefcase-sized Pelican case and one of the long cases. We put those in the bed of my F-150 along with my stuff and drove up to my shooting range.

Once we had arrived at the range, TJ looked around, whistled, and said, "Nice."

He opened up his little Pelican case and nestled in black foam were two pistols, a Glock G19 compact in 9mm and a full-sized Glock G17 in the same caliber. Both were threaded for the suppressors which were also nestled in the foam beside them. The suppressors were Gemtech GM-9's, which are very high-quality items. I noticed that the Glocks both had raised sights to allow for sighting over the suppressors when they were screwed on. The only pistol that I had brought along was my Czech CZ75 pistol. As all three pistols were 9mm, I had brought enough for both of us. I noticed what I thought were a few boxes of subsonic rounds in TJ's Pelican case. Coupled with the suppressors I got the feeling that he didn't like a lot of noise served with his shooting.

We set up some targets at 5 yards, 10 yards and 15 yards. I went first at 5 yards and managed to get all five rounds in a 2-inch circle in the black. TJ stepped up to the bench, racked the slide on his Glock G17, and fired five rounds so fast it seemed as if the muzzle blast was a single rolling sound. He had managed to put all five rounds in a hole that may have measured one inch across. We then shot at 10 and 15 yards. While my grouping spread out some, TJ's stayed tight at one-inch groups. To say that TJ had impressive skills with a handgun would be an understatement, which I suppose should have been expected considering his previous line of work.

I asked him what I needed to do to tighten my groups and get my shots off quicker.

"You're a good technical shooter, but you need to develop the instinct. You are still trying to line up the front and rear sight mechanically, as opposed to concentrating on the front sight and letting your subconscious worry about the rear sight. This is common in recreational shooters. We'll work on that when you get back from Kurdistan."

We put up the short guns and got out the long ones. TJ flicked the latches on his case and when he raised the lid, I recognized a Larue OBR in 7.62mm, with the 16-inch barrel. A very nice rifle. I flipped up the cover on my case.

"Nice. What is it?" TJ asked.

"That, my friend, is an Ed Brown custom made tactical rifle in 7mm Remington Ultra Mag. A 704 positive feed action, a 26-inch Shilen Number 6 Contour barrel, a Shilen jeweled trigger, all topped with Nightforce NXS 3.5x15 optics. The reticle is the NP-R2 format for those of us civilians who think in minutes of angle as opposed to military mildots."

"I thought Ed only made custom 1911 pistols."

"Most people do, and that is what he concentrates on now, but at one time you could get a custom rifle from him as well. This is one of his last ones."

We got in the truck and drove down the right-hand range to the 500-yard marker and set up two targets. Driving back TJ said that if he could consistently group in a 5-inch circle at 500 yards he'd be a happy man. I didn't bother to tell him that a 5-inch circle at 500 yards was shooting what is termed 'minute of angle' groups, which is pretty damned good in anybody's book.

"I didn't notice any optics in your case, you won't be able to hit squat at 500 yards without good glass," I commented.

"Yeah, I know. I damaged my Schmidt & Bender 3x12 Ultra Bright a few years ago and have been too busy staying below the radar to get it repaired. Mostly I have been practicing with the flip up iron sights at 100 yards."

"Alright, I'll stop at the 100-yard marker and you can run over to the middle lane and put up some targets there that you can work on later." Which we did.

After getting back to the firing line I set up on the sandbags. I also got out my old spotting scope and gave it to TJ so he could call my shots out to me. Getting set behind my rifle I took my time, controlled my breathing, made sure the rifle was not canted and squeezed off a round at the left-hand target at 500 yards.

"High and to the left at the edge of the black," TJ called.

On a cold bore first shot, before the barrel heats up, this can happen. I jacked in another round and set back up. I squeezed off another round and waited for the call.

"Nine o'clock at the edge of the ten ring."

I fired off another fifteen rounds, in groups of three, and had the rifle dialed in at sub minute of angle groups when I had finished. I loaded up five more rounds and let TJ shoot. He managed to hit the target with three of the rounds and seemed to be embarrassed at his performance.

“Nothing to be ashamed about. The fact that you are not a distance shooter, and you still managed to even hit the target at this distance, is pretty impressive. Long range shooting is simply technique, physics, and practice,” I assured him.

Moving back to the 100-yard range in the middle, TJ picked up the Larue, locked in a magazine and fired ten rounds using open sights and shredded the black on the target. I think he was either showing off or making up for the 500-yard shots. Regardless, this was impressive shooting over iron sights. Now I took the Larue, put in another magazine, took my time squeezing off the rounds, and managed to hit the paper with most of the rounds. Not my best outing, but I don’t usually practice with a carbine and open sights.

TJ smiled. “In the case of short-barreled rifles, it is not really technique and physics, just practice, practice, practice.”

“Alright, when I get back, we’ll need to get up here on a regular basis then.” I was a little annoyed at my performance with the carbine and was determined to get better with it. We policed up the brass, took down the targets and headed home. On the way back I asked TJ about the suppressors in his case.

“The vast majority of the time, in my old line of work, it was going to be up close and personal, and usually in an un-secluded location. Suppressors don’t really silence the gunshot at all, they simply bring the decibel level down to the point where it is easily lost in ambient noise and make it difficult to tell where the shot is coming from. Not at all like the movies. You still need a valid exit strategy,” he explained.

We were just enjoying the scenery on the way back, but I could tell he wanted to say something further.

“What’s on your mind, TJ?”

“After what Peio told you, you may have the impression that I was nothing but a hitman. To some extent, that is accurate. What has been left unsaid is that I never hit a civilian, that is, someone not in the crime game, and I never caused collateral damage. Like Peio, I was never going to be a part of the ‘family’, I had no connections and was generally working as a consultant on a call-out basis. If one of the ‘made men’ was getting out of line, or someone in any of the syndicates was not behaving by the rules, I’d get called in as a last resort.”

He continued, “I would appreciate it if you explained this to Rachel at some point.”

“Okay, mate, we’ll leave it at you were a hitman of hitmen if anyone needs to know. Personally, I don’t foresee the question coming up. We all have a history, you, me, Rachel, Bret and Peio. It is really up to you as to how much you want the others to know, but I can assure you that as long as you have their backs, they'll have yours. That is all that they are interested in. You'll see that the longer you hang around."

We got back to the house and took the guns up to the barn to clean and lube them. Once we had finished, I made some ham and cheese sandwiches to eat on the porch. There was a jug of sun tea Rachel had left on the railing, so I brought out some glasses of ice as well. We didn't feel the need for conversation so just ate and enjoyed the rest of the morning.

Around noon we heard the roar of the Whale Tail coming up the county road, so we waited to see what the occasion was, since Rachel rarely came home at midday. She made a sweeping turn and ended up at the steps to the porch.

"What are you two good for nothing rednecks up to?"

"Just finished showing the bald guy how to shoot," TJ said.

"What are you doing here at noon? I thought you had a job. Are you spot checking me now?" I added.

"Seeing as no other woman in a three-state region would have anything to do with you, I really don't have to worry about spot checking your mangy butt, but to answer your question, I needed to get TJ to help me drop the transmission and get the engine out of that old Mustang. As I am technically his boss, this is well within my sphere of authority," she explained.

"For your information, Ms. Chen, you simply could have called as TJ now has a set of wheels. I've given him the 1950 Chevy pickup to use."

"Well then, TJ, perhaps you can unass that couch and meet me down at the shop in an hour?" she said as she got out of the Porsche and headed up the porch steps.

"I'll eat lunch here and meet you there."

I followed her cut-off jean shorts covered backside into the kitchen. A vast improvement over coveralls in my humble opinion.

"This afternoon can you get TJ down to the courthouse so that he can get new tags for the old truck? I'll call and get insurance on it again," I asked.

"No problem," she said. "Are you going to make me lunch, or what?"

"The cost of lunch may be too much for you," I replied.

"And what is the cost for a lunch these days?" she said with a smirk.

"A 60-minute massage before bed tonight."

"Thirty minutes, and no hanky-panky afterwards," she negotiated.

"How about 30 minutes with some hanky and no panky?" I countered.

"Deal, now make me lunch. I've got things to do!

CHAPTER 7

AFTER LUNCH, ONCE TJ AND Rachel had gone back to work, I got on the computer to check that my airline tickets had been booked by the outfit I was consulting for. I then sent an email to the Erbil office to get an update on the drilling operations so that I knew what I was walking into. Finally, I sent an email to an untraceable account. I have not been entirely honest with Rachel and Peio. When I go to work, I usually go as a consultant Drilling Superintendent. This job requires a lot of travel. Sometimes I travel to places where I do some auxiliary work which has absolutely nothing to do with the role of Drilling Superintendent.

Years ago, while working a series of jobs in West Africa, I made my base of operations in Cape Town, South Africa. I frequented a pub called Brian's, in Seapoint, on my days off. It was one of your less salubrious drinking establishments, a dive I believe many would call it. I was not interested in the Cape Town nightlife, back in those days I just wanted to drink. Over the years I became one of the regulars and knew all of the other regulars. When strangers walked in the joint, they were instantly pegged. One afternoon a stranger walked in, sat down beside me and ordered a drink. After some polite conversation, he got down to business.

"Mr. Rose, I would like to speak to you about a business proposition, but not here and not now. Could you suggest another time and venue to have this conversation?"

First off, not many people in Cape Town even knew my surname. Fewer would approach me in Brian's to discuss business as it was essentially a dive and prospective business partners were few and far between. To say that I was startled, and a bit wary, would have been an understatement. But I was young and was willing to listen to any possible opportunity to get out of Africa.

“There is one pizza joint in Bantry Bay. Meet me there at three tomorrow afternoon and we’ll talk then.”

He nodded his head, finished his beer, and walked out the door. I asked around to see if anyone knew the guy, but nobody had ever seen him before. Deep in thought I took a cab to my apartment in Bantry Bay.

The following afternoon I was sitting in the pizza shop, across the main road from the beach, waiting for the stranger to show up. At exactly three, a taxi stopped in front of the shop and deposited the stranger on the sidewalk. Looking at him in daylight I could see that he was older than I originally thought, around 60. He was dressed in what would be called ‘smart casual’, as if he had come from an office, but not a fancy office. He was not carrying a briefcase, so any conversation we were going to have was likely preliminary.

He came through the door, looked around, saw me, and took a seat across from me with his back toward the street. I could tell that this made him uncomfortable, which should have clued me in that he was not in any normal line of work. He then took a device out of his shirt pocket, about the size of a pack of cigarettes, and thumbed a switch on the side.

“This will interfere with any sort of listening device known. It is not a recording device but will nullify any such device in the immediate area.”

Without any sort of introduction whatsoever, my lunchmate got down to business.

“Jebell Rose. Thirty-three years old. Colorado School of Mines graduate in Petroleum Engineering. Bachelor of Science. Parents deceased. Financially independent due to inheritance. Past 11 years working various roles in the international oilfield. Began as an engineer trainee offshore Brazil with a drilling contractor. Worked the drill floor as roughneck and derrickman. Ended up as Subsea Engineer in the North Sea. Through contacts, changed roles to consultant Drilling Superintendent. Presently working contracts on the West African coast while residing in South Africa. Have I missed anything of importance?” he asked while looking directly at me.

“That’s a fairly accurate summary. The question is why did you bother to look all of that up on my LinkedIn account?” This conversation was weird from the get-go.

“Did you know Trevor Shepard well?” he continued without answering my question.

"Yes, Trevor and I worked several jobs together. He was my mentor, for lack of a better word, when I broke into the consulting arena. No doubt you know that Trevor passed away 2 years ago."

"I am well aware that Mr. Shepard has passed on, which brings us to the question of his replacement."

"You've lost me now. I know just about every gig that Trevor took. When he passed away, he was working as the Drilling Manager in Tunisia for Compass Petroleum. Perhaps you can let me know who you work for before we continue this conversation?" I responded a bit agitated.

Without answering my question for the second time, he continued. "Let me ask you, while you were working with Mr. Shepard, were their times that he could have been out-of-pocket? You know, not in-country but calling in for the morning and afternoon reports. Calling and saying he was in a certain location, but never offering verification. The point being that although you stayed in touch with Trevor generally on a daily basis, you would not be able to confirm his actual location."

Thinking about it, he was absolutely right, although I had never had any reason to give it much thought.

"Once Trevor and I quit working the rigs and started taking consulting contracts, it was common for us not to see each other for the duration of the contract. He lived here in Bishopscourt, while I moved around with the work. There was no reason for us to physically be in contact while we prosecuted a drilling campaign anywhere in the world. Mobile phones, email and Skype were sufficient for communications. I would occasionally meet him here in Cape Town between contracts to figure out where we were going next."

"Trevor worked for us as well as working in the oilfield," he said.

Trevor had alluded to doing 'other' work the whole time I knew him, but I just assumed it was side deals finding equipment, organizing logistics for other folks, or consulting on the side. This conversation was not going in any of the directions which I thought it would, but I was very curious about his end game.

"Before we get any further, perhaps you can tell me who 'us' is? Any of the information you have presented could have been obtained off the internet. The question of Trevor's absences can easily be explained by the nature of our business. Who is 'us'?"

By this time the cute little Afrikaner waitress was heading toward our table to take our order. Once we had placed our order for a large half-pepperoni and half-

Hawaiian, and a couple of Cokes, the waitress went to place our order and the stranger continued.

"For the moment let's leave the identity of Trevor's, and my employer, undefined. What they do is to provide a supplemental, non-governmental surveillance or intelligence gathering service to a specific Western government. This service is unsanctioned, which means the personnel have no recourse to diplomatic intervention if things do not go well."

He did not speak while the waitress placed our Cokes on the table, but began again as soon as she was out of earshot.

"You, similar to Trevor, are able to travel extensively without drawing attention. Your cover is your job, and you are already in the governmental computers of the countries you work in, which negates creating a legend and documentation for you."

"I assume that there is some level of risk and danger inherent in what Trevor was doing for you. Is that an accurate assumption?" I asked.

"There is always a risk associated when acting as an undeclared agent on foreign soil. That said, it is usually minimal as we did not ask Trevor to do anything overtly illegal. It was simply surveillance of locations which we wanted watched, people we wanted watched, servicing dead drops, or performing brush passes when people, in the for now unnamed embassy, were all tagged and could not do this themselves without complications."

Now the pizza came, and we ate in silence while I considered what he had said. After polishing off the pizza I continued the conversation.

"Apparently you are trying to recruit me to replace Trevor, is that correct?"

"Correct," he confirmed.

"Three things come to mind. First, I am not trained in any of the tasks which you mentioned may be required. Second, what occurs in the event that things go sideways, and I end up with a problem in a foreign country? Third, what is in this for me as I see no upside to accepting this gig?"

"I understand your concerns and will address each point in the depth that I am able to at this time."

"First, if you decide to help us in this endeavor, you would be sent to a training facility for three of your 'off' work rotations to learn the skills necessary. This will be a concentrated curriculum which will include basic tradecraft, self-defense techniques, small arms training and operational scenarios. When you arrive at this facility, the location alone will confirm to your satisfaction which nation's interest you will be serving.

"Second, in the event that you are compromised while overseas, you will receive absolutely no assistance from the government you are assisting. The core idea is that you are not associated and therefore will not be of interest to any other party. It is a risk, but it is also your security blanket. Needless to say, any other assets in the area which we control will be tasked to assist you.

"Third, you will receive a retainer, each month, commensurate with what you could have earned in your position as a drilling consultant, whether you are working for us at the time or not.

"At the moment, your contracts are paid for every day worked on a 28-day on and 28 off rotation. This arrangement would pay you an equivalent salary each month regardless of whether you are working for us or not. If you are currently under contract, you would be paid on your month off and you would double your money on your month on. I am well aware that you do not need the money, but this is an accounting exercise. Also, you will put into 'debt' the government which you are assisting. Do not underestimate the value of a 'get out of jail free card' in the future. Finally, and correct me if I am wrong, you are tired of working in Africa and want out. You are bored to tears and are looking for something to spice up your life. This will do that for you. As an added incentive, we will ensure that you are employed as a drilling consultant within the international arena when not working directly for us. This will allow you to retain your skills as well as your cover. Also, you would never have to put yourself on the market, with the associated downtime, again."

He paused for a drink of Coke before he continued.

"I realize that this is a very strange approach, but due to circumstances which you are not aware of, necessary. I ask you to take 2 weeks to give it some thought before giving me your answer. If after 2 weeks you decide that you are not interested, do not contact me again. If you decide that you would like to pursue this further, meet me 2 weeks from now in room 417 of the Hilton Cape Town City Center."

Standing, he said, "Thank you for your time," and turned to walk away.

"What was Trevor's favorite book?" I asked.

Turning around with a slight grin, "I wondered when you would get to that. His favorite book was '*Shibumi*' by Trevanian," and he walked out the door. He had known Trevor.

The fact was, I was bored. When I am bored, I tend to become somewhat self-destructive, a ship without a rudder, and no clear goals to pursue. I also drink too much and get out of shape. The West African coast had been fairly exciting for a while and drilling complex wells from jack-up rigs off the coast of Angola had been a challenge for the past year. But the shine had worn off the penny, I was bored, and I wanted to get back to the States. Granted, there was a lot of unknowns about this new surveillance role, but I figured that I could bail out at any time. The role would get me back to the States and, if it worked as advertised, I would have a never-ending supply of contracts to pursue when I wasn't working for whatever intelligence outfit this was.

Being an engineer, trained at that previously mentioned penal colony known as the Colorado School of Mines, I got out a piece of paper and listed pros on the left side of the sheet and cons on the right. The pros were that I would be guaranteed a substantial income, which I really didn't need. I would be kept busy either drilling or being a junior spook. I could get back to Colorado and start restoring cars again. Finally, I would have direction, would cut back on the drinking and get back into shape. The con column contained one entry, 'May end up in a foreign jail or dead'.

Now a rational adult would have surmised that the 'con' column trumped the 'pro' column, but I had always been on thin ice when it came to the 'rational adult' category. I figured that if they trained me to a reasonable level of competence, that I would stand at least a 50/50 chance of avoiding a foreign jail or a coffin. I decided to throw the dice and go to room 417 in the Hilton at the prescribed time. Having a cranial-anal impact, that is, having your head up your butt, is a common occurrence among those who make a living in the oilfield. At times I think it may be required. Anyhow, 2 weeks later, I was in the Hilton Cape Town City Center knocking on the door of room 417. The door opened and there was my old lunchmate.

He put out his hand and said, "I am glad to see that you have decided to take us up on our offer."

I shook his hand and said, "How am I supposed to address you? It would make conversing with you a bit less stilted."

"Just call me Ansel," he replied. "Not my real name as you probably understand, but as you say, you need to address me somehow if we are going to go through this conversation in a civilized manner."

The meeting was conducted in a businesslike manner. Basically, Ansel described how the game would be played to allow me to continue with my present contract in

Angola while alternating between my presently scheduled rotations in the Luanda office and the required training. Further, he described the required training and where that was to occur. Once I returned from my next hitch, I was to spend one night in my apartment in Bantry Bay. I would find a business class e-ticket in my inbox that evening and would be required to travel the next day. My rent would be paid by electronic wire transfer for the next 6 months and a maid service had been employed to air out the place and keep it clean during that period. I was told to travel light as everything else would be provided when I arrived at my location. On the email containing my e-ticket would be a phone number which I was to call once I had arrived. And that was it, that is how I got recruited to be an 'amateur spy', for lack of a more definitive job title.

After a fairly uneventful hitch in Luanda, I flew back to Cape Town and took a taxi to my apartment in Bantry Bay. Sure enough, once I checked my email, I found an e-ticket for a business class flight to Washington Dulles International Airport in Washington, D.C., attached to an email from Sunway Travel in Kuala Lumpur, Malaysia. The subject line had a telephone number with a D.C. area code.

The next day I loaded up my North Face backpack with odds and sods, spare underwear and socks, and my toiletries. My roll-on bag had a couple of changes of clothes and some other essentials. I took a taxi to the airport to catch my British Airways flight out at six forty-five that evening. After a stop in London Heathrow, I arrived in Dulles International Airport 28 hours after leaving Cape Town. Since I didn't need to claim any baggage, I cleared Passport Control and Customs quickly, walked into the arrivals hall and used my iPhone to call the number which I had been given.

All I got once the phone was picked up at the other end was, "Go through the door directly ahead of you. Step to the curb and wait for a Black Yukon Denali to stop in front of you. The tag number is a white numeral 7774 on a blue background. Get in the rear door," and he hung up. So, I walked through the door and stepped to the curb. A black Yukon Denali with the license plate described pulled up, I threw my backpack and roll-on bag in and got in the back.

"Please fasten your seatbelt," said a disembodied voice apparently coming from the other side of the smoked glass screen separating my seat from the front seat, like in a limousine, and away we went.

It was now three in the afternoon. The sun was shining, and I was beat, so I took a nap while we went wherever it was that we were going. I felt the vehicle slowing to a stop, so I sat up and looked around at the fairly unimposing entrance of Camp Peary, Virginia, also known as The Farm, the training school for the CIA.

I can't go into detail about Camp Peary simply because I didn't see much of the place. I was driven through the woods to a clearing, enclosed by a chain link fence, which contained four Quonset huts arranged around a courtyard, the clearing was in a thickly wooded area. The driver drove the Yukon between the ends of two of the huts where the road entered the corner of the courtyard and came to a stop in front of the furthest hut. I was informed that we had arrived at our destination. This had to have been the administration building as it had a flag pole out front.

Each Quonset hut had a covered entrance sticking out of the middle, toward the courtyard. With no further instructions coming forth from the chauffeur, I got out of the truck, slung my backpack on my shoulder and walked to the entrance of the admin hut dragging my roll-on bag. Opening the door, I stepped inside. Directly in front of me, across the width of the Quonset hut, was a desk with a guy sitting behind it. The hut was partitioned into thirds, the room I was in, and one on either side. Each partition wall had a simple door in the middle to divide the hut into what appeared to be three separate rooms.

I walked up to the desk and said, "Jebell Rose reporting for duty!"

"Don't tell me, let me guess, you're the class clown?" he said without looking up.

"Possibly. This is as far as my instructions take me. Any idea what I do now?"

Looking up, he said, "Absolutely, Bozo." He reached into the left-hand drawer of the standard government issued gray desk, took out a key and slid it across the desk to me.

"Go back out the door you came in, hang a left, and go into that Quonset hut. That is the accommodation unit. Since you are the first trainee to arrive for this session, I've given you the key to room number 1. Others will be arriving this afternoon and tonight. Do not leave the area enclosed by the chain link fence. Dinner will be served at six in the hut directly across from the accommodation unit. The rest of the afternoon is your time. Your instruction will begin at six in the morning tomorrow. Be in this room at that time. Goodbye, dismissed or the equivalent in clown-speak." He looked back down at his paperwork.

This was to be my home for 3 non-consecutive months while I trained up as an Assistant Secret Agent or whatever the proper job title was. Except for training 'field trips', this is all of Camp Peary that I saw, or for that matter, wanted to see. I grabbed the key off the desk, slung my backpack over my shoulder, went out of the door dragging my roll-on bag, hung a left, and walked into the identical door of the accommodation hut. There was no foyer or central room in this hut. You walked down a short hallway made up by the walls of adjacent rooms until you hit the hallway running left and right at the middle of the building. At this point you could continue ahead to another short hallway leading to a fire exit or go left or right to your assigned room. Following the signs, I hung a left and walked to the end of the hallway. There were three rooms on each side of the hallway, room number 1 was the last room on the left. If you kept walking you would run into yet another fire exit.

I took out the key I'd been given, unlocked the door and stepped inside. Except for the curved ceiling and the fact that there was no window, the room was almost exactly what you would expect in a fairly nice hotel. As you walked into the room, there were closets on the left of the small entrance hall and a small, but reasonable bathroom on the right. Once into the room proper, there was a double bed butted up against the right-hand wall, a desk, chair and lamp butted against the curved outside wall and a small couch against the left-hand wall. Not bad.

I unpacked all the contents of the roll-on bag and my backpack onto the bed and put my kit away in the bathroom and closets as necessary. I set my alarm for dinner and took a nap.

I never heard anyone else arrive, but when I entered the chow hall just after six there was another guy and girl there. Obviously, they were as clueless about what was going on as I was, so they were sitting at separate tables and not making eye contact. I went up to the serving line, got meatloaf, mashed potatoes, green beans, Tabasco sauce and a bottle of water. Since I had not been instructed to avoid the others, I went over and sat across from the girl. Putting out my hand, I said, "Hello, I'm Jeb."

She looked around, I suppose to see if we were on CCTV, which we were, and said, "Are you sure that we are supposed to introduce ourselves?"

"Look, I am just as new to this stuff as you are, but I wasn't told to avoid anyone. Maybe that comes tomorrow, but tonight it is just a couple of people having dinner."

Thinking about it for a moment, she stuck her hand out to shake mine and said, "I'm Lisa."

About this time, the other guy sitting across the room picked up his tray and came over to join us.

"I wasn't sure about the protocol either. My name's Frank, pleased to meet you both."

After that, we just sat around making small talk until they closed the place at eight. Nobody was offering too much information as we were trainee secret agents, and it did not seem wise to divulge too much information.

The next morning, I was up at five, showered, teeth brushed, into new jeans and t-shirt, and across to the chow hall by five twenty. I loaded up on scrambled eggs, bacon and coffee before setting back down at the same table as the previous night. There was nobody else, except the cooks, in the building. A few minutes later Frank walked in, loaded his tray and sat across from me. Five minutes after that, girls take longer in the morning, Lisa came in for breakfast.

At six sharp we were all seated in the couches along the walls in front of the 'registration desk' waiting for whatever was going to happen. At six oh three, the same guy who had been sitting behind the desk yesterday opened the door on the right and said, "Come inside please." The room we found ourselves in was a classroom, the typical classroom you think of when you think back to high school except instead of a chalkboard there was a whiteboard. Again, no windows. The desk clerk went to the front of the room and stood behind the teacher's desk.

"My name is John, John Doe. This is how you will address me and no, it is not my given name," he said with a smile. "I am a facilitator; I will not be teaching you a thing. What I will do is bring in experts to teach you what you need to know. On occasion, we will take field trips to other facilities to allow you to receive instruction which is unavailable here. As you will not be assigned together, and it is almost certain that you will never be in the same region, you can talk freely amongst yourselves. You are not, repeat not, CIA agents nor were you ever intended to be. There are some clandestine activities and skills that we think you should be proficient at to allow you to accomplish your tasks. These are what you are here to learn."

Pausing to collect his thoughts, he continued, "The skills that you must master are arranging the pickup of clandestine material, evading hostile pursuers, situational awareness, memory retention and lock picking. In the parlance of the trade, these skills are referred to as 'drops', 'defensive driving', 'Kim's game' and 'picks and locks'. You will also be trained to a certain level in the handling of handguns and self-defense although you will likely never need these skills. There is a gym available, and I suggest you use it to stay in shape. You are all in excellent health and condition, but most of what you do here will be in the form of studying, and you will be tested extensively. You will need to get exercise to maintain your fitness, as well as to reduce stress. Do not bulk up further than you already are, to do so would raise questions when you return to your regular jobs."

John continued, "As far as domestic chores are concerned, you have none. Place your dirty laundry in the net bag you will find in your closet and place it outside your door each evening. It will be washed and folded during the evening and placed back outside your door by five o'clock each morning. If you require further clothes, toiletries, office supplies and so forth, give me a detailed list and I will have it provided to you. Any questions?"

THERE WERE NONE. "GRAB A cup of coffee or tea from the urns at the back of the room. Be ready to start in 20 minutes."

We took seats in the first row and waited for the first instructor to arrive. The door at the rear of the room opened and a man and a woman, both in their forties, walked in and went directly to the front of the room. The man leaned on the desk and said, "For simplicity you can call us Adam and Eve. We will be your instructors for the next 3 weeks on the subject of 'drops'. It is imperative that you know how to obtain and deliver information in a clandestine manner. You may, or may not, be tailed while passing or receiving information, that issue will be addressed during the 'defensive driving' part of your curriculum. Our job is to ensure that once you are in position, you can hand off or receive information without being obvious about it."

For the next 3 weeks we learned how to perform brush passes where material was passed during a brief encounter such as walking on the street, in a movie theater or in the supermarket. This also included learning how to pick pockets for the hand-to-pocket variation. We learned how to service dead drops and how to perform 'car tosses', where you surreptitiously pass an item to or from a vehicle. All basic tradecraft, as they called it, but effective. We also had to learn how to perform SDR's, surveillance detection routes, to ensure that we were not followed to wherever we were going. This entails going on a tortuous route, taking various forms of transportation, as well as walking, to either lose those following us or to identify the tail and call it quits. I felt this was nonsense. If the 'opposition' had enough people and assets, you'd never be able to identify them all. But that was my opinion and would not help me pass the course, so I kept quiet.

At the end of the third week, we went to the nearest town, Williamsburg, Virginia, to do hands-on training as well as to be tested by being given a dead letter drop to service, or a brush pass to perform after performing the required SDR. During the testing phase, Frank, Lisa and I took turns role playing the different characters working the various passes. It was a tough 3 weeks, but I was enjoying myself. It was something new, and sometimes all it takes is a change of routine to get you out of a rut and excited again. After being told that I had passed, I said goodbye to Frank and Lisa, packed my kit and was driven back to Dulles to catch a flight back to Cape Town in time to make it to Luanda for my next hitch.

After the grueling flight back to Cape Town, I arrived at my apartment in Bantry Bay via taxi. Opening the door, the air was not musty, and the place had been dusted. Proof that Ansel was as good as his word, at least as far as taking care of my place was concerned. I fired up my computer to check messages, and the travel arrangements back to Luanda, and found that I was booked to Luanda the next day.

I unpacked my kit, threw the dirty laundry in the washing machine and grabbed my 'go-bag' out of the closet. This was a bag that I kept packed so I could quickly head to the airport if required. It had two complete sets of clothes for work as well as a shaving kit with the required toiletries for a month. I threw this on the bed along with my MacBook Pro. I was now ready to go to work again.

Walking to the kitchen I opened the refrigerator and found it fully stocked. The 'sell by' date on the milk and cheese showed that it had been stocked up in the past day or two. I made a two-egg, cheese and onion omelet for dinner and washed it down with a beer. After cleaning everything up and taking out the garbage, I took a shower and got ready for bed. Tomorrow would be another long day.

The next day I caught the South African Airways flight to Luanda, via Johannesburg, at noon, and arrived in Luanda at around seven thirty that night. After the usual immigration fiasco, I walked out and found my driver. We arrived at the Alvalade Hotel around eight thirty. I registered and went up to my room on the fourth floor. The Alvalade is a decent four-star hotel, for Angola, and is located just up the street from our offices, which are located about 300 yards up Rua Emilio M'Bidi toward the Children's Hospital. I'd been working this gig for about 2 years now and this was all routine.

The hitch went fairly smoothly for a drilling operation in West Africa. We took a 'kick' which is usually gas entering the well, circulated out the gas and killed the well using the Driller's Method before continuing to drill ahead. After running 9-5/8" casing and cementing it into the ground, we performed the usual leak-off test, obtained a good result and continued drilling. We drilled another 500 feet into the reservoir and ran the 7" liner. Once the well was perforated, we were rigging up to run the completion and test the well when it was time for me to return to Cape Town at the end of my hitch.

Doing the Cape Town-Johannesburg-Luanda trip in reverse, I ended up back in my apartment just after one thirty in the morning the day after I had left Luanda. Checking emails again, I found that I was booked back to Dulles the following evening on the six forty-five flight again. I threw my dirty kit into the washing machine, showered up and went to bed.

Arriving back in Camp Peary, I walked into the admin building, and picked up the key to room number 1 from some guy whom I had never seen before. Walking back out I took a left, walked into the accommodation hut, and dumped my kit exactly as before. Once again, I took a nap and ended up in the chow hall at six fifteen that evening. I was the only one there.

The next morning at breakfast there were two other new faces in the chow hall. These two kept their heads down and were obviously not interested in conversation, so I ate alone before wandering back to the classroom in the admin building. John Doe was at the teacher's desk going over some paperwork, so I settled into a desk in the front row and waited for things to start. A few minutes later the two guys from the chow hall walked in and we began.

Once the two other guys had settled into desks, John stood up and without preamble said, "In this session you will be traveling to the BSR training facility outside of Windsor, West Virginia, for the entire month to learn and perfect your security, evasive and off-road driving skills. While there you will also be given firearms and self-defense training. Usually these courses are one- or two-day affairs, but not for you. You will spend a week learning how to drive anything evasively, on the road or off. Firearms skills will also take a week and self-defense is also a weeklong affair. After that you will return here. Go pack your bags, you are leaving in 15 minutes."

We each headed back to our rooms, packed our bags, and got into the van waiting to take us to West Virginia. The BSR facility is located in the Shenandoah Valley, and it only took us around an hour to get to the Hillbrook Inn in Windsor. We booked into the inn, which is really an upscale bed and breakfast about 2 miles from the BSR facility, then got back in the van to go to the BSR training area. The training area is located in an 825-acre complex consisting of three high speed paved road circuits, one low speed circuit, two unimproved road circuits, one off road training arena, seven firing ranges, three skid pads, twenty classrooms and the required support facilities. Suffice it to say that this session was an absolute blast. Where else can you drive someone else's vehicles to destruction, on and off road, and shoot other people's weapons and ammo to your heart's content?

The self-defense was fine, and I supposed I learned a few techniques, but there is no way you can learn enough in a week to keep someone who is actually trained in kicking your ass, from kicking your ass. To me, this is where the firearms training comes in handy.

I grew up shooting and hunting. I quit hunting when I got too busy to actually hunt, and I found that simply shooting gave me the same satisfaction, although no wild game. I will say that although I am highly proficient with just about any pistol or revolver, I did learn more grips, perfected magazine changes while keeping my eyes on the target, and offhand shooting skills. Which is actually quite a bit to learn in a week.

The evasive and defensive driving skills courses were impressive. They taught you how to handle cars and trucks at speed, and how to feel comfortable doing it. Unintentional skid control, intentional skid initiation and control, 'bootleg' direction changes, Pursuit Intervention Techniques and so forth. We also got to try our hand at similar techniques off road. Face it, 3 weeks is not enough time to become skilled at any of these disciplines, but it gave us the basics which we could hone on our own.

After we returned to Camp Peary, each of us was taken into the classroom separately to have our performance at the BSR facility reviewed and told if we had passed or not. We all did.

The following day we began returning to wherever we came from. I ended up in Cape Town with enough time to again wash my laundry, check emails and my travel arrangements back to Luanda, and get some sleep before returning to Luanda for my next hitch.

I arrived back at work just in time to 'plug and abandon' the well which we had just drilled. This does not indicate that the well was not a good well, in fact, it was. The problem is that the first well in a discovery is, by definition, an exploration well. If, during the testing phase, it is determined that there is an economical amount of oil that can be recovered in the discovery well, then an appraisal well must be drilled to confirm it before proceeding to the development stage. This hitch was spent plugging and abandoning the initial well and moving the jack-up rig to the appraisal location, pinning the rig on location, going through the pre-loading procedure, then jacking the rig up. Not a very demanding hitch, but those are nice when they happen.

Returning home, after a night at my apartment in Cape Town, I found myself once again winging my way to Camp Peary, and once again in room number 1, for my final training session. This session would focus on surveillance, memory retention and 'picks and locks', that is observing, being able to remember what you observe, and lock picking.

The 'Kim's Game' portion of the session took place in the classroom and was tutored by an old Army Ranger sniper. Now this might seem like an odd choice for an instructor for memory retention course, but keep in mind that most of the time a sniper is doing reconnaissance, not shooting people. He, or she, must have outstanding observational skills, and be able to remember what they have observed. The old dude, whom we named Old Dude, began the session by getting us to play Kim's games over and over and over. Kim's game is played by the instructor placing ten to twenty random items in a box. These could be pens, bottle caps, nuts and bolts, matchbooks, really any old thing that will fit in the box. The students would take the top off the box and be given a minute to observe what was inside it. Afterwards the top was put back on the box and each student would make a list of what they had seen. The student with the most items correctly identified, wins. This gradually builds your memory retention. Eventually we took the game outside. Various items would be placed around the huts or in the courtyard. We would be given 15 minutes to walk around and observe. Once back in the classroom we would have to write down all the 'out of place' items we had seen, and their locations. The final exam was to look in a box of items first thing in the morning, walk around the huts for 15 minutes, then attempt to list the items in the box from the morning session before listing the odd items outside and their locations. Again, this course was not attempting to get you to the level of a trained military sniper, it was to give you the skills to enable you to train yourself later.

The 'picks and locks' session took up the majority of the session. This was tutored by someone whom I assumed was a veteran thief or burglar. He explained the mechanics of locks, how they worked, and how to defeat them. For days we practiced with the basic pin tumbler lock, which makes up about ninety percent of the locks commonly used today. After going through the basic components of the lock: housing, key pin, springs and driver pins, we discussed the shear line and how to manipulate a lock, without a key, to get the gap between the key pins and driver pins on the shear line, thereby opening the lock.

We learned to do this with professional tension wrenches, rakes and hooks as well as with homemade tools made from paperclips and bobby pins. 'Bump keys' were discussed, but unless you happened to have the specific bump key blank required for the lock you were trying to defeat, they are useless. As we were rarely going to know what lock we might have to pick, we stuck to the basics and didn't spend much time on this method.

After we had attained a certain level of skill with the pin tumbler locks, we were shown specialist tools for defeating card keys used in hotels and office buildings. This really did not take any skill, just the right tools. Later, we were shown techniques for determining the code on a numeric keypad lock such as a security system. This was so complicated that, although I tried to follow it, I ended up nodding off. Finally, the series of training sessions was over. Once again, we were brought into the classroom individually and our recent performance was assessed. I was given high marks for standard lock picking, but I had failed miserably at defeating numeric keypads, but apparently this was not considered a critical skill for amateur secret squirrels. In a nutshell, I had passed and was now ready to go operational, whatever that meant.

Ansel was on hand for the 'graduation' and told me that I could now relocate out of Cape Town. I was told to select a location within the continental United States, which was a no-brainer as I had inherited the place in Colorado, and I needed to get there and renovate it. I told Ansel that I would return to Cape Town, settle my accounts there, and return to the Colorado as soon as possible.

He smiled and said, "I kind of figured that would be the case. We have terminated the rental agreement on your apartment in Cape Town, closed your accounts there and packed up everything in your apartment, and it is in transit as we speak. I have a ticket for you to Denver, and then onward to Glenwood Springs. There is a rental car waiting for you there. Stay in touch." I laughed, took the ticket, shook his hand and went to room number 1 to pack my kit before heading to Dulles for the last time. I was looking forward to getting back to Colorado.

Once I arrived in Glenwood Springs and signed for the rental Ford Explorer, I then drove west, then north for an about an hour until I got to Cadillac Springs. I didn't want to go out to the place at night, so I booked in at the Holiday Inn, then headed into town for a meal. The diner in town has always been a favorite from my childhood, so I headed there and had a chicken fried steak dinner and an iced tea. It was almost dark when I finished my meal, so I walked back to the Explorer. I stopped beside the driver's door and looked up at the darkening sky while inhaling that air which has a smell and texture which can only be found on the Colorado Western Slope. It was nice to be back.

CHAPTER 8

NOW BACK TO THE FUTURE. If you will remember, Rachel and TJ had just left for town, and I was getting ready to go back to work in Kurdistan and had sent an email to an untraceable account to find out if I had any secret squirrel tasks to attend to while in Kurdistan. Since the Kurds had essentially decimated ISIS recently, there was a good chance that I'd be given something to do. Operating with no official cover, NOC, in spook language, is always a risk. In Kurdistan, more so. The Kurdish security organization and primary intelligence agency is the Asayish. These guys and gals are good, very good. In a country which had been gassed by Saddam, crapped on by the politicians in Baghdad, and is trying to remain autonomous, you do not want to get on their bad side. At best, you will get deported, at worst, simply disappear. The Asayish plays hardball. That said, unlike most of the Middle East, the Kurds genuinely like Americans since we have tried to support them, as best we can, in the maze which is Middle Eastern politics. We have a large, functioning embassy in Erbil, the capital of the autonomous region, which is also where my office was located.

The message I got back from Ansel, and therefore from my secondary employer I now knew as the Jankowski Group, said that they did not need my services at the moment, but to stay in touch once I arrived in Erbil.

I was contracted out to Onyx Petroleum as a Drilling Superintendent and had two 1,500 horsepower rigs to get moved onto new locations prior to spudding new wells, so I was plenty busy with my day job. These locations were about halfway between

Erbil and Shaqiawa. After the recent incursion by ISIS, I had to organize security for each truck involved in a rig move as well as any truck moving the base camp. I also had to arrange security for any personnel going out to visit the drilling locations. To do this I had to coordinate with the Asayish.

To the best of my knowledge, nobody knows where the Asayish headquarters or offices are located. They maintained a villa within the English Village in western Erbil, which was handy as that is where Onyx maintained a villa, which was used as the office.

After calling ahead and making an appointment to meet with Colonel Sivan Ibrahim at two in the afternoon, I ordered out for a shwarma and ate in the office while going through the logistics required to move the rigs. A little after one thirty, I walked over to the Asayish villa and presented my Kurdish work permit card, complete with photo, to the young guard with the Kalashnikov AKS-74U Krinkov. He studied the card then opened the gate and let me walk to the front door and go inside. Just inside the front door was a desk with another similarly armed guard, although a bit older, who again took my work permit, looked at it then picked up his phone and called someone. After a short discussion in Kurdish, he pointed to the stairs behind him, and up I went. I had done this a number of times in the past and knew the drill. At the top I hung a left, went to the end of the short hall and knocked twice on the door on the left. Hearing a response, I opened the door, walked in and saluted an extremely fit, outrageously good-looking Kurdish woman in combat fatigues. Unlike most Middle Eastern cultures, the Kurds believe in gender equality, and at the moment roughly twenty-five percent of the Asayish is 'manned' by women. Most not as good looking as this one, but you have to start somewhere.

"Good afternoon, Colonel Ibrahim. Jebell Rose reporting for duty!" I barked.

"Why would I want an incompetent Drilling Superintendent in my ranks?" she said with a smile.

"For comic relief, unless you have something else in mind," I replied with a leer.

"You realize I could have you taken out front and shot for being so flippant with an officer of the Asayish, do you not?"

"That I do, Colonel, but if it was you pulling the trigger, I would die a happy man," I said as I approached her desk and gave her a peck on both cheeks.

I had gotten to know Colonel Sivan over the past couple of years. She was extremely competent at her job organizing security for the oil and gas operations north and west of Erbil. She had a well-developed sense of humor, and as I said before, she was not hard on the eyes. All of this made my job much easier, and pleasant. I flirted with her every time I saw her but kept it as professional as possible as her husband, Nebez, was a colonel in the Peshmerga, which are the military forces in Kurdistan. I had met her husband many times and had dinner with both of them on several occasions. He was well aware that I flirted with his wife and was also well aware that it was simply a game we played and not serious. Otherwise, my bones would have been found years later somewhere around Mosul.

"What can I do for you this afternoon, Mr. Rose?" she asked.

"Well, Colonel, I have to move two rigs onto locations roughly halfway between Erbil and Shaqiawa next month, and I need to request the required security details for the rig moves."

"Is it still about one hundred and fifty truckloads per rig?"

"Give or take a truckload or two. I'll have the final loadout plan ready by the end of this week," I told her.

"How many trucks per day and how many trucks per convoy are you planning?"

"About ten trucks per day is all that I can reasonably handle on each location. I'd like to run two convoys of 10 trucks each day, one to each location, so that I can start drilling in about 2 months," I replied.

"Are the locations ready now?" she asked.

"The locations are ready to move onto now. We are finishing up the perimeter fences and lighting, but I need to visit the oil and gas police to get the security worked out for each location," I replied.

She sat back in her chair with her eyes closed for a few minutes, then leaned her forearms on her desk and looked at me with those beautiful brown eyes and said, "Okay, we will start running ten truck convoys to each location daily starting as soon as you are ready. I will ask Colonel Nebez to contact the oilfield police and fast track your security requirements. Make sure that you touch base with them before you get ready to move either personnel, or material, to either location." I told you she was a professional.

She continued, "But this level of service will cost you. Nebez and I will expect you to take us out for a very nice dinner at the Al Bustan before you return to the States. This is non-negotiable," she said with a smile.

"It would be my pleasure, Colonel. Should I bring some suitable whiskey for the other colonel?" I asked. Kurds are not above enjoying a dram.

"I will leave that up to you, but if my husband becomes loud and boisterous, or embarrasses me in any way due to imbibing this whiskey, I will tie you to a stake and flay the skin off you personally. I have seen you boys drink together before."

"What are the chances that you could use a mink whip while inappropriately dressed?" I queried.

Pointing at her door she simply said, "Out!"

We had our dinner at the Al Bustan Lebanese Garden on Gulan Street a few days later. Nebez did not get too drunk on the Johnnie Walker Blue Label I had purchased at the Dubai Duty Free on the way in for just such an occasion, I was not staked out and flayed by any type of whip, and we had a very enjoyable dinner. The service was unbelievable, until you remember that I was at dinner with colonels from both the Asayish and the Peshmerga, in which case it was believable.

Before I left Kurdistan, the rigs were being erected on each location, on schedule. Nolan, my back-to-back, would need to get them both up and running to his satisfaction before accepting the rigs from the drilling contractor, and before commencing drilling operations. All in all, a very enjoyable hitch, which is not always the case.

I was only required to utilize my secret squirrel skills to attach a tracking device to a vehicle registered to the Belarus Consulate located on the Kasnazan Road. This was a walk in the park as I knew the vehicle would be at the Erbil Sports Center on Peshawa Qazi, roughly halfway between Ala and Koya Road in Zanayan, every weekday from noon to about one thirty. The only fly in the ointment was the driver of the vehicle, who sat in a café across the street having his lunch while waiting for his boss to sweat the vodka out of his system. I simply got to the café ahead of time each day and looked for an opening. Sure enough, each day at about one twenty-five, the driver would get up, pay his tab, and hit the head before going out to his vehicle and wait for his boss to appear.

I had been provided with a black box about the size of an old box of matches that had a sponge-like pad on one side. The instructions that came along with the tracking device simply said to pull off the backing on the sponge, pull out the little antenna on one of the narrow ends, find a fairly clean spot and stick the box to the vehicle. Using the skills learned during the 'drops' part of my training, I simply waited for the driver to get up to pay his tab, made my way to his vehicle, accidentally dropping my keys at the front of his car and stuck the tracking device to the inside of the front bumper while picking up my keys. Job done. A regular Jack Bauer.

Other than that, I was also required to forward a report concerning my meeting with Colonel Sivan, and the dinner with her and her husband.

CHAPTER 9

I FLEW OUT OF ERBIL, on the Emirates flight to Dubai, in the middle of the following afternoon after I had handed over to Nolan. I then caught the early morning British Airways flight to Denver via Heathrow, arriving in Denver around three thirty in the afternoon the same day. From there I caught the six fifty-five United flight to Glenwood Springs. I had Skyped Rachel before I left Erbil, so hopefully she would meet me in Glenwood Springs, take me home, and abuse me.

After bouncing around like a ping pong ball in the little puddle jumper over the mountains I arrived shaken, not stirred, in Glenwood Springs. Rachel waited for me as I walked onto the concourse. Jumping into my arms, she knocked my backpack off while giving me a very invigorating kiss with just the right amount of tongue. I could feel her warm womanly bits through the 1979 Outlaws Fall Tour t-shirt she was wearing. I am fairly certain she could also feel my manly pointy bits as well. I tried to remember how long it took to get from Glenwood Springs to Cadillac Springs.

After collecting my roll-on bag from the conveyor belt, we walked hand in hand to the parking lot. I tossed my bags into the bed of the F-150, Rachel threw me the keys and off we went. Getting on Highway 82, we headed north through downtown Glenwood Springs until we hit I-70 and headed west. At the Rifle Bypass we cut north to the 325 turn off and followed this until it came to the town of Cadillac Springs, beside the reservoir of the same name. If you carry on 325 for about another 8 miles through a small valley you will find my place off to your left about 200 yards from the county road.

Rachel rode snuggled up to me the whole way, like a couple of high school kids dating. It felt good. It was full on night by this time, and the mountain air had the fresh smell of evergreens and aspens, mixed with a slight peat smell. I always enjoyed the first evening back in the mountains after spending a month in the Middle East. Mountains, for me, are much more desirable than the flat, hot windy fields north of Erbil, but to each his own. Pulling the Ford in front of the barn I grabbed my kit, grabbed Rachel and went into the house.

"What's for dinner?" I asked.

"Frozen pizza," she replied with a smirk.

"Do I have time for a shower?" I replied straight faced.

"It's frozen pizza, moron," she pointed out. "You, with my assistance, have just enough time for a shower," she said as she headed up the stairs unbuttoning her jeans.

As it turns out, the frozen pizza was not actually consumed until the following morning as another, more important, issue arose and required attention. Sitting at the kitchen island eating coffee and cold pizza I asked, "So what's been happening while I've been away?"

"If you'd been paying attention last night you would have noticed that the drive from the county road to the house has been paved, along with a circular drive around the courtyard, and that you now have a proper concrete apron in front of the barn."

"I was paying attention last night, just not to my driveway," I said as I picked up my coffee, walked out on the porch and surveyed the new additions to my place.

Walking back to my kitchen, I said, "I suppose that needed to be done, but who made these momentous decisions while I was away?"

"Actually, it was a committee decision taken between Peio and myself. Peio had ordered too much asphalt for his place, and I was tired of getting gravel dings in the Whale Tail every time I come here."

I thought about this for a second before replying, "Peio ordered asphalt for the meadow in front of his trailer?"

"Actually, Peio is building a log home near where the trailer is parked. He needs the trailer to live in while his house is getting built," I was informed.

"Again, who decided Peio can build a house on my property?"

"If you remember correctly, Peio informed you at the last barbeque that he was fine where he was, for the moment. That moment passed while you were away, and the previously mentioned committee agreed that he should have a more permanent abode where he is. That being the case, it seems that he already had in mind a log house he wanted to build, called the outfit that supplies and erects them, and got them started," she said reaching for the last piece of pizza.

"Thank you for letting me know that these decisions were being made in my absence, we only talked on Skype twice a week." I was getting somewhat pissed off now.

"To what point? You'd simply bitch and moan, like you are about to do now, and at the end of the day you'd just knuckle under and allow it anyhow," she said while coyly looking at me over the rim of her coffee cup.

I really hate being that transparent, but she was right. Seeing as I was not getting anywhere with this, and that in the overall scheme of things having Peio as a permanent fixture, plus a paved driveway, were good things, I changed subjects and asked how the shop was doing. This perked her right up. It seemed that the GT500 was nearing completion and was only waiting on some original equipment suspension parts and a power steering pump.

"Is your house ready yet?" I asked.

"Why, want me to move out?" Some people actually think that there is no such thing as a stupid question. I refer the jury to this one.

"I kind of need the guest bedroom to turn into a place to build my toy train sets and layouts," I responded.

"You've never owned a toy train in your life," was the comeback.

She continued, "Actually, the house will be finished in a few weeks. The contract I have on the house will expire at the same time. I was wondering if we could continue with the same arrangement as we have now? I could pay you some rent." Perhaps my nefarious plans were coming to fruition faster than expected due to a disintegrating cottonwood tree. I'll take any assistance I can get, but I didn't want to appear too over-eager.

"I'm not so sure that this would be a wise idea. Perhaps we would be moving too fast in our relationship, and you keep accusing me of having 'commitment issues'," I said while trying to keep a straight face. "Maybe you could get a room at the YWCA while you give this some further thought before making such a momentous decision."

"Perhaps I could get a room at the YMCA and experience some real men while I give this some further thought, you asshole. Are you going to let me move in or not?"

"You'll have to cook and clean, it's only fair."

"You'd either starve to death or contract Hantavirus Pulmonary Syndrome."

"Then I will have to increase the rent, which you have never paid, to a level to cover the sweat of my brow associated with keeping us fed and out of the hospital," was my clever riposte.

"And I," she cleverly responded, "will need to figure out a fee scale for both your visitation rights to the guestroom, and Dr. Feelgood's visits to your room."

Before we left for town, we had reached an agreement. She would continue staying at my place without any increase in rent, which as I mentioned, she doesn't pay anyhow. I was still going to receive Dr. Feelgood visits at no charge, which I had not been paying for either. Essentially, we were back where we started, no hits, no runs, no errors.

Rachel got into her Porsche, I got into my truck, and we drove to her shop. TJ was already at work judging by the fact that my old 1950 Chevy truck was parked in front of the office. I parked in front, where the pumps used to be, while Rachel took a spot in front of one of the bay doors. When I walked through the office and into the shop, TJ was on a crawler under the front of the Mustang working on the front suspension. On a 'numbers matching' vehicle, you can't do what you'd really like to do and trash the old suspension and go with a more performance oriented one, you have to stay true to the original vehicle. I kicked his boot and said, "I guess Rachel is doing her affirmative action duty and is now hiring the totally incompetent and mentally afflicted."

To which he replied, "Somebody had to take your spot at the shop. I consider myself an upgrade to your mediocre and somewhat scatter-brained performance, shitbird." While he finished up what he was doing and rolled out from under the car, I took a look at what they had done. The car was back 'as built' from nose to tail and the interior had been redone to original black as well. The paint was a black cherry with gold pinstriping.

"I hate to bring this up at this point, but that black cherry with gold is not an original color scheme for this car."

"True, but the customer is always right, and this is what he wanted. He'd lose money at an auction, but I get the idea that he wants it for his personal ride," he said after wiping his hands on a shop rag and shaking mine.

"How did someone from your less than salubrious past become a fair to acceptable mechanic?" I asked. "Rachel also said that you guys were fixing to get a paint booth as well, and that you were a reasonable hand at painting."

"Believe it or not, my 'less than salubrious' vocation did not keep me exceptionally busy. You just can't go around popping people to stay active. I therefore offered my services and labor to a variety of chop shops which were associated with my employer, and simply learned on the job."

"And the body work and painting aspect?" I asked.

"Well, numbnuts, often you do not want a vehicle to look the same way coming out of a chop shop as it looked coming in. We didn't chop every vehicle that came in as occasionally we required vehicles to drive around and do our 'less than salubrious' stuff."

"Makes sense."

TJ went into the office to do something, so I walked over to the other side of the Mustang where Rachel was underneath the car, on another crawler, working on removing the old power steering pump.

"I wonder if two people could get on a crawler and squirm around under a car? It has potential you know."

"The only way you could get on a crawler with me is if either you lost 50 pounds, or we jacked the car up higher." I couldn't tell if she was serious or not, so I continued with my train of thought.

"If we were naked, we wouldn't need to jack the car up as high, and I wouldn't have to lose so much weight." Never let it be said that I could not think out of the box.

"When pigs fly, cowboy," was her reply. Sometimes thinking out of the box is a waste of time and overrated.

I could see that her mind was not on the same wavelength as mine, so I told her that I was going into the office to look over the books. To which she commented, "Don't you have to be able to add and subtract to do that?"

I kicked her in her fine, coverall covered butt, and went into the office to bullshit some more with TJ. He was on the phone with NAPA getting some parts, so I parked off in one of the overstuffed chairs in front of the desk.

When he got off the phone I asked, "I've got to run into town for a while, want me to pick up some burgers for lunch?"

"That'd be cool. I've got to get these parts located and I need to start looking at paint booths online to show to Rachel. How about two double cheese burgers, fries and a Coke?"

From underneath the Mustang a disembodied voice said, "I'll take the same, but onion rings instead of fries. Don't forget extra catsup!" She's got ears like a bat!

Walking back to the door from the office into the shop, I said, "How about only one burger, sweetheart? You're starting to look a bit saggy in the caboose."

"How about you fill my order exactly as I said and maybe I'll let you give the saggy bits the squeeze test tonight?"

"Your negotiating skills are as sharp as ever. Two burgers et al coming your way."

I drove over to The Foundry Machine Shop and shot the breeze with the guys for half an hour about reworking the heads on my 429, then stopped by Gold's Gym to harass Bret and see if he wanted to come by after work Friday for another barbeque with the white folks. He did. I then drove to the Double Z Bar and Grill and got the six burgers, two orders of fries, one order of onion rings, extra catsup and three Cokes, thus ensuring that an in-depth squeeze test of Rachel's saggy bits would be performed at some point that evening.

Getting back to the shop I had lunch with Rachel and TJ. I then drove back up the valley past my driveway, to the Bland Reservoir cut-off, and left a note in Peio's mailbox letting him know that we were having another barbeque on Friday, and that his presence was required. No RSVP necessary. I finally got back to the house, grabbed a beer and then sat on one of the old couches on the porch. Since the porch is on the east side of the house, it was in the shade. After finishing the beer, I stretched out on the couch until I heard the Whale Tail coming up the road.

Rachel parked the Porsche and sauntered up the steps onto the porch looking ravishing in a pair of cut-off jeans and my 1979 Led Zeppelin Live at Knebworth t-shirt knotted slightly lower, and dead center, of her pert, properly-sized boobs. She had built a small locker room cum shower at the shop so that she could clean up before getting into the Whale Tail. Giving me a peck on the cheek she went into the house, grabbed a beer and joined me on the couch.

"Where's your boyfriend?" I asked.

"Which one?" she replied.

"The squirrely Coonass that you've cunningly employed so that you can spend time with him while I am out of the country."

"Oh, that one. He'll be along shortly. Why do you ask, may I ask?"

"In an effort at efficiency, I was going to tell you both, at the same time, about the upcoming barbeque being held here next Friday after you working stiffs get off work."

Sipping her beer, she asked who was invited to the fandango and I explained that it was the usual culprits: Peio, TJ, Bret, her and myself. She informed me that TJ had met a girl and he may want to invite her along in an effort to increase the gender ratio and to make the fandangos more politically correct.

"If he is acting like a typical Coonass, she probably works the pole at some dive titty bar on the outside of town," I informed her.

"Actually, while you were away, I was working part-time at the same titty bar for some extra cash," she said while trying not to laugh.

"First, aren't you supposed to have enormous fake titties to work in a titty bar these days? They'd laugh those little Chinese melons, which you call boobs, out of the building."

Setting her beer down, she unknotted her t-shirt, pulled the neck away from her body and, while looking down at her chest said, "You mean these little things?"

Recovering quickly, I said, "You must realize that the crowds which frequent these places are generally uneducated heathens with no appreciation of the true female form." While I also inspected said Chinese melons through the thin cotton veneer, I continued, "Those are simply fine art which should be appreciated by someone with impeccable taste concerning the female form. I have a candidate in mind." Before we could get further into the discussion, we heard the purring of the 235 straight six in the 1950 Chevy pickup turning off the county road and onto the driveway. Rachel released the neck of her shirt and re-knotted it, much to my chagrin.

"Good recovery, big boy. If you behave yourself maybe you can appreciate these articles of fine art from a more favorable point of view later."

TJ parked in front of the bunkhouse before coming over to the house and up the steps. Without speaking he continued into the house to get a beer. Coming back outside he parked himself in one of the overstuffed chairs.

"What's up?" he says.

"Well, before you so rudely interrupted us, we were having a titillating conversation about your new girlfriend," I responded as Rachel rolled her eyes at my pun. "I was saying that you, being a typical Coonass, had found her working the pole at that titty bar outside of town."

"In an effort to set the record straight, and to ease your troubled mind, I will enlighten you as to my romantic endeavors." He continued, "Heather Sjofn is a healthy, somewhat curvaceous, 32-year-old graduate of the University of Denver with a Bachelor's degree in Finance and Economics, and a Master's in Business

Administration. She is of Scandinavian descent and has the associated ice blue eyes and platinum blonde hair. She is the Assistant Bank Manager at the Farmer's Bank in town. If you speak disparagingly of her again, I will be forced to kick your ass."

"Yeah, but does she have huge hooters so that she can work the pole at night?" TJ and Rachel told me to grow up simultaneously. I told TJ about the barbeque planned for Friday and told him to bring Heather if he was confident enough in his relationship with her that he would risk her becoming totally enamored with the owner of the premises.

"She's not into old, bald guys," was his catty response.

"You're damn near as old as me, and not near as sexy," was mine, as Rachel rolled her eyes.

After it started to get dark, we retired to the kitchen where Rachel and TJ discussed the next project, which was a Dodge Challenger R/T convertible with the 440 motor, the six pack carburation kit, the rare A32 Code Dana Super Performance Package rear end with the 4.10 gears, and the heavy duty A727 Torqueflite transmission. Meanwhile, I was busy putting together dinner which consisted of three egg Spanish omelets, bacon and baked beans. Afterwards, I let the kids clean up while I sat on the couch and caught up with my recorded episodes of 'Forged in Fire'. After the dishes were washed and in the drying rack, TJ retired to the bunkhouse and Rachel joined me in the living room. She curled up on the end and started going over some paperwork for the shop while I learned how to make a claymore. Granted, we tease each other incessantly, but we are comfortable enough in our relationship where conversation is not required every time we are together. I sometimes wonder why she hangs out with a guy 10 years older than her who is going bald. I tell myself it is my charming personality and sexual prowess.

After learning all that there is to know about forging a doublehanded Scottish meat cleaver, I kissed Rachel on the head and went up to my room to shower up and go to bed. A little later I felt Rachel crawl in beside me, press up against me and go to sleep. Life was good.

CHAPTER 10

THE REBUILD KIT FOR THE 429 motor had arrived from Barnett, so I went and picked it up from UPS and brought it back to the barn. For the next couple of days, I was in the zone putting my motor back together and made some serious headway on it.

Friday, I had to make another barbeque run into town to get the meat, potatoes, coleslaw, buns, and so forth. Getting back to the house around two, I again cleaned out the grill, loaded it up with mesquite briquettes, and prepared it to be fired up. At about five o'clock, Peio's old Suburban came into the courtyard and parked in front of the barn. Since TJ no longer lived at Peio's camp, he had to drive himself. I think this pissed him off, as he liked the idea of a chauffeur. I had a glass of Laphroaig ready for him and handed it to him as he passed me. He was headed for a couch on the porch, while I was on my way to light the grill. While getting the grill going, I heard the distinctive growl of Bret's low rider 1966 Impala SS coming up the driveway. He parked beside the Suburban in front of the barn and got out.

"Heard you white folks needed further instruction in the correct way to burn meat while cooking in the great outdoors." Typical Bret.

As he passed by the grill, I handed him the cooking utensils, "As I firmly support affirmative action, this grill is now your responsibility. Don't screw it up. I'll get you a beer so that you don't fake heat stroke and try to get out of the job." While getting a beer out of the cooler for Bret, I heard the hum of the 1950 Chevy pickup purring up the driveway. TJ parked in front of the bunkhouse, reached in the bed for a case of

Coors and came over to the porch. While I put the beer on ice in the cooler, TJ sat beside Peio, and they did some catching up.

Bret yelled up to TJ, “Man, when are you going to get a real ride? Nobody, and I mean nobody, rocks a straight six anymore!”

“Got it covered, Bret. Getting a 5-liter Coyote crate motor with a 4R70W automatic for it. Need to get the bald guy to figure out how to strengthen the frame as I’ll be running about 435 horses and 400 foot-pounds of torque.” I piped up that if TJ didn’t want to leave the rear axle lying in the road, he’d better upgrade that as well. Face it, working in a chop shop does not mean you know squat about building a decent ride.

About this time an almost, but not quite, silent vehicle approached us. We got quiet as well. Nobody except Peio brings a quiet vehicle to this house, it simply ruins the ambiance. It appeared to be a new Audi A4 with the S-line package and tinted glass. It backed up beside Bret’s proper ride, with the trunk toward the porch so that we had a grandstand view of whoever got out of the car. We waited to see what alien life forms would emerge from this foreign object. Both front doors opened, first one bare female leg emerges on each side, then the matching item comes out to join it. As the creatures slowly emerge, it is clear that the driver’s side creature is wearing a mid-thigh length dress while the other side has apparently nothing on! As they slowly emerge, the driver is attired in a navy-blue bandage dress, while the passenger has on some very nice high waisted pleated shorts in black and an off-the-shoulder midriff top in light blue. The driver has shoulder length platinum hair, while the passenger has raven hair which has been made into a thick braid down her back. The driver is a complete stranger, while the passenger looks vaguely familiar.

Obviously, Heather and Rachel had planned to make an entrance, and they did. All of us hard legs were standing around the porch speechless for several moments, before all hell broke loose. All the guys were yelling to get that piece of crap foreign car off the property and throwing their beer cans near, but not at, the girls or the Audi. I could read Rachel’s lips as she leaned over the roof of the Audi and said to a completely petrified Heather, “No class, I warned you.”

TJ finally quit laughing long enough to go get Heather and bring her to the porch for introductions. I went over as well and collected Rachel. “That was an entrance,” I said. “Your hair looks great, and I can’t remember the last time I saw you in something besides jeans, cut-off jeans, or Dickies.” Continuing, and in touch with my emotions, I said, “Damn you’re looking good!”

I had put my hand on her butt to walk her to the porch, but it was instantly raised to waist level. “Get your hand off of my butt while we are in public, and in polite company.”

I took an exaggerated look around, “Where would that be?” I could tell that I needed to be on my best behavior as she obviously didn’t want Heather to think we were a bunch of lecherous old men, although, truth be told, we actually were. Rachel took over introduction duties again, gave Peio a peck on the cheek and said, “Peio, I’d like to introduce my friend Heather to you.”

Peio, being the consummate gentleman, rose to his feet, kissed her hand like in some old movie, and said, “It is a pleasure to finally meet you, TJ has told me so much about you.” At this point I knew I’d been blindsided and that the only people there that were not aware of the budding romance were Bret and I. Bret was still manning the grill while trying not to drool into the fire.

While everyone else sat on the porch, I went down the steps to where Bret was standing and said, “Amigo, we’ve been had.” Taking a sip of Bret’s beer, “Everyone knew about the Norwegian goddess except us.” I asked him, “How could you possibly live in a town the size of Cadillac Springs and not know that such a creature was walking amongst you?”

“Obviously, I am getting old, near sighted, and my testosterone levels are dangerously low. We’d better eat.”

Heather was a knockout, if you happen to like 5-foot-7 Norwegian goddesses who are built like a brick shithouse. She was slightly shorter than Rachel but had more curves. As I like the swarthy, trim, and racy types, I still thought Rachel was the sexier of the two, but this is like comparing a Bugatti Veyron to a McLaren P1. It all comes down to your personal taste in perfection.

Bret and I gathered the food up, then went inside and placed it on the kitchen island so that people could serve themselves before retiring to the living room to eat. Peio had a place of honor in my recliner. Bret, Rachel and myself parked off on the couch, and TJ and Heather sat on the fireplace hearth. Everyone quizzed Heather about who she was, where she came from and how come no red-blooded American male in town had ever mentioned her.

Turns out that she had been working for a bank in Boulder since getting her first degree and was sick of the yuppie, liberal, bullshit lifestyle on the Front Range. When she was told about the opening in Cadillac Springs, she jumped at it. She’d been working at the bank here for 2 months or so and kept seeing TJ come into the bank each Friday afternoon to do the banking business for the shop, and thought he was cute. At this point TJ interrupted and said, “If any of you assholes ever call me ‘cute’, things are going to go sideways very quickly.”

Needless to say, Rachel batted her eyes and said, “But, TJ, you are cute, and from what I hear, in touch with your feminine side.” For a second nobody said a word, then everyone burst out laughing.

“Lucky for you that you are a skinny, under-developed strumpet, and my boss, or I’d have to take you out to the barn and spank you.”

At which point I piped up and said, “TJ, you’ve got your hands full, I’ll be glad to take her out to the barn and spank her. We’ll be back in about an hour or so.”

Heather really didn’t know us too well yet, so she paled a little, hard to tell with that complexion, at either the sexual innuendo or that she thought I really was going to take Rachel out to the barn and spank her. Anyhow, she continued her story.

She had essentially stalked TJ for a month, which I am certain he was aware of being a professional button man and confirmed that he ate his lunch at the bar, at the Double Z, every Tuesday and Thursday. She came up with a nefarious plan. She waited at a table in the back until he had placed his order one Thursday, then went up to the bar and sat on the stool next to him and said, totally out of character, “Hey, Sailor, buy me a drink?”

She says TJ went into anaphylactic shock, couldn’t breathe, was stuttering and turned beet red. She thought she’d have to give him mouth to mouth resuscitation, which would have meant her plan was working much better than anticipated. Instead, she laughed and said she’d been working up the guts to ask him out since she had first seen him walk into the bank. Eventually she got him calmed down enough to arrange a dinner and movie date for the next Saturday. And here she was.

Rachel had already briefed her on who the rest of us were, and what we did to get by, so we didn’t have to go around the room and do that nonsense. Peio, being the ladies’ man that he is, invited her and TJ to visit him at his new house once it was built on land that did not belong to him.

About nine o’clock, after a few more beers and a few more Laphroaig’s for Peio, the party broke up and everyone went their own way. Rachel and I tidied up a bit, and I put out the garbage in the bear proof bins beside the barn. Oddly enough, the Audi was still parked in front of the barn and TJ’s lights were out.

I was grinning when I got back inside. “What are you grinning about?” Rachel asked.

"Apparently Heather is explaining the finer points of finance to TJ. Her car is still here."

Thinking for a second, with her finger against the side of her head like she was pondering some abstract concept, she said, "I may not know a whole lot about finance, but if you shower up and get smelling good, I may be enticed to leave my room and introduce you to the finer points of 'full body massage'."

"Game on!" I said as I headed up the stairs, shedding my clothes and heading for the shower.

CHAPTER 11

The next morning, bright and early, I made a beeline to TJ's front door and knocked three times. After a few minutes the door opened, and a disheveled TJ opened the door.

"I happened to notice that Heather's car wouldn't start," I said pointing to the Audi. "You kids are invited to breakfast if you think that you still have enough energy to make it to the kitchen table," I offered with a grin. TJ couldn't make up his mind to laugh or to shoot me. I felt happy for him as I walked back to the house. Seems like things were starting to look up for him.

Today I was making French toast for breakfast, so I got out a half dozen eggs, milk, butter and the big skillet. While the butter was melting in the skillet, I got honey and syrup out of the cupboard, then began to cut up bananas. As I finished each batch of four toasts, I put them in the oven to keep warm until the natives became restless and started sniffing out breakfast.

The first native to appear was Rachel in her nighty heading for the coffee machine, which I had primed and readied prior to rousting TJ. "Darling, I love your outfit, and would like to slide it off you and have my way with you before breakfast, but I fear that shortly we'll have TJ and his Norwegian goddess coming over to join us. Unless she is dressed in a similar fashion, you may be underdressed for the occasion." Without a word she took her cup of coffee back up the stairs to her room to dress more appropriately. Sometimes I think TJ should turn me down for breakfast so that I could help Rachel dress properly. Before Rachel could make a reappearance, the front door opened and TJ walked into the kitchen followed, somewhat sheepishly, by Heather. Heather was not attired in her lingerie. A shame really. Heather sat down and I set a plate of French toast in front of her, then turned around to fix TJ a plate.

"Those Audis can be hard to start at times," I said with my back turned. TJ growled a warning, which I chose to ignore. "Similar to Porsches, they seem to develop ignition problems when the driver is feeling frisky. This is commonly known as the HFC problem amongst us car people."

A groan from TJ, while a sweet voice directly behind me said, "And what, pray tell, would HFC be an acronym for?" Rachel had snuck up behind me yet again, and now slapped the back of my head.

Without turning around, I said, "You would think that someone who restores cars for a living and drives a Porsche, is hot and occasionally frisky, would be aware of the Hot Frisky Chick syndrome." I fixed Heather's plate and took it to her. "There is nothing wrong with hot, frisky chicks, in fact I'm all for more of them," I told her.

"I fully expect to see the Audi experience HFC issues and be parked in that same spot in the future, just don't block in the Porsche. The HFC owner and operator of that vehicle has anger management issues. Which you have just seen firsthand."

"I'm dating an emotionally retarded dolt," Rachel explained to Heather.

"Let's go sit in the living room and have a decent conversation while these two muttonheads shovel French toast down their necks. I've seen it before, it's not pretty."

"So, what are your thoughts on lingerie, TJ?" I said as the girls retreated to the living room but loud enough that they could hear me.

"Racy teddy or silk cami set?" Heather missed a step. I just grinned at TJ, who surprisingly, grinned back.

After everyone had eaten and the kitchen was shipshape again, TJ and Heather said goodbye and the Audi, no longer suffering from HFC ignition issues, took off down the driveway followed by the 1950 Chevy. The Chevy had an arm out the window giving us a 'thumbs up'.

"Well, which is it?" Rachel asked. "Racy teddy or silk cami set?"

"Well, it all boils down to the one piece or two-piece issue, and which is easier to remove. It is really simply a question of self-control. As you mentioned previously, it is similar to opening your Christmas presents. The anticipation only adds to the thrill."

“Answer the question, cowboy!” she demanded.

“Without further study, I cannot definitively answer the question, Ms. Chen.”

“If you ever embarrass Heather in this house again, I will guarantee you that you will never, ever be able to answer that question, definitively or otherwise. Is that understood?”

Note to self. Never, ever embarrass Heather in my own house again.

Rachel had changed into her standard uniform of cut-off jeans and one of my t-shirts, this time, the 1979 Boston at Giants Stadium version, and only required the Dickie coveralls to be ready for work. As I walked her to the door she reached up, pulled my head down to her level and gave me a kiss that almost curled my toes.

“Racy teddy would have been the correct answer, you obviously need to be educated. School will be in session this evening. Don’t be late.” She then walked out to the Whale Tail without a look back and took off for work. Women are very strange creatures.

At about this point Rachel realized that she had actually arrived with Heather last night in Heather’s Audi and that her Porsche was still in town. She sheepishly returned to the kitchen and begged for a lift to her shop. This cost her an additional 30 minutes of racy teddy lessons that evening. Who said oilfield rednecks can’t negotiate?

CHAPTER 12

AFTER DROPPING RACHEL OFF AND returning home, I refilled the coffee machine and fired it up for round two. After shaving, and brushing my teeth, I went back down to the kitchen and poured about a quart of coffee in the big, insulated mug I use in the barn, and went out to continue working on the 429 motor.

While installing the bearings and shells I started thinking about TJ's Coyote motor. I was jealous, pure and simple. That said, a 429 Cobra Jet is old school muscle, and if I wanted to, I could do some upgrades later to at least allow me to keep his tail lights in sight.

After getting the bearings and associated hardware installed correctly, I had started to install the crankshaft when Peio showed up in his Suburban. This was an odd occurrence since he never shows up uninvited as a matter of decorum, although he is more than welcome at any time. I wiped off my hands while he parked on the apron in front of the barn, got out and came inside and shook my hand.

"We've got a problem," he said. From the look on his face, it was a serious problem whatever it was.

Grabbing my coffee mug, I said, "Let's take it in the house and talk about it over a fresh coffee." He nodded, turned and I followed him onto the porch and into the kitchen. Pouring him a cup of coffee and refreshing mine, I said, "What's the problem, Peio?"

"Have you noticed a few strange pickups and motorcycles going up and down 325 lately?" he asked.

"Not really, but I haven't been paying much attention."

"Well, there has been. As you know, I am building a house up north where my old trailer has been parked, thank you for letting me squat there by the way, and I have noticed the new traffic."

I interrupted at this point. "Just curious, Peio, did you get a permit to build that house?"

"Everything has been taken care of and is totally legal. You will find that your property taxes will increase some, but it is a pittance to pay for me being in the neighborhood. If you run into any financial difficulty due to my presence on your property, please let me know. Can I get on with my description of the problem now?"

"Pardon the interruption, please carry on." We like to keep things formal for the first few minutes of any conversation between us.

"I decided to follow one of these trucks one day in my Suburban. You know where 325 dead ends at the old homestead?" I assured him that I did as it sat on one of my property lines. "There are about six motorcycles, two pickup trucks and one large mobile home there. Apparently, they are camping out and it looks like they are planning to stay there for a while. I'd rather they didn't."

"Did you inform the sheriff?" I asked.

"With my background, TJ's as well, it may not be a good idea to get law enforcement involved. We do not want them arrested and then have to give a statement and identify ourselves, we simply want them gone and not to come back."

Standing up I said, "Let's go take a look. We'll take my truck since they may have seen yours. Let me get a camera as well."

Getting into the F-150 we drove to a point on 325 where we could get out and walk through the woods to a position above and behind the old homestead to take a look. The old homestead house was still standing and was usually utilized by the local high school kids for parties. Surprisingly, they hadn't burned it to the ground yet. There was no glass left in any window of the fairly large, two story house, but structurally it was holding out. Any outbuilding associated with the house had long ago been used by the kids as firewood for the bonfires at their parties. That thought actually brought back fond memories.

Using binoculars, I could see that the motorcycles and pickups were parked haphazardly in front of the house, but the mobile home was parked parallel with the back of the house, out of view from the entrance. The mobile home had all the windows except the windshield blacked out, and there was a strange set of exhaust stacks or vents coming through the roof at the back. I took some photos of the set-up with the zoom lens which came with the camera. The camera is Rachel's, and I am not a photographer, but looking at the photos on the screen they were clear enough for what I wanted.

Rolling from the prone position to my back, I looked at Peio, who remained prone, and said, "Peio, that's a mobile meth lab. Judging by the bikes, this operation will be run by an outlaw biker gang, one of the 'one percenters'. We may need to get law enforcement to help us out."

"Not an option. I assume that you have a plan?" he asked.

"Working on it. Let's get back to the truck." We got back to the truck unnoticed, and I drove us back to my place. I asked Peio to come by tomorrow night. I'd have a plan ready then.

After he left, I went back to the barn and cleaned up my workshop, put on some clean jeans and a t-shirt and drove to the sheriff's office. Blake Wiggins is an old Marine Gunnery Sergeant. He is also an old school law enforcement officer. I had known him for a few years as I used to upgrade the Sheriff's Department SUVs with Kevlar sheets in the body panels and bullet resistant glass.

Although it was a Saturday, Blake was at work. I walked into the sheriff's office and asked the receptionist if I could speak to the sheriff. She asked if I had an appointment, which I didn't, but Blake had come out of his office and told her it was okay. We retired to his office.

"What brings you in on a Saturday, Jeb?" he asked.

"Take a look at these photos," I said as I handed him the camera.

"When were these taken?"

"This morning," I told him.

"That RV appears to be a meth lab and the bikes mean it is being run by some outlaw gang. If I am not mistaken that is the old house at the end of 325?"

"You are correct. We need to get rid of them, but we don't want to start a war with these idiots. Furthermore, I would really not like to be identified in court as whoever they are, they will want payback, and Rachel is up at my place alone when I am out of the country."

"How did you talk her into that?" was his first question, but before I could answer, "Do you have a plan?" was his second. Didn't anyone else ever have a plan?

"I do, but I'll need to borrow a couple of hazmat suits and associated gear so that I'll look like I am officially checking for some terrible disease. A Colorado

Department of Health and the Environment van would add to the deception as well. Also a few stick-on GPS tracking devices."

"What's the plan?" he asked. So, I told him.

He agreed to my plan with the caveat that TJ and I would be wearing wires and that he, and his boys, would be hiding out at my place monitoring us in case things went sideways.

After dinner the following evening, Peio, TJ, Rachel, and myself sat down in my living room to discuss my cunning plan. First, Peio described what he had first noticed concerning the new traffic on 325. I told them about the reconnaissance that Peio and I had done that morning and showed them the photos. I then laid out the plan.

Tomorrow morning early, the sheriff would come by with his tooled-up SWAT crew to hold station at my place. They would be bringing the necessary equipment, suits and van, which he had borrowed from the Colorado Department of Health and the Environment, along with an expert to show TJ and I how to use it all.

Later in the morning, once everyone was satisfied with our performance, TJ and I would drive the van to within 50 yards of the old homestead house with the lightbar on the roof doing its thing. We would get out of the van and put on the hazmat suits and respirators. At this point we expected the bikers to get curious and come out to find out what we were doing. I would then go into my spiel about the house they were using was reported to be infected with the Hantavirus, and that we had to inspect the property to determine if it was or not. While poking around the property we would attach tracking devices to the RV. When we left, we would let the bikers know that the property was infected with the Hantavirus and strongly suggest that they get out of there as soon as possible. We would then go back to the van, take off the respirators and hazmat suits, and drive the van back to the sheriff's office to rendezvous with Blake and his crew.

Blake would have put a guy on the hill behind the homestead to monitor the situation, but it was assumed that the bikers would leave posthaste for parts unknown. Blake's boys and girls would track them by the GPS units attached to the mobile home and apprehend them once they were far enough away to keep me, TJ, and Cadillac Springs out of it.

TJ, being a rational adult, asked, "Are we going to be gunned up?"

"Is a pig's ass pork? Of course, we will be gunned up. Who knows how these 'one percenters' will react? We probably shouldn't mention this to Blake though," I said.

"What is my part in this devious plan?" Rachel asked.

"You will hide in your room until this is over. In the first place, I do not want you anywhere near the bikers. Secondly, if you go strutting around outside, the SWAT boys and perhaps even Blake, will be drooling like adolescent high school boys at a cheerleader convention, and will not be paying attention to our wires."

"So, if I am reading you correctly, I can't be actively involved, and Heather and I will essentially be prisoners. Is that correct?"

"You've got it in one, Sweet Cheeks." As soon as I said that, I knew that Rachel was hatching a devious plan of her own.

I kicked TJ and Peio out around nine o'clock and told them to get a good night's sleep in preparation for tomorrow's fun and games. If you remember, I was supposed to attend lingerie school tonight with Dr. Feelgood, and I didn't want to be late for class.

I woke up alone at six, which is probably good since I didn't have time to spend fooling around fondling hot, mixed-race, auto restorers of the female persuasion. I headed downstairs to get the coffee going. I didn't bother with any food as I was hoping that the SWAT guys brought donuts to share. After firing up the coffee machine, I went out and knocked on TJ's door to make sure that he was up and running. Going back to my house I grabbed a cup of coffee then sat on one of the couches on the porch to wait for everyone else to show up. About 15 minutes later TJ wandered out, I told him the coffee was on and to grab a cup. We had been sitting on the porch drinking coffee for about another 15 minutes when we heard vehicles coming up the driveway. First in was the SWAT van, followed closely by a Colorado Department of Safety and the Environment van. They parked in the middle of the courtyard, and everybody got out. There was Blake, four of his henchmen, and a scholarly looking chap I took to be the expert from the CDSE.

After the introductions, I told everyone where the coffee was and asked where the donuts were. Cops get tired of donut jokes, but I wasn't joking. One of the henchmen went to the back of the SWAT van and brought out a few dozen donuts from the shop in town. Now we were ready to get to work. The expert showed us how to put on the hazmat suits and respirators, and TJ and I practiced until we looked like we knew what we were doing. Next, he got out an air testing machine and ran me through the training on it as I would be the one operating it. While I was playing with that, he got out a soil sampling kit and showed TJ how to look like he was taking samples. After an hour or so we were deemed competent. The expert then gave us each proper

CDSE uniforms, so TJ and I went into the house, got another cup of coffee, and changed into the uniforms and our own work boots. Blake came in and gave us each a GPS tracking unit and showed TJ how to attach and activate them. I already had that merit badge from Kurdistan.

The crew had gathered on the porch to wait for the sun to get up. My back was to the front door. The burble of conversation went silent, as if a switch had been thrown. I thought everyone was looking at me, but I was sure I was zipped up and hadn't farted. I realized that they were not, in fact, looking at me, but at the zombie supermodel with the bed hair, pajama shorts and my 1969 Allman Brothers Band at Jacksonville Armory t-shirt on. Even in that condition she is ravishing and sexy, in a weird sort of way.

"What is with you stormtroopers? People are trying to sleep around here," she said as she came out on the porch to give Blake a peck on the cheek. Excellent public relations technique. "I thought you had better control of your people than this, Blake."

He was still stammering when Rachel turned around and walked back into the house, slapping one of the stormtroopers on the ass on the way by. He spilled his coffee.

"Okay, show's over, what say we go do this?" I said, while pitching my F-150 keys to the SWAT guy who would be over watching from the back of the house. At eight thirty TJ and I saddled up in the CDSE van and got underway after a communications check with Blake.

Everything was going fine. The sun was coming up, the birds were chirping and the lightbar on the roof was working as advertised. I wanted to turn on the siren, but TJ said that would probably be overkill. Fifty yards from the old house TJ stopped and slid the transmission into park. We got out, opened the sliding door on the passenger's side, and began putting on our hazmat suits and respirators. Sure enough, according to the script, a great big mountain of a biker came out of the front door headed our way, followed by two other normal-sized bikers. As we couldn't speak to them with our respirators on, we took them off.

The man mountain was dressed in what I assumed was the officer's version of the outlaw biker gang uniform. A filthy denim work shirt with the sleeves cut off to show arms the size of tree trunks, filthy oil-stained jeans, a wide leather belt with a Death's Head buckle, and steel toed boots. On each finger and thumb was a bulky ring of some description, negating the need to carry a set of brass knuckles. He was easily 6-1/2 feet tall and probably went 300 pounds. His head was shaved, but he was sporting a bushy ginger beard which hid the lower half of his face.

The other two had on what I supposed were biker enlisted fatigues, consisting of greasy worn-out jean jackets worn over greasy t-shirts of indeterminate color on top, with the requisite greasy jeans and work boots on bottom. We'll refer to these two guys as Heckle and Jeckle.

They all stunk.

Getting right in my face, the big fellow said, "What the hell do you think you are doing here?" His breath would have gagged a maggot.

"That house," I said pointing at the old farmhouse, "may be infested by vermin carrying the Hantavirus. We've been sent by the Colorado Department of Safety and the Environment to check it out and determine if that is the case. If so, we are authorized to quarantine the premises."

"Quarantine this, asshole," said Heckle pulling out a gigantic revolver he had been holding behind his back. While Heckle was doing his impression of a badass, TJ had been staring at Man Mountain's eyes. He pulled out a penlight from the pocket protector built into the hazmat suit, switched it on and motioned for Man Mountain to lean forward so that he could shine the light in his eyes, obviously checking for something.

"Have you been experiencing fatigue, fever and muscle aches, especially in the large muscle groups such as your thighs, hips, back and shoulders?" TJ asked while still shining the light into his eyes.

"I've always got fatigue and muscle aches, you idiot, I ride a motorcycle for a living and haven't slept in a real bed in months!" said the mountain.

"Open wide," says TJ. The guy actually did! "How about a shortness of breath, coughing, and a sensation similar to a tight band around your chest or a pillow over your face?"

"I've smoked for 30 years! Of course, I hack, cough, and get short of breath."

"Interesting," says TJ. "You also show signs of jaundice with possible complications associated with an overactive thyroid, better known as Grave's Disease. How do the others look, Peter?" I was Peter today; I had also gotten my penlight out and was performing a similar examination of Heckle and Jeckle.

"Same symptoms here, George." TJ was playing George today.

TJ had crossed one arm over his chest, gripping the elbow of the other arm, which was stroking his chin, while staring at the house in deep contemplation. "Gentlemen, we desperately need to inspect the house and surroundings to get a better idea as to what we have here."

The three biker clowns took a few steps back and had a private conversation amongst themselves. "You can look at the grounds outside of the house, but do not go into the house or the RV behind the house," said Man Mountain.

TJ was getting into his role by this time. "That is unacceptable, the vermin which carry the Hantavirus would be concentrated inside the structure, not on the outside. We need to get inside."

"Ain't going to happen, man, you can check whatever you can get to on the outside, but you're not going to be going inside."

"You realize that the Hantavirus has a mortality rate of thirty-eight percent, don't you?" I asked.

"What!" exclaimed Heckle.

"It's true," I said. "38 out of 100 people who contract the disease will die."

The rough, tough, hard to bluff bikers were starting to get uneasy by this time. Seeing a 50-gallon drum outside the house filled with KFC, McDonald's and Dominoes' bags and boxes, I had to twist the knife. "The Hantavirus is known to procreate much more rapidly in an environment where they can feed on used cooking oils commonly found in deep fryers and associated with junk food. Have you been disposing of any waste containing such oil in a proper manner?" I asked.

They all looked back at the fifty-gallon drum. "You'd best get busy. Don't go into the house or the RV and let me know what you find before you leave," said the big guy.

Putting our respirators back on and getting our sniffer and sample machines out of the van, we approached the house. I began testing the air around the foundation of the house with the sniffer probe while TJ made as if he was taking samples of the soil every 5 feet or so. Jeckle was following me around, while Heckle was following TJ. When I was at the back of the house, between the RV and the house, I acted like I had found something interesting. It was actually a dead marmot. Heckle left TJ on his own at the other side of the RV for a second while he came to see what the commotion was. TJ tagged the RV with his tracking device. At this point TJ started making a commotion and pointing down at the ground and mumbling something incoherent inside his respirator. When Heckle and Jeckle went around the RV to see what TJ was mumbling about, I tagged my side of the RV.

We continued around the house, finished up and walked to the CDSE van where we took off our respirators and hazmat suits. We were putting our kit away when the Three Stooges came back to talk to us.

“What’d you guys find?” asked Man Mountain.

“Well, without being able to access the inside of the house, we can’t say definitively. From what we’ve seen, I would say that there is a 50/50 chance of Hantavirus infestation in that house,” said George. I added that at fifty percent chance of infestation, the mortality rate would drop to 19 percent. But the odds were that it was much greater.

With that, we closed up the van, got in, made a three-point turn and headed back to the sheriff’s office, laughing all the way. We had called Blake to let him know that the tracking devices were in place, and he confirmed that they were working. He’d wait an hour at the ranch to see what the RV did before going back to town. Which I found odd as you can track the RV from anywhere.

Three hours later Blake and the stormtroopers arrived back at his office. “What the hell took you so long?” I demanded. The stormtroopers scattered.

“Well, a girl showed up in an Audi, and her and Rachel decided to sit out on your front porch,” explained Blake.

“And…” I asked.

“Well, they weren’t wearing much, although they assured me that they were wearing proper swimming attire,” he explained. “Once you guys started with your routine, I put it on external speaker, and we all laughed our asses off. You have to admit it was like a comedy routine. When you were on your way back, the girls fixed lunch for the boys, and it was damn near impossible to get them to leave. Honestly, it was like herding cats!” Blake exclaimed. “I do not know how you guys possibly live around those women. I’d never be able to concentrate on anything, and likely have a heart attack.”

“I’ve been told that it is a cross that I have to bear,” I told him. “I suppose someone is actually watching the trackers on the van, since that was the whole purpose of the exercise?”

“We’ll continue to watch it here once it moves out of the county, but I’ve passed it to the Highway Patrol and they, along with the Colorado Bureau of Investigation, will bust them once they are out of the area.”

About this time, Rachel and Heather showed up to give us a lift, still in swimming attire although they were now modestly wrapped from the waist down in sarongs, which did absolutely nothing to hide what was underneath. We decided to go to the Double Z for a late lunch. Big mistake. Although the place was packed on a Saturday afternoon, it went silent when Heather and Rachel proceeded TJ and I into the place and stayed silent until well after we were seated. It was like the clowns had never seen a pair of supermodels in bikinis and sarongs eating barbeque with their fingers. Some people really need to get out more.

CHAPTER 13

MONDAY ROLLED AROUND; I WOKE up alone as Rachel was in the shower. Putting on a pair of jeans and a t-shirt, I headed down to the kitchen to get the coffee going. As it was a work day, and I didn't feel like working, I got out the bagels, cream cheese, bananas, peanut butter, and put two bagels in the oven. I agree with Rachel, cream cheese, peanut butter and bananas are a perfect topping for bagels.

As usual, Rachel came down the stairs and headed for the coffee pot before saying a thing.

After a few sips of coffee, Rachel states, "I need to speak with the management. I pay an outrageous rent for this fleabag bed and breakfast, and all I get is bagels for breakfast."

"First off, you haven't paid management a dime since you've been here. Second, the management is concerned about your health and figure. You appear to be getting curvier, which the management does not feel is required, necessary or desired. The management has decided to cut your caloric intake in an effort to keep you slim, trim and racy."

Pondering my response, she finally replied, "First, said management did not seem to be disappointed in my health and figure last night. As to your second point, these bagels are essentially 'fat bombs', tasty but dangerous nonetheless."

"It is a difficult task for the management to balance your energy levels with your caloric intake. The best solution seems to be to feed you well, then work it off you later," was my cunning comeback.

"Judging by management's lack of stamina last night, you may need to enlist supplemental management to effectively keep me in shape."

"I doubt that there are any other suitable managers who could put up with your incessant whining. I suggest that we schedule a secondary workout, first thing in the morning, to alleviate management's concerns," I suggested hopefully.

"Don't be silly. You know that until I have had my first cup of coffee in the morning, I barely have a pulse."

"Management understands this issue and is willing to put a coffee machine beside the bed so that you don't have to exert yourself too much for that first cup of coffee, while still keeping you 'in the ring', if you will."

Smiling, she said, "Fat chance of that. What are you going to do today while us working stiffs toil for our coin?"

"Think I'll go into town and stock up on the groceries, then go hang out with Bret for a while before coming home and getting back on the 429. What do you want for dinner?"

"How about some fish? We haven't had fish in some time. As it's Monday, I'll be boxing with Bret after finishing at the shop, so I may be a little late," she said as she was heading toward the door.

"I'll get some fish at the Safeway and have it ready to go when you get home. Don't let Bret hurt you too much....and stop hitting like a girl!" I said as she got to the door.

With one hand on the doorknob, she turned her head and said, "Says the guy who couldn't fight his way out of a wet paper bag." Smiling sweetly, she left. I really need to consider taking up a martial art or something.

Driving to the Safeway I cleared my head of the lack of fighting skills by blasting 'Bat Out of Hell' by Meatloaf at reasonably elevated decibels. You've just got to love that piano! After stocking up on the usual 'meat and potatoes' items, I went in search of a suitable fish. After much deliberation I selected three nice pieces of Mahi-Mahi, can't forget TJ. I almost made a serious faux pas by forgetting coffee, but recovered nicely. From there, it was a straight shot to the liquor store to top up the beer supplies. At this point I was in a jam. I could go harass Bret and let the food spoil, I could go back to the house and unload the food before harassing Bret, or I could go with Plan C. I went with Plan C and drove over to the gym, carried all the perishables into Bret's office and put them in the refrigerator he has there. I then stole two beers and went back out to where the ring was located to find Bret.

I found him standing on the floor below the elevated ring yelling at, he says training, one of the two young Hispanic guys beating the crap out of each other in the ring. Tapping him on the shoulder I handed him a beer.

"Hey, mate, I'm looking for a short black guy who is going blind and has seriously low testosterone levels. Seen him around?"

Bret looked at me without blinking an eye and said, "Says the guy who couldn't fight his way out of a wet paper bag."

"Dammit! Rachel already called you and told you about her sass this morning. Is nothing sacred?"

"Not to that girl. You really should learn how to fight," says Bret.

"I'll have you know that I am trained in the secret art of Navy SEAL fighting."

"Yeah, what's that?" asked Bret.

"Go absolutely crazy for as long as you possibly can. Maximum violence delivered in minimal time," I expounded.

"And if that doesn't work?"

"Shoot them."

"Whatever works I suppose," was Bret's less than supportive comment.

We went back to Bret's office for another beer and a bullshit session. Bret kicked back in his chair with his feet up on his desk while I reclined on the ratty old couch against the wall. I told him about the fun and games over the weekend with the mentally deficient bikers, which had him laughing. I then got into the way Rachel and Heather had played the SWAT team and how their hormone levels had probably still not dropped to normal levels. I surmised that if they were married, they probably had worked out their hormonal issues with their wives by Sunday night, and that the wives would be somewhat sore and annoyed at the girls for a while. Or not, the wives might send them back out to the ranch for a testosterone top-up. Who knows?

"Speaking of which, how could you possible not know that Heather was in town? You know everyone in the single's crowd in town, and not one of them let the cat out of the bag?" I asked.

"Obviously, she wore some sort of disguise. Wigs, baggy clothes, walked with a limp, Groucho glasses, the basics. There is no way I would not have known had she acted and dressed normally. If I would have known, I'd have cut TJ out so fast it would have made his head spin," he said with a smile.

"Bret, Bret, Bret, we gotta find you a proper woman. A fine, sophisticated lady, preferably not a gym rat or a grease monkey like Rachel, they are dangerous.

Furthermore, except for the money you could extort from her, you don't need a banker. One in the gang is enough. Perhaps a lawyer, we need a good lawyer in the group."

At this point Bret got a faraway look in his eyes and softly said, "I'm working on it," but he said it with such emotion you could tell that there was a backstory there and that it was not a topic for light conversation.

After a while I grabbed my perishables out of his refrigerator and made my way home. I drug all the stuff into the kitchen and put it away before chopping up an onion, putting it in a large glass baking dish and squeezing three lemons worth of juice on top of it. I then placed the Mahi-Mahi in the dish, covered it with Saran Wrap and placed it in the refrigerator to marinate. Going into the formal dining room, which I use as my office, I paid some bills and called Blake to see what the story was on the meth lab. Seems the Highway Patrol and the Colorado Bureau of Investigation let the lab roll into Denver before busting it. Apparently, the bikers were part of the Flat Liners Motorcycle Club out of Phoenix. The gang was lawyering them up, but the amount of evidence did not bode well for them. The bikers were convinced that the old homestead was infected with Hantavirus and had spread the word, so it was unlikely that anyone else would use the place in the future.

With that sorted out, I went back to the kitchen and took the Saran Wrap off the fish and flipped them over before covering them again and putting them back in the refrigerator to soak. About that time TJ knocked on the door and came in when I yelled that it was open. I asked him when Rachel had left for the gym, and he told me about 2 hours ago. She would be home soon, so I set the oven to pre-heat to 425 degrees, grabbed two beers and met TJ on one of the porch couches.

"How's it going at the shop these days?" I asked.

"Moving along pretty well," he replied. "The GT500 will be finished in a week or so and then we'll move on to the 1970 Challenger."

"That's a pretty fast restoration for an old Mustang."

"True enough, but Rachel knows her business and has plenty of contacts, so we are never waiting long for parts. It's really just a matter of tear it down, build it up, paint it and move it along," he said.

"She must be making money hand over fist. I'd better check the books and make sure she's actually giving me a true ten percent. I should have known better than to mix business and pleasure, it only leads to deceit and heartache," I said with a grin while getting off the couch.

I had heard the Whale Tail pull into the driveway, so I went into the kitchen and got the Mahi-Mahi out of the refrigerator, unwrapped it, then wrapped each piece in a foil tent with some of the lemon and onion marinade. I cleaned the baking dish and dried it before placing the three 'tents' in it and putting the dish in the oven for 25 minutes.

Rachel had come in wearing tight, black Lycra workout shorts and a matching sports bra covered with a sweaty oversized muscle shirt. She said, "Hi, guys," as she headed into the house to shower up.

TJ turned around on the couch and said, "I can see where the deceit and heartache may be worth it."

"You should see it when it's cleaned up!"

By the time I set the table for three, made a salad, and grabbed the sun tea pitcher off the porch, the fish was ready to serve. Rachel had come back downstairs looking much more presentable in a loose, casual jumpsuit sort of thing, and sat down at the table. Once everything was on the island, everyone served themselves.

After a few minutes Rachel told us about several phone calls she had received from some guy inquiring about buying the shop. She had told him firmly that she was not interested, but he continued to call.

"The next time he calls, give him my number and have him call me. I'll sort it out," I told her.

"No, the business is mine, I need to sort this out. I'll ask him to come by the shop and we'll discuss it face to face."

"You seem to be taking this pretty seriously, cupcake, is there more to this?"

"This guy called just before I went to the gym. I told him again that I am not interested in selling and his comment was, 'you will be', like a threat."

I looked at TJ, "What do you think, intimidation to sell, or going for a protection scheme?"

"Hard to tell. I can't see where Cadillac Springs could support a protection racket. My guess is that if he is serious, he'll use intimidation and vandalism to force the sale." He was pensive for a moment, then said, "It must be some small-time hood. Anyone with the IQ of frozen yogurt would know that the business would fail without Rachel being on the letterhead."

"IQ of frozen yogurt. I like that. Can I use that line?"

"Feel free, but I get royalties." He continued, "Here's how we should play this. The next time he calls, set up an appointment at the shop to discuss the issue. They must know about me working there, so we get Bret and Jeb to wait out on Roosevelt Avenue in vehicles so that they can tail the guy either back to his house or to his business. Once we know who he is and where we can find him, we intimidate him to the point where he loses interest."

Rachel perked up at this, she probably wanted a little variety in her life and intimidating a Mafia wannabe sounded pretty good to her. I had to nip this in the bud. "You set him up, we take him down, Sweet Cheeks. No way I want you involved when we ding the guy."

"Hey! It's my shop and I need to be involved," she said indignantly.

"You will be, you're setting him up. If you were involved any further and things went sideways, you could go to court and lose the shop just the same."

She didn't like it, but she knew I was right. After we cleaned up the kitchen, Rachel went into the office room while TJ and I sat at the kitchen island.

"We need to get this sorted sooner rather than later. Hopefully, this guy will call tomorrow and we can follow him then. I need to get it done and dusted before I head back to Kurdistan," I told TJ.

"Understood. Depends on how much of a loser this guy is, but he may bring muscle to add to the intimidation. When the meet occurs, I'll keep an eye on Rachel, but let's hope it doesn't go sideways inside the shop."

TJ went off to the bunkhouse, and I went into the living room office to hang around with Rachel. She was still spooked about the caller, so I came up behind the office chair, put my hands on her shoulders and started massaging the tense muscles there. She leaned her head back against my stomach and sighed.

"All I wanted to do was have my own shop, have a good life, and not bother anyone. Now some complete stranger is trying to take it all away." Tears were forming at the corner of her eyes. This got to me as generally Rachel does not get emotional.

This was really bothering her, which meant it was really bothering me. "Don't worry about it, honey, between all of us, we have it covered. Let's go to bed and forget about it for today." Which is what we did.

CHAPTER 14

TUESDAY DAWNED AND RACHEL SEEMED her old self again. I got her fed, a couple of cups of coffee down her neck, and off she went to work. I could tell that she was still a bit angry about the whole 'selling the shop' business as she gave me a hug and a kiss while going out the door, but without the usual bantering.

I performed my morning ablutions, then got in the truck to go down and fill Bret in on the problem and the plan. Getting to the gym, I parked the truck out front and went in to find Bret. He was on the far side of the ring working out on a speed bag. I told you earlier about how fast his hands were, but you really had to see it to believe it. He was doing a figure eight with either hand where you start by punching the bag with the front part of the knuckles, follow through then hit it on the rebound with the top part of the knuckles, then catch that rebound with the front part of the knuckles on the other hand, catch the rebound with the top part of the knuckles on the other hand, and repeat. When normal people do this, it sounds like, tadada, tadada, tadada, and the bag is in a rhythm. When Bret does it the bag is nothing but a blur and the sound is a dull roar. When he had finished beating the crap out of the defenseless inflatable bag, I asked him if I could speak to him in his office.

"Must be serious," he said while pulling his gloves off and heading toward the office.

"At the moment, problematic, but could go to serious," I told him.

When we had gotten comfortable in his office, I told him the whole story and how we planned to sort it out. I told him that he needed to be ready to come by the shop and help me to tail this asshole, once Rachel had organized a meeting with him.

"No problem, amigo. I'll give Nicholas a heads up to take over the gym when he sees me leave and I'll be there." Nicholas is a huge black guy, with muscles on top of his muscles, and 3-foot-long dreadlocks. He looks like the Predator but is a nice guy if you don't piss him off too much.

"You might want to get something else to drive as your Impala tends to stick out," I suggested.

"I've got an old Dodge panel van I use for gym stuff. I'll use it."

"You might need a little more performance than an old panel van."

"Dude, it's running a 426 Hemi and the suspension has been upgraded, I think I'll be able to keep up with this cracker."

"Cracker is a derogatory term for white folks. I thought you were above that?" I smiled.

"I'd say get used to it, not only are you a cracker, but you're also oilfield trash. A double hit."

"You've got a point there. Keep your phone with you and I'll call you when the game is on."

I got back in my truck and headed over to the shop to see what Rachel and TJ were up to. Nobody was in the office when I got there, so I walked through to the back. TJ was under the driver's side of the Mustang again.

"What's up?" I said to his boots.

"This damn power steering control valve is acting up," he said while rolling out from under the car and standing up.

"They're always a pain in the ass once you get air in the lines. Better you than me. Where's Rachel?"

"She said she had to go do some chores about an hour ago. I imagine she'll have lunch with Heather while they figure out new and different ways to wind us up and spend our money."

"A small price to pay, my friend."

We went to lunch as well, at McDonald's, and by the time we got back Rachel was in the office. We had no sooner gotten in the front door when the phone rang. Sure enough, it was the persistent, wannabe shop buying asshole. Rachel kept a civil tongue in her head while she organized a meeting for four thirty at the shop that afternoon. I called Bret and let him know, while TJ went out to his truck to make sure his Glock was there with a suppressor handy. The guy takes looking out for Rachel seriously these days, I guess he needs a paycheck.

At about four fifteen, a relatively new, Black Chevy Tahoe pulled up under the awning where the gas pumps used to be. The driver, who looked like a 6-foot-tall steroid junkie in a dark suit, got out, went to the back-side passenger door, and opened it. Out stepped a medium sized businessman also in a dark suit. The driver closed the door before preceding his principal across the driveway and opening the door to the office. The principal then preceded the driver into the office. Intimidation 101.

Fifteen minutes later, Peio's old Suburban shows up and parked head-to-head with the Tahoe. Two old cowboy looking guys got out of the front, while Peio climbed out of the back, before they all headed over to the office. This was not in the game plan. Bret and I were out of sight on Roosevelt Avenue, one facing one way and the other facing the other so that we could start tailing as soon as the guy left, regardless of which direction he took. We had to stick with the plan since we didn't know what was going on. At least TJ was there with his suppressed Glock if things went sour.

Bret and I found out what had happened shortly after the gangster wannabe left. TJ called me in time to let me know not to follow the guy when he left, and I called Bret to let him know. What happened was, the guy had come in with his muscle to intimidate Rachel into selling the place to him. Unknown to everyone else was the fact that Rachel had not gone shopping and to lunch with Heather, she had run up to Peio's place to let him know what was happening. As I said earlier, Rachel is the daughter that Peio never had, so this situation seriously pissed him off. He told Rachel to call him as soon as the meeting was arranged. Peio then rounded up two of his old cronies, who were likely related to Billy the Kid or Wyatt Earp, and waited for Rachel's call.

When Peio's cowboy buddies walked into the office ahead of Peio, the amateur gangster's driver went to pull out a pistol from the small of his back. A poorly thought-out move. Peio's buddies magically produced their own old, well worn, gigantic revolvers and both were pointing them at the driver's head. At this point the actual amateur gangster turned around in the chair he was sitting in, one of those in front of Rachel's desk, to see what was happening. In walked Peio and the gangster turned white as a sheet.

"I thought you were dead?" says the aspiring gangster to Peio.

Peio replied, "I get that a lot. You and I need to talk. Actually, I will talk, and you will listen."

Peio then told the guy, we never found out his name, that from that point forward he was never to approach Rachel, or anyone Rachel associated with. In fact, it would probably be good for his health if he vacated Cadillac Springs for another location of his choosing, as soon as possible. If Peio ever heard that he was anywhere in the vicinity of Cadillac Springs, or more importantly, ever harassed Rachel again, that he would have him killed. Peio then asked if the gangster had understood everything that Peio had said. The guy was having difficulty breathing at this point and was sweating like a fat person in a sauna, but managed to nod. At which point Peio told him that he could go.

Billy the Kid and Wyatt Earp had disarmed the driver by this time and were arguing over who got to keep the .45 Springfield Armory XD that the driver had been carrying. The gangster wannabe and the driver then departed for destinations unknown.

When they left, Bret and I drove to the shop and walked into the office, everyone was laughing their asses off. But deep inside we all realized that Peio had pulled the stunt off far better than we could ever have hoped to do. The thing is, Peio was not joking. He had done this for Rachel.

Wyatt and Billy drove the Suburban back to Peio's place, and the rest of us went to the Double Z for dinner. Afterwards, TJ drove Peio to the bunkhouse, where he'd stay the night, before TJ drove him home the next day. Bret went back to the gym to ensure that Nicholas had not bent, spindled or mutilated anything, or anyone, during his absence. I went home alone and waited for Rachel to arrive. When she did, she first went over to the bunkhouse to give Peio a big hug and kiss, then she came into the house, and we snuggled on the couch in front of TV until bedtime.

CHAPTER 15

THE NEXT MORNING, WE HAD a full house for breakfast since Peio had spent the night at TJ's place. After Rachel had left for work, TJ and I gathered up our shooting kit, gathered up Peio, and drove him home prior to going shooting.

On the way to Peio's new house I noticed that the Butler Mine Road had recently been re-surfaced. I also noticed that the dirt trail into his meadow had been paved as had a circular driveway that now circled in front of the new log home. The house looked like it was finished on the outside and had an attractive green metal roof. It looked pretty nice.

"Heck, Peio, I didn't realize that you were going whole hog on the place! New asphalt on the Butler Mine Road and a paved driveway. What's next, a swimming pool and barbeque pit?" I asked.

"That's for next year," he said. "You guys want a tour?"

For the next 30 minutes Peio took us through his new house. His pride was evident. I think it was the first place that he could truly call his own. It would be a month or so before he could actually move in, as plumbing and electrical were ongoing. He'd already drilled his water well, put in his leach field and buried a suitably sized propane tank to the left side of the house.

At the end of the tour, we walked over to his old trailer. "You guys want a coffee?" Peio asked.

"We'd better give it a miss today, Peio," said TJ. "We're headed up to the range to do some shooting and really don't need the caffeine to give us the shakes."

"Well, you're the adult. Try to ensure that Jeb doesn't shoot himself in the foot, or more importantly, shoot you in the foot."

"Do you honestly think that is the way you should speak about the guy who let you carve out an estate on his property? Where is the respect?" I demanded.

"It is a simple cabin, not an estate. Keep in mind that I am actually doing you a favor and increasing the value of your property," he retorted.

"You keep in mind that you're taking care of the additional property taxes from here on. It would behoove you not to build a Club Peio. I'll be keeping my eye on you, old man," I said with a smile. Peio just waved us on as he went back into his trailer.

We got back in the truck and drove up to the range. Getting out our gun cases, we laid them out on the shooting benches and opened them up. TJ had his Glocks and Larue OBR. I, on the other hand, had brought the Ed Brown tactical rifle, an 870 Remington Express 12-gauge shotgun, which had the barrel sawn off even with the tube magazine underneath, and an old Colt 1911 that I had picked up at a pawn shop.

"Odd choice," said TJ.

"I've been playing around with a bullet design and wanted to try it out. Take a look." I opened up my old ammo can and got out a box of .45 ACP. Pulling out a round, I tossed it to TJ.

"Interesting, does it work?" he inquired.

"Let's find out."

What I had done was to take .45 ACP hollow point rounds and drilled a quarter inch hole a third of an inch into the bullet. I then inserted a Winchester 209 shotgun primer into the hole and epoxied it in place. In theory, the primer would detonate when it struck something, causing an explosive blast back into the bullet causing it to fragment like a little grenade. The issue I needed to investigate was; if the shock of firing the round, or the heat generated traveling down a 5-inch barrel, would cause the primer to detonate prior to leaving the muzzle.

We chambered one of the modified rounds into the old 1911, packed it in sandbags pointed down range, wrapped tape around the grip safety, and tied a string to the trigger. Standing well back, I pulled on the string until the gun fired. The weapon looked fine when we inspected it. We then loaded a full magazine of seven explosive rounds, stood well back again, and fired all seven rounds. Again, there were no issues with the weapon when we inspected it.

I then felt that the rounds were safe enough to fire by hand, so I went back to the truck and came back with a bunch of old phone books and catalogs so that we could test the effect. I placed a 2-inch-thick catalog standing up against a cinder block at 5 yards. I went back to the bench, loaded a round into the old Colt and fired it into the catalog. The bullet appeared to have gone all the way through the catalog before exploding.

Next, I placed two old phone books back-to-back against the cinder block and tried again. The results were spectacular. Apparently, the explosion initiated as the bullet went through the first catalog, which caused it to blow the second catalog into smithereens. At this point TJ managed to grow a set of balls and had to blow apart some catalogs. We spent the next 15 minutes blowing apart catalogs until we ran out of modified .45 ACP rounds and catalogs.

"What's the shotgun for?" TJ asked.

I showed TJ that I had done essentially the same thing with 12-gauge rifled slug rounds, creating even bigger exploding rounds. In practice, they failed simply because the mass of the slug was too great to fragment decently. I had more work to do.

Eventually we got serious, and TJ coached me on the finer points of tactical pistol shooting, concentrating on developing my 'instinctual shooting', the failings of which had been pointed out the last time we were at the range. We then got out the Larue and did some work at the 100-yard targets. As TJ said, short rifles require "practice, practice, practice" – so we shot up all the .308 ammo we had brought and called it a day.

Getting back to the house, I got out of the truck and saw a black streak heading up the hill into the woods behind the house. "Did you see that?" I asked TJ.

"All I saw was some big black animal headed for the hills. What was it?"

"It's some enormous dog-like thing that Rachel has befriended. It won't come near me, but apparently it lets Rachel scratch its ears."

"I suggest you treat Rachel nice, or you might become its dinner at some point."

Dog was still around.

We took the weapons up to the barn and spent an hour cleaning and lubricating them before locking them in the gun safe on the mezzanine level. By now it was getting on toward four in the afternoon so I gave Rachel a call to see what the plan for dinner was. I was informed that we, TJ and I, were going to take them, Heather and Rachel, to dinner at the Olive Garden on the other side of town at six o'clock.

This gave us enough time to clean up, put on some clean jeans and long-sleeved shirts, for a change, before heading to the shop to get the girls. TJ drove us in the 1950 Chevy since I was done driving for the day.

Getting to the shop, we saw the Audi A4, so we knew that Heather had already arrived. The girls obviously had planned this earlier as Heather did not look like a banker and Rachel did not look like a grease monkey. They had done their hair up, put on a little makeup and wore sundresses. Rachel's was a simple Tommy Bahama number in white, which set off her olive skin tone, while Heather wore a Tommy Bahama stretch jersey number in yellow. Some sort of fancy flip-flops completed the ensembles. Casual, but the outfits put your imagination in overdrive. Tommy Bahama had done well today, as I assumed they had gone shopping at some point in the afternoon.

After it was determined that we, that is TJ and I, were somewhat underdressed for the occasion, we climbed into the Audi as it was the only vehicle that could comfortably sit four. Heather drove with TJ riding shotgun while Rachel and I rode in back. While driving to the restaurant I tried to slide my hand up Rachel's dress, only to have it slapped in admonition, and "Behave!" whispered to me.

Turning my attention to more mundane issues, I asked, "So what's the occasion, girls? I have never seen you two so dressed up together, and beyond that, offering to take us to dinner."

"You'll have to wait," was all I got from Heather.

We arrived at the Olive Garden and were seated, and menus were distributed. While contemplating the menu we ordered drinks, white wine for the girls, iced tea for the boys. When the drinks were brought to the table, we ordered meals, veal for the boys, pasta stuff for the girls.

"Okay, enough is enough, what's the occasion?" I asked.

Rachel made that, two-handed palms up motion towards Heather, favored among Hollywood idiots, that I think means 'over to you'.

Looking a bit embarrassed and blushing just enough to make it noticeable, she told us, "You are looking at the new bank manager of the Farmer's Bank here in town." Thinking quickly, I said, "Great! When can we rob it?"

"Quit acting like a jackass," Rachel told me. "Congratulate her."

With a laugh, both TJ and I congratulated her with feeling.

"So how is this going to change your life?" TJ asked.

"Well at this level in the bank they do not really want to move you if you have become familiar with the community, so I suppose I am here more or less permanently now."

TJ beamed. I looked at him and said, "Don't ever play poker for money. Your poker face sucks."

The girls had a couple bottles of wine and got giggly, so I drove the A4 back to the shop, Rachel and I in the front, lovebirds in the back. I am sure I heard, "Behave!" whispered in the back seat.

At the shop, Rachel and I got into TJ's 1950 Chevy pickup and drove home while TJ drove Heather back to her place. He never showed up later that night, go figure. Since Rachel was tipsy, and I was a gentleman, I walked her up the stairs to her room and put her to bed fully dressed. Fifteen minutes after I got undressed and into bed, I knew I had wasted my time as Rachel, dressed in absolutely nothing but 'almost there' panties, crawled under my sheets. The rest was simply normal human interaction.

The next morning Rachel was complaining about an alcohol induced brain tumor and would not get out of bed, so I got up and went downstairs to brew up the coffee remedy. When it was done, I poured a large cup and took it back upstairs to the patient. When I got to the room, Rachel had the sheet pulled up and was looking down her body at something, and then said, "I'm naked."

"You weren't when you got here last night, you had on a pair of panties that probably were sewn together from the skins of jellyfish," I told her. She laid back in bed, took a sip of coffee and replied, "At least I had some form of clothing on and was not acting like a wanton hussy."

"To set the record straight, your 'clothing' remained on you for roughly a nanosecond, and it was you who removed them. Furthermore, you did act like a wanton hussy for a good 5 minutes before falling fast asleep. I'd give you a 7.5 or 8 out of 10 for effort, although your motor skills and endurance were failing."

Finishing her first cup of coffee and looking remarkably better, "Hmmmm…" she muttered while looking shyly at me. "Perhaps I need to work on my wanton hussy skills."

"I'm here to help. Can you attend class each evening for a month or so? I could have you being a first-class wanton hussy in no time," I offered. Getting out of bed stark naked, she started searching for her jellyfish skin panties, found them under her pillow, and headed to her room to get ready for work. Looking back over her shoulder she said, "Let me check my schedule."

After Rachel had gotten ready and left for the shop, I went out to the barn, put the REO Speedwagon CD 'You Can Tune a Piano, But You Can't Tuna Fish' on the sound system and finished rebuilding the 429 motor. Once I was happy with it, I rolled the engine stand under the chain fall, rigged up the lifting chains to the block and lifted the engine up high enough to clear the front of the truck and get the engine into the engine bay. As my chain fall hoist is on a trolley system on I-beams in the ceiling, it was a fairly easy operation getting the engine positioned over the engine bay and into the truck. At this point I went up on the mezzanine and got two modified engine mounts to fit the engine to the strengthened frame, bolted them up and lowered the engine onto them. After the engine was in place I tightened and torqued up the bolts from the engine mounts to the frame, and from the engine to the mounts. Enough for one day.

Going back to the house I made peanut butter and banana sandwiches for lunch, grabbed a glass with ice and went out to the porch. After pouring myself a glass of sun tea, I sat on one of the couches and ate my lunch while figuring out what to do next. First, I needed to order a four-link rear suspension kit from Heidts Products, so that it would be here when I got back from the next hitch in Kurdistan. Second, I needed to order a disc brake conversion for my 1956 F-100 pickup as well, and at some point, I would have to check the untraceable email account to see if I had an assignment from the Jankowski Group of spies.

Finishing my exceptionally tasty, yet nutritional, lunch, I took the glass and plate back to the kitchen, washed them and put them on the drying rack. I then went into the formal dining room office and ordered the brake and suspension kits. Accessing the double secret email account, I found that I had not been given any secret squirrel assignment as of yet. That said, there was a troubling message telling me to check again before I departed for Erbil. Sitting back, I relaxed for a second before jerking upright in a sweat. I had forgotten to order my new wheels from Cragar! What an amateur oversight. I quickly got back online and ordered a set of Cragar Black 'D' Window steel wheels to fit the bolt pattern on the new brake set-up.

Calling Rachel, I asked what her plans for dinner were and was told that I was cooking for four, the choice of entrée was left up to me. I asked if she was inviting two of her hot friends over and if I should set out the Twister game on the living room floor before heating up some oil?

"I would, darling, but I fear that your heart would give out before the game was over. We need to get you in shape first. But to answer and satisfy your curiosity, TJ and Heather are coming over for dinner," I was informed.

"Hold on a second," I told her, "my heart was not a consideration when you were applying to Dr. Rose's Wanton Hussy School," I retorted.

"Yes, but that would just be me attending. I just don't think that you are up to multiple partners yet."

"Wanna put some money on it?"

"Are you insinuating that I am not enough woman for you, Dr. Rose?" I heard her trying to stifle a laugh over the phone.

"In the spirit of full disclosure, Ms. Chen, I just don't think you are making a determined effort or utilizing your charms, as delightful as they are, to the full extent of your abilities," I countered.

"What do you suggest, Professor?"

"Have you ever read the Kama Sutra? It is required reading in Professor Rose's Advanced Wanton Hussy School. I suggest you buy a copy and show me what you have learned, chapter by chapter. Read fast, I have to go back to Kurdistan in a week!"

"You'd die a happy man. Go start dinner. See you soon, Professor."

I was a frustrated man when she hung up, but I had my marching orders and had to go figure out dinner. I had a frozen lasagna in the pantry freezer, so I took it out to thaw. I then made a salad and set out the parmesan cheese, Italian dressing, plates, silverware and glasses. I'd put the lasagna in the oven at around five o'clock. I was good to go.

At five the lasagna went into the oven and at five fifteen the crew started to arrive. First came Heather in the Audi, followed shortly by Rachel. Heather parked in front of the bunkhouse, got out and walked over to my front porch and gave me a peck on the cheek.

"Hello, cowboy," she said with a smile. She was dressed like a banker with a form fitting blue pinstriped pantsuit. She looked good.

"Too bad the others are coming to dinner, or you and I could find out what's under that pantsuit."

"I already know what's under this pantsuit. Secondly, that half-Chinese, half-Israeli girl, shortly to be headed this way, would beat you into the next county if she knew that you had propositioned me," she said with a smile.

"You can't blame a guy for trying," I grinned.

By this time, Rachel had parked the Porsche in the lean-to garage, had gotten out of it and was coming toward us.

"Guess who just propositioned me?" Heather asked her as I looked at her in mock shock.

"He does that to all the girls, just ignore him," Rachel replied.

Rachel was in 'distressed' jeans and my 1973 Aerosmith Get Your Wings Tour t-shirt, and in my humble opinion looked just as enticing as Heather in her expensive pantsuit. These two stunners were making me hungry.

"Let's retire to the kitchen so that I can get you two bombshells something to eat."

"What about TJ?" said Heather, standing up for her man.

"What about him?" I replied. "The food's hot, we're hungry, he's a grown man, and he knows what time dinner is served." It was a moot point as TJ arrived at that moment and parked his truck in front of the bunkhouse.

"About time you showed up to protect our virtue," said Heather. "This lecherous old fart has been propositioning us for the past 15 minutes."

"Should I shoot him?" asked TJ. I hoped he wasn't serious, and I wasn't sure how much of his background he had shared with Heather.

Rachel came to my defense, "If you shoot him now, we don't get fed. Maybe you can put it off until after we eat."

With that resolved we went in and ate. We'd become sort of a family, so everyone was relaxed during dinner and talked about their day at work, or in my case, at home. Heather was really getting into the bank manager thing, and Rachel and TJ were putting the finishing touches on the 1969 GT500. I asked TJ if he wanted to go fishing tomorrow, he said yes, and Rachel graciously allowed him the day off.

After dinner, TJ and Heather headed over to the bunkhouse while Rachel and I sat on the couch and watched another recording of 'Forged in Fire'. Actually, I watched it and Rachel read a book. After I had learned how to make a Chinese Dao, I turned off the TV and asked Rachel if that was a copy of the Kama Sutra?" She replied, "There's one way to find out."

The next morning, after I had discovered that the book in question had not been the Kama Sutra, but some boring tome dealing with automotive restoration nonsense, I was once again the first one up and running. Heading downstairs I turned on the coffee machine and began making omelets. I called TJ and asked if he was ready to go. He was, but wanted breakfast first, so I told him to come on over. Over coffee I enquired as to the disappearance of the Audi, and the associated HFC. Apparently the HFC syndrome expired around midnight, when Heather said she'd better get home and get a proper night's sleep so that she could concentrate on bank management issues today. Around this time Rachel showed up at the top of the stairs in bed hair, tap pants and a t-shirt, surprisingly not from my rock and roll tour collection. She took one look downstairs, saw the two of us staring at her, and turned around to find a robe.

"Even that would not be too bad to wake up to every morning," TJ said with a smile.

"You learn to take the good with the bad," I lamented.

A disembodied voice from upstairs said, "I heard that!" I refer you to the previously mentioned bat ears.

Eventually she found a robe and joined us for breakfast and coffee. I asked what she had planned for the day. "I'll go over the Mustang one last time to make sure TJ didn't screw up something, then get it ready to ship next week. After that I think I'll take half a day off."

"Oh, so you'll clean the house this afternoon? It's your turn, you know?"

"Actually, I might get around to it later, but first I am going to try to wash Dog." I gagged on my coffee and TJ just looked at her in awe.

TJ recovered first and asked, "You are actually going to try to wash that thing? How?"

"I have a plan," she replied. "You know that old round stock watering tank behind the barn? I am going to roll it out, fill it with water, get Dog into it with me....and wash him. He is beginning to stink a bit."

"Honey, you are the only one who can even get close to that monster to determine if he stinks or not. Furthermore, how are you going to get a 160-pound dog-like animal over the side of that tank? It must be 2-1/2 foot high at least and he outweighs you by at least 40 pounds."

"I'll figure it out. Maybe I can coax him in if I wear a bikini," Rachel said with a smile.

"That only works on me, this is a deer eating pseudo dog."

"Perhaps, but same mentality I'm guessing. You boys have fun fishing and I'll see you later." As she headed toward the stairs, the flapping robe showed off some incredibly sexy legs.

TJ and I finished up breakfast, cleaned the kitchen, then went outside to check that all the required gear was stowed in the back of my truck before heading off. We went south out of Glenwood Springs on 82, to Carbondale, where we stocked up on worms, beer and KFC. We then took 133 south until the cutoff for County Road 111, just past the Crystal River Baptist Church. We followed this until it became Prince Creek Road, then took County Road 6a to Dinkle Lake.

Now Dinkle Lake was not the greatest fishing spot, but then again, TJ and I were not the greatest fishermen. The idea was simply to get out of the house, drown a few worms, drink a few beers, gorge on KFC, and just relax. If we caught any fish, great, if not, no problem. After parking in the little lot on the northwest side of the lake, we drug our kit down to the lake and set up. After I baited up with Powerbait, and TJ hooked on a worm, we cast out and let the bobbers do the work. Sitting on our camp chairs, we got out the chicken and beer, and began our guys' day out.

"Ah, this is the life. Beer, chicken, the sun is shining, the birds are chirping and no girls to boss us around," I proclaimed. "Have you discussed robbing Heather's bank with her yet? That should spice up your romance and we could use the money."

"I really don't think that now, after her first few days as manager, is the appropriate time to discuss robbing her bank. Let's give it a few weeks." We drank some beer, ate some chicken and actually caught some fish. After rebaiting our lines, while waiting for the next bites, I got serious.

"TJ, you came clean with me awhile back concerning your background, so I think it is about time I do the same."

"Don't tell me you're gay, anything but that." TJ wasn't into serious mode yet, or maybe he was.

Anyhow, I continued, "This is serious, amigo; in case something would go sideways while I am away." Now TJ sat up a little straighter to pay attention.

"As you know, I work as a Drilling Superintendent in Kurdistan. What you, Peio and Rachel do not know is that I do some low-grade intelligence work as well when I am in Kurdistan. I got recruited about a year before I came back to the States. It turns out that my old boss had been doing work for these guys for years before he passed away. They felt I would be a good replacement as I was in the same line of work and could travel fairly easily, and they made their pitch while I was still in Cape Town."

"How did you know they were legit?" he asked. "They could have been setting up a false flag operation, or simply setting you up as well."

"I thought about all of that, but at the second meeting I asked him a question that only someone who really knew my old boss could answer correctly, and he did. After that, I did three separate months of training at Camp Peary in Virginia. It would be hard for someone not legit to have access to Camp Peary."

"What training did they give you?"

"It was the pickup of clandestine material, evading hostile pursuers, situational awareness, memory retention and lock picking. We also got some basic firearm and self-defense training."

"That's not very serious training for an agent, it could actually do more harm than good if you actually thought you were trained," observed TJ.

"That is just it, we are not thoroughly trained, but they don't ask us to do much either. The odd brush pass, attaching GPS trackers, like we did on the meth lab, and just keeping our eyes open for anything interesting."

"Are they ramping things up the longer you are with them? This would be a bad sign because eventually you would be asked to do something which you are completely incapable of pulling off." TJ was simply saying what I was thinking.

"For the past few years, it has been low level secret squirrel stuff, more as a deniable assistant, when they want somebody off the books to do mundane tasks. The thing is, I check an untraceable email account before I go to work and usually, say seventy-five percent of the time, there is no task to perform. Twenty-five percent of the time there is. But again, it is usually mundane bullshit and only takes a couple of hours, or a couple of days, to perform. Keep in mind that I have a real job as well, so it is not possible to be gone from my desk for extended periods of time. Yesterday, when I checked the account, there was no task required, but there was a message to check the account again before I left. This worries me as it indicates a 'rush' job is coming up."

TJ focused on the far side of the lake for a while, then turned to me and said, "Why are you telling me this now, it doesn't seem to be a critical issue at the moment, and it may be nothing."

"All true, but I've got a bad feeling about it, and I've learned to trust my gut. If something goes tits up on my next hitch, I want you to promise me that you will take care of Rachel. There is a Will lodged with my lawyer in town. If I do not make it back, I want you to take the whole crew down to the lawyer's office. I want Peio, yourself, Rachel, Heather and Bret, to be at the reading of the Will. Peio will be the executor of my will. Can you do that for me?"

"No problem, be happy to, but I think you may be reading too much into your gut feeling at this point. Let's cross that bridge when we get to it."

"Fair enough. You've got another bite, perhaps you can get off your dead ass and go reel it in."

We decided that we had had enough sport fishing at around two o'clock, besides, the chicken was gone, and we didn't want any more beer as one of us had to drive home. We packed up our kit and headed back to the ranch. Pulling up the driveway, just at the cut in the hill where it goes into the courtyard, I slammed on the brakes causing TJ to almost headbutt the dash. We sat in the truck, unspeaking, staring at the scene in front of us.

In the area between the left-hand end of the porch and the barn, someone had rolled out the old 6-foot circular stock watering tank that I had hidden behind the barn and filled it with water. Standing in the middle of the tank was Rachel in a pair of cutoffs and my 1978 Foreigner Double Vision Tour t-shirt. Standing with his front paws on the edge of the tank was Dog. This was the first time I had even seen Dog when he wasn't moving at Mach speed going somewhere else. To say he was an impressive dog would be like saying King Kong was an impressive ape. I had never seen a dog like this.

Dog, now that I could see him clearly, was jet black and appeared to be a cross between a Groenendael and a Mack truck. This dog would easily weigh between 150 and 160 pounds, it was a giant. The muscles on the animal appeared much bulkier than on a standard Belgian Shepherd, but not to the point of being grotesque, just impressive. Rachel had Dog by his 'armpits' and was trying to pull him into the tank for a wash. She was pulling for all she was worth, but Dog wasn't budging. When I hit the brakes and skidded to a halt, Dog took one look at the truck and lunged into the tank sending Rachel sprawling flat on her butt in the water.

I originally thought that we may have startled Dog, but the way he was standing, straddling Rachel with his massive front paws, it became apparent that he was protecting her. This was weird. Eventually Rachel scooted out from under Dog, got to her feet, waved at us, and began hosing down Dog. He had not moved at all and was staring at the truck. There was no way that either I, or TJ, was getting out of the truck now.

After hosing down the animal, Rachel, now in soaking wet shorts and t-shirt, and now that she was soaked, obviously no bra, reached down on the ground and got a bottle of shampoo. After shampooing the brute all over, she rinsed him off then reached for a different bottle and scrubbed conditioner into his long, black coat and rinsed him off again. Stepping out of the tank, Rachel grabbed some thick towels on the porch, then walked back to the tank and patted her thigh. Up to this point Dog had not moved a muscle and was staring directly at TJ and I. Once she slapped her thigh, Dog looked over at her then jumped out of the tank and was nuzzling her crotch while she dried him off. I was starting to develop a jealousy complex concerning this dog.

Rachel waved us over, which I thought was a bad idea, but we slowly got out of the truck and eased over toward Rachel and Dog. On the way over I pointed out that she was soaking wet, had no bra on, and that TJ was young and impressionable. Wrapping a towel around under her armpits she said, "I'd like you to meet the new, improved and slightly less aromatic Dog," putting her hand on Dog's withers.

"Is he hungry? Has he eaten his quota of wild game today? I don't want to get closer if he's hungry," I asked.

"Quit being a pussy and get over here!"

I just knew this was a bad idea, but what the heck, you can only get eaten by a monster dog once, and I didn't want to look like a pussy. I sidled over to Dog with my hand held out so that the back was facing those gigantic T-Rex teeth. With his eyes looking into mine, he sniffed my hand, likely trying to determine if it was something to eat, before finally lowering his big head.

"Scratch his ears," Rachel commanded. So, I did.

TJ, being the girly Coonass button man that he was, refused to come anywhere close to Dog. Okay, maybe he wasn't being girly, perhaps he was simply smarter than me. In my defense, it was not his HFC telling him what to do and calling him a pussy. I bet a dollar to a donut hole that if it was Heather, he'd have his arms around Dog's neck.

Rachel gave Dog a big hug, then pointed to the woods up the hill behind the house. Amazingly, Dog licked her hand then trotted off up the hill about 10 yards before doing that 'wet dog shake' thing that dogs do to get off the water that hot chicks with towels couldn't quite reach, then continued on into the woods.

We went onto the porch where I gave her a big braless hug, while TJ started hauling our kit to the barn. "You smell like a dog," I said. "And now Dog, King of the Jungle, smells like lavender and strawberries. He's going to get laughed out of the woods and hate you forever."

"He'll be back, and after I shower up and put on a minimal amount of clothing, so will you," said Rachel as she went into the house. I don't know about Dog, but I damn sure knew I'd be back.

I helped TJ clean out the truck and clean the fish at the sink in the barn. He was saying that he couldn't believe what he'd just seen. I told him that even the lizard brain of a prehistoric dog would be addled by the phenomenal set of legs, and a wet t-shirt, sans bra, on Rachel. I further surmised that if Heather showed up similarly scantily clad, that she could also wrap Dog around her little finger. Apparently, Dog had the same, well developed taste in women as TJ and I. We would have to keep an eye on Dog to keep him from stealing our action.

TJ took the fish to his place, and I headed back into mine. Freshly showered, and smelling like lavender and strawberries, was Rachel dressed in my 1978 Foghat World Tour t-shirt and little yoga shorts. "Now do I smell good enough to eat?" she said.

"One way to find out, but I need a shower first."

"Don't keep me waiting, I'm hungry. As appealing as you are, food is first in my book." Rachel has priority issues.

CHAPTER 16

WE WOKE UP THE NEXT day and decided, that since it was Saturday, and that the GT500 was ready for shipping, we'd take the day off and run up to see how Peio's house was coming along. Rachel dressed for the occasion in faded jeans, somewhat form fitting but not that 'skinny jeans' nonsense, and a proper long-sleeved shirt with the sleeves rolled up. A good, conservative look on the girl. I just did the jeans and t-shirt thing as I doubted Peio would care, one way or the other, what I wore.

We got to Peio's place about ten o'clock in the morning, and again, since it was Saturday, there didn't seem to be much going on. I walked over to the trailer and knocked on the door but got no response. Going back to the new house we saw that the door was open, so we walked up on the porch. I yelled, "Hello the house!" and the reply was, "Come on back." Peio was sitting at a round table with a large urn of coffee and a cell phone. Apparently just kicking back and enjoying the view from the back porch.

"There are clean cups in the kitchen cupboard over the sink. Go get a couple while I chat with this charming young thing," he said to me. Apparently I was the delegated servant today. I got the cups out of the kitchen, rinsed them and came back out on the porch. Rachel, by this time, was sitting on Peio's lap, with her arm around his neck, giving him a recap of the 'Dog Incident' yesterday.

While pouring coffee for Rachel, I asked, "Did she tell you the part about the dog knocking her, ass over tea kettle, into the stock tank? This is an incredibly smart animal as he knew what water does to t-shirts."

"I should have been there. Of course, at my age I probably would not have appreciated such a sight as much as you did. Then again, I may have appreciated it more," he said with a grin.

"Even if I would have been eaten by the hound, I would have died with a smile on my face," I mused.

"Hey, you lecherous old bastards! I am sitting right here! If you continue to embarrass me, I may need to remove myself from your company."

With that out of the way, I told Peio that the house seemed to be progressing rather quickly, and he'd no doubt be in it before winter. He explained that since no land clearing was required, getting the lot graded and the foundation poured only took about a week or so. Erecting the actual log frame was also quick since these log houses are actually erected at the company headquarters to double check fit and finish, then taken back down. Each log is numbered and then the whole kit is shipped as a package. So, getting the house erected and the roof on only took another 3 to 4 weeks. They were in the process of finalizing the heating, plumbing and electrical, which should be finished this week. The week after would be set aside for inspection and remediation of any faults found. After that, it would simply be a matter of the final touches such as insulation, trim work and finishing the cabinets and floors. Peio figured another 2 months and he could get rid of his trailer and move into his castle. He really seemed to be looking forward to it.

We finished the coffee, and Rachel had climbed off Peio's lap. I could tell that he wasn't happy about that, but when you are 70 years old you need to watch the old ticker. Rachel may have just saved his life.

We walked back out to my truck. Rachel gave Peio a peck on the cheek, then went around to the passenger's side to get in. Peio held my arm before I could climb in with a serious look on his face.

"You remember that asshole who wanted to buy Rachel's shop? The guy I asked to leave town?" he said.

"Actually, you essentially told him to get out of town or you'd have him killed, but yeah, what of it? I thought you scared him off pretty good."

"Well, apparently not good enough. He ended up in Kansas City, but he lost a lot of face out here. Keep an eye out for strangers and let me know if any turn up."

"Peio, I've got to head back to Kurdistan in a week or so, which will leave Rachel alone in the house. I'll give TJ a heads-up, but maybe you could drop by the shop, and the house, at odd times just to keep an eye on her?" I asked.

“No worries, son, you know that I would do that regardless. Let TJ know what is going on and I am sure he’ll keep things kosher, as Rachel would say.”

“Okay, that seems to cover the issue. Do you need anything from town?” I asked.

“Now that you mention it, I do. I need a bucket of Kentucky Fried Chicken, the spicy kind, and a bottle of your Laphroaig. Think you can handle that by dinner time?”

“No problem, see you around 6 o’clock.”

I got in the truck, and on the way back into town I asked Rachel if she had heard what Peio had to say. She said she caught most of it, but not all. I reiterated what Peio had said and made sure that she was aware that she’d need to keep her head on a swivel for a while.

Getting back to the house, we found TJ and Heather sprawled out on the couches on my veranda, drinking my tea, and apparently just taking it easy. Rachel got out of the truck with a malicious grin on her face, rushed up to Heather, did the girl hug thing, and they began whispering to each other before heading into the house. I picked up Heather’s glass, poured in some more tea, then sat on the couch that TJ wasn’t stretched out on. The day was warming up nicely, but we were in the shade and a breeze was stirring, so it was actually pretty comfortable.

I told TJ what Peio had said about the wannabe gangster in Kansas City and asked him to keep an eye on Rachel, as the dickhead seemed to be the vindictive sort. Since he lost face big time, he might want some form of payback.

“Never you mind, I’ll have it covered until you get back. At which point you can shoot him if I haven’t.” Good friends are hard to come by. Good friends who will hold off shooting some asshole until you get back to do it, are as rare as hen’s teeth.

TJ then asked, “Have you had time to make any more of those .45 exploding rounds? I’d like to keep some handy.”

“You’re a 9mm sort of guy, they wouldn’t do you any good unless you can figure out how to shove a .45 round down a 9mm barrel. Furthermore, they won’t load in your magazines.” Sometimes you need to explain these technical issues to retired button men or they may hurt themselves, or others, unintentionally.

“Dipshit, do you honestly think that I showed you all the tools of the trade? I keep an HK45 Tactical pistol in another box, which I chose not to show you as you’d probably want to steal it while I was at work.”

“Is that the one already prepped for a suppressor?” I asked.

“Yes,” he confirmed.

"Damned right I want to steal it! But as I already have a .45, and not that old 1911 Colt we used as a test gun, and since I do not want hard feelings with the neighbor, I won't." Continuing, I told him, "We fired all of the explosive rounds I had the other day, and I'll have to make some more. I'll make up some more before I go and give you a box. Why do you want them?"

"Just like to keep my options open," was all he would say.

About this time, the girls came out scantily clad in bikinis, carrying lawn chairs. This looked interesting and cut our conversation short. Heather was attired in a black bandeau style bikini that really highlighted her pale complexion, while Rachel had on a classic triangle bikini in yellow. These two could stop traffic. They set up the chairs in the sun, facing away from the two slobbering guys on the porch, who were trying to keep certain body parts from becoming noticeable. As the girls were applying suntan oil on each other and driving us nuts, I asked TJ, "What do you think is the most erotic part of a girl in a bikini?"

Rachel was now oiled up and on her back in the left-hand chair, while Heather was on her stomach on the right-hand chair. Their heads were closest to the porch where we were having our debate, giving us a good head-to-toe view.

TJ pontificated, "Look, if you will, at the two little dimples on either side of Heather's spine, just above the bikini bottom that is just showing the crack of her firm little behind. That, my friend, is so sexy it makes my teeth itch."

I remonstrated, "To each his own I suppose, but for me it is where the bikini bottom forms those two little gaps between where the hips and the stomach, flat as it may be, hold the material just off the skin between them, mere inches above the naughty bits, while the subject is on her back. It just causes your imagination to run wild. You can almost see 'the Promised Land'. Please focus on the model on the left."

"We can hear you guys," said Rachel.

"Is it making you horny?" I replied.

"I'll let you know after dinner. Speaking of which, you need to run into town and get KFC for Peio, and pizza for us girls. Don't forget the Laphroaig for Peio."

"Yes, dear, TJ and I will get right on it. What type of pizza do emaciated supermodels eat?"

"After all this time you do not know what types of pizza allows us girls to maintain our coltish figures?" was Heather's comeback.

"The term 'coltish' is defined as 'adolescent or not fully developed'. You,

Heather, do not fit that description. Rachel on the other hand, with her slim, trim, racy and slightly less rounded figure comes much closer to fitting the definition." Rachel sat up, turned, and threw the suntan lotion at me, which forced her to stretch and reveal her coltish figure. Carrying on I said, "In my experience, Hot Frisky Chicks, such as yourselves, seem to have an affinity to pepperoni and Hawaiian pizzas. Is that correct?"

"That would do nicely, as long as you get two large of each," replied the one with the more coltish figure.

"Consider it done," I said as TJ and I got off the porch and headed to his truck while trying to hide our knobby bits.

Driving into town to Pizza on the Rocks, which was cunningly located between two large boulders on the nearest side of town, I asked TJ when he was going to get his Coyote motor and new transmission installed in the old 1950 Chevy pickup we were riding in. He said it would be installed before I got back from Kurdistan. His old straight six 235 was cool, but that 5.0-liter Coyote motor with a 4R70W automatic transmission, putting out 435 horses and 400 lb.-ft of torque, would be much cooler. Which was annoying me greatly as my '56 Ford truck wouldn't be able to catch it then.

Still contemplating what I could possibly do to my old truck to make it competitive, I ordered the pizzas, then we ran over to KFC to get Peio's spicy chicken before doubling back to Pizza on the Rocks to collect the supermodel forage. When we drove back into the courtyard the girls were now on their incredibly flat stomachs showing off their pert little butts. I parked the truck, TJ and I got out and admired the view for a few seconds, then took the pizzas into the kitchen, put them in the oven, and cranked it to warm.

Going back outside I told the girls that we were heading up to drop off Peio's chicken, that we would be back shortly, and not to touch the pizza until we were back.

We got back in TJ's truck when Rachel pipes up, "Did you remember the Scotch?"

"Damn," I said as I climbed out of the truck and trudged up to the barn to get a bottle of Laphroaig.

Twisting the knife, Rachel informed me, "At your age, short term memory loss can be an issue. You'll likely forget all about those 'bikini gaps', and the promised land you mentioned earlier, by the time you get back."

“I could have full blown dementia and still remember ‘bikini gaps’ and promised lands, child.”

We dropped off Peio’s dinner, for which he was thankful, especially when he saw that I had not forgotten, as far as he knew, the Laphroaig. He brought TJ up to speed on the Kansas City idiot and we headed back to the girls.

When we walked into the kitchen, the girls had made themselves presentable by putting on some short, clingy wraps, which did absolutely nothing to hide the fact that they still wore their bikinis. They also sat at the table with a plate in front of them, a fork in one hand and a knife in the other chanting, “Pizza, pizza.”

I got the pizzas out of the oven, put the opened boxes on the table, and stood back while the feeding began. How these girls maintained their incredible bodies was beyond me. Tanning obviously made you ravenous. TJ and I took our plates, pizza, and beer to the living room to eat like civilized people, without the distraction of exposed female flesh.

Afterwards, TJ and Heather retired to the bunkhouse to study Heather’s body geography, while I stumbled around like a blind man until Rachel unwound her wrap, again revealing her bikini, and said, “Is this what you’re looking for?”

CHAPTER 17

RACHEL WENT TO WORK THE next day even though it was a Sunday. I think it was a result of the guilt from not working yesterday. I was not sure what she was doing, as the Mustang was ready to be shipped this week, and the Challenger would not arrive until next week; the books I guessed. I told her that she should really be going to church this morning after what she put me through last night.

"In the words of Bachman Turner Overdrive, 'B-B-B-Baby, you ain't seen n-n-n-nothing yet,'" she replied while mimicking the tune.

"A very appropriate musical reference as the first line of the tune is, 'I met a devil woman, she took my heart away,'" I crooned.

"I was reaching on that one, cowboy, BTO was before my time," she said with a sweet, innocent smile.

"I'll need to bring you up to speed on your classic rock and roll. Tonight's lesson will be 'Slippery When Wet', a Bon Jovi album from back in the day, but as relevant now as it was then," I replied with a sweet, innocent smile of my own.

"Are you familiar with the tune 'Dream On' by Nazareth?" enquired Rachel.

"Damn girl, that is even before my time! Are you sure you are 29 or are you a well preserved 60?" I asked as I kissed her before pushing her out the door.

I then took a few hours to clean up the house and do a few loads of laundry. After that session of domestic chores, I filled up my big coffee mug with the cold coffee left in the machine, then went out to the barn to clean it up as well. After the tools were all cleaned and put back in their respective places, I swept and mopped the floor. It is sealed concrete, painted storm gray, and looks pretty good cleaned up.

After that it took a few more hours to make up a couple boxes of explosive rounds of .45 ACP, one for TJ and the other for myself. I had a feeling that he had something in mind for these rounds, I also had a feeling that I didn't want to know what it was.

I then got in my truck and drove over to Bret's gym to shoot the breeze with him. I picked up a case of beer for him on the way, since I am always drinking his at the gym. Nicholas and Bret were in the office when I got there going over the books. It seemed that everybody was working on Sunday. I took the six packs out of the case and put them in the refrigerator while getting three cold ones out and passing them around.

"What are you muppets up to?" I asked.

"World domination," said Bret.

"Pretty adventurous of you. Could take some time."

"True. It's giving me a headache anyhow," Nicholas added.

I brought Bret up to date regarding the Kansas City gangster and asked him to keep an eye on Rachel when he could. Especially when she was leaving the gym. Which prompted Nicholas to say, with a leer, "I'll happily watch out for her."

"Nick, Nick, Nick. First off, she'd beat you like a drum if you touched her inappropriately and secondly, I'd have to shoot you when I got back."

"But damn, it would be worth it," he laughed. He likes Rachel as much as the rest of us and flirts with her any chance he gets. Nicholas finished his beer and went out to make sure nobody was stealing his weight piles.

"Want to do another barbeque this Friday?" I asked.

"Same time, same place?"

"Same bat time, same bat channel." Anyone who understood that reference to the Batman TV show of 1966-1968 would be showing their age.

"Are you going to bring an HFC this time? I need to plan the chow, beer and so forth." Bret got the '1000-yard stare', shook his head a little and said, "Not this time, amigo." Now this is the second time I had seen him get a bit weird when a girl was mentioned. None of my business, he'd tell me when and if he wanted to. I got up, said "Adios," and went out to my truck.

On the way back to the house I thought I'd drop in on Rachel and see if she and TJ wanted to grab a bite in town. Turns out she wasn't doing her books, but her and

TJ were putting in a paint booth between the back of the old station and the fence of the property behind it. It looked like a quality unit from Tools USA. They had bought the reverse flow semi-downdraft unit which was 15 feet wide, 27 feet long and 11 feet tall. They had slotted it in behind the old garage, with the front access doors facing the same way as the bay doors of the garage. It looked like a perfect fit with plenty of room along the sides for access and maintenance.

"Those things cost about $9,000. Hope that's not coming out of my part of the profits," I said with a smile. Rachel and TJ had obviously been working up a storm to get the paint booth installed and operational, but I could still see the electrical hookup wasn't done, so I jumped in to help.

"I can pay you back in weekly installments of Dr. Feelgood visits, if you're interested?"

"How many visits would that be?" I enquired.

"At my going rate of $1,000 a visit, nine visits."

"A thousand bucks a visit! That's highway robbery. I think I have been getting the Dr. Feelgood Cliff Notes version in the past."

"That is true, you have been. If you're interested in the deluxe house call version, then I'll have this paid back in a month."

"You're on!" I said with a smile. There are better things in life than money. TJ just shook his head.

Monday morning rolled around, and after a single deluxe visitation from Dr. Feelgood the previous evening, I was feeling pretty majestic. As usual, I was the first one up, and the first one down the stairs, so I got the coffee going before making a couple of ham and cheese omelets. Rachel's omelet went in the oven to keep warm, while mine went down my neck. I was on my second cup of coffee when Rachel stumbled down the stairs and headed for the coffee maker. While she was reviving herself with coffee, I got her omelet out of the oven and placed it in front of her along with the required cutlery.

"You seem pretty full of yourself this morning, Mr. Rose," she said between bites.

"After the deluxe Dr. Feelgood session the past evening, coupled with the Wanton Hussy lesson which followed, I am lucky to be alive. That said, I am feeling fairly Olympian this morning."

"Really? You only got the intermediate version of the session last night. You need to start slowly and work up in stages at your age. Your heart, you know," she said with a grin.

"Oh really? I will have you know that what you experienced last night was not the full-on Wanton Hussy lesson either. It was a tamed down version to prepare you for the real thing. Honestly, you need more flexibility before progressing," I retorted.

"Said the man who can barely touch his toes either standing or sitting on the floor."

"True, it will require a number of full body massages before I can touch my toes for any length of time without cramping up. The benefits to yourself would be multiplied greatly." Obviously, I was trying to work a deal here. Getting up from her stool, she came up behind my back and said, "You do yourself an injustice. Perhaps I do not need any more benefits from these sessions. I need to get to work." Kissing the top of my bald head, she headed for the stairs to get ready for work.

"There is always room for improvement, Sweet Cheeks," I threw at her back. "Furthermore, I think that you had better put on something besides my t-shirt and your panties before heading out. The one barely covers the other."

"I am trying to attract new business," she said from the top of the stairs.

"That would do it," said I.

I was still drinking coffee when she came back down the stairs with her hair in a ponytail and her Dickies on. I walked her to the door where she gave me a kiss. I returned the kiss and grabbed her butt while wishing her a nice day.

Once the Porsche had departed, I had to figure out what to do with my day. The parts for the 1956 Ford pickup were not in yet, so I couldn't do anything there. I needed to give TJ his explosive bullets but could do that anytime. I was at a loss. I wandered up to the barn to look for something to do and saw the old box for a CZ 2075 RAMI BD I had bought a few months ago as a concealed carry weapon. I hadn't had it out since I bought it. The pistol was no longer in the box, as I usually lock everything up in the gun safe on the mezzanine deck. Going up to the safe, I got the pistol out and took it back downstairs to the workbench to disassemble it, clean it and lube it up. A CZ 2075 BD is a neat little weapon. It is built on the usual slide-in-frame design common to CZ pistols, which adds strength to the gun. Although it is a sub-compact, it has a barrel just over 3 inches, weighs in at 26 ounces, its overall length is just 6-1/2 inches, with a maximum width of 1-1/4 inches. It still fires the 9mm Luger (Parabellum) round and comes with a double stacked ten round magazine. It is quite a nice, concealed carry piece. About the time I had finished with the pistol, Jake pulled up in his Sheriff's Dodge Durango and parked in front of the house. I shoved the pistol into the cargo pocket of my shorts and walked out to meet him. I caught up to him at the front door and invited him in for a coffee, he's a big coffee drinker as well.

After I had the machine going, I sat down and asked, "What brings you out this way, Jake?"

"Just loafing and needed a coffee really. Thought I'd bring you up to date on the meth lab thing." I got up to get some cups and filled them with coffee before I sat down, and he continued.

"Seems like it will go to court in a few months after the usual dance between the prosecutor in Denver and the defense lawyers provided by the Flat Liners Motorcycle Club. That said, I have been assured that the case is rock solid, and they'll be put away for a lengthy stay at the Rebar Hotel. Also, short of having a crystal ball, they will have no idea how they were twigged. The cops in Denver are claiming a phoned-in tip from a payphone and have a recording to prove it," he said with a smile.

"Good to know. I'm gone half the time and would worry about Rachel if they got off. Thanks for the info."

"Thanks for the coffee, but I've loafed long enough and better get back in the saddle."

I walked him back to his truck and waved him on his way before heading back into the house. I had decided to shower and shave before going into town to see how the paint booth project was getting on. I rinsed the cups and put them on the drain board and started to head up the stairs when something dinged into the corner of the kitchen island. It was the CZ RAMI that I had forgotten I had in the cargo pocket of my shorts. Since I didn't want to go back out to the barn and it was highly unlikely that any kids would be in the house, I took it out and put it in the magazine pouch that was concealed on the side of the couch. I'd put it away later.

Showered and shaved, I hopped in my truck and drove to the shop. Since the Challenger was yet to arrive, and there was nothing being restored, both TJ and Rachel were in the paint booth putting in the final touches.

"Hey!" I yelled. "You can paint this truck if you want to give the booth a test run." I bought my truck used in Denver, and it had been painted a bright orange. You won't find this color listed on any Ford paint scheme, but years ago some Denver city official vehicles were this color, so I can only surmise that my truck had been an official Denver city vehicle at some point in its past.

"No way! We'd never be able to keep an eye on you," replied TJ.

"Not to worry, TJ, I've got a tracking device on that truck." I hoped Rachel was joking.

"What are you kids doing this afternoon?" I asked.

"I've got a mountain of bills to pay and need to check on the whereabouts of that Challenger, so I'm stuck here until five o'clock, then I get to go kick the crap out of Bret in the ring. I'll be home around seven or seven thirty," was Rachel's reply.

"I've got a dinner engagement with a hot bank manager. Don't wait up for me," was TJ's cheeky response.

"As I can't seem to corrupt either of you to leave work early and do something fun, I'll head over to K-Mart and get some new jeans for work and pick up the toiletries for the next hitch, Rachel, can you pick up some pizza for dinner, I don't feel like cooking tonight?"

"Yes, Bwana, your wish is my command." A pause, "Wait! Cancel that last comment, but I will pick up pizza."

TJ was laughing his butt off. I drove across town to the K-Mart and bought a couple of pairs of 501's, and all the kit I'd need in Kurdistan, before I headed back to the ranch. As I had nothing better to do until dinner, I just grabbed a beer, laid on one of the couches on the porch, drank the beer, and took a nap. Rachel got home around seven thirty that evening, and we had a quiet pizza night at home in front of the TV. She had some paperwork to do in the office while I cleaned up the pizza boxes and took out the garbage. A fairly domestic evening all in all, but sometimes these are what you need.

Rachel and TJ spent the rest of the week getting ready for the next project, the 1970 Challenger, while I made sure the house was in shape to leave for a month, and that I had all my ducks in a line to go. The Challenger arrived on Friday, which kept the shop busy all weekend tearing into it and figuring out what would be required to restore it. I just hung around, packed my kit, and got ready to go on Monday. Sunday night I cooked a nice fish dinner for Rachel before we retired to the bedroom for our last Dr. Feelgood session for a while. You need to practice if you want to avoid muscle memory loss while you're away.

CHAPTER 18

MY FLIGHT OUT OF GLENWOOD Springs was at five o'clock in the afternoon on Monday, so we slept in a little and had a late breakfast. I threw my stuff in the back of the truck and we drove to Glenwood Springs so that Rachel could do some shopping in the malls there before we had lunch at the Red Lobster. After lunch, we drove to the airport on the south side of town. We got to the airport at about two thirty that afternoon. I got my backpack and roll-on bag out of the back of the truck, gave Rachel a big hug and a nice kiss, with the proper amount of libido, then walked into the terminal. Neither of us were fond of long goodbyes.

While waiting for the flight to Denver, I got my MacBook Pro out of my backpack and logged into the airport Wi-Fi so that I could check my untraceable email account. It seemed that I would be required to tail a gentleman on a certain evening and see where he went. This didn't sound very challenging as I was also told that he would be staying at the Erbil Rotana Hotel on Gulan Street, and that he would be leaving the hotel around seven in the evening.

I caught my flight to Denver but had to wait until the following day for the 21 hour Emirates' flight to Dubai. I booked into the Westin at Denver International Airport, had dinner, and went to bed. I was up early the following morning as the security procedure at the Denver International Airport is a pain in the butt, and my flight to Dubai left at ten-thirty. After standing in line for hours for the opportunity to take off my shoes, belt, watch and so forth, I was finally allowed to move on to Concourse B to catch my flight.

I arrived at the madhouse, which is also known as the Dubai International Airport, at seven thirty in the morning, on Wednesday. I was sick of traveling, but still had one more hop to make. I flew Royal Jordanian from Dubai to Erbil, arriving at four twenty in the afternoon. After clearing passport control and collecting my roll-on bag at the carousel, I walked out the front of the terminal to where a company vehicle was waiting to take me to my villa in the Royal Villas community. I arrived at my residential villa, as opposed to my office villa, which is in the English Village across the unnamed road that runs between the two, around seven in the evening. The house girl had left some dinner on the stove, so I ate, laid out my clothes for tomorrow, showered, set the alarm for five the next morning, and went to bed. International travel is not the great adventure that it is cracked up to be.

The next morning, I walked across the unnamed road to the English Village, and my office villa there. Before going upstairs to my office, I made a cup of instant coffee in the kitchen, to the right as you walked in the front door. Instant coffee was invented by the Marquis de Sade and tastes terrible, but it's all we had. Once in my office, I found the handover notes which Nolan, my back-to-back, had left for me. Our travel arrangements did not allow for a face-to-face handover this time, but he left good notes and I could call him at home in Australia if I needed any clarification.

One rig was drilling ahead in the 12-1/4 inch hole section while the other was cementing their 9-5/8 inch casing. If there were no problems, we should finish drilling both wells while I was in town. There were no problems with any of the third-party services, and the logistics seemed to be working out. It looked like the hitch should be fairly straight forward and easy money, but being that this is the oilfield, I wouldn't be holding my breath.

The morning call to the rigs consists of just me, the Senior Drilling Engineer, Eddie, from Malaysia, and the Logistics Manager, David, from Australia. Many companies have everybody on the roster at these morning calls, but I think that this just adds to the confusion, so I employ the KISS Principle - keep it simple stupid!

After the morning call with both rigs wrapped up, I called the Drilling Manager at the head office in Kuala Lumpur and gave him a rundown on the operations. He asked me to keep an eye on the timeline. Completion equipment, and personnel, were at a premium and would need to be booked as soon as we knew when the wireline tools would be out of the hole. After this, I just caught up on what had been happening, ordered some shish tawook kabobs for lunch, and tried to find a real coffee maker for the office.

That afternoon I called Colonel Sivan's secretary and made an appointment for three o'clock. Walking over to her villa office that afternoon, I showed my identity card to the submachine gun toting guard at the front gate. He inspected the contents of my backpack before granting entrance. I then went through the same procedure with the guard at the front door to the villa. He seemed satisfied that I was who I said I was and got on the phone to Colonel Sivan and informed her that I was downstairs. She must have told him to send me up as he waved me forward, then ignored me.

Arriving at Colonel Silvan's office door I knocked and was told to enter. "Good afternoon, Colonel Ibrahim. Jebell Rose reporting for duty!" I barked.

"Don't you ever get tired of that line?"

"I find it best to be totally correct whenever I see you again at the beginning of the hitch. To 'test the waters' if you will, to determine if you still want to have me taken out and shot," I replied.

"I might have you taken out and shot simply for using that line for the hundredth time. You should really try to get more creative," she said with a smile while waving me to a seat in front of her desk.

"Is everything well back in Colorado? How is that gorgeous, brain addled girl you are cohabitating with?"

"She's doing great. Her shop is keeping her busy and out of my hair most of the time, and it is turning a profit. I can get rid of her if you tell me that you and Colonel Nebez are separating."

Sivan has a great laugh and she laughed now. "Only you would dare talk to the wife of a Peshmerga colonel like that," she said.

"Colonel, may I remind you that you are Asayish. If you took offense, there would be nothing left for Colonel Nebez to take out his anger on."

"Truer words were never spoken," she said.

"In an effort to get me back in the graces of both colonels, I would like to make a peace offering," I said while digging through my backpack. I pulled out the usual bottle of Johnnie Walker Blue Label for her husband and set it on her desk. I also pulled out a bottle of Jam Jar Sweet Shiraz from Paarl, South Africa.

I went into my spiel. "This Shiraz is a fresh, fruity, semi-sweet wine that displays aromas and flavors of ripe blueberries, blackberries and raspberries with dark chocolate overtones. Refreshing and approachable with a perfect balance."

Sivan took the bottle from me, looked at the label, looked at me and said, "That was thoughtful. What is it that you want?"

I put on my best 'innocent' look and replied that I didn't want anything, it was simply a gift so that she would not have to drink that foul stuff I brought for her husband. She laughed again. After we discussed the security situation and schedule for the foreseeable future, I said goodbye and made my exit.

Back at my office I made sure everyone was slaving away, reiterated to David that his continued employment depended on him finding a suitable coffee maker, then took a walk to the Holland Bazaar to stock up on snacks and things for my residence before heading home.

Amira, our house girl, always cooks me a dinner and leaves it on the stove, so I rarely go out for the evening. I do stop at the Holland Bazaar for snacks, but Amira does the real grocery shopping.

I ate whatever it was that was left on the stove. I am not familiar with Kurdish dishes; they are all tasty, I just don't know what you call them. After cleaning up the dishes and silverware, I got on my laptop and gave Rachel an update and let her know I was fine. Since Cadillac Springs is 9 hours behind Erbil when they are on normal time, and 10 hours behind when they are on Daylight Savings Time, and considering Rachel's abhorrence of getting up early, we had decided that staying in touch by Skype was not necessary for the month I was away. A simple email each day was okay. I then cleaned up for bed and pulled out the latest Janet Evanovich novel, caught up on what Stephanie Plummer was up to, then called it a night and went to bed.

The next week or so went by as per the routine: get up, eat breakfast in my villa, walk to work, have the morning call, make sure everything is organized to keep drilling the wells, call the Drilling Manager in Kuala Lumpur and brief him, check with our liaison with the Kurdish Regional Government (KRG) and the Ministry of Natural Resources, make sure all of our bills are paid, eat lunch, harass the staff, do the four in the afternoon rig call with the Senior Drilling Engineer and Logistics people present, go home, eat dinner, shower, read, bed. Repeat.

Thursday evening, 2 weeks after I had arrived, was the 'certain evening' that I was required to tail a certain gentleman. I knew the town well enough, and I could not have one of my guys drive me, so I decided to use my personal company Hilux four door pickup that evening. My truck was generic white, like most of them in Erbil, and it did not have any corporate logo on it. I sure as heck could not do anything to twig Colonel Sivan that I was doing a little more than just drilling oil wells in Kurdistan. That could go bad quickly.

My untraceable email account had provided a photo of the man I was supposed to tail, and a time interval in which he was supposed to exit the Rotana Hotel on Gulan Street. The gentleman in question was roughly 6-foot-tall, about 60 years of age with longish blondish-gray hair, wore black framed nerd style glasses, and was in fairly good shape for his age. He also walked with a walking stick. He should be easy to spot. I had a feeling in the back of my head, which I could not shake, that I had seen this guy before, but since I was not supposed to actually interact with him at all, this was not an issue.

I parked the Hilux outside of the hotel security checkpoint around six so that I could get to it without a hassle. I then went in and sat in the lounge, in front of the registration desk, and began reading the local expat magazine while actually keeping an eye on those coming and going. Sure enough, right on the dot of seven, my guy walks out of the elevator and goes to the registration desk to discuss something with them. This was my cue to get outside to my truck. If he took a cab, I'd need to be ready to follow it, if he left on foot, I could simply leave the truck.

From where I had parked the truck, I had a good view of the front door of the hotel, so I waited for him to come out of the door. The downside of being a solo tail, is that if he thought that he was under surveillance, he could choose another exit and I would be left with nothing. Then again, I assumed that the Jankowski Group knew that a solo tail was a risk, and I was just going to do what I was told.

A few minutes after I had gotten into my truck, the target walked out of the hotel and asked the doorman to hail him a taxi. It was too early to be very busy, so a local orange and white taxi pulled up in a few minutes, after passing the security checkpoint on the road into the hotel. I looked carefully for distinctive details of the taxi in the event I got separated in traffic. Two giveaways, it was running a space-saver spare tire on the driver's side rear, and there was a Manchester United sticker on the rear bumper. As they drove past the parking area I was in, I simply fell in behind them as they got on Gulan Street heading into Erbil. I let a few vehicles get between us as we stayed on Gulan Street making the loop around the city to the north. They made no attempt at a surveillance detection route, so this was easy as long as I did not get burned.

Approaching the Ainkawa exit, the taxi helpfully indicated his intended turn off from Gulan Street to Ainkawa Road. At the bottom of the exit ramp, he continued to indicate a right turn so that he would be headed south on Ainkawa. At this point I was directly behind them since no other vehicles had taken this exit. I had a fairly good idea where they were headed at this point, and sure enough, after traveling almost 200 yards, the taxi again indicated a right turn and pulled in front of the T-Bar. I had no choice but to continue on Ainkawa until I could get out of sight and make a U-turn. This also allowed the target to get settled in the bar while I parked out of sight.

When I finally walked into the T-Bar, the target was sitting at the bar nursing a beer. I went to the other end of the bar and ordered a beer, wondering how long I would have to stay there. After we had both had a couple of beers, and an hour had passed, the target asked the bartender where the restrooms were, then walked toward the toilets. Now this is not good if you are a tail. The target can just walk out the front door, or any other exit, leaving you at the bar. On the other hand, if you go looking for the target and he spots you, you are finished for the evening. I decided to sit and wait when my phone vibrated. I had a text message saying, 'I am your target, meet me in the restroom now. Trevanian.'

I was shocked, scared, and pissed off all at the same time. I made the assumption that the target was actually Ansel, my original contact with the Jankowski Group when I was recruited in Cape Town. The only time I had heard the name Trevanian in years was in the pizza shop in Bantry Bay, South Africa, when I had asked him what Trevor's favorite book was. Why had he asked me to tail him in the Asayish's back yard? If they discovered that I was doing any sort of intelligence work in Kurdistan without their approval, things would go very bad, very quickly.

I was thinking all of this when I got off my barstool and made my way to the men's room. I walked in the door and saw Ansel standing at the sinks. He had taken off the blondish- gray wig and the black framed glasses, and just stood there.

"We are alone," he said while indicating that the stalls were empty.

"What silly assed game are you playing?" I hissed. "If I get caught by the Asayish doing any intelligence work, of any kind, regardless of how amateur it may be, I may never leave this country again!"

"Before you work yourself into a lather, give me a minute to explain," Ansel said as he raised his hands to chest level, palms out, in the universal 'calm down' gesture.

"You've got exactly as long as it takes for some other guy to come in here to get rid of his rented beer. When that happens, I am gone."

"The owner of the T-Bar and I have an arrangement; this restroom is presently out of service as of when you walked in the door. We will have concluded our discussion, one way or another, within the next 5 minutes."

Reaching into his pants' pocket, he took out a Sony 3.1 Gen 1 32 gigabyte memory stick and passed it to me. "You need to get that to Colonel Sivan Ibrahim as soon as possible, tonight if you can."

"And how the hell do you expect me to do that without compromising myself to the Asayish and spending the next decade in a cold, damp cell, or worse?" I demanded.

"Simple actually, you go home and call her, I assume you have her mobile number, and tell her that you must see her immediately concerning a matter of national security."

"And why would I need to do that? As far as she knows I am nothing more than oilfield trash, drilling oil wells in Kurdistan." This situation was going from bad to worse.

"Generally, you will need to sail as close to the truth as possible. You went out for a drink at the T-Bar to get out of the house. Once you were here you had a few beers and then went to the restroom. A few minutes later, while you were washing your hands, a gentleman approached you, handed you that memory stick, told you to get it into the hands of the Asayish, and left. Feel free to describe me in detail since I am already on a video which is on that stick, and it will not matter in the long run."

"What is on this stick? I am giving her something I know nothing about. Who's to say that whatever is on this stick won't implicate me in something else that puts me in another cold, dark cell, or worse?" I asked.

"You'll need to trust me on this. The Kurdish Regional Government has a mole who is passing detailed information concerning the oil strategy in Kurdistan. It is being used against Kurdistan, and it is time sensitive."

"Why me? Why don't you just waltz into the Asayish, give them the stick, let them arrest the mole, and get the credit for finding him or her?" It seemed like a reasonable question.

"As I said, it is time sensitive information. If I were to walk into any government office here with this information, I would immediately be detained and questioned to verify my identity. Afterwards the information would travel through the bureaucracy, perhaps tipping off the mole, before anything was actually done. You, on the other hand, already have a relationship with a member of the Asayish and can get it into their hands immediately. As you know, the Asayish will simply bypass everyone in an immediate effort to detain the mole and interrogate him or her. If you care anything at all about this country, you'll do this. We will both likely be detained for some time, but at the end of the day they will shake our hands and let us go."

"You realize that if I do this, I will be burned in Kurdistan and will be useless to the Jankowski Group, in this country, from this time forward?" I pointed out.

"That is understood. This is vital. Your financial agreement and all other parts of our original agreement will remain in effect until you decide to retire. If you take work in another country at a later date, where we may require your services, you can decide to be reactivated at that time."

"And if I decide not to go through with your plan?" I needed to explore that option.

"Simply, you will force me to approach the Asayish myself, the scenario I described earlier would occur. You and I would both be arrested and detained, and the mole would most likely escape the net."

"So, I am pretty well screwed either way, is that it?"

"In a nutshell, yes."

CHAPTER 19

NEEDLESS TO SAY, I WAS sweating bullets by the time I drove back to my office in the English Village. I had thought about going home, but I decided that the office was more 'professional', and it was a short walk to Sivan's office. I unlocked the gate to the carport at my office and pulled my truck under the carport. There was no sense in locking the gate as the Asayish would be here shortly. Unlocking the front door, I walked to the kitchen and got a large bottle of water out of the refrigerator before walking upstairs to my office.

Pulling the memory stick out of my pocket I placed it on the desk, then reached into my other pocket and pulled out my iPhone and laid it on the desk as well. I drank about half the water, leaned back in my office chair to pull myself together, then grabbed my phone and called Colonel Sivan at home before I lost my nerve. As it was only ten in the evening, I hoped that I caught her before she went to bed.

"Good evening, Colonel Nebez speaking." Damn, I'd gotten the wrong colonel! Nothing to be done but press forward.

"Good evening, Colonel Nebez, this is Jeb calling. I need to speak to Sivan urgently, I believe it is a matter of national security."

He was instantly alert, "This is no time for joking, Jeb." I assured him this was no joke. He yelled for Sivan to come to the phone. "Is my presence required?" he asked.

"Let me explain the situation to Sivan and we will let her make that decision. Perhaps it may be a good idea if you could put it on speaker, so that you can both hear what happened this evening."

Sivan got on the phone, "Good evening, Jeb, judging by the look on Nebez's face this is not a social call. You are on speaker with Nebez and myself. Please go ahead."

I then went through the story exactly as Ansel had coached me. I had gone to the T-Bar for a drink, and to get out of the house. I had two beers, then went to use the restroom. While in the restroom a man had handed me a memory stick and told me to get it into the hands of the Asayish. I assumed that the man had seen Sivan, Nebez and myself at dinner over the years, and that I had been selected for that reason. I also told them that I had driven directly back from the T-Bar to my office and was waiting there with the thumb drive.

Sivan was the total professional now. "Jeb, you will stay in your office until Nebez and I arrive, do not go anywhere else. In a few minutes, an Asayish detail will arrive and come to your office. They will not come inside your office. Do not touch this thumb drive, just wait for us. Do you understand?"

"Yes," was the only rational answer to that question.

Sivan hung up, and 5 minutes later there was a screech of tires outside as the Asayish detail arrived. As the front door was open there was no need to kick it in, and three sets of boots pounded up the stairs. A young captain, about 30 years old, came to the door with his Glock drawn, and asked if I was Mr. Jebell Rose. I said that I was. He told me to just relax and wait for the colonels, then asked if I needed anything. I'd polished off the water that I had brought to the office earlier, so I asked for another bottle. The captain said something in Kurdish to one of the other guys, and a bottle of water appeared at the door. I had to stand up to get it. When a colonel of the Asayish, tells a captain of the Asayish, not to enter the room, they tend to follow orders to the letter.

Thirty minutes later both Sivan and Nebez walked into my office, in uniform, and sat down in the chairs in front of my desk. They asked me to repeat my earlier story, which I did. Sivan said something to the captain outside the office, and several minutes later he returned with a Sony laptop. The captain appeared to be some kind of IT geek as well. He asked me if he could sit in my office chair as he went to work on the thumb drive. It is not one of those times when you refused such a request. He visually inspected the drive, and satisfied, he plugged it into the USB slot on the side. The Sony_32X icon came up on the desktop, he clicked on it, and it opened without requiring a password. There were several photos, a video file, and a single text file on the thumb drive. At this point Sivan asked for me to be escorted into another office while they studied the files.

Two hours later Sivan shook me awake. I had fallen asleep in the Senior Drilling Engineer's office, in his chair. She looked tense, so I knew that they had found the information concerning the mole.

"Jeb, I cannot thank you enough for bringing this to my attention. It is a serious matter which I cannot discuss with you at this time. Also, we need to keep an eye on you, and the best way to do this is to put you under 'house arrest'. You will be able to go to and from your home to this office, but nowhere else. You will have an Asayish escort at all times, and one will be with you at home, and in this office, at all times. I am sorry, Jeb, but it must be this way, and I am not sure how long these measures will be in place. You can contact Rachel at home as usual, but do not discuss this matter with anyone. We will likely require your assistance in the future, so do not plan on going home on your normally scheduled rotation. My men will take you home now."

For 2 weeks I was on pins and needles just going to and from work. Amira, my house girl, made dinner each night for me and my escort, so I didn't need to worry about that. Breakfast and lunch were brought to the office, but I could not get out to the rigs. I really didn't need to as the Drilling Supervisors on the rigs were more than up to the task, but I felt like a prisoner. I was wondering what would happen when I next saw Colonel Sivan.

As it turns out, Colonel Sivan surprised me. She called me to her office, so I trooped over there with my escort, wondering if I would be a free man later that afternoon. I was escorted up to her office and found Sivan and four other high ranking Asayish officers, three men and a woman, waiting for me there.

"Again, thank you for bringing this issue to our attention, Mr. Rose," Sivan was being formal, so I knew this was a serious meeting. "The memory stick which you delivered to me has caused much concern in the Asayish and in certain departments within the Kurdish Regional Government. Major Bashur will explain. Tara, continue." Sivan indicated the other woman officer.

"Mr. Rose, first let me thank you for this information. From the video on the thumb drive we could easily identify the source as a Mr. Ansel White, who is employed by the Jankowski Group, as he did not take any steps to conceal his identity. The Jankowski Group is a private intelligence firm. These private intelligence firms are generally legal and are usually private, non-governmental or quasi-non-governmental organizations, devoted to the collection, analysis, and exploitation of information, most commonly through the evaluation of public sources, open-source intelligence, and cooperation with other institutions. Some private agencies make their services available to governments as well as individual consumers; however, most of these agencies sell their services to large corporations with an interest or investment in the category. In certain cases, functions previously performed by intelligence agencies are now outsourced to private intelligence firms."

"You wouldn't know anything about these firms, would you?" queried Sivan, with a sly smile.

Major Bashur continued, "Apparently, while doing some work for an unnamed, international, integrated oil company, the Jankowski Group found some 'inconsistencies' in the way the Russians and OPEC were responding to the oil strategies being developed within the Kurdish Regional Government and the Ministry of Natural Resources. Specifically, production estimates and development strategies. The Russians and OPEC were adjusting their tactics based on closely held information in Kurdistan, before the information was being made public. This is detrimental to the long-term goals of the KRG."

At this point one of the other officers took over the tutorial without benefit of an introduction.

"During the past 2 weeks we have been able to locate the mole within the Ministry of Natural Resources, and he is being closely monitored. He apparently is a fitness fanatic who frequents the Erbil Sports Center on Peshawa Qazi. This gym is also a favorite of the Policy Officer for Trade and Economic Affairs at the Belarusian Consulate in Erbil. It seems that our mole has been passing information to this policy officer for some time. It also appears that the policy officer is passing this information on to the Russians, who then disseminate it to OPEC. Not only do we need to interrogate our mole, we need to interrogate this policy officer as well to determine exactly what game is being played. He may be a middle man, but then again, he may be a principal player."

I was getting worried, as I had been the one to attach a GPS tracker to the vehicle of this Belarusian diplomat while he was in the gym. If the Asayish knew this, I could be in a world of hurt. I looked over at Sivan who was reclining in her office chair, with her fingers locked behind her head. She grinned, tried not to laugh and looked away. Another unnamed gentleman from the Asayish took over the story. "Contrary to popular opinion, embassies are the sovereign territories of the country they are located in, not the county whose diplomatic mission is resident there. You will have seen some embassies housed in buildings which also contain other embassies or banks, for example. The reality of the situation is that the Vienna Convention states that the local government foreswears the right to enter an embassy and that diplomatic immunity protects the diplomats working within the embassy. This does not mean that the physical embassy is foreign soil, or legal territory for law enforcement purposes. That said, we do not wish to cause a diplomatic issue or a media circus to get at this policy officer, which is where you, Mr. Rose, come into play. Over to you, Colonel."

Sivan unlaced her fingers from behind her head, sat up straight, rested her elbows on her desk, with her chin on top of her hands, then looked at me and said, "This is what you are going to do for me, Mr. Rose. You will lure Mr. Roma Navitski, Policy Officer for Trade and Economic Affairs for Belarus in Kurdistan, to a location where we can take him. Once you have a plan in mind, we will meet again to go over it and approve it. The quicker you can make this happen, the better. Understood?"

"Yes," I replied as, again, there was really no other acceptable response.

I was due to rotate in a few days, but there was no way that I could leave Kurdistan at the moment. I had to call Nolan and make up some excuse that I needed 2 months off the next hitch, and that I wanted to work a 2-month hitch this time. He had no problem with that, so I was over the first hurdle. I then Skyped Rachel and told her that I had to work another month. I told her that Nolan had some family business he needed to take care of during the next hitch, so instead of me having a short off-hitch, I would just do a double and get 2 months off the next time back. Finally, I had to find some way to get Roma out of his consulate to a place I could have him kidnapped by the Asayish. As he was the Policy Officer for Trade and Economic Affairs, I needed some sort of financial lure, either for Belarus or him personally, to get him out.

Belarus has an oil and gas company, Belorusneft, operating in Belarus, Venezuela, Ecuador and Russia. I needed to find something which they had that I apparently wanted. After calling their offices in Gomel, where they thankfully spoke fairly good English, I fished around by phone and ended up with the Department of Foreign Economic Activities. From them I was able to get a list of surplus drilling equipment sent to me. Looking at the list I found, unbelievable as it may sound, two new National Oilwell Varco FD-1600 triplex mud pumps. These are the type presently on my two rigs, so it was conceivable that I would be interested in them.

I then called the Belarus Consulate and asked for the Policy Officer for Trade and Economic Affairs. As I expected, from such a small consulate, Roma Navitski answered the phone in heavily accented English. I explained to him that I was a Drilling Superintendent running two rigs for Onyx Petroleum in Kurdistan. I was having trouble with some mud pumps on my rigs, and was shopping around for suitable replacements. I had contacted Belorusneft in Gomel and had obtained a list of surplus equipment from them. On the list were two new National Oilwell Varco FD-1600 triplex mud pumps, and I would like to discuss the possible purchase of them at his convenience. As a 'tickler' I added that I was willing to pay a fee for any assistance with the paperwork and logistics required to get the pumps from Belarus to Kurdistan as soon as possible. Roma got very excited, asked for my email address and mobile number, then said that he would get back to me once he had a chance to investigate the proposed sale.

While Roma was figuring out how to maximize his kickback from the mud pump deal, I still had two rigs to run. Since one was logging at total depth, the planned depth of the well, I could safely leave that in the hands of the Senior Drilling Engineer and the well test gang coming in-country. I had remembered to give the Drilling Manager a heads-up when we ran the logging tools into the well, so that was all in hand. The other rig had drilled their 8-1/2" hole section and were about to run a 7" liner, so I needed to get with the Senior Drilling Engineer and the Drilling Supervisor on location to make sure everything was ready to go, and that the cementing calculations and program were prepared. All while trying to plan the abduction of a foreign diplomat.

The next day I received a phone call from Roma saying that Belorusneft would like to enter into negotiations for the mud pumps. That was quick, so Roma was greedy. He informed me that Belorusneft had appointed him as their agent in Kurdistan, and that he would be charging ten percent of the net price for both pumps, as an agent's fee. I told him that I needed to run some numbers and would get back in touch with him the following day. I actually let him stew a day longer, then called him and told him that I was willing to pay $75,000 US dollars for each pump, and a seven percent agent's fee. I would have paid anything really, but I had to make the negotiations look authentic.

The next day he countered with $80,000 per unit with a nine percent fee. I waited a day then called back with my final offer of $78,000 per unit and an eight percent fee. I reminded him that the fee would be paid in Kurdistan, in cash, and would be $12,480 in his pocket. He bitched and moaned, but his greed won out and he agreed. To make it even more authentic I told him that I had organized an inspector from

National Oilwell Varco to visit the Belorusneft warehouse in Gomel the next week to inspect the units, and that the sale was dependent on the outcome of the inspection. He was not happy with this, but I sweetened the deal by offering him another eight percent agent's fee if he would arrange for the shipping from Belarus to Kurdistan. I would have to agree to the arrangements, but I suggested he get them on the weekly IL-76 cargo flight out of Minsk, as it was the MD variant, it could handle both pumps plus other cargo.

The next day Roma called again and said that the terms of $78,000 per unit with the eight percent agent's fee was acceptable. The delivery fee using the IL-76 was $23,500 with the agent's fee being eight percent of that paid, in cash, to the agent in Kurdistan, or $1,880. I told him that I agreed to that and would take possession at my warehouse in the Energy Logistics compound located on the Airport Road going toward Mosul. I asked him when I could expect delivery and he said a week from today as the IL-76 flight would arrive on Wednesday and he would need 2 days to clear Customs. I then called the inspector and made sure that he could have the inspection performed and written up before the pumps were loaded the next Wednesday, but to call me if there were any serious issues with the pumps.

At this point I called Sivan and asked for a meeting in her office. She told me to come over at three in the afternoon. As I seemed to be sweating more than usual since my last meeting with Sivan, I freshened up some and put on a clean shirt before walking to her office with my escort. Needless to say, I was not required to hand over my work permit this time and I was escorted directly to Sivan's office. My escort knocked, stuck his head in the door like he was sticking it into a lion's mouth, whispered something politely, then backed away and indicated that I should enter. I entered; he closed the door.

I was not sure how to present myself this time. In the past my visits had essentially been social calls, but with this mole issue, I was not sure. "Good afternoon, Colonel Sivan," I said, figuring that was formal enough. Sivan looked at me with a frown on her face for a moment, then the corners of her lips started twitching, then she burst out laughing so hard she had tears in her eyes. When she finally got control of herself, she indicated that I should take one of the seats in front of her desk. I was now totally confused.

"You should have seen the look on your face the other day when you were brought into my office after your encounter at the T-Bar, it was priceless," she said while getting a tissue to dry her eyes. "The way you are behaving now is also priceless."

She leaned back in her chair with her arms along the chair arms, "Honestly, Jeb, did you not think that we knew that you were doing some of that adolescent spy work for the Jankowski Group? This is the Asayish, we know everything."

"How long had you known?" I asked.

"Ever since you tagged Roma's car at the Health Club. We actually had a girl in the café next to the one you were in, who was there to place a GPS tracker on Roma's car, but once you showed up, we wanted to see what was going on. Once you tagged his car we simply piggybacked onto the signal. At that time, we knew you were working for another party. Once you gave me the thumb drive it was obvious that you had been working with the Jankowski Group," she explained.

"Why didn't you pull me in for interrogation or whatever the equivalent is in the Asayish? Obviously, I was doing low level intelligence type work for another player," I asked.

"Jeb, you and I are friends. The type of work you were doing for the Jankowski Group does not hinder our work in the least, as a matter of fact, in this case, you actually did our work for us. Once we knew what was going on, we could keep an eye on you fairly easily as there is a tracker on your vehicle now, as well as on all of the vehicles registered to Onyx Petroleum. Last, but not least, we now had something on you, and could get you to do some tasks for us in the future, unless you wanted to visit the cells. Do you want to visit the cells?" she asked raising one eyebrow.

I gave a sigh of relief. Not only was my friendship with Sivan and Nebez intact, I no longer had to go around playing secret agent man while in Kurdistan. "No, Colonel, I have no desire to see the cells. Could you please ask someone to get me a Coke? I am parched due to the fact that you have successfully scared the crap out of me and have cruelly drug it out for weeks."

She yelled something at the door and minutes later a tray with a can of Coke and a glass of ice appeared. I opened the can, filled up the glass and drank half of it in one gulp. After getting some lubrication down my throat, I asked Sivan if she would like to hear the nefarious plan which I had devised to get Roma out of the consulate so that her, and her minions, could abduct him.

"Be clear and concise, as I will be recording this," she said as she pulled a digital recorder out of her desk drawer and set it up.

"Okay, next Wednesday, the usual IL-76 flight from Minsk to Erbil will arrive.

Onboard will be two mud pumps which I have purchased from the Belorusneft surplus warehouse in Gomel, Belarus. I have worked this deal directly through Roma and he is taking an eight percent agent's fee on the sale of the pumps, and for organizing delivery to Erbil. That is $14,360, untraceable and tax free to Roma for a week's worth of work.

"The pumps will arrive on Wednesday and clear Customs on Friday. I have arranged to take possession at my warehouse at the Energy Logistics compound on the Airport Road, on Friday. I will ask that Roma be at the warehouse when the trucks hauling the pumps arrive at the warehouse, so that I can sign any documents required and give him his agent's fees in cash. I am sure that he does not want to do this at the consulate for obvious reasons. At this point, Colonel, the ball will be in your court, as they say."

Sivan turned off the recorder, rested her elbows on her desk and her chin on top of her hands, gave me a big smile and said, "Well done! I am sure that we in the Asayish could have done better, but that is a very clever plan and is based on greed, which almost always works. You could have a future in this spy business, as long as you only work for me." Still smiling she continued, "Keep me informed on how this plan progresses, and let me know, as soon as you can, what time these pumps will be delivered to your warehouse."

"There is one thing that you can do for me to make things work smoothly. Can you contact Customs and make sure that the pumps are cleared on Friday, but only on Friday?" I asked.

"Consider it done," she said. "As it is Friday today, and I am sure that you are tired of your house arrest, I suggest that you take Nebez and I to dinner tonight at Naranj. We can meet here and walk, as it is just on the corner with Vital Village Road. Let's say seven o'clock. Do you think you can do that?"

After contemplating my lack of options, I said, "Consider it done."

I walked back to my office villa, sans escort, and simply decompressed while waiting for seven o'clock to arrive and then going to dinner. I could finally relax without the axe of the Asayish hanging over my head. I took the time to actually do some of my day job and called the rigs to make sure that everything was in order for either testing, or 'plug and abandoning' the wells, dependent on the results of the logs.

At six forty-five I walked back over to Sivan's office, and once through security, went up to her office to find both her and Nebez trying to keep from grinning. "We had you worried, didn't we?" Nebez asked.

"Colonels, you will never know the depths of my despair. Are you two going to sit here and bust my chops all night or am I taking you two miserable reprobates to dinner?"

We walked the few hundred yards to Naranj and had a wonderful dinner. Belboula salad for starters, then Sivan had the Harak Issbau, while Nebez ordered the Hamshouka, and I had the Kibbach Naboulsi as our main courses. Dessert was vanilla ice cream with mint. All in all, a nice meal, and we seemed to be back to our old relationship. Later, Nebez's driver collected Mr. and Mrs. Ibrahim from the restaurant, and I walked back to my residence in the Royal Villas.

The day of the abduction rolled around, and we met in Sivan's office at seven in the morning to review and finalize the plan. Attending the meeting was Sivan, myself, and a young trooper introduced as Major Tomar whose men, I was informed, would actually perform the snatch. I went over the plan up to the point that Roma would be at my warehouse to complete any required paperwork and to get his cash. At this point the young trooper took over. He told me to just go ahead with the deal, give the money to Roma, and to let him leave the warehouse area with the money. He and his men would take it from there.

"I thought that you were going to take him at the warehouse?"

"Think about it," Sivan said. "Roma, as paranoid as he appears to be, will be sure to have informed his people at the consulate as to where he is going. If we take him at your warehouse, and this became known, you would likely have visitors later in the day asking how we knew that Roma was going to be there at that time. It is better to let him be caught on your CCTV cameras arriving and departing from your warehouse. It would also be wise to make sure that you are caught on camera giving him the cash, as you will no doubt have a visit from his consulate security team after he has been reported missing. You will need to be able to show them the completed paperwork, and the CCTV footage to get you out of the picture. We will take him while he is on the way back to the consulate."

"Are you going to give me my 'agent's fees' back?" I needed to put those funds back in the company account.

"Depends on if you perform your role correctly and all goes well. Otherwise, I will let Major Tomar keep it," Sivan said with a grin. She was enjoying busting my balls just a little too much these days, but as discretion is the better part of valor, I decided not to mention it.

At this point my phone rang. It was Roma calling to tell me that the mud pumps had cleared Customs and would be arriving at my warehouse at ten o'clock. He indicated that he would be there around ten thirty to finalize our business. After hanging up the call I let Sivan and Major Tomar know that the game was on, and then made a call to ensure that the 30-tonne crane would be at my warehouse at ten to unload the mud pumps.

I left Sivan and Major Tomar plotting in her office and went back to mine to take the morning call from the rigs and to take care of any necessary business resulting from the calls. At nine thirty I had my driver take me to the warehouse, where I waited for the trucks to arrive with the pumps. As the pumps weighed in at just under 24 tonnes, without the fluid ends, I would need to store them outside so that, in the future, a crane could load them back onto another truck to deliver them to the rigs. I decided where I wanted them placed and had the crane standing by there waiting for the trucks to arrive.

Just after ten o'clock the trucks came through the gates, and I had my driver explain to them where I wanted them put. One after the other, the trucks pulled into position and the crane operator lifted them off the trucks and put them where I needed them. As they came on shipping frames, there was no need to lay down timbers for them to sit on. The entire operation took just over half an hour, at which time Roma had arrived in his embassy car with his driver. I assumed that it still had the GPS tracking unit on it, that I had placed inside the bumper weeks ago.

I had placed the pumps across from the concrete apron directly in front of the bay doors at the front of the warehouse since it was handy for me to access them, and the fact that this area was covered by a CCTV camera which was mounted under the eaves at the apex of the roof over the bay doors.

Roma was obviously nervous and wanted to be gone as quickly as possible, but I wanted him on camera for a reasonable amount of time. I had him accompany me around the pumps to visually inspect them for shipping damage before asking him if there was any paperwork to finalize. He had some forms in his briefcase which required my signature, so I asked him to follow me to the office inside the warehouse. Once I was seated at the desk and he was sitting in a chair in front of the desk, he passed me the paperwork, which was thankfully in English. I read through the documents, signed where required, then passed them back. He placed these back in his briefcase but did not bother to close it. This was my cue to reach into the desk drawer and take out a plain manila envelope with the agent's fee inside. I passed this to Roma who, as expected, took the time to count it. Once he was happy with the count, he placed it inside the briefcase, closed and locked the case, then stood up to shake my hand. Afterwards, he walked out to his waiting car and driver, and left. The pinhole camera behind the molding in the corner of the ceiling caught it all.

My role in the matter was finished, now it was up to Major Tomar and his boys. I walked back outside and took a good look at the mud pumps I had just purchased. Since I knew that the pumps on one of the rigs were on their last legs, this was a good buy as long as I got my agent's fee back. I found my driver smoking in the warehouse. Once he had finished his cigarette, we drove back to the office in the English Village. I sat around nervously doing my day job until I heard from Sivan that everything had gone satisfactorily. She reminded me that, without a doubt, the Belarusian Consulate security team would be visiting me later today or tomorrow, and to act normally, show them the paperwork and drive them out to the warehouse to view the CCTV tapes. Easy to say when you are not the one getting grilled.

Sure enough, when I arrived at my office the following day, there was a black, up-armored Toyota Landcruiser parked outside. As soon as I walked up to unlock the front gate and go inside, two rather large men in ill-fitting suits, which seem to be the fashion in ex-Iron Curtain countries, got out of the Landcruiser and approached me. They both pulled out small wallets with identification in them indicating, in English, that they were employed by the Belarus Consulate in Erbil. The one with a shaved head asked in heavily accented English if they could discuss a sensitive matter with me in my office. I asked what this concerned, as they would have expected that, and was told it would be better to discuss this in my office. I nodded, walked to the front door and opened it. I ushered them inside and asked if they wanted some instant coffee, I had not prevailed on David to purchase a real coffee maker yet; perhaps with the 'agent's fee' when it was returned? They wisely declined, so I grabbed a bottle of water and headed up the stairs indicating that they should follow me. I unlocked my office and motioned them inside. Pointing to the two chairs in front of my desk, I went around the desk and sat in my office chair.

After taking a drink of water I asked, "Gentlemen, what can I do for you?"

"Do you know a Mr. Roma Navitski, Policy Officer for Trade and Economic Affairs for Belarus in Kurdistan?" asked Shaved Head.

"I know him simply due to a business arrangement which we concluded yesterday. Why do you ask?"

Without answering my question, he continued, "What business arrangement did you conclude yesterday?"

“I had purchased two mud pumps for my drilling rigs from the Belorusneft surplus warehouse in Gomel. Mr. Navitski facilitated the sale and delivery of the pumps,” I replied.

Shaved Head’s buddy, I’ll call him Mustache, as that was his defining feature, a big bushy mustache, took over the questioning. “Do you have the paperwork to confirm this sale?”

I reached into the bottom drawer on the left side of the desk and pulled out a sheaf of paperwork held together with a clip, and placed it on the desk. “I think that you will find this in order.”

Mustache reached over and took the paperwork. He and Shaved Head inspected it for a full 5 minutes before placing it back on the desk. “This appears to be in order,” from Mustache.

Shaved Head then asks, “When was the last time that you saw Mr. Navitski?”

“The pumps cleared Customs yesterday morning and arrived at my warehouse around ten o’clock yesterday morning. While they were unloading, Mr. Navitski arrived with his driver. He and I inspected the pumps for damage, then went to my office to complete the paperwork. Mr. Navitski left shortly after that with his driver,” I replied.

“Do you have some way to confirm this?” from Shaved Head.

“Gentlemen, this is not Belarus, and I am not required to prove anything to you. You have come to my office asking questions, and up to this point I have remained courteous to you, but now you are pushing my hospitality. Perhaps if you told me what is going on, I could help you. If not, I will need to ask you to leave.”

They both scowled at this, but they knew that I was correct, and that if they pushed it, I would simply call the police. At which point, being consulate staff, the Asayish would be brought in, something nobody wanted. After a moment they both relaxed a bit before Mustache said, “Mr. Navitski disappeared yesterday, sometime before eleven in the morning. We are trying to locate him and would appreciate any assistance which you could offer us.”

“Why didn’t you say so!” I responded. “Disappearing in Kurdistan is not to be taken lightly. Why don’t you follow me out to my warehouse, and we can look at the CCTV tapes? Perhaps they will tell you something.”

They looked at one another, then back at me. “You have CCTV tapes of Mr. Navitski’s visit yesterday? With a time stamp?” this from Mustache.

“We have a CCTV camera set under the eaves at the front of the building for security reasons. As this is where the pumps were offloaded, he should be on them."

"That would be much appreciated," Shaved Head replied.

I called my driver to come get me and explained that we would be going out to the warehouse again, but we would be followed by the black Landcruiser, and not to lose it. We arrived at the warehouse, and I waited for Shaved Head and Mustache to walk to the front door to the right of the bay door before unlocking it and ushering them in. I got the CCTV feed up on my desktop computer, then motioned for then to come around the desk so that they could see the monitor. Backing the feed up until just before ten yesterday morning, I asked if they would like to sit at my desk and review the video. Shaved Head took the seat and the controls, while I got a Coke out of the refrigerator and let them view to their hearts' content. After about 20 minutes of viewing, Shaved Head stood up and came over to where I was sitting and asked if he could get a copy of the tape from ten o'clock to eleven o'clock yesterday morning. I told him that I really didn't know how to copy the tape. If he did, he could do it now from the desktop, and email it to himself at the consulate.

First, I am a computer idiot and actually did not know how to do this. Secondly, if he did it himself, he could not accuse me later of tampering with it. He nodded his head, went back to the computer, and 5 minutes later he was finished. They both came around the desk, thanked me and shook my hand before heading toward the door. I let them know that if there was anything else I could do to help, just to ask. I sincerely hoped that this was the last I would see of anyone associated with the Belarusian Consulate in Kurdistan.

After the little episode with Roma, the rest of my extended hitch went fairly easily. Both wells had reached their planned total depth, and both were logged. After the logs were evaluated by people much smarter than I, one well was deemed to contain enough hydrocarbon bearing geology to warrant a well test, while the other wasn't. So, I got everything organized to run a test string in the 'good' well and went about plugging and abandoning the 'bad' well.

Nolan flew in 2 days before I was due to leave so that we could have a proper handover after a 2-month hitch on my part. After going through the paperwork his first day, we went out for a proper dinner. Thankfully, he didn't ask about the reason I needed 2 months off, so I didn't have to lie to him, and then have to remember that lie later. The second day we visited both of the rigs and had lunch with the Drilling Supervisor of one rig, and dinner with the Drilling Supervisor of the other. It is good practice to visit the rigs and hang out for a while with the guys actually doing the work. Getting back to town I packed up my kit at the residence villa and got a good night's sleep.

I flew out of Erbil on the Emirates' flight to Dubai in the middle of the following afternoon. I then caught the British Airways' flight to Denver, via Heathrow, arriving in Denver around midafternoon the same day. From there I caught the late United Express flight to Glenwood Springs. I had Skyped Rachel before I left Erbil, so hopefully she had not run off with the mailman and would be waiting to pick me up.

As it turned out, the mailman had not gotten lucky, and Rachel was waiting in the arrivals hall to greet me. After a serious kiss, with the appropriate amount of passion and associated butt grabbing, we walked out to my truck. I threw my bags in the back and we drove home. I do not think that I was ever so happy to be home.

Rachel had 'cooked' dinner, which for her meant she had taken out one of the frozen lasagnas which I keep in the freezer, and let it thaw on the kitchen island. I turned on the stove to let it pre-heat while I dumped my kit in the laundry room at the back corner of the pantry, near the back door. Back in the kitchen I put the lasagna in the oven and made a salad. Rachel had gone upstairs to freshen up, so I set out the plates, silverware and two Coors beers. Once the lasagna was hot, I yelled to Rachel to come to the table. Funny enough, most of her clothes were missing. I could tell that she had on my 1976 Electric Light Orchestra Face the Music Tour t-shirt, but it was difficult to tell if she had anything else on. There were no visible panty lines.

"I've suddenly lost my appetite, perhaps we should just forget about dinner," I suggested.

"Eat up, cowboy, you're going to need your strength," she said with a grin.

I started to eat like a ravenous piranha but was told to slow down as anticipation was half the fun. "Wherever you read that, the author has probably never been sitting across the table from a scantily clad nymph, while eating in anticipation of some gratuitous sex afterwards. I suggest you do not pay attention to such rubbish."

"Regardless, I am quite sure that you will need your strength. I have been studying diligently while you were away, and now hold a black belt, third degree, in the art of Wanton Hussy. I am eager to show you my new moves."

Suffice it to say, she did, I barely survived, it was a wonderful evening.

CHAPTER 20

THE FOLLOWING MORNING, AFTER RACHEL got untangled from the sheets, she located and put on the previously discarded ELO t-shirt, and went to her room to get ready for work. I threw on some cargo shorts and went downstairs to start the coffee, clean up the dishes, which were never properly taken care of the previous evening, and put the first load of my work clothes in the washer.

By the time I had finished and walked back into the kitchen, Rachel was sitting at the island drinking coffee in her Dickies coveralls, and apparently had a pulse. I walked up behind her, and utilizing all of my secret squirrel skills, began nibbling on her ear while I looped my right hand under her right arm and grabbed the zipper of her coveralls, pulling it down. Looking over and downward, I was dismayed to see that she had on my 1978 Eagles The Long Run Tour t-shirt and shorts underneath.

"You wouldn't survive another round bubba," she said while raising her right hand, with her coffee cup, up and over my hand which still held the zipper. A very complicated, yet graceful, move.

"Perhaps, but I would die with a smile on my face. People underrate a happy demise."

She finished her coffee, rinsed the cup, stood up while rearranging her shorts and t-shirt, zipped up her coveralls and headed for the door. I walked behind her, admiring the wiggle in her walk. She gave me a peck on the cheek and said that it was her boxing night, so she would be home late and would require chili dogs for dinner. I told her I had that in hand and would willingly trade her chili dogs for her clothes when she got home. She said, "Deal," and headed out to her Porsche.

After I had another cup of coffee, I went out to the barn to see if my suspension parts, disc brakes and wheels had arrived. I had asked TJ to keep an eye out for them, and to put it all in the barn if it arrived. Sure enough, all my new toys were there. I was like a kid at Christmas while I opened up all of the boxes and surveyed my new stuff. Maybe I would get the 1956 finished this time home. Walking back to face out of the barn door and survey my kingdom, I caught a glimpse of a black shadow scooting up the hill behind the house. I guessed Dog was still in residence. I didn't blame him, if Rachel would wash me, I'd stick around as well. With that mental picture in my mind, I got in the F-150 and drove to town to get hotdogs and buns.

On the way back from Safeway I stopped at Rachel's shop to say hello to TJ and just to see what was going on there. About the time that I had left for work in Kurdistan, they had finished and shipped a 1969 Shelby GT500 Mustang and were waiting on a 1970 Dodge Challenger R/T convertible to arrive. I pulled my truck up under the awning out front and walked in the front door. Nobody was in the office, so I kept walking through to the bays in the back.

The Challenger was a beauty! They had painted it the correct EV2 hemi orange with the V6W longitudinal white stripe. The interior was black, while the convertible top was white. There was also an extraordinary female backside, covered in stretched tight Dickies, bent over the engine compartment. Walking up behind Rachel, I slipped my hand into the right-hand slit pocket and felt around in there.

"Is that all you ever think about?" Rachel said while continuing to work on the six-pack carburetion linkage.

"That and food is about it. I can only concentrate on one or the other at any given time."

"Okay, concentrate on going and getting TJ and I some lunch. Burgers and fries are fine. We need to get this car finished."

From under the car, on the other side, came, "How's it going, Jeb? Make mine two cheeseburgers and fries."

"Since when did I get demoted to food runner?" I demanded.

"Since you refused to pick up a wrench and help out. You may as well make yourself useful," said Rachel. If she wasn't a black belt in 'Wanton Hussy', I'd consider kicking her out of the shop.

So off I went to make a lunch run. After I got back, and they took a break to eat, I drove home and got the grill cleaned up, and organized my shop to get ready for the suspension and brake installation project. I took a quart Tupperware container of homemade chili out of the freezer in the pantry, and put it on the kitchen counter to thaw, then went out and loaded up the grill with mesquite wood and charcoal briquettes. Going back into the kitchen, I put a couple of beers in a cooler with ice and took them to the porch while I waited for TJ to arrive. After a while, I heard an odd engine coming up the driveway from the county road, but it was TJ's 1950 Chevy pickup. He pulled in front of his bunkhouse and came over for a beer.

"I am guessing," said I, "but your old pickup seems to have grown some balls. I would venture to say that your Coyote motor and transmission arrived, and that you installed it while I was gone?"

"You are correct in your assumption," he replied. Then with a big grin he said, "And she goes like a bat out of hell, you'll have to give her a test drive."

"All in good time. At the moment I need to drink this beer, get the fire going and heat up some chili. Did you upgrade the rear end? Speaking of rear ends, how's Heather?"

"First things first. Give me a beer." After a long draw on his beer, he continued, "I chopped a Dana 60 to fit the four-link suspension I installed, so it will handle the 5.0 Coyote motor tied to the 4R70W automatic. Furthermore, the frame has been totally rebuilt out of box section tube steel and everything is geared up to handle the 435 horses and 400 lb-ft of torque." Another draw on the beer. "Asking about my girl's rear end is disrespectful and would normally get you reprimanded. That said, I am sure that you are only asking out of concern for her wellbeing, so I will tell you. It is still firm and round. Rachel has got her going to that Bikram stuff on Tuesdays and Thursdays, and the results speak for themselves."

We finished our beers, and I started the fire in the grill while TJ went to clean up. After I got the fire going, I went in to the kitchen, put the chili in a pan over a low fire and set out plates and silverware for three. I got the sun tea jug off the porch and put it on the island as well. Should have been good to go.

At seven forty-five the Whale Tail growled into the courtyard and headed left into the lean-to garage. Out popped Heather and Rachel gesticulating, laughing and acting like silly little girls. Both were dressed in workout kit, the tight spandex looking shorts and sports bras, which is a fashion statement in its own right. Being the proper host, I gave Heather a peck on the cheek first, before giving Rachel a big sloppy kiss while fondling her backside.

"Where's my butt grab?" demanded Heather.

"If I grab your butt, I will get beaten up by Rachel, and then shot by TJ. As much as I would enjoy grabbing your backside, common sense says not to," I said with a pout.

"Oh well, your loss," she said with a grin.

I was curious, so I asked, "Why are you in sporting attire, Heather? Rachel just got the crap beat out of her by Bret, but I didn't think you were the masochistic type."

"Nicholas has put together a routine for me on the heavy bag and the speed bag. I now go with Rachel on Monday and Wednesday to cheer her on and get a bit of a workout."

"Does Nicholas stand behind you when you are working out on the bags?" I asked.

Thinking about it for a minute, she turned bright red and said, "Yeah…"

"Then while you are working out on the bags, Nicholas is working out his eyes on your butt. Don't get me wrong, Nick is doing you right, but this would be termed an 'ulterior motive' for the guy. I think I'll stop by and watch on Wednesday," I commented.

Rachel had been listening and came up behind me putting her arm around my waist. "If you show up Wednesday you had better be looking at one butt, and one butt only, if you know what's healthy for you." Now seemed a good time to get everyone into the kitchen to eat.

"You guys go ahead into the kitchen; I'll get TJ and we'll be there in a minute. Rachel, the stove is the flat thing with the rings on the top which make fire. Could you turn the fire off, so we don't burn the chili?"

"Keep it up goof ball and we'll see if you get any sugar tonight, and I am not talking about dessert," was all she said going into the kitchen.

I knocked on the bunkhouse door and told TJ that dinner was served, then walked back onto the porch and into the kitchen. The girls were yakking like turkeys and hadn't noticed that Heather did not have a place set, so I had to do that as well. Going back out to the grill I piled the dogs and buns onto a tray and handed it to TJ as he went by to the kitchen, "May as well make yourself useful," I said. What goes around, comes around.

We took our time eating our chili dogs and I caught up with what everybody had been up to. Rachel was doing well at the shop and TJ was slotting in their just fine.

His mechanical skills were fine to start with, but under Rachel's tutelage, he was quickly becoming a master. His skills at bodywork and painting, gleaned at chop shops in the south, were also getting to the point where Rachel felt he was good enough to straighten and paint the high-end vehicles which she restored. Heather had taken to managing the bank like a duck to water and continued to add both commercial and private accounts to the bank. Peio had dropped by to see Rachel on a few occasions but was busy getting his new house in order. I'd run up and see him in a few days. Bret was another issue.

"Something is really bothering Bret," Rachel told us. "He is still running the gym and trying to remain upbeat, but he isn't working out much and he just doesn't seem motivated these days. He has bags under his eyes like he isn't sleeping well, and he is short-tempered at times. All of which is extremely out of character." Looking at me she added, "You need to go find out what the problem is." I assumed that I was chosen as I was the only adult in attendance.

Now Bret never had problems, everybody else did, but not Bret. He'd shown up about 5 years ago and had bought the run-down Gold's Gym franchise in town. In relatively short order he had gotten the place back in shape and he began increasing the membership. He personally vetted the personal trainers which used his gym for a fee and made sure that they were proper trainers. Once he started making a profit, he turned it back into the gym and began upgrading the equipment. He was a self-made guy who seemed to enjoy what he was doing. We'd met him when he brought in his Impala to upgrade and make into a proper lowrider. Eventually he got Rachel into boxing and once the MMA crowd got going, she began training in Krav Maga again. We all became good friends, and once he met Heather and TJ, it was one big happy family. We usually had a barbeque at my place on Fridays when I was in town. To hear that he was agitated had me concerned. I told Rachel that I'd run by the gym tomorrow.

TJ started up about the 1970 Chevelle SS 454 that was his and Rachel's next project. This vehicle is arguably the ultimate muscle car and was a nice feather in their cap. Rachel and Heather chatted about girl stuff while TJ and I went out on the porch for a last beer. Setting down on one of the old couches I asked TJ if he knew anything about the situation with Bret. He said that he hadn't really seen much of him while I was gone, but that whatever the problem was, it was getting to Rachel.

We finished our beers and went back inside. Heather was saying goodbye to Rachel and stopped on the way out to give me a peck on the cheek. I grabbed her butt and said, “Now you can sleep well tonight.” Heather and Rachel burst out laughing while TJ had no idea what was going on, which is probably a good thing.

While I cleaned up the kitchen, Rachel went to shower up before coming down to the dining room we use as an office, to start researching the Chevelle. When I finished in the kitchen, I went into the office to try to find out more about Bret. Rachel was sitting behind the desk in yet another of my sacrosanct rock and roll t-shirts, the 1986 Bachman-Turner Overdrive North American Tour edition, and black lace panties. When she curled her legs underneath her, I could see about 6 miles of incredibly toned leg, with just a hint of panty. I lost my train of thought for a second.

“Sweet Cheeks, do you have any idea what is the matter with Bret? He would have told you if he told anyone.”

She sat back in the office chair, thought for a minute, then said, “This is only woman’s intuition, but Heather and I have talked about it, and we think it is something that happened back East before he got here. Also, I would say it may be family oriented, but he has never talked about his family. That, in itself, is telling.”

“Bret has never, since we’ve known him, gone into himself like this. Usually, he is an open book. I’ll go have a chat with him tomorrow and see if I can get this figured out.” Continuing, I asked, “When are you coming to bed? I am trying to exercise restraint here, but those black panties are calling out to me.”

“An elderly gentleman like yourself? I would have thought that you would need a night off, after last night’s ‘Welcome Home’ event, to recoup and recover. I don’t want to put you in traction.”

“Elderly gentleman, huh? I am only 10 years older than your practically adolescent self. I am in the prime of life and it is my job to train you properly in the physical satisfaction derived from erotic experiences.”

“I’ll be up after you clean up and smell good. I’ve been reading the Kama Sutra like you suggested, and I’ve got a few things I need to ask you about.” She was trying not to laugh but was only marginally successful. I was not paying attention as I was busy flying up the stairs toward the shower while undressing. Think that is easy? Try getting out of a pair of jeans and a t-shirt while running up the stairs!

The next morning, I woke up and felt as if I had ruptured every vertebra in my back. That Kama Sutra stuff will kill you. Smacking Rachel on her finely formed, and firm, backside, I told her to get her lazy butt out of my bed and go to work. I then put on some shorts and a t-shirt and headed down to start the morning coffee ritual.

After last night's workout I felt that pancakes were in order to replenish our energy levels, so I got the batter going and the skillet out.

I heard the shower in her room running so I knew she was up, and if not running, at least ambulatory. Eventually she came down the stairs in a big fluffy robe and headed to the coffee pot, her first stop on any given day.

"Did I hear you right? Did you say I have a 'lazy butt'?" she asked.

"I think you were still asleep and misheard me, darling. I think that I ruptured every disc in my back last night trying to recreate the pictures in your book. There may be man-eating parts of your anatomy, but I can attest to the fact that there are no lazy ones. Eat your pancakes."

She eventually got off to work, and I went up to the barn to start installing the four-link rear suspension kit from Heidts Products. I'd finished one side by noon and decided to clean up and go see Bret.

Putting on some jeans and my black Sig Sauer t-shirt, I jumped into the F-150 and scooted across town to Gold's Gym. Getting out I started walking toward the front door when Nicholas came out. You'll remember that Nicholas is a huge black guy with muscles on top of his muscles, 3-foot-long dreadlocks and is also the assistant manager of the gym. Nothing ever rattles Nicholas. If something tries to rattle Nicholas, he usually just swats it aside and keeps moving. Today he looked rattled. He motioned me around the side of the building.

"Jeb, you got to talk to him. Something is going sideways in his life, and he can't handle it on his own, he's trying, but it's wearing him down."

"Has he told you anything?" I asked.

"Not a word. He's keeping it all inside," he replied.

"Do you have any idea at all what is going on?"

"No, I don't, but he spends a lot of time on the phone these days. I called the phone company, there are a lot of calls to and from Philly."

"Okay, mate, leave it with me and I'll get back to you."

Walking inside, I could see Bret in his office with the door shut, which was odd as his door is always open. I knocked on the door and waited for Bret to tell me to come in. It took a few minutes.

"What's happening, brother from a different mother?" I said while reaching out to shake his hand.

He got up slowly, shook my hand and then sat back down. He looked like he hadn't slept in a month, and his usually immaculate clothes were wrinkled.

"Good to see you, Jeb, but I'm a little busy today. Can I hook up with you later?"

"No problem. I got back in town a few days ago and the girls said you looked like you could use some help so I thought I'd come and see what I could do for you."

Bret got a weird look on his face, leaned forward in his office chair, crossed his arms on the desk in front of him and spat, "I don't need your help, or anyone else's help. Whatever is going down is a personal issue, and you should respect it as such. You think your rich white ass can help a brother out? Go live your own life and leave me out of it. Don't let the door hit your ass on the way out!"

I was a bit pissed off, but something was so wrong with the picture that I couldn't really blame Bret. On the way out the front door I saw Nicholas in the parking lot. He walked over while I was getting in the truck.

"I heard most of that Jeb. You know and I know that he didn't mean it. Something ain't right."

"Nick, keep your ear to the ground and see if you can find out anything else. I'm going to do some digging as well. One way or the other we'll get to the bottom of this, hopefully sooner rather than later."

Driving back to the house, I kept thinking that Bret was now into Jekyll and Hyde mode bigtime, which was not like him at all. Something was bothering him bad, and he needed help whether he wanted to ask for it or not. I drove by the shop and told Rachel and TJ what had occurred at the gym, and that I wanted everyone to get together at the ranch that evening after work. TJ would collect Heather after she got off work and I would go get Peio. Somebody needed to let Nicholas know the plan, so that he could attend if he wanted to. I also told the muppets not to worry about dinner, I'd grill some brats.

I left the shop and headed directly out to Peio's new place. Pulling to a stop in front of his porch, I hopped out of the truck just as Peio came to the door with a couple of beers.

"Since this is an unscheduled visit, and judging by the look on your face, I'd say something serious is going on," Peio said while handing me a beer.

"It's serious, but I don't really know what is going on," I said. I then told him what Rachel and Nicholas had told me, and then described what had happened at the gym. Peio got a thoughtful look on his face.

"You say that he was making and receiving a lot of phone calls from Philadelphia?"

"According to Nicholas, that is what the phone records showed."

Looking thoughtful, Peio asked, "And Bret arrived here how long ago?"

"About 5 years ago, more or less," I answered.

"Do you remember when I first met Bret at one of your barbeques several months ago and Bret said something to the effect that my reputation preceded me?" I thought back and nodded. "I may know what this is about but will need to make some calls and do some research. I'll get back to you on this as soon as possible." Peio is a handy guy to have around.

I thanked Peio for his help and told him that the crew was meeting at my place after work to see if we could figure out what was going on and to come up with a strategy to sort Bret out.

Waving through the window, I drove out of Peio's place, back onto the Butler Mine Road, then onto the Bland Reservoir Road to the county road and home. I parked on the apron in front of the barn and got out to set up the grill. I then went inside and got the brats and buns out of the freezer to defrost. This was Tuesday and Rachel would normally go to yoga after work, but I knew she would be worried about Bret and come home right after work. Around five thirty, I put the brats on the grill and the buns on the sideboard to warm up, then went inside to put the condiments and tea on the table along with a stack of paper plates.

Just like clockwork, I heard the growl of the Whale Tail followed by the throbbing rumble of TJ's new and improved 1950 pickup. Rachel pulled into the lean-to garage and TJ parked in front of the bunkhouse. He had collected Heather at the bank, so she went into TJ's place to get on some casual attire, and Rachel went upstairs to clean up a bit and put on something non-work related as well. TJ and I loaded up the cooked brats and warm buns, then took them into the kitchen so that we could eat once everyone arrived in one place.

Once the girls arrived in the kitchen, everyone fixed a plate and got a glass of tea before setting at the kitchen island to eat. While we ate, I told everyone what I had learned from Nicholas and then gave them a blow-by-blow description of what had happened in Bret's office. I also told them that Peio was now aware of the situation and may have an idea as to what was going on.

TJ brought up the fact that this was the first time that anyone had gotten anything out of him at all, so perhaps this was a good sign. We brainstormed trying to come up with a plan to help Bret, but unless he wanted to confide in us, there was not much we could do. I said that I'd get back with Nicholas and try to get a list of the numbers called to, or called from, in Philly and take it from there.

Rachel looked at me funny and asked, "How do you plan to get a list of those numbers, and furthermore, how will you figure out who they belong to?" This was skating on thin ice, as I had never told her about my part-time job with the Jankowski Group. "I have some contacts which may be able to help. I won't know until I try. The numbers will appear on the gym's phone bill, so Nicholas can get those to me."

It was getting dark now and had cooled off, so everyone went out on the porch to continue the discussion. The girls had a glass of wine while TJ and I had beers. We'd been sitting out there on the couches for no more than 20 minutes when we heard an unfamiliar vehicle coming up the drive. It was Nicholas's 1970 Cadillac Coupe Deville that Rachel had done up for him. He pulled up beside my truck on the apron and Nicholas got out of the driver's seat, and lo and behold, Bret got out of the passenger's seat! He was obviously exhausted emotionally, mentally and physically. Nicholas had to go around and help him over to the porch. We got him inside to the living room and sat him down in one of the overstuffed chairs. I asked Nick if they had eaten and he said they hadn't, so I fixed them both a plate of brats. When I went to get beers, Nick looked at me and shook his head no, so I got two glasses of ice-tea instead. Putting this on a tray I went back to the living room and got out two dinner trays that we use when eating and watching TV and put one in front of Bret and another in front of Nicholas.

"Bret, you're among friends now, so you just go ahead and do what you have to do, or say what you have to say, but first you need to get some food down your neck, so go ahead and eat. You too, Nick," I told them.

While they were eating, the rest of us just made small talk about work stuff until they were finished. We had heard a vehicle drive up and Heather went and opened the door for Peio, who took a seat at the kitchen island. It got dead quiet until Nick looked at Bret and said, "Tell them, bro."

Bret took a deep breath, then told us his story.

Seven years ago, he had been running a rough and tumble boxing gym in the Allegheny West neighborhood in North Philadelphia. This was in the slums and many of his members had gang connections and were not the most upstanding clientele he would have preferred. That said, a good percentage of the guys who frequented the gym were drug free, just interested in working out, boxing and staying off the streets. These guys would often hire out as security guards or bouncers since not much other employment was open to them. Some guys were 'shades of gray' and floated around near the edge of the criminal pond.

There were two brothers, Jeremiah and Joseph, Bret never knew their last name, who dabbled in drugs and the usual street crime. They were lean and mean, but eventually became friendly with Bret. This is where the trouble started. Jeremiah and Joseph hatched a plan to hit a local drug house where the dealer stocked his merchandise. The idea was to hit the house hard and fast and get the drugs. Quick in, quick out. After the heist, the brothers would get out of town until the heat died down, then split the drugs into smaller parcels and sell them wholesale in other cities on the East coast.

They had planned the heist meticulously. They even had a guy on the inside that would tell them when there was a reasonable amount of merchandise in the house and would let them in the door on the night of the hit. The problem was, they needed a wheelman to drive them to the house on the night of the heist, then come back and get them after the action. Bret had been fairly young and impressionable, needed some adventure in his life, and wanted to build his street cred. He agreed to be the wheelman.

On the day of the robbery, Bret had gone into Philadelphia and stolen a 2000 Chevy Impala sedan. In another neighborhood, which he had checked out earlier, he switched out the license plates with those of an identical Impala. In the event that a cop called in the vehicle for whatever reason, the car would not be reported as stolen. After switching the plates, Bret had driven back to the apartment which Jeremiah and Joseph shared in Allegheny West.

Jeremiah and Joseph had been busy as well. They had gotten hold of two stolen Ruger Security-9 pistols and two stolen Remington Model 11-87 semi-automatic twelve-gauge shotguns. The shotguns stocks had been sawn off, contoured and smoothed out just behind the grips to allow them to fit in the old army duffle bags which they would take inside the house to carry out the stolen drugs.

After going over the plan one final time and making sure that the guns were loaded, they piled into the Impala. Jeremiah sat in the front passenger's seat and Joseph sat behind him so that they would both be on the curb side when they pulled in front of the house. They set off to arrive at the drug house at exactly two in the morning, as that was the agreed time with their inside man. They pulled in front of the house right on time, Joseph and Jeremiah bailed out and Bret drove to a nearby Safeway parking lot, empty at that time of the morning, to wait for his phone to ring. If it rang and showed either Joseph's or Jeremiah's number on the Caller ID, Bret would race back to the house immediately.

The phone rang at roughly two fifteen, showing Joseph's ID. Bret threw the car in gear and took off fast for the house. When he got there, Joseph and Jeremiah were both on the porch, on either side of the open front door, firing the shotguns back into the house. When they saw the car, they fired one last volley into the house, grabbed the bulging duffle bags and ran to the car. Both the duffle bags and Jeremiah went in the back, while Joseph got in the front. Before the doors had closed, Bret was hightailing it out of the neighborhood. The plan called for Bret to drive to a storage unit in Philadelphia, drop the guys and the duffle bags off, then drive the car to a vacant lot a few miles away and burn it. Bret would walk back to an all-night diner for breakfast before taking a taxi back to the gym. One of the brothers would call later in the day to arrange for Bret's payoff.

Bret never heard from the brothers all that day. The next day, the rumors were flying. Apparently, when the brothers got back to their apartment around six in the morning on the day of the heist, there were people inside waiting for them. They must have somehow been identified during the heist. In the ensuing shootout, both brothers had been killed. As they were supposedly the only ones that knew of Bret's involvement, that knowledge should have died with them.

As it turned out, the drug house which they had hit belonged to a gang which had a policy where the drug proceeds, for all of the area which they controlled, were collected periodically and taken to a different stash house on a rotating basis. This 'bank' was where the money was counted and banded up in bundles. It just so happened that Jeremiah and Joseph had hit this house on the day it was the designated 'bank'. The duffle bags had not been full of drugs but had been full of the gang's cash. Apparently, the brothers had gotten out with between three and four million dollars in untraceable cash. But nobody knew where it was.

After the heat had died down, Bret had gone back to the storage facility several times but could find no record of the brothers ever renting a unit. They must have simply been throwing out a red herring by having Bret drop them there in the event that someone knew that Bret had acted as the wheelman. The money trail went cold at the storage facility and died out with the brothers. For months Bret had lived on pins and needles, constantly looking over his shoulder. He had saved up some money over the years, and when he heard about the run-down Gold's Gym in Cadillac Springs, he had jumped at the chance to get out of Allegheny West and make a new start. Things had been going just fine until about a month and a half ago when he'd received a phone call from someone simply saying, "We know you were at the wheel. We'll call back later to discuss the money. Think long and hard on it." A week later he received another call from the same number, according to the Caller ID, and a man who identified himself as Owen McGrath told him a story.

Apparently, the drug house cum bank belonged to the Northeast Philly Irish Mob, sometimes called the K&A Gang. Once the heat had died down after the heist, and the cops had not gotten anywhere, the K&A Gang started their own investigation. Eventually they identified the brothers inside man and questioned him vigorously until he died. All that he could tell them was who the robbers were, which they already knew, and the name of the wheelman, which he wasn't supposed to know. The brothers must have let it slip at some point.

By this time Bret had made the move to Cadillac Springs, bought the gym through a front company and stayed off the grid. It had taken them years to find him, but they had. Now they wanted the untraceable millions, in used, non-sequential bills, back.

Bret was now playing for time to come up with a plan. He had no idea where the money was and could not lay his hands on anything approaching three or four million dollars in used bills. He had told McGrath that he'd eventually changed all the money into used hundred-dollar bills to make the volume easier to handle, but in the process had to pay a percentage and the total was now just over 3.2 million dollars. Bret had no connections to launder the money, so it was still in cash. McGrath said that this was understandable, and he would be willing to settle for this amount. Bret then told him that the money was in a safe deposit box in a small town in Wyoming. It would take him a few weeks to collect it, as he had to have a valid reason to take time off from the gym and make a trip north to collect it. McGrath was losing his patience but understood that the easiest way to collect the money was to let Bret do the legwork, but he was also smart enough to realize that he needed leverage.

McGrath had called Bret late yesterday afternoon and told him that he had 4 weeks from tomorrow to collect the money and make arrangements to hand it over to whoever McGrath designated to pick it up. The he dropped the bomb which put Bret over the edge.

"It seems you were a bit friendly with a lass named Alyshia Grier, the librarian at the Historical Society of Pennsylvania Library. We know all about her. She's apparently on vacation to Jamaica at the moment. We'll be watching her both in Jamaica, and when she returns. If we do not get our money, you'll not get her. Understood?" McGrath did not wait for a reply, just hung up.

Dead silence again until Rachel asked, "Who's Alyshia Grier?"

By this time Bret had relaxed a bit, I think it was simply having someone to unload his story on. "You guys used to give me grief all the time as I never had a lady with me, and I know at times I got a little upset with you. Alyshia is why." Heather had gotten him a beer by this point, and he took a swig now. Continuing, he said, "I always wanted to get out of the Allegheny West slums, and I always like to read. Eventually I made my way to the Historical Society Library. I really enjoyed the peaceful, quiet atmosphere and I started going there almost every afternoon and reading. I would read anything that caught my eye, books on history, chemistry, accounting, poetry, just anything. When I began going there, I noticed this librarian who worked there. She was obviously of Caribbean descent, a few years older than me, quiet, shy and a real stunner. It was love at first sight. The problem was I had no idea how to approach a girl who wasn't from the 'hood'. Okay, we went through that 'catching each other looking at each other' phase and the 'how to make small talk phase' and eventually we started going out. We would go out on her side of town, because sure as hell I wasn't taking her to my side. Anyhow, I had told her about the gym, and she must have checked it out online, as one day she just told me that she knew I was from the bad side of town. I actually drove her around Allegheny West one night so she could see where I was from and what she was missing. It didn't faze her at all. She knows all about the brothers and the heist and the fact that I am laying low out here. The idea was to let it blow over and me return, or let it blow over and she comes out here. Looks like it ain't going to happen either way now."

Peio cleared his throat to catch our attention, "Can I say something here?" We had all forgotten that Peio was sitting in the kitchen with the lights out.

"The floor is yours," Rachel said.

"First things first. Can you contact Ms. Grier now?" Peio asked Bret.

"I believe so, I was supposed to call her in an hour anyhow."

"Okay, give me half an hour. Do not call her until I get back to you." Turning to me he asked if he could use the living room office and I said that was not a problem.

While Peio was working his phone and my desktop in the office, I had to ask Bret a question. "Bret, remember when you first met Peio here during a barbeque, you said to him, 'Your reputation precedes you, sir.' Want to explain that? It has always baffled me."

"If you were involved, even peripherally, in crime back East, you would be aware of Peio. Although he was never actually a criminal, in the strictest sense of the word, he was the go between for anyone wanting to do business either with Cosa Nostra, or in their territory. He was untouchable. When he whacked those assholes, who had kidnapped that woman, he acted out of character, without sanction, and had to go. He was so well respected that they let him go peacefully and without any strings attached. I think he still acts in a consulting capacity at times. Even to this day, Mr. Apaiz is a man to be reckoned with."

I chuckled, "I have never known Peio's surname."

"You still don't. Nobody does. He is called Mr. Apaiz. Apaiz means 'priest' in the Basque language. He got the name because rumor had it that he often administered the 'last rites' to those that crossed him. I have no idea if that is true, but it is something to keep in mind."

Peio came back into the room and asked Bret to come into the living room office. "Can you call the young lady on Skype? It will make things much easier."

"That's what we usually do," Bret said.

"Okay, call her now, introduce the rest of us, then tell her about the situation you are in. At that point, let me sit down and talk to her." Bret called his lady, got her on Skype, introduced the rest of us, then told her what was going on. I must say she took it well and did not crack up or ask a bunch of idiotic questions. "What do you want me to do?" was all that she asked.

"Aly, there is a gentleman here who you need to listen to. I trust him completely and you need to as well. I will explain all this when I see you again. I'll turn you over to Mr. Apaiz now. Listen very carefully as your safety depends on it." Peio traded places with Bret at the office chair in front of the computer.

"Ms. Grier, my name is Peio, and I am a friend of the moron that has placed you in this difficult situation," said Peio with a smile. Alyshia actually grinned back. The girl had some backbone for a librarian, heck, for anyone in a situation like this. Did I forget to mention that the girl was a looker, even on Skype?

"Where are you staying at presently?" asked Peio.

"At the Traveler's Beach Resort in Negril, on the west side of the island," she said.

"Okay, two large, black gentlemen of Caribbean descent will be in the foyer of the main building in 2 hours. These men have worked with me for years and you can trust them implicitly. The taller of the two is named Ajay, the slightly smaller one is named Keneil. For identification purposes, ask them what the cubed root of seventeen is. Keneil will answer 'blue mushroom two'. If Ajay answers, something is wrong. If Keneil answers with any other phrase, something is wrong and do not leave with them. Call us immediately. Only take a backpack with what you will need for 24 hours. Do not check out of the resort you are now in. Ajay and Keneil will drive you to Kingston. There they will accompany you on a chartered flight to Anguilla. Once there you will be driven to the Altamer Hotel, on the extreme western side of the island, where Ajay and Keneil will watch over you until this problem has been resolved. Everything is taken care of, Ms. Grier, do not worry. You will need to go shopping after you arrive in Anguilla, get whatever you need and do not worry about the cost. You may as well enjoy yourself until Bret sends for you. Have you understood everything which I have said?" asked Peio.

"Got it," she said making some notes. Smart, efficient and hot. Good combination in a lass.

Peio vacated the office chair so that Bret could talk to Alyshia in private. He then called Ajay and Keneil and told them the plan. The rest of us went back to the living room, where Nick was asleep in the overstuffed chair recently occupied by Bret. Bret finally walked back into the living room and asked Peio how he could ever repay him. Peio grinned and asked if Alyshia had any sisters.

"Okay, down to business," and Peio got the ball rolling on a plan. "We need to buy some time to plan, and we need to get this McGrath character on his back foot and greedy. I made a call to the head of the Northeast Philly Irish Mob, a fairly decent fellow named Liam, and it turns out that the K&A Gang does not officially exist anymore as their group was folded into the Northeast Philly Irish Mob years ago. McGrath is not his real name; his real name is William 'Irish Bobby' Shannon. He started a splinter group crewed with disaffected K&A Gang members when the Northeast Philly Irish Mob absorbed them. This was sanctioned as long as the group, now known as the Craic Crew, stayed north of Highway 1, west of Interstate 76, and only ran drugs and protection rackets."

Peio continued with his marching orders. "Bret, you drag this out for at least 2 weeks. At the end of 2 weeks, I'll send you a video of a substantial amount of used one hundred-dollar bills, in packets of ten thousand dollars, being put into three duffel bags. At that time, you can tell him that you have the cash and are ready to do the handover."

Turning to me, Peio said, "Jeb, you'll need to find us a fairly remote location with some structures where we can control the handover. Not too remote or he will smell a rat, not too close as he will then bring a large crew and there will likely be too much shooting to get this done correctly.

"TJ, you provide security to the operation. Granted, you can only be in one place at any given time, so I suggest that you roam and look for people who are out of place. Once Irish Bobby knows that Alyshia is in the wind, he'll be looking for other leverage. If he associates Heather and Rachel with Bret, they will become prime targets. If you think that anything is out of place, you call for help.

"Bret, you just relax and stay near your phone. You will need to bait this roach into coming for the money. Under no circumstances do you agree to go back East. Also, once he realizes that Alyshia is no longer available, he will assume you had something to do with it. You deny it and say that you have never even been to the island of Jamaica, which I assume is true. At some point you will need to disappear so that it appears you are headed to Wyoming to get the cash. We will plan that later.

"Nicholas, I do not know you, but Jeb swears by you, which is good enough for me. You will need to work with TJ, to keep Rachel and Heather safe. I must ask you to listen to and obey TJ in this matter as he has considerable experience with this sort of situation."

Nick nodded and said, "No problem."

At this, Rachel and Heather looked at TJ, who was studying his boots. Peio twigged to this, "I am making the assumption that Mr. Aucoin has not shared bits and pieces of his past with the ladies. We can discuss this later once Mr. Shannon has been dealt with.

"Everyone keeps their phones charged and with them. If anyone sees anything that looks suspicious or out of place, let everyone else know immediately. It is guaranteed that at some point the Craic Crew riffraff will come to town for the handover."

After giving everyone their marching orders, Peio got up, stretched and said that he was heading home as, at his age, he needed his sleep. We all saw him to the door and both Rachel and Heather gave the old coot big hugs and pecks on the cheeks. I hope I get the same attention when I'm his age.

Later, back in the living room, Bret had tears in his eyes and apologized for his rant at the gym and admitted that he should have trusted his friends. Being the good friend that I am, I said, "Damn right you should have! You're just lucky I didn't beat you like a drum for dissing me like that." Needless to say, everybody had a good laugh at my expense, likely due to the fact that I had zero chance of beating Bret like a drum, or any other percussion instrument for that matter. Which was a good way to leave it for the evening.

Heather decided to grace TJ with her presence that evening. I assumed she would take the opportunity to find out the true story of the man she was sleeping with. I did not envy the lad, girls don't handle lying very well, even if it is with the best intentions.

Bret and Nick got in the Caddy lowrider and went home, leaving just Rachel and I in the house. "What's my best time for getting you in your birthday suit starting from a cold start at the bottom of the stairs?" I asked Rachel in all seriousness.

"It's been a while since we've timed it, but I believe your personal best to this point was about a minute flat," she replied in all seriousness while moving toward the bottom of the stairs. "Think you can better your record?" she added.

"Well, I am a bit older now, and I am still recovering from throwing out my back during the recent Kama Sutra session, but I still think I have some life left in me."

Her foot hit the bottom stair and over her shoulder she said, "Your time starts now!" and sprinted up the stairs.

You may not believe this, but my new personal best is 51 seconds.

CHAPTER 21

WE ALL HAD OUR MARCHING orders. Rachel went to work as usual, but TJ would just cruise around scoping out the town, so she was on her own at the shop. Nicholas' Coupe Deville would attract too much attention, so I lent him the Ford F-150 truck for the duration. He would also be quartering the town looking for anything out of place. Not the best surveillance, but the best we could do at the moment.

I'd gotten the 1956 up and running and would run around in it. I drove the backroads around Cadillac Springs looking for a fairly remote structure to do the handover in but was not having much luck. It is a lot harder than you think to find abandoned buildings that are 'fairly remote, but not too remote', especially for what I think Peio had in mind. I also took the time to get plates and insurance for my 1956 pickup now that I was using it full-time.

We did this for a week with no strangers taking an interest in us and no further calls from 'Irish Bobby' Shannon. We'd meet each evening at Rachel's shop after everyone got off work, just to touch base. The problem with no action is that it breeds complacency.

The Thursday after Bret had clued us in to his problem, Rachel and I got a small break from the routine, which paid big dividends which we had not even thought of. I'd been driving around the county looking for a suitable place to lure Irish Bobby and his crew to, but was not having any luck, so I needed to regroup and rethink. I drove over to Rachel's shop around two o'clock in the afternoon and parked in front of the left side work bay door. She was still waiting on the arrival of the 1970

Chevelle SS, so the bay door on the right was open but the bay was empty. Rachel was in her coveralls scrubbing and washing down the floor when I pulled up. I got out, smacked her on her magnificent backside, and said, "If you were in a t-shirt and shorts, I'd grab that hose and wet you down." She turned off the nozzle, handed me the hose, stripped out of the coveralls and said, "Talk is cheap, I'm sweating bullets here, hose me down!"

What can you do at a time like this? I did as I was told. To be honest though, she had on a pair of those tight workout shorts, my 1982 AC/DC Back in Black Tour t-shirt and a sports bra, so the end result was not everything that I was hoping for, but better than a sharp stick in the eye!

Shortly thereafter, we were standing in the shade of the open bay, just catching up on the day's events, when a 1987 Monte Carlo lowrider, leaning a bit to starboard and painted a ghastly metallic gold with white scallops, flowed into the lot and made a U-turn in front of the paint bay. Coming back toward us, it parked so that driver's side was facing where Rachel and I were standing inside the bay. The driver's window was open and two Latino gangbangers in jeans down to their asses, wife beater t-shirts, and bandanas rolled up and used as headbands, were in the car jamming to some sort of Spanish rap crap. Turning down the tunes, the driver whistled at Rachel while scrutinizing the tight shorts and wet t-shirt motif.

"Hey, momma! If you get tired of that lame old white bread you can come take a ride with me and Felix," said the driver.

I may have mentioned earlier that Rachel has a deeply hidden, but volcanic temper. The driver was about to discover it for himself. When the driver had finished his spiel, Rachel started out of the bay toward the Monte Carlo. While all eyes were on Rachel, I scooted around the back of the Monte, and sidled up just behind the passenger's window pillar of the Monte Carlo, out of sight of the passenger. Knowing what was about to occur, I reached around my back with my right hand and pulled out the CZ75 9mm I had been carrying lately. I just let it hang down by my right leg until I needed it. Rachel was now at the driver's door, leaning down so that she could look eye-to-eye with the driver. "And what do they call you, handsome?" she asked sweetly.

"I am Gervaso, means 'warrior' in the language," said Gervaso the warrior.

"I can see that you are well named, you look like a fighter." This had Gervaso smiling and showing his two gold teeth, one up top, one down below. "What exactly did you and Mr. Felix have in mind while I take that ride you mentioned?"

"Mi querida, we would do anything and everything to you, and for you, to satisfy your fine self! You would be squealing with delight and begging us to return for more," explained Gervaso with a leer.

This was not the correct answer. Rachel cocked back her fist and hit Gervaso right in the nose with vigor, then repeated herself. Gervaso's nose exploded on the first punch, the second knocked out the upper gold tooth. The volcano was erupting. Rachel then opened the door, grabbed the dazed warrior by the hair, and drug him out of the car, where she proceeded to kick the living daylights out of the stunned ex-warrior.

While this was going on, once he recovered from the initial shock of a drop-dead gorgeous woman in a wet t-shirt beating the crap out of his compadre, Felix turned toward his door and made to get out of the car. He stopped when I put the muzzle of the CZ against his forehead. Generally, it is not a good idea to actually touch the guy which you may eventually be shooting, with the muzzle. It is best to stand back out of arm's reach, but I didn't figure Felix was that much of a gun fight technician, and would get the point. He did, he froze.

"You two dumbasses started this dance, so you just sit there, very still, while my girlfriend beats the crap out of your buddy. When she is finished, we'll talk."

The volcano eventually got tired of kicking Gervaso's ribs, head, back and butt. He was curled up in the fetal position against the front tire, while Rachel was checking her nails to see if she now required a manicure. I told Felix to get out of the car and go sit beside Gervaso in the shade of the car. He did as he was told.

"Judging by your tats and head rags, you two morons run with the Aztec Lords gang, is that correct?" Rachel asked.

No answer was forthcoming, so she kicked Gervaso in his already broken ribs and asked again. Since Gervaso was having a hard time talking, Felix admitted that they were Aztec Lords.

"The last I heard, Tito Ramírez was the 'sin nombre' for all the Latin gangs in this part of the country. Is that correct?"

Before she could kick Gervaso again, Felix said, "Chica, you know we cannot answer that question!"

I had not chambered a round at this point, so I made a show of racking the slide then aimed the pistol directly at Felix's balls. Since I was standing and he was sitting with his back against the car, if I pulled the trigger there wouldn't be any ricochet. I would blow his balls off, but he would likely survive. If you are a rough, tough

Mexican gangbanger, you probably wouldn't want to survive without any balls. I know I wouldn't.

"Mr. Ramírez is the 'sin nombre'."

Rachel pulled her cell phone out of her back pocket, put it on speaker, checked her contacts list then hit a number. She let it ring until someone answered.

"Is this the gusano grande of the vicious Latin gangs I keep hearing about?" Rachel asked. There was silence for a moment, then a burst of laughter from the phone. "Mi amor da vida! Why have you waited so long to call me? Are you ready to leave that gringo Jeb yet?"

I said, "Keep it up Paco, I'm the last friend you have that you don't actually have to pay."

"Ah, Jeb, I had to ask. Perhaps there is hope for me yet. Anyhow, as Rachel has indicated, I am the Big Worm for various business entities in the region. How may I assist you?"

Rachel took over the dialogue. "I've just kicked the crap out of one of your homies named Gervaso, and Jeb is contemplating shooting the balls off his compadre named Felix. They drive a hideous 1987 Monte lowrider. Does this ring a bell?"

"I know of whom you speak. That car is rather hideous. Why are you beating up, and considering emasculating, my homies, if I may ask?"

"These two morons just stopped by the shop. I think that they wanted new bags on their ride as it is leaning to starboard, but Jeb had just hosed me down to cool me off. I think this addled their minds and they made the mistake of offering me a 'ride', if you know what I mean?"

"Yes," Tito replied, "that would explain it. May I ask if the two morons in question are ambulatory?"

"Felix, yes. Gervaso needs a hospital."

"I assume we are on speaker and the gentlemen, and I use that term loosely, can hear me?"

"Correct," said Rachel.

A torrent of Spanish erupted from the phone. Gervaso and Felix were jerking around like they were being machine gunned. Eventually, the voice on the phone reverted back to English.

"I have explained to these men that you, Jeb and your shop are untouchable as you are friends and my go-to shop for personal auto work. Again, thanks for sorting out that new suspension and paint on my 1968 Fleetwood, very nice. I have instructed Felix to put Gervaso in the car and then he is to drive it to my office immediately. I would like to express my apologies in person, will you and Jeb be there in half an hour?"

"See you then, Tito. Hey! Any chance you can bring some of those real green chili and pork burritos when you come?" I asked. He gets them from somewhere special and they are a gastronomical delight.

"My pleasure, consider it done."

After I had assisted Felix in loading Gervaso into the passenger's side seat, Felix drove off with a look of impending doom, which was probably warranted when Tito is annoyed at you. Rachel went inside to the changing room in the back, and I went and got a beer out of the fridge and poured Rachel a glass of white wine that she keeps there as well. She came into the office in her faded jeans and a purple polo shirt looking nothing at all like the Amazon who had just beaten the living daylights out of a gangbanger. She went behind my old desk and sipped her wine while we waited for Tito to show up.

A few minutes later a satin black 1968 Cadillac Fleetwood, with charcoal ghost scallops, drove in the front and parked in the shade under the awning. You would think that satin black and charcoal ghost scallops wouldn't work well together, but Rachel had made it tasteful. Also, it was not a lowrider as such, it had been lowered and had an air suspension to lift it when the road required it. It was actually a pretty cool ride.

Tito got out dressed in a charcoal gray lightweight wool suit, a light blue button-down shirt, and a scarlet tie. He was a snappy dresser, and you'd never guess he was the 'sin nombre' of the regional gangs. In gang speak the 'sin nombre', the 'one without a name', is similar to the Capo di Tutti Capi in the Mafia, or 'Boss of the Bosses'. Tito was a distinguished looking guy in his early to mid-fifties, about 5'10" tall and in very good shape, but not bulky, more rapier than a cutlass. As he walked to the front door, Rachel rose to greet him and gave him another one of those annoying, to me anyhow, when performed on someone besides me, hugs and pecks on the cheek.

"Nice to see you again, Tito. You haven't stopped by in ages," Rachel told him.

"Business, chica, always the business."

Tito came over and shook my hand. "Jeb, you're looking well. Thanks for not shooting the balls off Felix. He does come in handy at times for certain types of work."

Turning back to Rachel. “Remind me never to make an off-color remark to you in the future. It appears that Gervaso has suffered a ruptured spleen and three broken ribs. He will be out of the game for some time I’m afraid. Plus, you broke his nose and knocked out one of his prized golden teeth. He will harbor some ill will for a time, but I have convinced him that seeking revenge on the owner of my personal body shop would have terminal consequences, so I do not think that you will need to worry yourself about that. Could I ask you for a beer?”

I jumped up, indicated the other chair in front of the desk and went to get Tito a cold one. “I have developed the manners of a pig,” I exclaimed jokingly, “I should have had one waiting for you.”

“It is not your fault, Jeb; it is your lack of Spanish blood that precludes you from developing proper manners. Obviously, this is not an issue with those of mixed Chinese and Israeli blood such as Ms. Chen,” said Tito raising his beer to Rachel.

“Everybody’s trying to keep the white man down these days,” I grinned.

“So how have you been keeping, Tito?” Rachel asked.

“As you know, these young gangsters have no respect for the rules which have been developed over the years. I am constantly having to mediate between this group and that group. Everyone is greedy for more. That said, I am keeping well.”

“And no Mrs. Ramírez on the horizon?” queried Rachel with a raised eyebrow.

“As you seem to be besotted with the gringo there, I have had to search further afield. There are several possibilities, but you do not want to rush these things.”

“How have you two been doing, and the shop?” Tito asked.

“To be honest, Tito, the gringo keeps me amused for the moment, and the shop is doing well. I have a 1970 Chevelle SS coming in soon for a makeover, and I am looking forward to working on what is, arguably, the epitome muscle car of the era.”

“Ah well, when the gringo no longer amuses you, and keeps you smiling, you have my number on speed dial.” A lot of truth is said in jest.

I had just had an epiphany. “If you two are finished slagging us white folks, I need to get serious,” I said. “We have an issue concerning a friend of ours, which we could really use your help with.”

“If I can provide you this assistance, I will. What do you require?”

“We have a situation in which a friend of ours is being pressured by a group from back East who, for lack of a better description, are gangsters. No offense intended. They have threatened to kidnap, or worse, a woman who is close to our friend. We have that under control. The problem is that this group will likely be coming into town in a week or so and we need to know as soon as they get here, and where they are staying. At the moment we only have TJ and Nicholas keeping an eye out, but if you could get your boys to also keep an eye out for any strange white guys who show an unexplainable interest in Gold's Gym or Rachel's shop, we would be in your debt," I explained.

Rachel could see where I was going with this and nodded her approval.

Tito thought for a second. "Okay, if it is an out of state group making some sort of play in my back yard, then I am obliged to pay attention. As you mentioned Gold's Gym, and that Nicholas is running interference, I have to assume that the friend you mentioned is Bret. You do not have to confirm or deny that, just know that Bret has helped get a few muchachos off the street and into the gym. Even I understand that the gangs are a dead-end and getting these ninos into another environment is appreciated. I will gladly help you out with surveillance, but keep in mind that anything else required will be up to you, you will understand why with my line of work."

"That is great, Tito! If your guys even think that something is not right, or they actually see these guys, please give either Rachel or myself a call immediately as time is of the essence now. I need to warn you though, these guys are an offshoot of the old K&A Gang which did not fold into the Northeast Philly Irish Mob. They are not amateurs and may be dangerous."

Standing up Tito said, "The Latino gangs have been around for many, many years, just as the Irish and Italian gangs have been. The difference has been that we originated in California while they originated on the East coast. Many people think that since we are Latino, that we are not as organized as the Irish or the Italians. This is not true. We can handle these interlopers efficiently, if necessary, especially as they are now on our turf. That said, if I am only providing surveillance, I will not need to worry about any violence. That will be up to you. It is all that I can do."

Rachel told him, "It is much appreciated, Tito, you know that." She gave him another hug and another peck on the cheek while I shook his hand at the door.

Before he got in the Fleetwood he turned back and said in all seriousness, "Do I get a tune up out of the deal?"

At five that afternoon, everyone showed up at Rachel's shop to go over the day's events. I told them about Tito's assistance on the surveillance, which got an "amen" from TJ and Nicholas. Bret said that he had received another call from Irish Bobby asking for an update. He felt that it was time to think about appearing to make the run to Wyoming. Since tomorrow was Friday, I told everyone to come up to the house for a barbeque again tomorrow. I'd get Peio down and we'd have another planning session.

When everyone split up, Rachel and Heather went to their Bikram yoga class, Bret and Nicholas drove back to the gym in Bret's ride, and TJ stayed at the shop to finish up some things he'd been ignoring while on surveillance duty. I left the 1956 F-100 at the shop, and since Nick didn't need my truck any longer, took my F-150 to the Safeway to stock up on all the items needed for tomorrow's barbeque. I also picked up a bucket of KFC for dinner, then drove up to the mailbox at the Bland Reservoir turnoff and left a note for Peio about the planning session tomorrow. Raising the flag on the mailbox so that Peio knew he had mail, I turned around and went home.

Pulling into the courtyard I saw a black streak shoot off the left-hand side of the porch and up the hill behind the house, so it appeared Dog was still hanging around. Rachel must be domesticating him to some extent, as I had never seen any sign of him actually on the porch. I parked in front of the house so that I could take the groceries inside to stow them in the pantry, freezer, or fridge as required. After that, I pulled the F-150 onto the apron in front of the barn and put the CZ pistol in the gun locker on the mezzanine deck. I then walked to the house, grabbed a beer, and sat on the porch until the crew showed up.

As it turned out, TJ and Heather stayed in town, and only Rachel showed up that evening. When I saw her drive up, I went in and got the bucket of chicken out of the oven where it had been keeping warm and put it on the table. While Rachel went upstairs to clean up and change out of her yoga gear, I got out the paper plates, put ice in the glasses and poured the tea. Rachel came down the stairs in some baggy tracksuit pants and my 1975 Aerosmith Toys in the Attic Tour t-shirt, pulled her chair up to the table, grabbed a couple of pieces of chicken and started eating.

"Good call on the KFC, I think I could eat the whole bucket," she told me while gnawing a thigh bone.

"If you eat the whole bucket, we'll have to figure out some way to burn off all those calories, as you will have just defeated the purpose of the Bikram yoga workout," was my clever reply.

"We'll think of something, I'm sure." Grabbing another piece of chicken, she continued, "I'm baffled as to how you ever made any money building cars? I stopped by the shop on the way home and took a look at that 1956 pickup you've been working on. The 429 Super Cobra motor is a nice old school touch, although TJ's Coyote motor will probably smoke you, but the stance is all wrong! It needs to be lowered a bit, the suspension needs tweaking and you need a custom exhaust system on it, among other things. Also, it needs to be painted."

"Knock yourself out, you're the artist," I said.

"Already on it. Ordered the drop spindles and the paint before I came home."

"What's this going to cost me?" I pondered.

"Your body on a number of evenings, plus a number of visits to that new Shiatsu massage place in town."

"Done, I can start paying you back this evening if you like?"

"I get to call the shots," she said while looking me in the eye and gnawing on thigh bone number two.

"No problem," I replied, "I am a firm believer in gender equality and innovation."

We ate our KFC in silence for a few minutes before she said what was really on her mind. "The other night you said that you had contacts who could check out phone numbers, and you also do not seem to be overly concerned about what is going on around here. I get the feeling that there is something you are not telling me, and that bothers me."

Well, it was bound to come out at some point in our relationship, and now was as good a time as any. "Let's finish the chicken, grab some teas and go sit on the couch. I'll tell you the story."

That evening I told Rachel the whole story concerning the Jankowski Group. I started with the first meeting in Bryon's Bistro in Cape Town, went through the training sessions, and detailed the whole abduction of Roma in Erbil. She didn't seem too annoyed that I had kept my secret squirrel life from her, and really didn't seem fazed by my revelation at all. It made me wonder if she already knew. Keep in mind that her dad is somehow connected to the Israeli embassy in DC, they know everything.

"And you think that this has prepared you for dealing with this Irish Mob?" she asked.

"Not at all. It has given me some skills which I would not normally have had, but if things turn violent, I'll leave that to Peio and TJ. I will say that 18 years working in the drilling business has prepared me, to a point, for dealing with moronic alpha type males. The fact is that Peio, TJ and to some extent Bret, are used to dealing with people like these, and I'll follow their lead. We don't have a lot of choice in the matter if we want to get Bret out of trouble and Alyshia back home. Simple as that."

Looking me in the eye, she asked, "Do you think that you could actually shoot someone if you had to?"

I closed my eyes for a few seconds, then said, "I would say that for the right reason, in the right circumstances, I could shoot someone if I had to. But from what I have read, even soldiers, or for that matter, trained snipers, can't answer that question until they are actually put in that position." More on this later.

"And what would constitute 'the right reason?'" she asked.

"I have thought about that often, and the answer has two parts. First, if someone was seriously threatening someone I truly cared about with physical bodily harm, I'd shoot them. I have no illusions about my ability as a fighter, but I can and do shoot well, with handguns or rifles, and I would revert to those skills to neutralize the threat, as they say. The second scenario is similar to the first, except that I would not necessarily need to be familiar with the person being threatened. If someone I thought was helpless and innocent, were being threatened with physical bodily harm, I would again attempt to neutralize the threat."

She grinned, "Good answer. Do I qualify as someone you truly care about?"

"Again, that answer has two parts. First, I am not convinced that you actually need someone to protect you, Exhibit A would be Gervaso earlier today. Second, I can show you much better than I can tell you." Big grin from me at this point in the conversation.

Standing up and holding out her hand, she asked, "Well, what are you waiting for, cowboy? Let the games begin!"

Following her up the stairs, while ogling her backside, I had to ask, "Is this counting as payback for fixing my truck?"

"No, this is a freebie," as she dropped the tracksuit bottoms.

The next morning, I got Rachel fueled up on coffee and omelets, and out the door. There wasn't much I could do as Rachel had taken possession of my 1956 pickup, and as far as I knew, all the bases were covered. I decided to go shooting.

After packing up the Ed Brown rifle, the CZ75 (9mm), the CZ 97 (.45), and a ton of ammo into the F-150 pickup, I drove up to Peio's place and confirmed he was going to make it to the barbeque that evening before heading up to my shooting range. Once there I moved onto the 1,000-yard range bench and got my rifle and spotting scope set up. I then drove out to the 500-yard line and set up a couple of targets there, then out to the 800-yard line and set out a couple more before heading back to the firing line. Getting back to the bench I loaded up three rounds of Nosler Trophy Grade 160 grain rounds. These puppies are rated at a muzzle velocity of 3,225 feet per second, and at 800 yards, are still moving at 1,902 feet per second, which means they have not dropped back through the transonic velocity of 1,000 feet per second, and all the nasty things that does to your ballistics. Also, at 800 yards they are still carrying 1,286 foot-pounds of energy, about one and a half times the energy of a .44 Magnum handgun round fired point blank.

The rifle was sighted in at 200 yards, so with no wind and the crosshairs on the bullseye, I expected the rounds to print about 30 inches low at 500 yards, which they did in a nice tight group. I then adjusted the elevation on the scope 6-1/2 minutes of angle (MOA) up and fired another group of five. These were hitting just above the bullseye as expected. I fired another group of five just to confirm I was set up correctly. I dialed the scope back to the 200 yard zero, where I like to keep it.

Setting up the Nightforce glass for 800 yards meant I had to take into account the drop of 120.5 inches from a 200 yard zero. A minute of angle is a simple mathematical calculation. The 'Rule of Thumb' is that at 100 yards a minute of angle is one inch, at 200 yards it is 2 inches, and so forth. At 800 yards one minute of angle is equivalent to roughly 8 inches, so I dialed in 15 minutes of angle and got ready to try the long shots. Many people get all worked up about windage on long shots, but I follow the Chris Kyle school of thought, that since wind is constantly changing, by the time you adjust for the wind, the wind changes, so why bother? I just watch where the first bullet hits and adjust from there. Elevation and physics are constants, so adjusting your scope for different elevations at different ranges makes sense.

I fired the first group of three, then got on the spotting scope and saw that they were in the black, which for me was pretty good. I proceeded to fire four more groups of three and managed to tighten my groups and felt good about the shooting. I then went out to the 200-yard line and put up three more targets so that I could re-zero at 200 yards. Once I was happy with that, I put the rifle away and went down to the pistol range and put up three targets at 5, 10, and 15 yards. Pistols are all about practice and muscle memory, so I fired two hundred rounds of 9mm out of the CZ75 at the various distances, then put out three new targets and fired two hundred rounds of .45ACP out of the CZ97 at the various ranges. I was hitting what I was shooting at, so I figured it was time to pack it in, go home and get ready for the barbeque.

Back at the house, I got the grill set up near the front porch and got the meat out to thaw. After setting out the paper plates and plastic utensils on the kitchen island, I rounded up all the condiments and put them on the island as well. I then went out to my truck to get the guns out for cleaning at the workbench in the barn. After I got the guns cleaned, lubed and put back in the gun safe, I walked back to the house to grab a beer, sit on the porch and wait for the miscreants to show up for free food. As it was Friday, Rachel would be practicing her Krav Maga while kicking the crap out of the MMA wannabes at Bret's gym, and would not be home until around seven thirty. The other reprobates should start arriving around five so I fired up the grill at that time so that everyone could grab a beer and relax before the food was ready.

Sure enough, just after I got the fire going in the cut down drum, I heard the growl of TJ's 1950 Chevy pickup on steroids. To be honest, I was jealous of his truck and that Coyote engine set-up. I just hoped Rachel would work some of her magic on my 1956 F-100 so that I could at least compete in the 'cool' category. Pulling up in front of the bunkhouse, he got out and sauntered over. I handed him a beer and we sat down on the old couch to wait for the rest to show up. Sometimes conversation is neither required, nor desired.

Next up was Peio in his old Suburban. He parked beside my truck on the apron in front of the barn. I was walking that way when he got out since I had forgotten to get out a bottle of Laphroaig for him. Shaking his hand, I told him that I'd forgotten his Scotch and if he'd wait on the porch with TJ that I would rectify the situation immediately. He muttered something about youth, lack of responsibility and respect for our elders while he walked to the porch. Grabbing a bottle of Laphroaig from the case I keep up on the mezzanine deck strictly for Peio's visits, I walked back to the kitchen and got a glass out and filled it about half full, Peio considers ice or other additions to his Scotch as sacrilege. Walking back onto the porch I handed Peio his drink.

"Does that excuse my youth, lack of responsibility and disrespect of those elderly people illegally squatting on my property?" I asked him.

"It's a beginning," was all he would say. Tough audience.

Eventually we heard Bret's Impala rumbling up the driveway. He parked beside TJ and he and Nicholas got out and headed our way.

I told TJ, "It's your turn to flip burgers and brats," and handed him the spatula. He looked at it as if I had handed him a snake. "You realize that I don't cook, and quite possibly could burn water, don't you?"

"You're a Cajun! Of course you can cook!"

"I'm not from the cooking variety of Cajuns," was his sorry excuse.

"Well, you'd better come to some sort of arrangement with Bret then," I retorted.

TJ gave it some thought, then handed the spatula to Bret. "What's this for? I flipped last time," Bret asked.

"If I flip, the burgers and brats will be inedible, if you flip this won't happen," responded TJ.

"No way, this is why we had the civil rights movement and affirmative action! I refuse simply as a matter of principle!" Bret was grinning.

"If you do this for me, I promise not to shoot you in the foot today." TJ was now into his 'negotiating mode'.

"What you going to shoot me with, Mr. Badass? Don't see you packing anything."

TJ reached behind his back and pulled his little Glock 19 out of the pancake holster he wore. He then reached into his hip pocket and pulled out the suppressor for it. Screwing one onto the other he held it up for Bret to see.

Bret pondered this for a moment, then, "What about after today?"

"Let's just go one day at a time, as neither one of us has a crystal ball. But I promise to give it serious consideration while I eat," was TJ's reply.

"And I promise not to spit on your burger."

"Deal," replied TJ.

After this exhibition of 'the art of the deal', we all sat around shooting the breeze until about six-thirty before I put the meat on the grill. We were all starving and decided not to wait for the girls. We did the 'male bonding' thing on the porch, which consisted of telling lies and eating burgers and brats while drinking beer, or Scotch in Peio's case. At around seven-thirty we heard the Whale Tail pull onto the driveway off the county road, so Bret slapped some more brats and burgers onto the grill while Rachel parked the Porsche under the lean-to. Her and Heather got out and headed toward the porch. All conversation stopped on the porch, and I am sure the girls felt like gazelles walking toward a pride of lions. It really wasn't our fault, as all they had on were those short, tight workout shorts, and sports bras. Any male with a pulse would have stopped and watched.

"You boys eyeballing us?" from Heather. Obviously, she'd been hanging around Rachel too much lately.

Heather went up to TJ for a kiss and Rachel simply walked past me, slapped my butt and kept going to give Peio a big hug and a peck on the cheek. Peio was starting to give me a 'second hand' complex. I'd need to speak to Rachel about this, hopefully while discussing the health benefits of the Kama Sutra later in the evening.

Anyhow, everyone got fed and watered by around eight-thirty, so we all piled into the living room for an update and to make a plan. With Peio in one of the overstuffed chairs flanking the fireplace, TJ in the other, Rachel and Heather on the couch facing the fireplace, Bret and I on the hearth, and Nicholas on a kitchen stool behind the couch, I called the session to order.

"Okay, as it stands now, Alyshia is safely stowed in Anguilla, no known bad guys are in town, and we know that Irish Bobby is getting antsy. Let's go around the room and get updates from everyone before we try to plan ahead."

Looking to my left I nodded at Bret on the hearth.

"So far I've been able to keep Irish Bob happy with the fact that I am making plans to visit the bank in the unnamed town in Wyoming to get his cash. I'm not sure how much longer I'll be able to do this and think that I should shortly disappear for a few days before showing back up at the gym. Once I do this, we won't have much time left before Irish Bob and his boys come to town for the handover. Also, I get the feeling that Bob has a watcher on me as he seems to know when I am in the gym and makes sure that he calls then. It'd be nice to ID the watcher as we'll need to keep him under wraps as well when Bob comes to town."

I then nodded at TJ to give us his thoughts.

"Not much happening on the surveillance front. Since Rachel beat the crap of Gervaso and Tito got involved, we've had a pretty good net looking out for strange white guys in town, especially those with an interest in the gym or shop. So really, nothing to report."

I asked Heather if she had anything to say, but as she really wasn't involved, she just shook her head 'no'.

I then looked at Nicholas, who was sitting behind the couch on a stool, but next in line going around the room. "Anything on your end, Nick?" I asked.

"Nothing to add to what TJ said, nobody of interest appears to be in town yet."

"Rachel, you have anything for us?" I asked.

"Nobody seems to be paying any attention to the shop at the moment, but if they do have a watcher in town, they'll know that Heather and I frequent the gym often. If they tie us to Bret, and with Alyshia no longer available to them as leverage, I think that Heather and I become the next in line."

"Peio mentioned this in an earlier meeting. We'll need to consider that," I said. She was right, with their leverage gone, they'd be looking for new meat.

Next up was Peio. He appeared deep in thought for a moment, "Okay, kids, first off, Alyshia is safe, happy and is apparently enjoying her little vacation on Anguilla. We do not need to be concerned about her at this time," he said while giving a nod to Bret. "This supposed watcher does give me some concern. I will speak to Tito tomorrow and see if we can flush this person out. Heather and Rachel, I may need your help on this. Finally, I think we should put the ball in play regarding Bret retrieving the money in Wyoming. Let's give it one more week. Bret, you need to come up with some reasonable excuse to leave the gym for a few days and make sure everyone knows that you are leaving, and that Nicholas will be in charge while you are away. We need to make this look as realistic and as reasonable as possible. While you are supposedly away, you will stay with me, at my house, strictly to keep you undercover but accessible to me while we lure Mr. Shannon here. A few days after you apparently leave for the bank in Wyoming, we will send Mr. Shannon a photo of duffle bags full of stacks of used, one hundred-dollar bills, along with a newspaper from some small town in Wyoming showing the date. This should keep him satisfied, but it will also get him moving this way. Under no circumstances do you agree to meet him anywhere but here."

Peio then looked at me and said, "We haven't had an update from you yet, Jeb. Have you found a suitable location to make the drop?"

"Peio, I've driven hundreds of miles in the past week or so, and to find a place that is 'remote enough to not be observed', but 'not so remote as to look like a set-up', is a tough call, but if you think about it, we've already found a suitable place and reconnoitered it," I said.

Peio looked a bit confused and said, "Explain yourself."

"What about the old homestead where 325 dead ends? Where we had to get rid of the bikers and their meth lab. It is remote, only one road in, high ground around it, and they will have to pass both my driveway and the turnoff to Bland Reservoir to get there, making it easy to keep an eye on them. What do you think?" I asked Peio.

He was grinning like the Cheshire Cat in Lewis Carroll's 'Alice's Adventures in Wonderland'. "Perfect! I cannot believe that we did not think of that earlier. Well done!" Clapping his hands together, he continued, "Today is Friday, so next week will be crucial to our plans. On Tuesday and Wednesday, I want Bret to take Rachel and Heather to lunch on both days. Bret, you will first drive to the bank to fetch Heather at twelve-thirty, then from there go to Rachel's shop and collect her. On the Tuesday, I want you to go to the Double Z, and on the Wednesday to the Italian

Garden. I do not want TJ or Nicholas to follow in the event that the watcher knows of them. I will have Tito blanket both restaurants and have his people looking for a tail. Once we identify this watcher, I'll ask Tito to watch the watcher until we decide what to do with him. Let's meet back here next Friday to further our strategy."

Now Peio's expression got very dark and serious. "There is something which we need to discuss as a group before we go any further. Without beating around the bush, some people are about to die. I could have said 'disappear', but you are all adults. We simply cannot afford for these people to surface again, including after a stay in prison, which means we cannot involve law enforcement. These people are violent criminals who would have certainly kidnapped, and worse, Ms. Grier to further their aims. Furthermore, once they have this cash, they would begin to clean up loose ends, which means anyone they feel was involved in this business. We do not know who the watcher has included in his reports to Mr. Shannon, which at this moment, could be all of us if he has tailed someone to this meeting and noted who has arrived. Some of you have been associated with the criminal underworld previously, even if peripherally, others have not. After this business has been concluded, you will all be an accomplice to a crime." Reaching into his shirt pocket, Peio pulled out a folded piece of paper and opened it before putting on his reading glasses. "Just so we know the legal definition, let me read you this:

"'One who is complicit is said to be an accomplice. Even though an accomplice does not actually commit the crime, his or her actions assisted someone in the commission of the crime. The concept of accomplice liability means that an accomplice will face the same degree of guilt and punishment as the individual that committed the crime'."

Taking off his glasses and refolding the paper and putting it back in his pocket, he looked around the room and continued, "Although I would have preferred not to tell you this, I feel I must. I have much experience in this sort of thing from my past life. I know how these things should be done and I, with or without you, will do this thing. Even though that will be the case, you will need to be prepared to live with the knowledge that we, as a group, will be causing the death of Mr. Shannon, whoever he brings with him, and the watcher. There is no other way to keep everyone in this room, plus Ms. Grier, safe in the future.

"I would have preferred that you all had kept thinking of me as a grumpy old man who enjoys your company, but at times like this, you must do what it takes to keep not only yourself, but those you hold dear, safe.

"Now I ask each of you, can you live with yourself knowing what I, or we, are about to do, will make you guilty by association and an accomplice in the eyes of the law?"

Turning to his right, he asked Bret, "Can you, son?"

Bret nodded. Going around the room he looked each of us in the eye and asked the same question. Everyone nodded assent.

"Okay then, I bid you all a fond adieu. Us older gentlemen need our rest. I will see you all for a barbeque at the same time next Friday." We all got up and walked Peio to the door in silence. The guys all shook his hand, and the girls gave him a hug and a peck on the cheek before he climbed into his Suburban and drove off.

It was a solemn bunch who finally went their own ways that evening. Heather and TJ retired to the bunkhouse, Bret and Nick drove back to town, and Rachel and I lounged on the couch, with her laying up against my chest watching TV in silence.

After a while she said, "You can't honestly tell me that you are going to let Peio shoulder this load by himself. That would be extremely out of character, and perhaps even cowardly."

"Oh, ye of little faith. Myself and my trusty sidekick TJ, also known as Tonto, have already discussed this and have a nefarious plan in place to ensure that Peio is not alone, and is covered however this goes down. I will also have you know that I went shooting today to ensure that I still have some skills out to 800 yards with my trusty Ed Brown shooting stick and with my pistolas. Keep in mind that I only have my pistols to ensure that I can get back to the rifle, in the event that I am dumb enough to put it down in the first place. I am way ahead of you on this."

"It is good to know that I am not the kept woman of some spineless piece of oilfield trash. Furthermore, I am way ahead of you in other matters," was Rachel's comeback.

"And what matters would those be, pray tell?"

"Well, while you have been yapping, my hands have been busy underneath this blanket, and I have managed to get my workout shorts almost over my hips. Perhaps you could assist me at this point?"

So, I did, and the rest of the evening was somewhat of a blur.

CHAPTER 22

SATURDAY STARTED MUCH LIKE ANY other day, with me shoving Rachel out of the bed and heading her toward the shower, while I went down to the kitchen to fire up the coffee machine and start the French toast. Rachel finally emerged smelling of sandalwood and dressed in a pair of those skinny jeans, I didn't even know that she owned a pair, and a white broadcloth button-down shirt. She looked and smelled great.

After she had a coffee and a pulse I said, "I know it is none of my business, but I thought the 1970 Chevelle SS was due in today, and correct me if I am wrong, but that outfit really does not fit the usual 'grease monkey' motif that I adore so much."

"I am taking the day off and doing girl things with Heather. TJ can accept the Chevelle, and this girl needs to get with other girls, and away from this lecherous, testosterone fueled environment, which is known to Heather and I, as the El Rancho del Loco Gallos. For you uneducated oilfield types this translates to 'the Ranch of the Crazy Roosters', which is an appropriate name for this place."

"I have never heard you complain about my testosterone fuel in the past. Are you ever coming back?" I asked.

"Only to be ravaged and pillaged. Civilization may not be all it is cracked up to be," she said with a smile.

"Works for me. I will gladly ravage and pillage you to your heart's desire, anything to get the stink of civilization off you," I offered.

"Your pointy bit is starting to show, cowboy. Best get your mind on something else, like feeding me French toast. I may need my energy later." So much for getting my pointy bit worked on at the breakfast table.

While she ate, I told her to keep an eye out for the watcher, the sooner we found him, the better. She finished her enormous pile of apparently non-fat French toast, on her at least, finished her coffee, and twerked me as she went out the door. The shameless, teasing hussy.

As my 1956 F-100 was in Rachel's capable hands, I'd already done my shooting for the week, and Peio had already lined everyone out, I decided to loaf around town for the day. I cleaned up the kitchen after Rachel's feeding frenzy, then went upstairs to change. I put on a pair of old jeans, my 1978 Cheap Trick Live at the Budokan t-shirt, which I found in Rachel's closet, my Nikes, and headed out to the F-150. I was just out the door when I heard a really deep growl on the end of the porch toward the bunkhouse. It scared the crap out of me. Lying in the shade at the end of the porch, was the Hound of the Baskervilles himself, gnawing on the bone of some unfortunate large animal. This was a surprise, usually all I saw of him was his backside while he was headed back to the woods. As he didn't try to charge and kill me, I kept on going up to the barn to get my truck. Rachel must be bonding with the beast, that is all I could figure.

Getting into my truck, I drove down to the shop to shoot the breeze with TJ, as I knew he was on his own while the girls were out doing girly things. I pulled up under the awning out front and walked through the office to the work bays. Backed into the work bay was a totally original, numbers matching, metallic olive green with white racing stripes, 1970 Chevelle SS with the cowl inducted 454 motor. I am not a Chevelle guy, but to many folks this car was the embodiment of the 'muscle car'. TJ was underneath the passenger's side getting it set up on the lift to take a look underneath, so I kicked one of his boots and said, "Hey, the boss isn't here, let's go get drunk and chase some loose women."

Sliding out from under the car on his Craftsman Creeper, he stood up while wiping his hands on a shop rag and said, "That would be a good idea if you were never going to see the boss again, so that she couldn't kick your ass into next week, and you actually forced yourself to drink enough to get drunk. From my side, I kind of like having Heather around and my days of visiting titty bars are far in the past."

"They just don't make button men like they used to," I said with an exaggerated sigh. "Okay, get done with what you are doing, and I'll let you take me to lunch."

"How gracious of you. Give me an hour to get this thing in the air and take a look around underneath."

I took a look at my forgotten 1956 F-100 in the next bay. Hopefully, they'd get this Chevelle out of here quickly so that they could get working on my ride. I walked back into the office, grabbed a coffee and leafed through some parts catalogs while TJ did his thing. I happened to look across the street and saw a new white Toyota Camry parked in the alley behind the liquor store across the street. This struck me as odd, as the liquor store wouldn't open until noon and the only things in that alley were dumpsters. I walked outside to my truck and got out a pair of binoculars I keep behind the seat to watch animals out on the ranch. Wrapping an old rag around them I walked back into the office. As the windows of the office are tinted, I knew that whoever was in the car could not see in. I took out the binoculars and focused on the driver through the passenger's window. Lo and behold, the driver was pointing a pair of binoculars at the shop.

I yelled for TJ to get in here. Due to our present situation, he was beside me like a shot. "Take these binoculars and scope out the driver of that white Camry in the alley behind the liquor store," I told him while handing him the binoculars.

"That bastard is scoping us out," observed our highly observant resident Coonass.

"Correct, take a good look at him, from what you can see from here, and describe him to me."

"Red receding hair, not bald but getting there. I think they refer to it as a 'widow's peak'. Unlike yourself, who is well on his way to truly bowling ball bald. Can't tell his height as he is leaning against the driver's side window. Fair build, no facial hair, pale complexion. May have blue eyes. I think he may have some tats on his forearms," said TJ.

"That's what I saw. So, the red hair and pale skin could indicate an Irish bloodline, the fact that he is scoping us from what appears to be a rental, and with our present concern about a watcher, what do you bet this is our guy?" I asked.

"I'm guessing you're right," he replied. "How do you want to play it?"

"We can't give the game away at the moment. Go get cleaned up and we'll head out for lunch. I'll drive across Roosevelt Avenue on the side street the bay doors face on. He'll likely duck down as we go by. When he does, take a picture with your phone of the license plate. I want to see where it was rented and what name it is rented under. Maybe we can find out where he's staying."

After TJ closed the bay doors and locked up the shop, we got in my truck, and I went around by the bay doors and got on the side street which crossed Roosevelt Avenue. Once it was apparent that we were going to cross Roosevelt Avenue, and drive directly in front of the Camry, the redheaded guy leaned over into the passenger's side seat and got his head below the dash. TJ took a few photos of the front of the car, and we kept going until we got to the Double Z for lunch.

Over incredibly large, juicy cheeseburgers and a mountain of fries, amateur secret agents and retired button men need their energy, I called Tito and asked him if he happened to know anyone who could run a plate for me. He replied that he wouldn't be much of a 'sin nombre' if he couldn't even run a plate. I told him it was likely a rental, but I needed to know where it was rented, and what name it was rented under. I explained to Tito about the watcher and that we thought we had seen him. Maybe we could find out where he was staying, if he registered under the same name as he rented the car. Tito said he'd call me back that afternoon.

TJ meantime had called Heather, the girls were at some sushi joint eating raw fish and told her about what we had seen and to be on the lookout for a late model white Camry driven by a guy with receding red hair. Heather replied that she had no idea what a late model Camry looked like. I took the phone and told her that if the wench sitting beside her could not recognize a late model Camry, then she is in the wrong line of work. Heather then informed me that she had been on speaker phone, and that I was now in the doghouse.

Dropping TJ at the shop, I then drove over to Bret's gym and strolled into the office, where I found him and Nicholas having a chat. I told them about the guy in the Camry and that Tito was trying to get a name so that we could check hotels. Bret let me know that the Gold's Gym in Cheyenne was having an open house a week from this Thursday, so he could use that as a reason to travel up north during the timeframe Peio had mentioned. I told him that I would run it past Peio that afternoon, as I wanted to run by his place and talk about the watcher issue as well. I'd call Bret later that night and let him know what Peio thought.

Saying adios, I walked out the front of the gym and took a good look around. The watcher should be paying more attention to the gym than to the shop, unless he was told to find more leverage now that Alyshia was sunning herself in Anguilla. I didn't see any late model white Camrys around, so I got in my truck and took off for Peio's place.

You'd never know that Peio had built this place and moved in within 8 months. The old trailer he called home had been removed and the place had been expertly landscaped. It was a fantastic log house, and the views to the south toward my place were fantastic. Walking onto the front porch, I noticed the security camera over the door, and the others on each end of the porch. No doubt this place was as secure as Fort Knox. Using the knocker, I knocked three times and waited for the old coot. Suddenly the door clicked open and somewhere a speaker told me to come in and to go out back. Peio had just finished putting some chips and guacamole on the table and was filling two glasses with tea.

"What brings you by this time of the day?" Peio asked.

So, while eating his guacamole and drinking his tea, I told him about the redheaded guy in the Camry who we thought may be the watcher, and about Bret's plan to use the open house at the gym in Cheyenne as the excuse to disappear.

"This thing may be coming to a head then. Let me know what Tito finds out and we can take it from there. Ask Bret to come by your place after work on the Wednesday before the open house on Thursday in Wyoming. I will collect him then and bring him here. We need to get some eyes on this watcher as soon as possible since he will no doubt meet up with the Irish crew once they arrive. If we know where they are in town, we can get Tito's boys to follow them and let us know what they are up to."

We finished up the guacamole and sat sipping our tea, just enjoying the afternoon, when Peio put his elbows on the table and looked directly into my eyes.

"When the final act of this tragedy is played out, I will be in the old farmhouse waiting with the money. I will have TJ with me since he has been through similar situations before and knows what to watch for, and what to do when the shooting starts. There will be shooting. Irish Bob will put a shooter somewhere in the hills surrounding the farmhouse long before the meeting. I need a highly competent shooter on that hill as well, hopefully above the other one. I am not a rifleman, but I would guess my man on the hill will need to make at least one shot from something like 400 yards at a downhill angle. Rachel says you are an amazing shot with a rifle, and that you keep in practice with a specialty rifle that you own. Is that correct?"

"Peio, I have been shooting my whole life. With the rifle and optics that I have, a 400-yard shot should be fairly easy," I told him.

"The shot you take could be the difference between whether TJ and I walk out of that bowl in the hills or get carried out of it. Now I ask you again, can you, and will you, take that shot? If not, and there is no shame if you say you cannot take the shot, I will need to source someone else quickly."

I took a sip of tea, looked Peio right in the eye, and told him a story.

"In June of 2014, ISIL began a lightning offensive in northwestern Kurdistan to capture the city of Mosul. They took the city and rebranded themselves as ISIS, while they consolidated their position in Kurdistan. The Peshmerga stopped them from advancing further south toward Erbil, but the Kurds were taking a beating due to the fact that they had no heavy weapons. While the West, specifically the US, began shipping heavy weapons and resupplies of small arms and ammunition to them, the Kurds had to hold until these shipments arrived. I was stuck in Erbil when all of this occurred. I could either sit in my villa and wait for the result, or I could offer my services to the Kurds. I am not a trained sniper, and I had no military training whatsoever, but I am good with a rifle and could provide overwatch for the real soldiers as they fought. I went to my Asayish security liaison and explained all of this to her. Initially they were skeptical. They took me out to a shooting range, where the Peshmerga zeroed their weapons, and handed me a fairly new Russian Dragunov SVD sniper rifle equipped with a PSO-1M2 scope. This scope takes some time to get used to as the reticle is complicated. They paired me with one of their snipers to familiarize myself with the weapon. After that I was asked to make shots at 200, 400, 600 and 800 meters. Which I did."

Drinking some tea, I continued, "I fought in the battle to liberate Tikrit in March of 2015, in the northern Sinjar region in November of the same year, and in the battle to recapture Ramadi. I have no idea how many people I killed since keeping score is meaningless when you are trying to keep other guys alive. Suffice it to say, I killed a lot of people before I was finally allowed to board a flight for Dubai, and then home."

Finishing my tea, I put the glass on the table, "So to answer your question, 'Can you and will you take that shot?', my answer is, most assuredly, yes."

He looked at me for a long time then said, "I guess I am not the only one with a history. I apologize for putting you in the situation where you felt I should know your story, but I believe you understood my reasoning. We will not mention this again. I assume Rachel is unaware of this?"

"Rachel was scared to death while I could not get out of Kurdistan, and I didn't think it would be very smart to tell her what I had done. It is better if she thinks I am just some old oilfield trash she fell in love with, not a killer," I said.

"She will not hear of this from me, I assure you. That said, I think our little Rachel will surprise even you. She is not the shrinking violet type."

My phone rang at this point. It was Tito. "Your watcher is using the name Owen Madden. He is staying at the Holiday Inn on Roosevelt Avenue, at the opposite end of that street from Rachel's shop. Do you want me to put a blanket on him?"

"Tito, you are a star! Do you mind keeping him covered for a while? We need to know when his buddies get here, and we need to make sure he doesn't get anywhere near Rachel or Heather, TJ's banker lady friend."

"No worries, amigo. My boys need some practice, and I will personally cut the cajones off the redheaded pendejo if he disturbs Rachel. Speak to you soon." Tito hung up and I relayed the information to Peio.

"This is a good break for us." Peio stood up, "Now you go home and take care of Ms. Chen while I do some planning."

At the front door, I turned to Peio and said, "I'm curious, why don't you get a mobile phone so that we can do a lot of this legwork over the phone?"

"I do have a cell phone, and I do much work from it. The issue is that this is where I am retiring, but not yet. There are still a few loose ends that I want to clean up. If I had a cell phone, with your names and numbers on it, and I failed at one of these 'loose ends', and they got my phone, then you, Rachel, TJ, Heather, Bret, Nicholas and anyone else on it would be in danger from some very bad people. I would not have that on my head."

With that on my mind, I got back in my truck and drove back home.

Walking in the pantry I pulled some handmade frozen manicotti out of the freezer along with the green chili and pork burritos that Tito had brought by the office the other day. Putting them on the counter to thaw, I grabbed a beer and sat on the porch just relaxing and waiting for people to show up. First came TJ in his 1950 Chevy sleeper. He parked in front of his bunkhouse and came over to the porch. I told him to grab a beer and join me. When he did, I filled him in on what Tito had found out about the watcher, and that his boys were now watching the watcher. Tito would let us know when the rest of the crew got into town. I then told him about Peio's idea concerning how we would set up at the old farmhouse on the day, me on the hill and TJ inside with Peio. TJ thought about it, then said that was good as far as it went, but a lot would depend on how many of the Irish hooligans came to town, and how many actually showed up at the old farmhouse. Up to four and we were probably good to go, more than that and we'd be in a bind. At the end of the day, we'd just have to see how the situation developed.

Eventually Rachel and Heather showed up in Heather's little Audi A4. She parked alongside TJ's pickup and the girls came over carrying their recent purchases, gave their respective studs a peck on the cheek, then went into the house to sort through their loot and try stuff on. Heather informed us that they had already eaten so we were on our own for dinner.

"Manicotti or pork burritos with green chili?" I asked TJ.

"I'm feeling like burritos," he said.

"Let me get the manicotti back in the freezer and put the burritos in the oven to warm up. I'll grab us another beer on the way back."

The sun was going down behind the house so the courtyard in front of the house was getting dark and cooling down.

After taking a few sips of beer, TJ looked at me and asked, "Have you ever actually shot someone? It most definitely is not like the movies." He obviously had the same concerns as Peio had earlier, and I did not blame him in the least considering what we had in mind, but I didn't feel like going through it all again and just told him to talk to Peio. Which had him looking at me kind of weird, but I didn't say anything else and just sat there enjoying the evening and drinking my beer.

Eventually I got up and took the burritos, wrapped in foil, out of the oven, put them on a tray on the island and got plates and silverware out. If you have never eaten real Mexican pork burritos, with real green chili, you have missed out on one of the unsung culinary delights of the world. Needless to say, Tito had brought us the original items. They were outstanding.

While we were eating, we were treated to a fashion show as the girls modelled their recent purchases by changing in Rachel's rarely used guest room, then prancing down the stairs and making a circuit around the porch before heading back up the stairs again, where the next model was on deck to come down. I have learned long ago to never offer a negative opinion. The fact is, either of these girls could have come down the stairs in potato sacks and still looked stunning. It was a great way to pass the evening, drinking beer and watching hot chicks model their new stuff, all on the comfort of your own porch.

Eventually they ran out of new stuff, put back on their old stuff, and came out to the porch to have a beer with the boys. I brought them up to speed on the watcher, and Peio's instructions for Bret to come by two Wednesdays from now so that he could be relocated to Peio's, while Irish Bob thought he was up in Wyoming getting his cash. Once the girls had finished their beers, Heather and TJ went over to the bunkhouse to play Monopoly, I'm guessing, while Rachel and I sat on the porch just enjoying the evening.

"You realize that you failed to address my 'pointy bit' this morning at breakfast before you went to work. Furthermore, it was your fault entirely that my 'pointy bit' had become pointy," I pointed out.

"So true, and I felt bad about it all day. Let me grab a shower and I'll meet you in your room to ease the pressure on your pointy bit. Would that make everything better?"

"Depends, are you going to wear that latex Cat Woman outfit?" I asked, knowing full well she did not have a Cat Woman outfit, or any other latex outfits, to my knowledge. But I had to ask.

"I think I threw that out. Latex doesn't let my body breath. I was thinking more of a Cleopatra motif for the evening," she said while heading inside and up the stairs.

"Works for me. I'll need to dig up my Mark Antony outfit to set the mood," I said as I followed her mesmerizing backside up the stairs.

CHAPTER 23

SUNDAY ROLLED AROUND, AND SINCE nobody had to work today, I gave Rachel the Wanton Hussy Lesson #7. After she had successfully passed the exam for that lesson, she gathered up her Cleopatra outfit and retired to her own room to shower up and make herself presentable again. She tended to work up a sweat while working her way through the Wanton Hussy syllabus. I on the other hand, smelled like a Rose, pun intended. I found my boxers, put them on, found my jeans, put them on, and headed down to the kitchen to start the coffee and pancakes.

Rachel was not in zombie mode this morning due to our early morning horizontal, well mostly horizontal, workout. She bounced down the stairs, got her own cup of coffee and waited patiently for her pancakes. While I was sorting out the grub, I asked her what she was going to do today.

"At some point I'll need to wash Dog again, but before that I think I'll lay out and get some sun and just relax. How about you?"

"Right now, I'm thinking that I should stick around and act as the Official Applier of Coppertone. But as I've already molested you once today, I think I'll run into town and just see what's shaking. What about lunch?"

"After you apply the suntan lotion to my parts which I can't reach, and you are finished running around, could you pick up a couple of buckets of KFC, one original, one spicy?" she asked.

"Two buckets? I thought that you were watching your figure these days. Why two buckets?"

“I do not need to watch my figure, that’s your job, and I heard no complaints earlier. We need two buckets, as I have invited Heather over to enjoy the sun and to hang out with. TJ will eventually arrive, as you will no doubt inform him that Heather is here and scantily clad. I know you don’t feel like cooking lunch, so two buckets of KFC are required. Don’t forget sufficient coleslaw, mashed potatoes and gravy. Also, can you roll the old round stock tank from behind the barn to the usual dog washing spot?”

“A slave in my own house. You realize that this is my day of rest as well, don’t you?”

“Every day is your day of rest, you knothead! Besides, if you quit whining, I may let you shower the suntan lotion off me later.” She is a very adept negotiator.

“Deal, I’ll see you around one,” I said as I went upstairs to put on a shirt and shoes and brush my teeth before heading into town. On the way out I asked Rachel if she still remembered how to clean up the kitchen. She flung a piece of pancake at me, so I took that as a ‘yes’ and headed out the door.

I figured that TJ was at the shop as his overpowered 1950 Chevy pickup was not in front of the bunkhouse when I left, so I headed there first. The bay doors were open, so I pulled around to that side and parked the truck outside the bay with the Chevelle in it. Although his truck was parked outside, I didn’t see TJ anywhere. I yelled, “Anyone at home?” I heard a reply coming from under my 1956 F-100 in the other bay. When I made it through the obstacle course of tools, air hoses and the tire repair/balancing machine, I saw TJ getting to his feet on the far side.

“What are you doing, amigo? Sabotaging my ride so that I don’t kick your butt in that old Chevy of yours, stoplight to stoplight?” I kidded him.

“Let’s see, you’re running an archaic Super Cobra Jet rated at 370 horsepower and 450 foot-pounds of torque through a 1969 M-21 Muncie four speed, while I am running a 5.0-liter Coyote motor rated at 435 horses and 400 foot-pounds through a performance four speed automatic transmission with an electronic overdrive. I’m pretty sure that I’ll kick your ass,” was his annoyingly perceptive reply.

“You Coonasses definitely have the gift for gab. I noticed that you quoted stock performance figures for my old 429, while quoting Coyote performance numbers for yours. Keep in mind that you have no idea what cam is in mine, nor do you know if I have installed lightened con rods and pistons. Comparing apples to apples, a 429 Barnett crate engine is putting out up to 550 horses and 580 foot-pounds of torque,” I retorted.

“True perhaps, but you are not running a Barnett crate motor.”

“Hey, at least I built my own. Once I get my Edelbrock 7166 carb and intake manifold set-up installed, and the motor run in, you and I are going to run a quarter mile and put this argument to bed. What are you doing to my baby?” I asked him again.

“Rachel has declared that during the actual work week we’ll be working on the Chevelle only, which means these charity projects get worked on during the weekend. I was told to get the drop spindles installed this weekend. I’m about finished.”

“Charity project! I hate to bring this up, comrade, but I still technically own this shop,” I said with a grin.

“Technically perhaps, but for all intents and purposes you have signed it over to Rachel and totally emasculated yourself.”

“If you consider getting the girl, ten percent of the profits, and the spindles switched out on your truck without getting dirty, emasculated, then I can fully understand why they ran you out of the Crawfish State.”

“That just goes to show your lack of education, the nickname for Louisiana is the Pelican State. That said, you did end up with a pretty sweet deal. Why’d you come by?”

“No reason really. I wanted to touch base with Bret and Tito before I picked up the two buckets of KFC Rachel wanted,” I told him.

“Two buckets, huh. You’d better keep her well exercised or she’s going to get fat.”

“I do my best, but keeping up with a half-Chinese, half-Israeli dynamo is not as easy as it may sound. But to get back to the point, the KFC is for Rachel and Heather, who are planning on sun tanning in bikinis in front of the house this afternoon. A real Coonass would tell me to go about my business, and that he would meet me at the house around one this afternoon to watch the show, while drinking beer and eating chicken,” I explained to him.

“Why are you still standing there! Go see Bret and Tito, get the chicken and I’ll see you on the porch at one.”

Tito didn’t usually work on the weekend, but I drove by his office anyhow. His office is in an old brick, two story building about halfway down Roosevelt Avenue in the old, original part of town. His office is on the second floor and consists of a big room facing the street with wood floors, a reception desk, complete with a distinguished black lady in her fifties named Mrs. Robertson, and tasteful, yet comfortable, furniture. His office is to the left as you walk in and takes up the back half of the floor. I do not know what he does for a living apart from providing adult supervision to gangbangers, and never bothered to ask. It must be lucrative, and evidently keeps him occupied while managing the gangs in western Colorado and elsewhere. I think he is sort of like Peio, but like everyone else, he differs to Peio. I'll never figure this out.

Anyhow, Tito's Fleetwood was not in the reserved spot directly in front of his office, so I figured he was at home, wherever that was. I called him on the phone to see if there was any news regarding the watcher. He said the guy was still shadowing Rachel, Heather and Bret, but that was all. His friends were not in evidence yet. I thanked him, hung up and drove over to the gym.

Bret was in the ring instructing some young Latino guy in the fine art of boxing, so I went in to the office, grabbed a beer, and sat ringside to watch. Nick came over and sat beside me, and we started shooting the crap as guys in gyms tend to do. I told Nick that as he was now officially one of the gang, he should start attending the barbeques and should bring his girl if he had one.

"Thanks for that, man! It'll give me something of a social life besides this gym."

He got quiet for a second, then said, "I may have an issue with my girl though."

"Why is that? Is she ugly? We won't hold it against you if you have an ugly girlfriend," I definitely have the gift for polite conversation.

"No, she's mixed-race."

"What Rastafarian and Martian? I really can't think of any other mixed-race girl who would consider dating you."

"I'm serious man," and he looked it suddenly. "She's mixed-race, white and black."

I looked at him as if he was an idiot. "What has that got to do with the price of tea in China?" I demanded.

"She worried that she would not be accepted in the crew or would be looked down on. I tried to explain that you guys are color blind, and it doesn't matter, but she is still a bit uncomfortable with it," he explained.

"You did explain that Rachel is mixed Chinese and Israeli, didn't you? It doesn't get weirder than that, unless you throw in that Martian blood."

"I did. She's a bit young and just a little insecure about the race thing. She never knew her white dad and was raised black by her mom. Maybe this has something to do with it," he elaborated.

"When you say 'bit young' I assume she is of legal age. You guys with dreads tend to think 14 is legal," I smiled.

"Yes, she's 2 years younger than I am, she's 24," he smiled.

"Okay, stud, here's the deal. Friday we are getting together for another planning session. You are tasked with bringing this insecure, half-white, half-black chick. What's her name anyhow?"

"Jemima, and don't even think about saying what you're thinking about saying."

"To continue, your job is to bring Aunt Jemima to the barbeque, even if you have to hand cuff her to get her there. Once she gets ruined by Heather and Rachel, she'll feel right at home. But I warn you, she'll never be the same!"

"I told you not to say it, but you just had to do it, didn't you? Do you have any idea how old that gets?"

"You better get used to it, partner, this crowd takes no prisoners," I advised.

At this point Bret climbed out of the ring and Nick sauntered off laughing. I told Bret that Peio wanted him to make sure that everyone knew that he was going to the open house in Wyoming a week from Thursday. He should come by my house the Wednesday afternoon before that, packed up and ready to go. Peio would have him collected and he would stay with Peio for a few days while he was supposedly collecting the money. They could send the photo of the money to Irish Bob from Peio's place. Finishing my beer, I told him that I had to go get KFC then back home to watch Rachel and Heather tan. He suggested that I watch the gym for the afternoon, and he'd take over my chores.

"In your dreams, buddy," was my reply, as I headed back out to my truck.

I picked up the chicken, one bucket of original and one of spicy, as ordered, then drove back to the house. As expected, there were two bikini-clad, nicely proportioned, young ladies laying out in chairs in front of the porch catching the midday sun. I drove slowly to the apron in front of the barn so as not to dust the lovelies. Getting out I grabbed the buckets of chicken out of the cab and yelled, "Lunch is served!"

TJ had been lounging on the porch in the shade while watching the scenery and came over to take one of the buckets off me. Putting my bucket on the porch, I went in to get paper plates and napkins, and was pleasantly surprised to see that Rachel had remembered how to clean the kitchen. She probably did not want to be embarrassed by bringing Heather into a kitchen after a Rachel feeding session.

Taking the plates and napkins outside, the girls had come onto the porch to have lunch. Each couple took a couch and dug in. I had developed an appetite just looking at the flesh on display. Boys will be boys. After everyone had their fill, I took the remains into the kitchen and wrapped them up for later while TJ took the garbage to the trashcans beside the barn. The girls had gone back to tanning and talking, so TJ and I went behind the barn and rolled out the old stock tank and filled it with water in preparation for the main event, washing Dog. If the girls could keep their bikinis on it should be sort of like mud wrestling, if not, it would be like adult mud wrestling.

About an hour later, the girls went inside to prepare for the event, I supposed that bikinis were not going to be part of it. Damn! A few minutes later they came back out in cut-off shorts and bikini tops. I assumed that bikinis were still on underneath the shorts, but that defeats the whole purpose of bikinis!

I asked Rachel how she was going to find Dog in the middle of the day. She told me to watch and learn. Turning to the gap between the house and the barn, which goes up the hill into the woods, she gave a whistle. A few minutes later a big black streak shot between the house and the barn and came right up to Rachel and sat down! Rachel and Heather scratched his ears and made goo-goo talk to him, and he just ate it up. This is all well and good, although I, and TJ, were at a loss as to how the girls had befriended a werewolf. There was no way we were going to get any closer to that animal.

Eventually Rachel got in the stock tank and called out to Dog. He came up to the edge of the tank and put his massive paws on the edge. He was now nearly as tall a Rachel. Rachel grabbed him by the armpits again and began pulling. Meanwhile, Heather was trying to push his butt toward, and hopefully into, the tank. Dog just stood there letting the girls exercise for a while before calmly stepping into the tank. Needless to say, this caused Rachel to fall backwards into the tank while Heather damn near did a header into the dirt but recovered gracefully. While Heather stepped into the tank, TJ and I grabbed another beer and continued watching the show.

Rachel, Heather and Dog frolicked in the tank for about an hour. During this time Dog was shampooed and conditioned a few times, then rinsed with the hose until his coat gleamed. This was the cleanest werewolf on record. After the rinsing, they got him out of the tub simply by climbing out themselves and whistling to Dog. With a bunch of old towels from the shop they dried him off, fed him some chicken they had hidden in the barbeque grill, then pointed back up the hill, and off Dog went. It was simply an amazing display of werewolf obedience training.

The girls came back on the porch, but TJ and I were pinching our noses in the universal sign of 'you stink'. Which they did. Heather headed over to the bunkhouse to clean up, and Rachel went upstairs. As much as we were tempted to go assist the ladies, they really did stink, which kind of took the edge off our ardor.

While the girls were cleaning up, TJ and I folded up the lounge chairs and towels and put them away in the wash room. Grabbing another couple of beers, we retired to the porch to wait for the girls to show back up. Eventually they did, in t-shirts and gym shorts. I'd put a bottle of white wine in a bucket of ice and two glasses on the table between the couches, and the girls joined us for a drink.

The sun sunk to the west while we sat on the porch and talked about everything except the problem with Irish Bob. About five, I had gone in to put the previous night's manicotti out to thaw, and around six-thirty I went in and put it in the oven to heat up and make a salad. At seven thirty we all went in and had dinner sitting around the island. All in all, a fairly mild, but entertaining day.

TJ and Heather went out to the bunkhouse around nine, and I cleaned up the dishes and the kitchen. I couldn't possibly ask Rachel to do that twice in one day without risking bodily harm. Rachel was sitting on the couch watching the History channel when I finished. I sat next to her and said, "Hey, aren't you forgetting something?"

"What are you on about?"

I replied, "Earlier today you said that if I behaved myself that I could wash the sun tan lotion off of you later."

"Sorry, you forfeited your chance when you would not go upstairs with me after I was finished washing Dog."

In my defense, "That is arbitrary and unreasonable, you smelled like a dog. Would you have climbed in the shower with me if I smelled like a dog?"

"A very valid point, Mr. Rose. How do you propose that I get back in your good graces?"

"If you are serious about this, you could go upstairs and put on that red baby doll outfit of yours and I could meet you in my room in say, 5 minutes?" I suggested.

With a grin, she got off the couch and did a slow, sexy walk up the stairs. Five minutes later, I followed.

CHAPTER 24

MONDAY DAWNED, AND FOR A change Rachel kicked me out of her bed. I'm not too sure how we ended up there, but variety is good. After finding my clothes, I put on my boxers and jeans, then headed down the stairs to do the breakfast routine. I didn't feel like cooking, so just put out bowls of granola stuff, which I keep around for just such an occasion, and milk. When the coffeemaker was finished doing its thing, I poured a cup for each of us and waited for her Highness to appear. She did, and after the first cup of coffee, began to speak.

"What is this gravel-like substance you are forcing me to eat?"

"That, my dear, is what I bring out when I don't feel like cooking breakfast or if I feel you are getting too curvy. Your pick."

"In an effort to maintain our relationship and exercising self-control so that I do not jump over there and beat you senseless, I will assume that you are simply too lazy to cook breakfast this morning."

I thanked her for considering my physical wellbeing, then asked her what was on her agenda today. Under her new work plan, each and every day, except weekends, would be spent on the Chevelle until it was completed. My job was to pick up lunch every day and bring it to her and TJ at noon. I thanked her for giving me something worthwhile to do, something to occupy my spare time, and something to keep me from considering joining one of Tito's crews out of sheer boredom.

As she already had the Rachel's Restorations uniform of a Dickie's coverall on, she finished her gravel, threw the spoon in the bowl and headed out the door before I could check to see if she had anything on under the coveralls. I cleaned up the kitchen, filled up the old wok by the back door at the end of the pantry, which had been re-purposed as Dog's water bowl, and went upstairs to do my morning ablutions and to shave.

Feeling like a new man, I jumped into the F-150 and drove over to the Safeway to load up on non-perishable items for the pantry, then went by the NAPA store to see if my Edelbrock 7166 carb and intake manifold had come in. No such luck. I then parked several blocks away from the shop on Roosevelt Avenue, and walked into the alley which eventually came out behind the liquor store across the street from the shop. I walked toward the liquor store keeping dumpsters between me and where I thought the Camry would be. Sure enough, Red was parked at the same spot. He obviously was not the sharpest surveillance guy in the business. Walking back to my truck, I got in and drove over to the Double Z to get some Jamaican jerked beef sandwiches and potato salad for lunch, then delivered it to the shop.

It was now only about eleven-thirty, but that didn't stop Rachel and TJ from dropping their tools and heading into the office when I told them what was on the menu. TJ got some Cokes out of the fridge and, using Rachel's desk as a table, we all dug in. I told them that Red was still scoping them out as of about an hour ago, from the same place as last time, which caused TJ to snort and roll his eyes.

After finishing lunch, TJ and I cleaned up, as Rachel seems to have a mental block about cleaning up after any meal, regardless of where it is at. I needed to speak to her about this genetic flaw in her make-up. While Rachel went back to the shop proper, TJ held back and asked me if I could make him up a box of those explosive tipped .45 ACP rounds which we had shot up at my range. I said I'd get on it today and didn't bother asking him what they were for. As I was low on .45 rounds, I had to stop by Al's Gun Shop and pick up a few boxes before heading home. I also needed some more Winchester 209 shotgun primers for the business end. That done I headed back to the ranch.

Getting back to the house, I took the supplies from Safeway into the pantry and put them away before taking the new rounds and primers to the barn to start making my still unpatented, better-than-those-mentioned-in-the-'Day of the Jackal', exploding bullets. I set out two boxes of .45 ACP rounds and put the rest into the gun safe. Going back to the workbench I set up my smaller drill press to drill a ¼-inch hole, a 1/3 of an inch deep. After that was done, I drilled the nose of each of the hollow points, two boxes were one hundred holes. I then took a break, as leaning over the drill press was killing my back. Getting back to work, I mixed up a batch of epoxy and brushed some on each primer before seating the primer in the hole with my thumb. I left them on the workbench so that the epoxy could harden while I cleaned up my mess. Going to the fridge in the barn, I grabbed a Coke and drank it while walking around my workshop, making sure that everything was in its place and not rusting away. Due to the fact that Rachel had my '56 truck, my tools had nothing to do. Tossing the Coke can in the garbage can by the door, I went back to the bench and assured myself that the epoxy had dried before putting the rounds back in their plastic holders, then put the holders back in their boxes. I marked each box with 'Exploding Rounds' before locking one box in the gun safe and taking the other with me to the house.

I really had nothing to do now, so I went in the dining room office and got up to date on the bills. It was now only about four in the afternoon, so I took all the kitchen knives out of the block and onto the front porch, where I proceeded to put an edge on them with a whetstone. Putting the sharpened knives and the whetstone back in the kitchen, I grabbed a beer and sat on the porch waiting for TJ to arrive. Rachel would be doing her boxing routine with Bret this evening and would not be home until around seven thirty. While I was drinking beer and contemplating what to cook for dinner, TJ arrived in that noisy old clapped out, '50 Chevy pickup of his. Pulling in front of the bunkhouse, he got out and headed my way. I'd gone in and grabbed two more beers and the box of Dr. Rose's Special Kablooey rounds. As he hit the top step, I handed him the box and a beer. After he had a chance to wet his whistle, my curiosity got the best of me, and I had to ask what the explosive rounds were for.

He looked at me and said, "Jeb, you know the old saying that 'curiosity killed the cat', don't you?"

"Well, I'm not a cat and you don't shoot .45 ACP, so in our present predicament, I wondered what you had in mind for these beauties?"

"They're for Peio," he told me.

Surprised, I asked, "Can Peio even shoot?"

"That old man will surprise you," was all he said. Which was enough, since Peio surprised me just about every time I ran into him.

TJ finished his beer, thanked me for the rounds, and walked back to his place. I just sat on the porch contemplating life until the Porsche growled its way into the lean-to garage and Rachel got out in her boxing get up. She carried her backpack, with her street clothes in it, and two pizza boxes. The dinner issue had just been resolved.

After giving me a kiss with just the right amount of 'urge and desire', we went into the kitchen where she put down the pizzas and then headed up the stairs to stow her kit and freshen up. I got out the paper plates, silverware, and two bottles of water. Rachel came back down the stairs in her Daisy Dukes and my missing 1979 Bad Company Live at Wembley t-shirt. I think she stole my whole collection. As I valued her company, her mind, and her body, I decided not to mention this larceny. We polished off one Hawaiian pizza while just discussing the day's events, and I put the pepperoni in the refrigerator for later. We then watched some TV before she headed up to her bed saying she was too beat for any romantic nonsense. I followed her up the stairs while explaining to her that this is what happens when you get old and don't take care of yourself, just before she closed the door in my face. Oh well, tomorrow is another day.

Tuesday was pretty much like Monday. I was reminded to bring lunch to the shop at noon as Rachel hit the road after breakfast. I eventually went over to Bret's gym to shoot the breeze with Bret and Nick before doing the lunch run. Bret had called Irish Bob on the number he'd been given and informed him that he would be heading up to the bank in Wyoming on Thursday, a week from this Thursday, to get his cash. He had explained to Irish Bob that there was an open house at a Gold's Gym in Cheyenne, Wyoming that Thursday, so he had a reasonable excuse to go up to Wyoming. I reminded him that once he supposedly left for Wyoming, that the clock was ticking. I said goodbye to Bret, then walked out of his office to the gym proper to find Nicholas. I found him by the speed bag instructing a kid on how to get into a rhythm and told him that I'd like to speak to him when he had a chance.

I went over to the ring and sat down to watch two ropy muscled black kids hammer the crap out of each other. Thankfully, I am old enough not to feel it necessary to consider this foolishness. Nick came and sat down by me, and I asked him if he had invited Aunt Jemima to the barbeque on Friday.

"I told you, man, quit calling her that!"

"I would, except I know how it winds you up, so how can I stop? Now did you ask her or not?" I demanded.

"Yeah, she's up for it, but still a little nervous about it."

"Don't you worry. You just get her there and I'll sort out the rest, and I promise you that I will not call her Aunt Jemima again, at least to her face. Deal?"

"Deal."

I then got back in my truck and drove over to Taco John's, on the other side of town, and bought six burrito Supremes to take back to the shop. If you've never had a Taco John's burrito Supreme, they are addictive. Getting back to the shop I announced, "Lunch is served!" and began clearing Rachel's desk so we could eat. Rachel followed TJ into the office, and we had lunch. TJ told us that Heather had to go to Denver for a bankers' meeting tomorrow and would be back Thursday. In the present situation he felt that he should go with her just in case. Rachel and I agreed, but Rachel added the caveat that I must take up TJ's slack in the shop. Keep in mind that although Rachel and I have been cohabitating, and mapping each other's body geography for years, we had never actually had to work together. This 'taking up TJ's slack' had all the earmarks of a disaster since we were both set in our ways regarding how to properly restore an automobile. But it had to be done.

With that in mind, I met Rachel at the Bikram studio that evening when she was finished and took her out to dinner at the Lebanese joint in town. In the event that things went belly up while working together the next few days, at least we had a nice evening out beforehand. After dinner, I took her back to her car and followed her home. That evening she was again too beat for any romantic nonsense. I thought that 29 years of age was a bit young for menopause. I'd need to research this.

Wednesday arrived, and we both got up and showered, not together. I shaved before I got the coffee and eggs going. After breakfast, I got the kitchen cleaned up, we got in the Porsche, and went to work. This felt weird. First off, I hadn't been in the Porsche in months, and I felt like my butt was just a few inches off the asphalt. Sitting this low, even going 40 miles an hour seemed like Mach speed. Sports car enthusiasts are demented, I'd take my pickup over this any day. Also, I think both of us were wondering how this 'working together' was going to pan out.

We arrived at the shop, and I got the coffee machine in the office going. I needed coffee to work. Heather went straight into the workshop, opened the doors and got busy taking off the hood, and front fenders. I got busy removing the doors. The work continued with minimal conversation. Rachel obviously didn't want to order me around, and I did not want to be ordered around. Something had to give. Eventually we broke for lunch and grabbed a quick burger at McDonald's.

As an engineer, I am trained to always think in the 'worst case'. The worst case was happening. Once I knew we were going to be stuck working together, I had asked TJ to stop by the sex shop beside the tattoo parlor and pick up something for me. He said that I now owed him big time, for making him even run the risk of being seen going in there. I had stuck this item underneath the rear seat when Rachel had left work yesterday to go to her Bikram class.

Once I had the doors off and the front bucket seats out, I began to take out the rear seat.

"Whoa!" I exclaimed loudly, while backing up like I'd seen a rattlesnake in the car. "Rachel you'd better come have a look at this," I said somewhat theatrically, but with concern in my voice.

She rolled out from under the front bumper where she'd been loosening some of the bumper bolts and came over to my side to see what I'd found. Lying on the floor pan, underneath where the rear seat had been, was a psychedelic colored, 12-inch long, female sex aid with the words 'Midnight Rider' printed on the side in white.

"What do you suppose that is?" I asked, while keeping a straight face.

"You really don't know?" she asked skeptically.

"Well, it looks strangely familiar, but I just can't place it."

Rachel was looking at me like I was an idiot, but I had to play this hand.

"You bonehead," she said somewhat annoyed. "That's a dildo!"

"Really? Are they supposed to be that long?"

"Only if you want satisfaction," she said. I would need to revisit this comment with her at a more appropriate time.

"You want to get it out of there?" I asked.

"I'm not going to touch that thing! Who knows where it's been?"

I reached in, grabbed it, and took my time examining this unrealistically long item.

"How does it work?" I asked.

"Use your imagination."

"I think we need to test it out to see if it works," I told her while grabbing the back of her coveralls.

The game was on! I still had a grip on the back of her coveralls, but she had kicked off her shoes and wriggled out of her coveralls like a snake shedding its skin. I chased her around the shop telling her to stop running, and that I'd be gentle, while trying not to laugh too hard. She was shrieking hysterically.

"Come back here! How do we know it works or not unless we try it out? Maybe we can clean it up and sell it?" I yelled while trying to pin her behind my 1956 pickup in the other bay.

She ducked down so that I couldn't see her. I looked under the truck, but she had climbed into the bed and took off for the other side of the shop, using me as a springboard. I finally trapped her in the parts room in the back, by the bathroom. The only way out was through me which, if we are being honest, she could have done in less time than it takes to blink an eye, except she was laughing so hard I thought she might pee in her shorts.

"Come on, 5 minutes of your time and we can see if this thing really works. You might even enjoy it! Where is your adventurous spirit?" I asked as I finally got hold of her. Putting the sex aid on the shelf, while keeping a good grip on her, I reached down for the zipper on her cut-offs, "You'll need to lose these," I explained.

"Jebell, if you touch me with that thing, I'll kill you!" she shrieked.

"Whip me, beat me, make me write bad checks, but we need to try this baby out! Who knows, maybe you really don't need a man. Think about how much emotional distress you could save with a pocket buddy like this!" I postulated.

"I'll wear my French Maid's outfit tonight if you let me go," she negotiated while still trying to regain her composure and her breath.

"And Little Bo Peep tomorrow night?" She was not the only one who could negotiate.

She agreed to the deal, so I zipped her back up and let her get back into the shop where she put on her coveralls again. She put her hand on her hip, pointed her finger at me, and was about to chastise me, but broke down laughing again and got back under the Chevelle. For the rest of the afternoon, you could hear chuckling whenever she happened to think about the 'Midnight Rider'. After getting this out of our system, the work on the Chevelle went fairly quickly. By the time we knocked off, the car had been stripped down to the unibody shell on the frame with the running gear still installed.

When we got home, I put the frozen pepperoni pizza in the oven while she put on her French Maid's outfit. Both the pizza and the outfit disappeared quickly.

Thursday showed itself. I was in my bed, with Rachel wrapped around me, snoring softly. The maid's outfit was flung all over the place. It was a night to remember, but duty called.

"Get up, sunshine, time to go to work," I whispered in her ear.

"I ache in places I didn't even know I had, Mr. Rose. What did you do to me last night?"

"I just let my imagination run wild. I was not aware that French maids provided half of the services I experienced last night. I think I may have a slipped disk," I commiserated.

"Serves you right taking advantage of an innocent young woman like that."

"Was there one of those here last night? I really can't remember a threesome. Don't forget the deal, Little Bo Peep tonight!" She rolled off of me with a groan.

"Can we have an ambulance on standby?" she asked as she gathered up her outfit and hobbled into her room to prepare for the day.

Once again, I headed down the stairs to get the coffee started and took out four bagels to heat up while getting out the cream cheese, bananas and honey. Remarkedly, Rachel came down the stairs with a spring in her step; perhaps we should have a costume night every week! She filled a cup with coffee as I took the bagels out of the oven, split them and put two in front of her and two in front of me. Chuckling, she said, "How did that sex toy get in the car? It still had the price tag on it, so I knew it was not a relic from the past."

"I knew that things were going to be a bit strained with us working in the same shop together, so when you went to yoga the night before, I asked TJ to stop by the sex shop, the one beside the tattoo parlor, and get the gaudiest, most outrageous, female sex aid that he could find. I put it under the rear seat before I came home. If things were going fine, I would not have had to use it, but we were not even talking, so I had to revert to Plan B."

Pointing her bagel at me, she said, "If you ever, ever chase me around my own shop with a big, psychedelic dildo ever again, I will hurt you in ways that you can't even begin to imagine. Do you understand me, Mr. Rose?" she asked while trying not to laugh and blow bits of bagel all over the kitchen.

I said that I did, but that I had a serious question to ask her. "Are 12 inches a minimal requirement for satisfaction, or can you get by on less? Enquiring minds want to know!"

After almost choking on her bagel, she informed me that she had been making do with less for a while now, but it wasn't the size of the ship, but the motion of the ocean that counts. I filed that mentally and avoided an inferiority complex.

We got to the shop and carried on with the Chevelle. It took both of us working together to remove the drive line and drop the transmission. Every time Rachel started getting bossy, I took the Midnight Rider out of my pocket and tapped her wherever I could tap her. When she saw what I was tapping her with she'd bust out laughing and threaten me with bodily harm. A much better working environment than yesterday morning. After lunch, Rachel was in the office organizing to get the transmission overhauled, while I removed the motor from the mounts.

About three, TJ and Heather showed back up, so we all went into the office to chat. I took the Midnight Rider out of my pocket, pointed it at Heather and said, "How'd the meeting go?" Heather's eyes got as big as Oreos, and for a second, she simply stared at the dildo. Rachel and TJ burst out laughing.

"You should have seen the look on your face, just before you went beet red," Rachel exclaimed.

Heather looked at me and demanded to know what I was doing with a big, psychedelic dildo. I told her the whole story, and everyone was laughing uncontrollably before I finished.

The bankers' meeting had gone well. Heather and TJ had a nice romantic evening strolling on the 16th Street Mall, and a dinner at Otra Vez Cantina on the mall. Being me, I said, "That's all fine and good, but you weren't chased around a shop by a madman with a huge sex toy, were you?"

"Give it to TJ, maybe later," was her clever riposte.

Heather went home to her place in town to unpack and get ready for tomorrow, while TJ, Rachel and I, went back to the Ranch of the Crazy Roosters. TJ begged off early to rest up for tomorrow, while Rachel and I retired to the living room. We curled up on the couch and watched some TV before I reminded her of the Little Bo Peep deal. She claimed exhaustion, so I got a rain check. Life was good.

Friday rolled around and it was going to be a busy day. Rachel spent the night in her bed, so I got up early and got things going in the kitchen. The resident zombie finally came to the kitchen and got her coffee infusion, with cheesy scrambled eggs before going to work. Thankfully, TJ was back, and I no longer had to take up his slack. Eventually working together would have caused issues between Rachel and I, so I was happy to pass the reins back to TJ.

Once the kitchen was back in order, I went out to the barn and got my Ed Brown rifle, the 870 Remington Express shotgun, my CZ 97BD pistol, and plenty of ammo for each. I also grabbed a box of clay pigeons and five old plastic milk jugs full of water. Arriving at my shooting range, I took the guns and ammo to the shooting tables. I then drove out to the 400-yard line and set out three full-sized silhouette targets. From a look at Google Earth and using the ruler function, it looked like my intended perch was going to be roughly 400 yards from the fire pit in front of the farmhouse's porch. I wanted to keep my 200-yard zero but see where I was printing at 400 yards.

Back in Kurdistan I had been using a Russian SVD Dragunov rifle, which is a semi-automatic rifle that automatically loads the next round, and your follow up shots are much quicker. My rifle is a bolt action that takes a bit longer for a practiced rifleman to get the second shot ready to go. As we had no idea how many bad guys were going to show up, I wanted to know what correction I would need. Also, the SVD fires the 7.62x54R round which, unless you are shooting very light rounds, generally has a muzzle velocity of around 2,500 feet per second. I would be shooting a 160 grain 7mm Remington Ultra Mag round with a muzzle velocity of 3,225 feet per second, so a much flatter shooting round. Saying that, the time in flight of my 7mm Remington Ultra Mag round would be about half a second at 400 yards, which is not a lot of time to get the second round chambered and on its way. I needed to be on my game when the time came.

Setting up behind my rifle I held the crosshairs between the eyes of the silhouette target on the left, let out my breath while gently squeezing the trigger and was slightly startled when the rifle fired. This is what you want, you do not want to be anticipating when the round will fire and concentrate on holding the crosshairs steady, and on your breathing. I did this four-more-times before leaving the bolt open and laying the rifle back on its case. Getting out my spotting scope I could see where the five rounds were grouped in about a 2-inch circle roughly 16 inches below a line drawn between the eyes of the target. I repeated this exercise on the remaining two targets before driving out to the targets to actually measure the drop from my aim point. The average drop for all three targets was about 16 inches to the center of each group, which was what I expected when using 160 grain Nosler AccuBond ammo. I drove back to the firing line and put away the rifle as it was sighted in to the best of my ability, without knowing the exact range I would be firing from.

Grabbing the 870 shotgun and the CZ pistol, I walked down to the pistol side of the range and set them down out of the sun while I went back to the truck and got out the box of clay pigeons. I found clay pigeons to be perfect static targets for shotguns and pistols, and they were fun to shoot. After lining up five clay pigeons on a board at 20 yards, I loaded the tube of the 870 with five rounds of double ought buck, jerked it tight into my shoulder and fired all five rounds while working the pump action as smoothly as possible. All five clay pigeons exploded. I did this a few more times, just for grins and giggles, before putting the shotgun down.

Going back to the truck I grabbed the five milk jugs full of water and carried them out to the 10-yard line and lined them up as well. I wanted to see how the special Kablooey rounds worked against a liquid filled target. Loading up a CZ97 magazine with my explosive rounds, I took careful aim at the center of the left-hand milk jug and let her rip. Granted, any large caliber bullet hitting a water filled milk jug is spectacular, but this exceeded my expectations. The jug simply exploded, and water went everywhere. This was good fun, so I did it four more times before locking the slide open on the CZ and walking up to the ex-milk jugs. I can only assume that the hydrostatic shock was multiplied several times by the explosive nature of the bullet as each milk jug was in several pieces. Usually, the milk jugs stay together with an entry hole and several splits, these rounds actually ripped the jugs to pieces and there were bullet fragments in many of the pieces. I began to think of patenting these rounds, assuming it is actually legal to even make them.

After cleaning up the ranges and sweeping up the firing line, I put the guns in their cases and put them back in the truck. I stowed the spotting scope and grabbed the remainder of the box of clay pigeons before I left for home.

After arriving home, cleaning the guns and putting the shooting stuff away, I took inventory of what I had, and what I needed, for the barbeque that evening. Piling back in the truck, I headed to Safeway to stock up. After Safeway, I stopped at the liquor store across from the shop to get several cases of beer and to see if Red had gotten bored yet. Apparently, he had, as the Camry wasn't in the alley. Leaving the liquor store, I drove across Roosevelt to the shop, to touch base. The unibody shell was coming off the frame and it looked to me like they were making progress. I asked when my truck would be done, Rachel threw a nasty shop rag at me, and I headed back out to my 'normal' truck and drove home.

Getting home, I took all the supplies into the kitchen and put everything away, the burgers and brats in the fridge, and the rest of the stuff in the pantry. I walked through the pantry, to the back door at the corner of the house, to check on Mr. Baskerville's water wok. It was dry, so I filled it back up so that he could wash down the deer and elk he must have been dragging down for sustenance.

Walking back out the front door, I loaded up the grill with mesquite chips and barbeque briquettes before going back to the kitchen, washing my hands and started making hamburger patties by the dozen. After making the patties, I sprinkled salt and pepper on both sides of each patty before stacking them in piles of four with waxed paper between them. I then put the stacks in a big tray and put them back in the fridge for later. Brats are low maintenance as far as preparation is concerned, unless you want to soak them in beer and diced onions, which I did not. Going into the barn,

I grabbed my second to last bottle of Laphroaig and took it to the house so that Peio could partake of it during the evening.

Fridays are usually a Krav Maga day for Rachel, but she had decided to let the boys recover for another week and would be home shortly after five for the barbeque. So, I'd start the fire just before five. I decided to take a shower and put on some clean jeans and a clean t-shirt before grabbing a beer and heading out onto the porch to kick back. While grabbing a beer I heard something slurping water out of the wok behind the house, so I figured Dog was still alive, well, and terrifying the local wildlife.

At four fifty on the dot, I fired up the grill and waited for the miscreants to arrive. First up was TJ, so I grabbed him a beer out of the cooler full of ice on the porch, and we just bullshitted for a while until the next heathen arrived. Up next was Bret. I tried to get him interested in cooking duties, but he just shrugged me off, grabbed a beer and went up to the porch to harass TJ in the shade. Peio came next, the apron in front of the barn was now full: my truck, Bret's Impala and Peio's Suburban. For the first time in recorded history parking may be an issue at El Rancho del Loco Gallos. I went into the house to grab the tray of burgers and brats, and also to fix Peio a glass of Laphroaig. Peio was already sitting on one of the old couches, so I handed him his drink before heading to the grill to load it up with meat.

Heather showed up next in her little A4 and parked beside TJ's truck in front of the bunkhouse. We all shut up while we watched to see what kind of slinky outfit Heather had worn to the festivities. She climbed out wearing Daisy Dukes and a tube top. This brought a chorus of approvals from the lechers on the porch. She walked up the steps to the porch, sat down beside Peio and raised an eyebrow at TJ, who quickly scooted into the kitchen to grab the bottle of white wine from the fridge, and prepare a glass for his squeeze. She was getting him trained, I'd need to have a word with the boy.

Rachel was fifth over the line and pulled the Porsche into the lean-to garage. Again, the porch went quiet in anticipation. She slowly put one bare leg out, waited a moment, then the other bare leg came out, then she unfolded from the car wearing what I think girls call a skort, which is like a pair of shorts, but the front looks like a wraparound mini-skirt. The skort was black. Her upper portions were covered in my black 1980/81 AC/DC Back in Black World Tour t-shirt, rolled up and knotted just below and dead center of those perfectly formed, grapefruit-sized breasts. Again, the peanut gallery exploded in applause. Rachel curtseyed and came over to the porch for a beer. On the way there, I got a slap on the butt and a peck on the cheek. The girl knows how to make an entrance. Of course, it helps if you are stunningly good looking and have legs that go from here to Cleveland. I'm fairly certain that I couldn't have pulled it off.

The first round of brats and burgers were ready for consumption, so I put them on a tray, took them into the kitchen, and put them on the island along with the condiments. Everyone came in after me and the feeding frenzy began. I had taken the second tray of meat out to the set beside the grill, when a rather tired looking 1968 Camaro drove into the courtyard, hesitated a minute then pulled over beside Heather's Audi. Nicholas unfolded himself from the bucket seat, then went over to the passenger's side and opened the door. I assumed it was Jemima that climbed out looking a bit apprehensive. Nick took her hand and they started toward the house. Jemima's Camaro needed some work, Jemima did not.

Now I don't care what anyone else says, mixed-race people just look better than us single race folks, they seem to get the best of each race's features and attributes. Jemima was no exception. She was of medium height, around 5-foot-6, with dusky skin, mellowed African facial features, and that unbelievably cool hair which doesn't know whether to be curly or straight and tends to run wild. It sort of looks like a loose Afro, and the way she was wearing it; it fell across one side of her face. She had slightly less curves than Rachel. Her figure was to Rachel's, what Rachel's was to Heather's, but at 5-½ foot tall it all came together in a very attractive package. The only problem I could foresee was that she was wearing a nice yellow sundress with a green bamboo design printed on it. I had no doubt that Heather and Rachel would sort that out sooner rather than later. She'd need to show some skin to run with those girls.

I walked out to meet them. "You must be Jemima, welcome to El Rancho del Loco Gallos. If you ever want to ditch this oversized chaperone you brought with you, please let me know, but don't tell Rachel!" I grinned while shaking Nick's hand and giving him a wink. Taking off my apron and handing the spatula to Bret, I pried Jemima's hand out of Nick's, she was still a little apprehensive, and I said, "Let me introduce you to the crew."

Walking up to the porch I introduced her to Peio, then TJ, Bret and finally to Heather and Rachel. They were already dialed in to Jemima's mixed-race issue, so without further ado they took her into the house, fixed her a plate and in less than 2 minutes had her deep in conversation. I turned to Nick and told him he may as well grab a plate and a beer as Jemima would be busy for a while. I grabbed a burger, a brat and a beer and circulated among the crew making sure everyone was doing well.

The girls were sitting on the couch in the living room, Jemima in the middle, and I could hear Rachel getting a bit excited, so I kind of eased over in that direction. The issue seemed to be that Jemima felt that being mixed-race relegated her to a less than equal status to that of the rest of the human race. Rachel was explaining that she was mixed-race, and that, as far as she was concerned, she was of an elevated status to the rest of the human race. Furthermore, Jemima's mother was also a little overprotective of her only daughter and was also apprehensive of her being up here with the riffraff.

Hearing all of this, I came up behind Jemima and touched her on the shoulder, causing her to leap out of her skin. I asked her if she had her phone on her. She said she did, so I asked her to call her mom, and let me speak to her. She did, but you could tell that she didn't want to. While the phone was ringing, I asked Jemima what her surname was, she told me it was Robertson. I was shocked! She had to be Tito's secretary's daughter!

The phone was picked up, "Hello?"

"Mrs. Robertson, this is Jebell Rose. We are having a barbeque at my ranch this afternoon, and earlier I invited Nicholas and your daughter to join us. They are here now, along with several other folks. During a conversation that your daughter was having with my significant other, Jemima indicated that you were somewhat apprehensive about her being up here with a bunch of strangers. I fully understand your concern. I would like to make a suggestion that may alleviate your concern, as well as get you out of the house if you do not have plans for the evening. May I share that suggestion with you?"

She hesitated for a moment, but then said, "Please continue."

"If I am not mistaken, you work in Tito Ramírez 's office. Mr. Ramírez will likely be arriving here sometime this evening. I could ask Tito to collect you on his way here, you could then have dinner with us, and you could see for yourself if we are suitable company for Ms. Jemima. What do you say?"

She thought about it for a minute, then replied, "If you are sure that this would not be an imposition on Mr. Ramírez or yourself, I will gladly accept. I do not think that I have been to a barbeque in years."

"I assure you that you will not be an imposition in the least, and I look forward to meeting you again. Let me give Tito a call, then I will let Jemima know what time he'll pick you up, and we'll see you shortly thereafter."

"Thank you, Mr. Rose."

"Just call me Jeb," I replied and handed Jemima her phone.

Pulling my phone out of my back pocket I called Tito. When he picked up, I told him the whole story, and told him that I would feed him if he would pick up Mrs. Robertson and bring her here. He told me that this was a very Christian thing to do, inviting Mrs. Robertson out for the evening. He said he would pick her up in 30 minutes. I relayed this to Jemima who called her mom and told her the plan.

Rachel's eyes were a bit moist as she reached around and put my phone in my back pocket with a little squeeze. "That was a nice thing to do," she said. I must be getting soft in my old age.

I mingled for a while, made sure that the food and drink was still flowing and turned the porch lights on. Rachel had fixed me a plate, and I was sitting next to Peio, when Tito's 1968 Fleetwood pulled into the courtyard, trying to find parking. He finally just parked it behind Rachel's Porsche. Tito, dressed in proper slacks, a long-sleeved shirt and proper Oxford brogues, got out and went around to the passenger door, opened it, and offered his arm to Mrs. Robertson. After closing the door, Tito walked her over to the porch where I took over and introduced her to everyone. Since none of us drinks to excess, I didn't need to worry about someone making a fool of themselves. I saved Peio for last and kicked Bret off the couch beside him so that Mrs. Robertson could sit next to him. Jemima had prepared a plate for her mom and brought it out while Tito was chatting to Heather and Rachel.

I keep a bottle of Don Julio Anejo tequila in the crate with Peio's Laphroaig, so I asked Tito if he'd like me to get it for him.

"Who drinks that swill? It is like paint thinner mixed with rat poison! I am ashamed it is associated with Mexico. What is Peio drinking?"

I told him that I kept some Laphroaig on hand for Peio.

"Now that is a proper drink for a man. Would it be too much to ask for about three fingers of that nectar in a tumbler?"

"Coming up," I told him.

Going back toward Peio, I heard Mrs. Robertson ask Peio what he was drinking. He told her that I kept some Laphroaig on hand for when he showed up. She asked if he thought that perhaps she could have a small glass.

I thought Peio was going to go into shock, "You drink Laphroaig?"

"Not often, as I really cannot afford it, but when I can, I like to read a book and sip it."

I looked at Peio and gave him a thumbs up, "I'll take care of it, Mrs. Robertson. Tito would like a glass as well." Note to self, restock the Laphroaig.

The barbeque was a roaring success if you rated it on how well Jemima seemed to come out of her shell, began to be corrupted by Heather and Rachel, and also the totally unexpected outcome of Mrs. Robertson and Peio chatting all evening, and really seeming to get along. Who would have thought that would happen? Eventually, Tito drove Mrs. Robertson and Jemima back to town, leaving only those involved in the upcoming dance with Irish Bob and his crew at the ranch.

Everyone took a seat in the living room again, and once again we went around the room giving our respective updates. The only item of interest was that Bret would apparently travel to Wyoming on Thursday but would actually be coming here to be collected by Peio late on Wednesday. Peio would arrange for the photo of the duffle bags full of money to be sent to Irish Bob. At that point the game would begin in earnest, and we could expect Irish Bob and company to descend on Cadillac Springs. Tito's boys would tip us off when they arrived.

Peio, TJ and myself decided to reconnoiter the site at the old farmhouse the next day and to make sure that nobody was camping there. We would need to ensure that the site remained uninhabited until the deed was done. I suggested that we post signs warning of a Hantavirus infection, where the county road entered the bowl which the farmhouse sat in. Rachel and Heather were already up for this after the run in with the meth lab bikers.

Nicholas was reminded that he would be running the gym from Thursday until Bret returned back on Saturday morning, a week from tomorrow. He'd need to man the phones and let everyone know that Bret was out of touch for a few days, and to just keep it vague.

Peio informed us that as far as he could ascertain, the Craic Crew mob was essentially composed of eight principals. Irish Bob and Red being two of them. We could rationally assume that all eight would come to the party and it was imperative, that none left it. If they all simply disappeared, the remaining lieutenants and sub-lieutenants would be in the dark. Without a doubt Irish Bob would not have told them where he was going, and that he was collecting several million dollars of untraceable cash. Everyone was told to keep vigilant, as everything would be in flux until we could confirm that the bad guys were in town, and Tito's crew could shadow them until the handover at the old farmhouse.

After this, it was getting late so Peio, Bret and Nicholas went home. Heather and

TJ stayed around and helped clean the place up before retiring to the bunkhouse, and Rachel and I relaxed on the couch. I had one more beer and Rachel had a final glass of wine. I reminded her that she owed me a Little Bo Peep rain check. She asked me how I could possibly be thinking about Little Bo Peep when we had just finished planning the demise of Irish Bob and company. I played the 'possibly my last chance to see her in that outfit' card, but it went nowhere, and she went up the stairs to her room shaking her head at my unbelievably one-track mind.

Saturday dawned, and I got up a little early to get the coffee set up before heading over to TJ's to make sure that he was up and running. Going back to my kitchen, I sliced some bagels in half and put them in the oven to warm up. TJ knocked on the door and walked in. We talked about our impending drag race, and compared numbers between our trucks, while we ate bagels and drank coffee. Rachel had not appeared yet, so I wrapped two bagels in foil and left them warming in the oven. There were still a few cups of coffee in the machine, so I didn't need to worry about that. Leaving a note saying that bagels were in the oven, TJ and I headed out to my truck to go collect Peio.

Peio was sitting on his front porch drinking coffee when we drove up, so he piled in the cab, and we drove up to the old farmhouse.

To put you back in the picture, the county road dead ends at the old gate to the farmhouse. The farmhouse sits in a small bowl in the mountains. The old gate is about a 100 yards due south from the farmhouse and is directly in front of it. About 10 yards out from the front porch, and in line with the old gate, is a firepit surrounded by football-sized stones which the high school kids had put in place over the years. The bowl around the farmhouse is cleared of vegetation except for some refrigerator-sized boulders sprinkled about, and the odd patch of serviceberry bushes. As you start getting higher and higher up the slopes north, east, and west of the farmhouse, you have the house-sized boulders from which the refrigerator-sized boulders had broken off in the past. Also, you start to have aspen groves sprinkled with spruce and pine.

The original outbuildings had collapsed into piles of rotten timber over the years and really did not form any noticeable feature.

While TJ and Peio went into the old farmhouse, I found an old barrel beside the house and drug it out to put it in the middle of the firepit. I then angled up the slope to the west of the house, looking for a good hiding place to set the rifle up to cover the fire pit. I'd gotten into the trees and found a nice boulder, the size of a good, two story house, with some brush and serviceberry bushes growing on top of it. To get to the top I had to start on the south side of the boulder, climb up about 5 feet to a lower shelf, then climb about another 25 feet or so to get to the top. The first shelf would have made a fairly good hide, but I wanted to be on top with a good view of the farmhouse and the surrounding area so that I could scout for Bob's marksman. The view from the lower shelf was obstructed to the north by the main body of the boulder.

From my position at the top, I found that I was almost due west of the old farmhouse with a good, unobstructed view of the porch and the firepit. Reaching into my backpack, I pulled out my trusty Bushnell Tour V4 Jolt rangefinder. This is a laser rangefinder built specifically for golf, but it works equally well for shooting out to 1000 yards, with an accuracy of plus or minus one yard. Taking it out of its case, I used the five-power magnification to find the barrel in the fire pit and hit the button. The readout showed I was 393.6 yards from the barrel. I took a few more readings to confirm the distance then put the rangefinder back in its case and put the case back in the backpack. As my rangefinder already compensated for the down angle to the target, I didn't have to figure out the angle, then get out my trusty Hewlett-Packard calculator, and do that 'cosine of the angle' thing to get my true horizontal distance to the target. People make a nine-act Greek tragedy out of shooting at an angle, either uphill or downhill. The only thing that you really need to keep in mind is that the range of interest to the shooter is only the horizontal distance to the target, and to adjust your zero accordingly. Sometimes being an engineer comes in handy.

Walking back down the slope to the house, I saw TJ and Peio by the fire pit discussing something. As I walked up to them, Peio asked if I'd found a suitable location. I pointed back toward the boulder and told him I would set up there, giving me a good view of the porch and fire pit. When he asked about the range, I told him it was just under 400 yards horizontally, and not an issue. He was a little worried about my shooting a light, 160 grain bullet, but I told him that it would be carrying about 2200 foot-pounds of energy when it hit from 400 yards, which would be roughly the equivalent of twice the energy of a 240 grain .44 Magnum round fired point blank. This seemed to satisfy him.

I asked them if they had gotten their plan together, and they had. The unknown was how many of Irish Bob's crew would actually come to the meeting, and where they would be standing. As TJ would be on the porch behind Peio on his left, and we figured that Irish Bob would be doing the talking to Peio directly in front of him, that

I would get the ball rolling by shooting anyone to the right of Peio while TJ took anyone to the left. Peio said that he would sort out Irish Bob. Anyone else who came to the party would be my responsibility.

I said this was a good plan as far as it went, but if there was more than one man to Peio's right, I would need to chamber a second round and shoot. The bullet would take about half a second to get there, and a lot could happen before my second shot arrived. We discussed finding a semi-automatic sniper rifle for me, but that would leave a trail and I would still have to zero it and get comfortable with it. The fact is, when my first round arrived it would make a noise like someone hitting a heavy punching bag with a baseball bat. When the guy dropped, there would be a moment of confusion which should give me time for a second shot if required. As both TJ and Peio would be armed, we should be okay. If the whole crew showed up, we'd need to figure something else out.

With this in mind, we piled back into my truck and drove to Peio's place where he fed us a brunch of homemade guacamole and tortilla chips. I love that stuff. Peio seemed to be in somewhat of a hurry and was to the point of shooing us out the door, when I asked him what the problem was. He said he had a lunch date.

I grinned and said, "Would that happen to be with your new Laphroaig drinking buddy from last night?"

"None of your business. Now get out of here and let me get ready," he retorted. TJ and I were laughing ourselves silly as we walked to the truck, when Peio came back to the front door and told me not to forget to stock up on Laphroaig. We laughed even harder.

Getting back to the house, TJ got out of the truck and said that he'd better go to the shop and assist Rachel before she worked herself into a lather. I told him to call me if they wanted me to do a lunch run. Walking into the house I tried to think of something constructive to do but couldn't think of anything. I knew I had to take Rachel to the range tomorrow and give her some instruction on the Remington 870 shotgun, but that was for tomorrow. I then started thinking that she should be carrying something with her until this was over and walking around with an illegally sawn-off shotgun was not the answer. Going out to the gun safe in the barn, I opened it and couldn't find my little CZ 2075 pistol. I had never misplaced a gun before, and it was driving me nuts. I tore the mezzanine level apart but couldn't find it. Finally, it dawned on me. Several weeks ago, I had the little shooter in the house when Jake the sheriff had dropped by. After he left, I'd stuck it in the magazine pouch on the side of the couch. Walking back to the house I went to the living room and, sure enough, the little CZ was nestled in the magazine pouch on the couch. Making sure that a round wasn't chambered, I set it on the kitchen island so that I would remember to take it with me tomorrow when we went to the range.

About this time my phone rang, and Rachel was requesting a Taco John's burrito run for a late lunch. Climbing back into the F-150 I drove to Taco John's, got six more burrito Supremes and headed for the shop, hopefully Rachel had not gone into insulin shock yet. As luck would have it, she was still conscious when I arrived, so we all piled around her desk to eat. While we were eating, I asked TJ if he had taught Heather how to shoot and given her a weapon. He said that he and Heather had gone to the range here in town a few times, and he'd bought her a subcompact Glock G43, and a pancake holster from Wolf Creek Leather, so that she could carry it. She'd also attended a concealed carry course given by Jake at the sheriff's office, and that she was now licensed to carry a concealed weapon.

Rachel gave me the 'what about me?' look, so I told her I had her covered, but she'd have to organize the course with Jake on her own. I also told her that we'd be going to the range tomorrow to get some practice.

After we had finished eating, I left the wrappers on Rachel's desk, turnabout is fair play, and went home to start the spaghetti that I had planned for dinner. TJ and Heather had plans, so it was just going to be Rachel and me. I had just finished cooking when I heard the Whale Tail growl into the courtyard, so I got out the plates, silverware and glasses while Rachel sashayed into the house. Looking over my shoulder, she said it smelled good. I told her to make herself useful and put ice in the glasses. After dinner we decided we really had nothing to do, so while I cleaned up, she went up and took a shower before coming back down in her shorts and another one of my t-shirts, the 1978 Thin Lizzy Live and Dangerous at the Rainbow one, and curled up on the couch while I put the movie Rio Lobo in the DVD player. We watched the Duke and cuddled until it was over, then went to bed and just slept for a change.

Sunday morning arrived without any fanfare, I nudged Rachel awake and told her we had to go shooting before it got too hot. She disagreed, so I shoved her over the side of the bed and onto the floor. She came up somewhat annoyed and was ready to beat the crap out of me, when I told her that it was for her own good. She got that 'I'm processing what you're saying' look, then she lost the tension in her shoulders and ambled off to her room to shower.

Surviving the first brush with death of the day, I got on clean jeans, my Colt Diavel t-shirt and some socks, before heading to the kitchen for the morning coffee and feeding ritual. I got the coffee sorted out and then made scrambled eggs on toast while waiting for her Highness to arrive. When she did, I watched carefully until I saw the caffeine taking effect before putting a plate of eggs and toast in front of her before backing away to a safe distance. I got a plate of my own, and a cup of java to wash it down with. About midway through breakfast, I was informed that if I ever unceremoniously shoved her off the bed and onto the floor again, that first off, I would be beaten black and blue, and secondly, I would not enjoy her company in my bed ever again. I thought that this was cruel and unusual punishment but had sense enough to keep my mouth shut.

Eventually she seemed to get this aggressive behavior out of her system, finished her coffee, and headed up the stairs to brush her fangs and get ready to go shooting. I finished my coffee while admiring her fine-looking tailgate going up the stairs, barely concealed by her silk dressing gown. I cleaned up the kitchen before going up to my room to do my morning ablutions before we headed out to the range.

Going back downstairs, I poured coffees into 'to-go' mugs, collected the little CZ 2075 I'd left on the counter yesterday, and took them out to the truck. I put the CZ in the glove box and stuck the mugs in the old school cup holders hung on the bottom of the window frames, before going into the barn and up to the mezzanine deck to get the cut-down 870 Remington shotgun, the box of remaining clay pigeons, some pistol targets and enough ammo to have some fun. Taking all of this back to the truck, I put them in the toolbox behind the cab and waited for Rachel to show up.

Eventually she came out of the house in her signature cut-offs, t-shirt and flip-flops. Today's t-shirt was the 1980 Tom Petty and the Heartbreakers 1980 Whiskey A Go-Go version. Climbing in the truck she made that twirling motion with her finger, which is Rachel-speak for 'Let's go'. So, we did. Arriving at the range, I laid everything out on the tables in the shade, then gave Rachel a detailed lesson on how the shotgun worked, how to reload it and how to work the pump action. Once I was sure that she could function the weapon to my satisfaction, I set five clay pigeons on a board 15 yards away. I then went back to the firing line and showed her how to properly shoulder the gun, concentrate on the front bead and squeezing, not jerking, the trigger. Once she had this down, I had her load five rounds into the weapon and chamber a round. This done, I told her to just shoot the clay pigeons.

As expected, she didn't pull the gun into her shoulder tight enough on the first shot and suffered the consequences of 12-gauge recoil. After cussing like a sailor while holding her shoulder, she tried again. She is definitely not one to admit defeat and let the gun get the best of her, so she tried again. This time she pulled the gun tight into her shoulder, and blew the first four pigeons, left to right, to smithereens. Giving me a high five, she told me to put out four new pigeons while she reloaded. She got the hang of it quickly and started having fun. I'd put pigeons at different ranges, and she'd transition left to right and dust them. At the end, I'd toss the pigeons into the air, and she'd try to nail them, not easy with a sawn-off gun, but she hit more than she missed.

Having expended our shotgun ammo, I had her lock the breech of the shotgun open and lay it on the bench. I then went over to the truck and got the CZ 2075 out of the glove box, dropped the magazine out of it, and started thumbing rounds into it. Rachel came over, grabbed the magazine out of my hands and said she had it covered, so I went out and put up two NRA 25-foot slow fire targets at the 10-yard line and walked back. Rachel was just slapping the magazine into the pistol. She told me to stand back, and she'd show me how it was done.

She wiggled herself into a proper Weaver Stance, which was stimulating to watch, got the gun in a good 'thumbs forward' grip, and fired off all ten rounds in a measured cadence. When the slide locked open, she turned and gave me a thumbs up. Walking to the left-hand target, all ten shots were in the seven-ring, or all in the black. I asked her to do the whole routine again, and again all ten shots were in the black.

Many women shoot instinctively and use the pistol like an extension of their index or trigger finger. They can generally hit what they are 'pointing' at. This was not the case with Rachel, she was obviously familiar with the Weaver Stance, the 'thumb forward' grip and how not to fixate on the sights, but how to mate the front sight with the target. I was curious and asked her how she learned all of this, as I hadn't taught her. She explained that her father had taught her how to shoot pistols when she was a teenager simply because he thought girls should know how to defend themselves. Since the last thing I wanted to do was try to teach her how to do what she could clearly already do, I packed up our stuff and we drove into town. Picking up TJ at the shop, we went for lunch at the local deli.

After lunch I dropped TJ back off at the shop and told him that since it was the weekend, his boss said that he could work on my 1956 pickup. Rachel said my stuff didn't make her any money and overruled me. It wasn't worth arguing about, and since it would probably be finished while I was in Kurdistan on my next hitch, I didn't.

Getting back to the ranch, I took the guns, the remaining clay pigeons, and the excess ammo into the barn and got busy cleaning and lubricating the guns. When I had finished, I took both the little CZ and the 870 back to the house. I put the shotgun in the office on top of the desk with a box of buckshot loads, then took the CZ into the kitchen, where Rachel was making sandwiches, and told her to load it and keep it with her in her backpack. She doesn't believe in purses.

We tidied up the house and our respective rooms before I got out the vacuum cleaner, and got busy with it, while Rachel dusted and polished the furniture. She does have some of that domestic DNA, but not a lot. After sorting out the house, Rachel went into the dining room office and got busy with the paperwork and bills for the shop, while I laid on the couch and read the latest Mark Greaney book. Eventually we heard the rumble of TJ's truck pulling in. Looking out the front door I could see that Heather was with him, so I defrosted four brats and four burgers left over from last Friday's barbeque for dinner.

Heather came straight over to the house to gossip with Rachel, while TJ went to the bunkhouse to clean up. I grabbed a couple of beers and took them to the porch, then set about firing up the grill. TJ arrived and we popped the top on the beers then sat on the couches and shot the breeze until the fire was ready, and I went inside to get the meat and started grilling. The girls finally came out to join us and while I cooked, they just chatted until the brats and burgers were done. I asked Rachel to go into the house and get the paper plates and condiments, since we had decided just to eat on the porch while the sun went down. All in all, it felt like it was a nice, relaxing afternoon, but underneath you could feel the uneasiness of the situation we had found ourselves in, and the knowledge that our thin veneer of civilized behavior would take a beating before it was all over.

Monday began the week which would see our plan either come to fruition or see some of us no longer in the land of the living. The quicker we could sort out Irish Bob and his crew, the quicker we could all get back on an even keel. It wasn't that our collective lifestyles had changed outwardly, but until the issue was resolved, we couldn't move ahead with our lives. It was also in the back of our minds that, even if everything went our way in the next week or so, eight people would die and disappear.

After breakfast, Rachel went to the shop to continue restoring the Chevelle, and I drove over to the gym to check on Bret and see how his pulse was beating. Going into the gym, I saw Nicholas over by the speedbag and detoured over to him. He thanked me for sorting out the issue with Jemima and her mom, to which I replied that he'd better take a second job as once Heather and Rachel got ahold of Jemima, she would start emulating their behavior and spending habits. I asked how Bret was holding up and he said, so far, so good. Like everyone else, he was ready for it to be over.

I left him at the bag and strolled over to the office. The door was open, so I knocked on the jamb and went in. Bret was on the phone but motioned for me to take a seat. Once he got off the phone, he looked at me and said, "It's coming to a head this week."

"Yeah," I replied, "we need to get this over and done with. How are you holding up?"

"Like a cat on a hot tin roof. I am not exactly comfortable about what is going to happen, but they brought it on themselves, and I want Alyshia safe and not looking over her shoulder."

"Speaking of Alyshia, have you spoken to her lately?" I asked.

"Spoke to her yesterday from Tito's office. It sounds like she is doing fine, but she wants to come home. She'll be okay for a week or so."

"Alright, good to hear that. If you need me for anything before your trip, give me a ring, otherwise I'll see you on Wednesday."

We shook hands and I headed out the door. I then drove over to Tito's office. Walking in the door I said hello to Mrs. Robertson. We chatted for a few minutes, and she thanked me for the invitation to the barbeque last Friday. I told her the pleasure was all mine and that we'd do it again soon. She also told me that Jem had really come out of her shell over the weekend, and she wanted to thank Heather and Rachel when she got a chance. I told her not to worry, the girls had really enjoyed having Jem over, as they felt there was a gender inequality issue at these barbeques. She just laughed and told me I could go see Tito.

I walked into Tito's office and shook his hand when he came around his desk. As usual, he was nattily attired in black slacks, a white button-down shirt, no tie and expensive loafers. A very nice sport coat was on the coatrack behind the door.

After a few pleasantries, I got down to business. "How's the shadow on Red going?"

"Our friend is still in town, although he has changed hotels to the Regal 8 Motel, and has changed rental cars to a late model blue Malibu. We are on him like the white on rice."

"Tito, you realize that Bret will be disappearing Wednesday evening, apparently heading up to Wyoming to get something that these jokers think belongs to them. Once he gets back to Cadillac Springs on Saturday, the game will well and truly be on. We desperately need to know the minute his compadres show up in town, we'll need to know exactly how many there are and where they are, at all times. The game will be over a few days after they arrive, but while that crew is here, we need to know where they're at."

"There is no need to be secretive about your plans, Jeb. Peio has told me about Bret's problem, and as much about the plan to resolve it as he decided that I should know. We'll keep a blanket on all these men until the game is over. You have my word."

I replied, "Thanks, Tito, your word is all that I need. I am not sure that we could have pulled this off without your help." Making a shooing motion with his hand, "What are friends for?"

After picking up six Big Macs and three large fries, I drove back to the shop to feed Rachel and TJ, and also to see if they had done anything with my old truck. Parking outside the bay doors I grabbed the McDonald's bags, held them high and said, "Lunch is served!"

We congregated in the office and began to eat. Rachel was giving TJ a list of things which he needed to do that afternoon, while she was ordering paint and organizing to have the rebuilt transmission shipped back from Denver. Essentially TJ had to rebuild the motor and get the body shell and fenders ready to paint. As I had nothing better to do, I offered to get on the engine so that TJ could start prepping the body to paint. He gladly took me up on the offer. From my side, I needed to keep my mind off the Irish Bob issue and building engines had always been therapeutic for me.

So, while Rachel did paperwork and made phone calls, TJ got the unibody and other bits into the paint booth and prepped, and I got the bottom end of the 454 motor put back together. At five we called it a day, I went back to the ranch, Rachel went to Bret's gym for her boxing session, and TJ stayed to do some work on his truck. As I didn't feel like cooking, I stopped by the Subway shop on the way home and picked up four meatball sandwiches on oregano bread. If TJ and Heather didn't show up, the extra sandwiches were good for a day if I left them in the fridge.

I needed to keep myself occupied or I'd go nuts waiting for things to happen. I checked my untraceable e-mail account with the Jankowski Group, nothing there. I filled up Dog's water wok, and finally just went to the barn to clean it up again, although I really hadn't done anything in there since Rachel had taken over my 1956 F-100 project.

I heard the growl of the Porsche pull into the lean-to garage next to the barn, so I turned out the lights and walked around the corner to see if Rachel needed any help carrying stuff into the house. She handed me her gym bag while reaching in and grabbing two pizzas. While walking into the house I told her that great minds think alike, as I had picked up sandwiches on the way home. It seemed like neither one of us was in the mood for much of anything that evening so we each heated up a sandwich and two pieces of pizza, got a glass of sun tea, then parked in front of the TV to watch 'The Magnificent Seven', one of the greatest films of all times. Once the movie was over, Rachel actually helped me clean up before we called it a night and retired to my room.

Tuesday morning rolled around bright and clear, and I decided to follow Rachel to work so that I could get more done on the 454 motor. Our grab ass sessions were becoming few and far between due to the tension building as the end of the game got closer. I was to the point that I'd personally whack Irish Bob if it meant I could chase Rachel around the house scantily clad again. A man can only put up with so much sexual non-abuse.

TJ came in, said hello and retreated to the paint booth to continue with his prep work. I flipped the motor around on the engine stand and started working the top end. Rachel was in the office keeping the place running. Time passed, and before I knew it Rachel was at the door to the office with Double Z bags in her hands saying, "Lunch is served!" for a change.

As we ate at the desk, Rachel wanted an update from TJ and I. TJ told her that he should be ready to start painting by next week, and I told her that the motor should be back together by the end of the week. She seemed happy with that. She told us that the next project was not a restoration, but a hotrod build on a 1950 Mercury. Apparently Tito had called and asked if Rachel could take a rolling chassis, in good condition, and make a unique hotrod for one of his favorite nephews, who had just been accepted at the University of Denver. She really couldn't say no after all the help Tito had been giving us, but Rachel hates building cars to anybody else's specifications. Tito knew this and told her that she would have total control over the build, his only caveat was that it could not resemble a cheap Mexican lowrider piece of crap. Rachel told Tito that she'd call him for the rolling chassis after she had finished up the Chevelle. Rachel lives for total control of a hotrod build, as opposed to the much more lucrative, but far less creative, numbers matching restorations. The Mercury was bound to be interesting.

Again, we wrapped up at five, and TJ and I headed home in our trucks while Heather and Rachel went to sweat out their poisons in the Bikram yoga studio. TJ went into the bunkhouse to do whatever it is he wanted to do, while I set up in the kitchen to make a large batch of unbelievably unhealthy macaroni and cheese with bacon bits. I hadn't done this in a while, but it seemed everyone was ready for a change. Once the mac was finished, I made a large bowl of salad to drive away the guilt, and put it in the fridge. Grabbing a beer, I went and sat on the porch to while away the time until the girls arrived. Eventually TJ showed up, grabbed a beer and we just sat on the porch and watched it get dark.

Hearing the Whale Tail and the A4 coming up the driveway, I went into the kitchen and started heating up the mac while putting the salad and a variety of dressings on the island. TJ had followed and was putting out the plates and silverware. The girls came in jabbering about something that had happened at the yoga studio, but finally got seated at the table. Rachel's eyes got big when I set out the mac. For a fitness freak she loves food which is, shall we say, not usually available on the training table. She told me that she knew that she loved me for some inexplicable reason, before digging in. Everyone had a laugh, then we all dug in.

Rachel and Heather offered to clean up, so TJ and I grabbed another beer and headed back out onto the porch. Looking off into the night, TJ said, "You know, if things go tits up later, we may not be doing this for much longer."

"At the risk of telling you something that you likely already know, don't miss your shots and we'll be fine," I elucidated sagely.

"Good point."

Wednesday was the actual start of the game, as today was the day that Bret would vanish and apparently head to a small town in Wyoming to get Irish Bob's cash. I think everyone was thinking about this since there was not much small talk at breakfast, or at the shop.

During lunch I ran over to the gym and huddled up with Bret and Nick to discuss how we were going to get Bret to my house without anyone being the wiser. We decided that I would call Bret when I was about to leave the shop. He'd get his bags sorted out and put them beside the rear fire door, which accessed the alley behind the gym. When I was a few blocks away, I'd call Tito and have him do a quick check with his guys to ensure that Red was nowhere near. If he was, Tito's bunch would somehow keep him occupied. I'd then ring Nick that I was close. I would drive down the alley slowly, with the passenger's door facing the fire exit. When I was just coming even with the fire exit, I'd open the passenger door and Bret would jump in and stay below the dash. Nick would follow him out and throw the bags into the bed of the truck as I continued on. This would limit Bret's exposure, and I would not have to stop. Bret's car would be left in the parking lot in front of the gym. This would add to the illusion that he was on a secret mission to get the cash. Nick would let us know if anyone came in looking for Bret.

Back at the shop I explained to TJ and Rachel what I had in mind, then kept wrenching on the Chevelle motor until close of business. At five I called Bret and told him I was headed his way. I then called Tito for an update on Red's location. As luck would have it, Red was in the drive-thru lane at McDonald's and was third in line. He should be out of play for the time necessary. Driving into the alley I slowed down to a walk and opened the passenger's door just before coming abreast of the fire exit. As planned, Bret came straight out of the door and into the passenger's footwell, while Nick threw his bags in the back and shut the door. I motored to the end of the alley, hung a right on the side street and was back on Roosevelt Avenue, headed to the ranch, in less than a minute after I had entered the alley.

Heather and Rachel were staying on routine and would be headed to the gym for a boxing session. TJ was on the porch when we arrived to make sure that everything had gone to plan, he also had been into my house uninvited and had a cold brew ready for Bret and I. We just left his bags in the bed of the truck and sat on the porch waiting for Peio to show up.

Around seven thirty, Peio showed up in his old Suburban. While TJ and Bret loaded Bret's gear into the Suburban, I went to the barn and got out my last bottle of Laphroaig to give to Peio. Needless to say, he asked me if I had ordered more, which I had. With that done, Peio and Bret said goodbye and headed up to Peio's place. The game was now on.

CHAPTER 25

THURSDAY, TJ AND RACHEL WENT to the shop as usual, while I just hung around the house waiting for something to happen. I knew that it was too early for that, but I really didn't want to get involved in anything else, just in case. Eventually, common sense won out. Bret would need to be at Peio's place at least until tomorrow before sending out the photo of the money. I might as well do something constructive, so I pulled the F-150 into the barn, changed the oil and oil filter, changed out the air filter and tuned the engine, before I admitted that I was simply burning daylight and had one of the leftover Subway sandwiches for lunch.

Going back to the pantry freezer I got three big steaks out to thaw and cut up some potatoes for hash browns. I wanted to get prepped for dinner, although Rachel would be going to yoga later and would not be back until seven thirty or so.

Red the Watcher would have a day off today, since Bret had called Bob earlier in the week and confirmed that he would be heading to Wyoming yesterday or today. Bret disappearing would have been expected.

Finally, I just laid on the couch, grabbed my Janet Evanovich novel, and read a few chapters before falling asleep. I woke up when I heard TJ arrive. Since it was six forty-five, I got the grill going and made the hash browns. TJ came over when he saw me kicking around, but by mutual consent, we were not drinking any more beer until this thing was over. We settled on a couple of Cokes and sat on the couches until the girls drove up in separate vehicles. I informed everyone that there were only three steaks, and I wasn't sharing, so they'd have to figure out the rationing on their own.

Turns out the girls weren't too hungry, so TJ and I got a steak while the girls shared one. The hash browns were a nice change.

We paired off and went to our respective abodes. I had told Rachel that I was tense and bored waiting for this thing to kick off. Dr. Feelgood was back on call, and she decided a back massage and heavy petting were recommended. She didn't get an argument from me.

Friday, I got Rachel out the door in running order, then took a run up to Peio's to see what was going on. I got there around ten and used the door knocker to get someone's attention. Peio answered the door, then showed me into the kitchen where Bret was scrambling eggs. Since I really had not eaten breakfast, I asked him if he'd make me a plate as well. I then grabbed a mug from the cupboard and got a cup of coffee before sitting down. After breakfast we took our coffees to the back porch before getting down to business.

First, I asked if they had sent Irish Bob the photo of the duffle bags full of money yet. Peio said that he wanted to let Irish Bob stew for a few more hours, with Bret apparently out in the wind, before sending the photo. He wanted Irish Bob well and truly hooked. I then got down to my real reason for visiting, I wanted to know exactly what the plan was once Irish Bob and his crew showed up in Cadillac Springs, and specifically, if Bret needed to be physically present at the farmhouse.

Peio said that until Bob and his crew were actually in town, we could not work out a timeline, but essentially it would go down as we had discussed earlier. First, once Bob and his crew were in town, Tito's crew would put a blanket on them and let us know their movements. Bret would stay out of sight to ensure that they did not try to grab him before the handover. After a short period of time, Bret would call Bob and let him know that he had the money and was ready to hand it over. At no point in the conversation would Bret allow Bob to determine the location of the handover. Eventually Bret would give Bob the GPS coordinates for the farmhouse and tell him that the meet would take place the following morning at eight o'clock.

Peio would then call Rachel. The girls would take a run up to the farmhouse and ensure that there were no campers or high school kids there, if there were, they would give them the Hantavirus story and get them moving out. Once they confirmed there were no other people in or around the farmhouse, they would put up the Colorado Department of Health and the Environment signs, which we still had from the meth lab incident, on the porch of the farmhouse, at the gate where the county road ended, and on either side of the side of the gravel road approaching the house. Hopefully, nobody would question the signs, or camp at the farmhouse, until the deed was done.

Once the time and place for the handover were settled, I would need to get my kit up to Peio's place, then take one of his four-wheelers cross country to the farmhouse, so that no unexplained tire tracks were on the gravel road at the end of the county road. I would be set up on my boulder long before the sun came up. In the meantime, Bret, TJ and Peio would also make their way up to the farmhouse long before sunrise and get settled in. Peio and TJ would be armed with their choice of handguns with three spare magazines apiece in case things went haywire. Bret would not be packing, since he hated guns, and would hopefully be out of the way when the shooting started.

The girls would watch the county road passing by my driveway. They would let Peio know when Bob and his crew passed by using Iridium 9555 satellite phones provided by Peio, one with Rachel and one with Peio. Tito's boys would have passed Rachel the make, model, color and license numbers of any vehicles they associated with Bob and his boys. Once Rachel called Peio and told him that Bob and company were headed toward the old farmhouse, and how many there were, Bret would place an old chair we had found in the farmhouse just outside of the firepit, with the back toward the house. The blue duffle bags seen in the photo sent to Bob would be in the firepit. Bret had to be outside and visible. As far as Irish Bob was concerned, nobody else was involved in the handover and Bret would be easy to take care of once the handover was completed. We wanted him to be over-confident and cocky.

Now, when Bob and his boys showed up, things could get interesting. They could either drive directly up to the firepit, or they could stop at the gate, leaving a man there to watch the road while the rest walked to the firepit, or some combination thereof. I would need to prioritize my targets. Eventually some, or all, of the crew which Bob had brought along would walk up to the firepit and start a dialogue. At the instant they got to the firepit, Peio and TJ would walk out of the front door of the farmhouse. Peio would walk up to the firepit behind Bret, while TJ moved to the left of the front door while remaining on the porch, giving him a good field of fire. Again, this could go sideways in a hurry if the bad guys went for their guns at this point. We'd need to be very alert while everyone was getting positioned at the firepit. Assuming that everybody realized that they were now at the negotiating stage, Bret would walk back into the farmhouse. Peio would take his seat and we would be at the penultimate stage of the plan.

I would start the ball rolling by shooting the guy furthest right from Peio's perspective, when I pulled the trigger was up to me, but I could not let them get their guns out. The first guy would be hit before the sound of the shot reached the pit. It would sound something like a cinder block dropped in wet cement; both TJ and Peio were familiar with the sound. Once they heard it, TJ would start shooting folks from left to right, from Peio's perspective, and Peio would take out Irish Bob. By this time, I would have jacked in another round, and I would be working from right to left. If a guy was left at the gate, I'd have to address him as well. Once the shooting was over, Peio's sheepherders would come out of the hills to clean up the mess and sanitize the area, so that the Craic Crew boys would simply disappear.

Peio now brought up something that we were all thinking about but had not mentioned. What if all eight members of the Craic Crew were not at the farmhouse? We had to hit them all at roughly the same time or our plan wouldn't work. Peio said that he would contact Tito immediately after the event to get an update on any members who hadn't shown up at the farmhouse, and have Tito grab them. As far as plans went, it was the best we could come up with at the moment, but as soldiers say, no plan ever survives contact with the enemy, so we'd need to be ready to adapt as events unfolded.

I thanked them for breakfast and told them to let me know as soon as Irish Bob got to town. I then got in my truck, drove to the shop and briefed TJ and Rachel before heading over to the gym to check that everything was cool with Nicholas. That done, I called Tito to get an update. Red was still watching the gym and the shop but didn't seem too energetic. This was to be expected as Bret was still 'out of town', and the photo of the money bags would only have been sent to Irish Bob within the last few hours. Once he started getting antsy it would likely mean that Irish Bob was on his way.

I hit the KFC for some comfort food to take away, I then headed back to the house to wait. Deciding that waiting was unproductive, I got out the little CZ, the Remington sawn-off, my Ed Brown rifle, my CZ97, and re-cleaned and lubricated each one. I checked ammo. I did a lot of useless tasks to keep from going nuts.

Eventually TJ showed up after work and we sat on the porch and shot the breeze until Rachel showed up about seven thirty, after her Krav Maga workout. I went into the kitchen and made grilled cheese sandwiches to go with the leftover macaroni and cheese. After dinner, TJ said he had things to do in the bunkhouse, so Rachel and I cleaned up the kitchen and then parked on the couch to watch Sniper, with Mark Wahlberg. Maybe I could pick up some tips. The only thing I took from the movie was that left-handed shooters should not be shooting right-handed bolt guns. I already knew that. Turning off the TV, I headed up the stairs to bed. Rachel had become bored with my movie and had gone to bed in her room. I really needed this thing to be over before all my hormones left me for lack of meaningful employment.

During the Saturday morning coffee and breakfast ritual, Rachel informed me that out of the goodness of her heart, she and TJ would be spending the day working on my truck. Furthermore, as I had no creative input into the project, that I should stay away from the shop until it was finished so as not to ruin the surprise. Fair enough, but I told her if they painted it pink, she'd be looking for new digs. She just poked out her chest, ran her hands over her butt, and said she didn't think so. She obviously required some disciplining; I'd have to sort that out once this other thing was finished. I looked forward to it.

I was drinking coffee while standing on the porch, when she came out the door to go to work. I got a hearty slap on the butt, a peck on the cheek and a big smile, which is not bad for first thing in the morning. Now I had to figure out how to stay occupied, and the shop was out of the picture. My cell phone rang. It was back on the kitchen island, so I walked back into the house and picked it up.

"Hello."

"Jeb, Bret here. Bob got the pictures of the money bags yesterday afternoon. He's chomping at the bit to get here, but I told him that I would not be back in town until Monday morning. We think that the handover will happen Tuesday. Can you let all the players know?"

"No problem. Let's all meet at Peio's place around five o'clock Monday afternoon just to make sure that we are all on the same page."

"Gotcha."

Since I was banned from the shop, I called Rachel and gave her the update along with the plan to meet at Peio's place at five in the afternoon on Monday. I also asked her to pick up some pizzas for dinner.

Driving into town, I stopped by the gym and let Nick in on the update. I called Tito to tell him that things were coming to a head, that the out-of-towners may be on their way, and to keep an eye out for them. He said Peio had already called, so his boys had been told to stay sharp.

Getting back to the ranch I once again had nothing to do, so I checked Dog's water wok, cleaned the house up some more, then went out to the barn and got my old ghillie cape out of the gun locker and began working it over to blend in a bit more with the vegetation around the old farmhouse. A ghillie cape is simply a camouflage cape designed to blend in with the background from which you will be shooting from. It is simple, but effective, and necessary. You modify it to fit the environment by plugging in local twigs and leaves from the area you'll be working in.

Putting it away, I locked up the gun safe and walked back to the house. Admitting defeat, I got out my Janet Evanovich novel and caught up with Stephanie Plummer and her crew while sitting on the porch drinking tea. TJ and Rachel eventually showed up, and neither of them would tell me a damn thing about my truck. I took the pizzas inside and put them in the oven to keep warm while we waited for Heather to arrive. Going back out and sitting on the porch we discussed the plan for the next few days, but none of us really wanted to talk about it. The plan had been hashed and rehashed in our minds. The fact that the plan could go sideways, at many different points along the timeline, was something that we couldn't plan for and didn't really want to think about.

Heather finally arrived, so we retired to the kitchen to eat pizza and drink tea. I was missing my beer, but that could wait until after the big event. The girls chatted about fashions, work-outs and shoes, while TJ and I talked about whose truck would be the coolest, fastest, the biggest chick magnet, and so forth. At the mention of 'chick magnet', we both got the look that said, 'You will never try to entice any other chicks into your trucks if you know what is good for you.' We laughed. Jealousy can be a healthy thing.

Sunday dawned. I got out of bed carefully and let Rachel sleep while I got dressed and went downstairs to fire up the coffee machine and make up some pancake batter. After putting out plates, silverware and all the stuff which you may want on your pancakes, I crept back up to my room and set about waking Rachel up. This took a while as she is definitely not a morning person. She finally kicked into gear and walked to her room to get ready for the day. I watched her walk away. There is something about seeing an incredibly sexy woman with long legs, dressed in a short nighty, walking away. Giving my head a shake, I went back downstairs to make pancakes, pour orange juice and slice bananas.

Rachel eventually came down the stairs and walked directly to the coffee machine without a word. Filling a mug, she sat down at the end of the island and got half the mug down her neck before the spark of life returned. This was my cue to load up a plate with flapjacks and get it in front of her. After putting butter, honey, banana slices and walnuts on her pancakes, she dug in. Once the sugar reached her bloodstream, she asked me what I was going to do today. I told her that I really didn't know. It was the calm before the storm, and I really had nothing on my plate for today. She said she needed to get away from the situation, and the town, for a while and suggested that we go to the Glenwood Hot Springs Resort hot springs and soak, before having dinner at the Brava Modern Trattoria. I said it sounded like a good idea. First, I could ogle her in the new bikini she bought when her and Heather were on their girls' day out, and secondly, I'd get some good Italian food that I had not cooked for a change. The downside was that if I fooled around with Rachel in the hot springs, it would take a while to recover so that I could exit the pool without embarrassing myself. You've got to pay to play.

She went back upstairs and threw on some cut-offs and one of her girly t-shirts, as opposed to one of my collectable rock and roll ones, and packed a daypack full of stuff for the outing. I went to my room and did roughly the same thing, except for the girly t-shirt part. I wore my fashionable black Sig Sauer P220 version. We piled in the truck and headed to the Glenwood Hot Springs Resort.

If you've never been to the Glenwood Hot Springs Resort, you need to make a plan to go there one day. It is extremely relaxing, even if it is snowing. You're in pools fed by hot springs, so it makes no difference what the weather outside is doing. That said, on a nice sunny day, it is simply a great way to burn daylight. Afterwards, when you get out feeling like a boneless chicken, you just go across the river to the old town and grab a drink and a meal before heading home.

We got to the resort and paid the $23.75 adult ticket fee each for the day, then Rachel headed to the women's change room, and I headed for the men's locker room. Needless to say, I was changed and in the pool 15 minutes before Rachel appeared. Now I am biased, but Rachel is an extremely good-looking woman in that natural, girl-next-door, healthy sort of way, as opposed to the 'glamour girl' nonsense you see in magazines or on TV. That long black hair just accents that honey colored Chinese-Israeli complexion, and her body is fit and sexy from all that yoga, boxing and Krav Maga stuff. Also, I hate enormous breasts on women, they look like unnatural growths. Rachel has perfect, pert, grapefruit-sized breasts. To top all of this off, she was wearing, what I found out later, was a Wicked Weasel Electric Palms Tri top and Brazilian bottom bikini. You put that girl, in that bikini, have her walk out in public, and what happened, happened. The pool went dead silent while she walked over to me and slithered into the pool. The guys were in hormonal shock and the women were simply jealous.

Now every guy worth his salt loves this stuff, my girl just turned every head in the pool old enough to drive, and many that were not quite there. It was like back in the days of drive-in movies when your girl walked to the concession stand, and nobody watched the movie until she disappeared from sight. Which was repeated when she walked back to your hotrod. You just feel like the king of the world.

Anyhow, we soaked in the pool for a while before getting out and laying in the sun on the lounge chairs provided. We then got back in the pool to soak again, at which time I tried to peel her bottoms off underwater. This brought forth a shriek and a half-hearted slap. She didn't let me get the bottoms off, but she dragged out the struggle for quite a while. After a few minutes of this, Rachel had enough and went to the changing room to get dressed. I, on the other hand, had to sit in the pool for an additional 15 minutes so that my pointy bit wasn't too noticeable, and then I hobbled to the locker room with my towel in front of me.

Meeting in the lobby, we walked hand-in-hand out to the truck, and then drove across the river to the old part of town, until we could find some parking near the Brava Modern Trattoria. Once we were seated in the restaurant, and could smell the cooking, we became ravenous. Soaking in a hot spring will do that to you. For starters, she had the Calamari Fritti, and I had the Mussels Fra Diavalo. Tasty. For our main courses, Rachel chose the Linguine al Frutti di Mare while I had the Shrimp and Lobster Ravioli. Both were outstanding.

After a fantastic meal, we drove back home feeling supremely satiated. Getting home, I parked on the apron and grabbed our backpacks. Walking onto the porch, Rachel turned to me and said with an innocent grin, "I have my new bikini on under this pair of shorts and this t-shirt. Want to try your luck getting me out of it again?" There is such a thing as a rhetorical question.

"I only failed originally because you screamed like a little girl and everyone was looking at us," I said in my defense. "I'll meet you on the couch as soon as I dump these packs in our rooms," I said with a lecherous grin.

I don't think she was fighting as hard as she could have, as I had her out of her cut-offs, t-shirt and Wicked Weasel Electric Palms Tri top and Brazilian bottom in just under 5 minutes. We slept well that evening.

Monday finally arrived. Rachel and TJ again went to work while I did one more check of my gear to make sure that I had all the kit I was going to need. Packing it in a proper backpack, I rolled my ghillie cape up and tied it on the bottom. Going out to the barn, I went to the gun safe on the mezzanine deck, and got the Ed Brown rifle out and put it in a drag bag along with a box of Nosler Trophy Grade 160 grain AccuBond ammo for the 7mm Remington Ultra Mag. The CZ97BD .45 pistol, along with two spare mags and a box of my special Kablooey exploding rounds came next. Putting the ammo in a burlap sack, I took the guns and ammo back to the house and laid them out on the kitchen island by my backpack and ghillie cape. Three bottles of water and six energy bars rounded out the load in the backpack.

Going into the dining room office, I grabbed the 870 Remington shotgun off the desk where I had left it, jacked all five rounds out of it, then reloaded it again with the double ought buck rounds I had ejected. There were still a full box of buckshot loads on the desk if she would need it, but I hoped that she wouldn't. She was carrying the little CZ 2075 with her, so she should be safe until this thing was finished.

TJ and Rachel closed up an hour early so that they could get to Peio's for the five o'clock meeting. The bank closed at four, so Heather didn't need to do anything out of character to make the meeting. I left my place at four thirty with the drag bag, the backpack, the rest of my kit, and drove up to Peio's. Everyone was already there when I drove up and were already seated around the table on the back porch waiting for me. Peio had made a big bowl of taco meat and had set it out on his kitchen table along with taco shells, chopped up onions, tomatoes, cilantro, sliced limes and grated cheddar. Everyone grabbed a paper plate and made their tacos to taste before heading back out on the porch. A big pitcher of tea was on the table as well.

You could feel the current vibrating around the table while we ate. Everyone was amped up and ready to get the deed done, but at the same time we were all a little apprehensive as our plan could go sideways due to a variety of circumstances beyond our control.

After we'd eaten, Peio got down to business. He'd gotten a call from Tito; Irish Bob and six others had arrived in Cadillac Springs earlier in the day. Counting Red the Watcher, this gave him a total crew of eight guys. They had all checked into the Regal 8 Motel and had taken four rooms on the same floor as Red. Tito had them blanketed by his guys and would keep Peio informed by sat phone as to their movements. Peio had given Tito an Iridium phone as well.

Bret would phone Bob later in the evening to give him the GPS coordinates and directions to the farmhouse. Bret would wait until after Heather and Rachel had run up to the farmhouse after this meeting and ensured that there were no campers or kids there, then put up the Hantavirus warning signs. Peio did not want to chance giving

Bob the location before that and run the risk of him sending up his crew at the same time that Heather and Rachel were doing their thing. We expected Bob to send up a few guys to reconnoiter the site this evening, so Peio had a couple of his sheepherder buddies watching the farmhouse to ensure that they did not leave someone behind to surprise us, and also to let us know if any campers or kids showed up later in the evening. Either way, we would know the situation before we made our move.

Peio then gave Rachel an Iridium 9555 satellite phone and made sure that she knew how to use it. Once Rachel and Heather got the signs put up, Rachel would call Peio and let him know that she and Heather had completed their tasks. At which point the girls would go back to the ranch and start watching the county road as it goes by my driveway. Tonight, they would watch for Bob's crew doing a recon and let Peio know.

TJ seemed to always be ready and Peio didn't quiz him too much. They obviously had a history together of some sort, and apparently this was good enough for Peio. I, on the other hand, was grilled fairly well. Both Peio and TJ went over my equipment and kit. This did not bother me in the least. In my mind, the more eyes on your equipment, the better. I told them that I planned to leave Peio's house around four the following morning on the four-wheeler and get to within a mile of the boulder I would set up on. I'd then walk the rest of the way. If none of Bob's boys had stayed behind earlier, I'd be in place long before daylight. If someone had been left behind, I'd have to sort him out and then get set up. Regardless, I'd be in place by the time my services were required. I did ask them to make sure that the barrel I'd placed in the firepit to use my rangefinder on was moved beside the farmhouse. I did not want anything in the way when the shooting started.

There was nothing else to be said, so the girls left to check out the farmhouse for unwanted visitors and to put up their signs. About 15 minutes after they had left, Tito called to say that Irish Bob had rented a late model silver Dodge Caravan. This meant that they had this vehicle as well as Red's late model blue Malibu. Peio got on the sat phone and passed this information to Rachel.

Around seven thirty, Bret called Irish Bob and gave him the coordinates and directions on how to get to the farmhouse the next morning for the handover. The agreed time for the handover was eight in the morning.

At roughly eight-thirty that night, Rachel called and said that Red's blue Malibu had just gone past my driveway. Sure enough, Bob was scouting out the handover location. Peio's sat phone rang around nine-thirty, it was his sheepherder buddies calling to say that two guys had shown up, looked the area over thoroughly then left. Nobody was left behind. They did say that one of the guys had taken an inordinate interest in a rock formation to the west of the farmhouse. Peio looked at me and I nodded, they were going to put a shooter on the west side, probably on or near my boulder as it was the most likely spot to shoot from. I'd need to be careful while going in, and I would definitely need to find this guy and sort him out before the party started.

Peio showed me the four-wheeler I was going to use to get to the farmhouse. I fired it up to ensure it started, then checked the fuel and fluid levels before pulling it around to the front of his place and loading my gear on it securely. As I did not have any night vision devices, and no experience driving with them anyhow, I'd use the headlight to drive to my jump-off point and hope that getting off a mile away would be sufficient to keep anyone from knowing what I was up to.

After that, there was not much else to do. Peio showed TJ and I to our rooms. I set my alarm for three-thirty and tried to get some sleep.

I slept soundly. When the alarm went off, I rolled out of bed, slipped on my old jeans, Timberline boots, faded Levi's shirt, watch cap, gloves, and my old Carhartt jacket before getting on the four-wheeler and heading off to my boulder. There were plenty of old logging trails in the woods north of Peio's place, but there was no direct route to the farmhouse. I knew the area fairly well, but it still took me about an hour to get to my drop-off point, where I would leave the four-wheeler and walk in. I made it to within 100 yards of the boulder, coming in from the back side. From here on in I went slowly forward, keeping an eye out for Bob's shooter. I made it to the boulder without seeing anyone else, so I climbed the boulder and began setting up my hide on the very top of the rock, facing east toward the farmhouse. Once I had my mat out on the rock, and the rifle resting on its bipod, I took out my ghillie cape and wove some twigs and leaves from the serviceberry bushes that grew on top of the boulder into my cape, to better blend in with the environment. Putting on my cape, I drank half a bottle of water, ate an energy bar, and settled in behind the rifle to wait. It was now just after six in the morning. I dialed in another 4 minutes of angle elevation on my Nightforce optics. This would put me dead on at 400 yards from the 200-yard zero I kept on the rifle.

Not long after I had settled into place, Peio's old Suburban came off the county road and parked behind the farmhouse. Watching through my scope I saw Peio, TJ and Bret get out of the Suburban and haul three full duffle bags and an old camp chair out of the back of the Suburban and into the house. Bret then carried the duffle bags through the house, out the front door and dropped them in a row on the north, or farmhouse side, of the firepit. While at the pit, he grabbed the old drum I had used to sight in on and took it back to the side of the house. Going back into the house, he got the old camp chair and placed it just outside the firepit, behind the duffle bags, facing the firepit.

While I was watching all this through the scope, I heard a rustling and scuffing noise coming from the lower shelf of my boulder, the area that I had earlier thought would also make a fairly nifty hide. Slowly, inching my way to the right, I got to a position where I could look down about 20 feet onto the first shelf, and there was Bob's shooter. He may have been a good shooter, but he wasn't very good at concealment, he just had a mat and was lying on it with no cover at all. His rifle was a Remington 700 Sendero, but I couldn't tell what caliber it was. This is a pretty good rifle, but as always, the quality of the shot largely depends on the shooter. He also had a handheld radio. This was not good; at some point before I started the ball rolling with my first shot toward the firepit, I'd need to pop this guy.

Easing back onto my rifle, I reached over to my pack and eased out my CZ97 from a pocket on the side, and quietly chambered a round before laying it beside the rifle. Getting back on the scope, I just relaxed and waited.

At eight o'clock straight up, a late model silver Dodge Caravan pulled through the gate at the end of the county road and stopped. Bret came out of the house with his hands out to his sides and walked to the old chair and sat down. The Dodge then drove slowly to the opposite side of the firepit and stopped about 15 feet from the pit, at an angle so that it was facing slightly northeast giving me a good view of the entire driver's side of the van. Both front doors, and both sliding side doors opened at the same time, and four guys got out. The two on the passenger's side got out and came around to the front of the van, so did the driver. The fourth guy got out of the sliding door on my side, and just stood there. He would be my second shot.

While the guys at the front of the van were focused on Bret, TJ and Peio came out of the farmhouse, TJ going left on the porch while Peio, with a blanket wrapped around his shoulders to keep off the chill, kept walking toward Bret. The guys at the van perked up, but Peio just kept walking. When he got to Bret, he said something to him, and Bret got up and walked back into the farmhouse. Peio took the seat.

I had studied the photos of Irish Bob that Peio had provided, he was a medium-sized guy with a full head of gray hair, kept short. He was in good shape for a guy who was 60 years old, but his most telling features were paper thin lips which never smiled, and evil green eyes looking out of a craggy face.

Irish Bob and his two guys walked the 15 feet to the firepit opposite of Peio and stopped. One guy on Bob's left, one on his right, and the remaining one standing beside the open driver's side sliding door on the van.

"I thought you were dead," Bob said while looking Peio over.

"I get that a lot these days, Bob. As you can see, it is not so."

"What is your stake in this, Peio?" asked Bob. "Is this your money?"

Peio leaned forward and unzipped each duffle bag revealing nothing but old magazines. "There is no money here, so how can it be mine?"

At this point the handheld radio in Bob's left hand squawked, raising it to his ear he said, "Go ahead." After a second, he put the radio away in his back pocket and told Peio, "That was my guy out in the hills, he says he's in position and has you in his crosshairs."

Once Bob and his guys started walking toward the firepit, I had once again slowly inched to the right until I could look over the edge at Bob's shooter 20 feet below me. This time I had my pistol with me. Once I heard him say, "I am in position and have him in my crosshairs," I shot him in the back twice, and once in the back of the head for good measure. Those explosive .45 rounds really tore him up.

Back at the firepit, Irish Bob had just told Peio that his shooter had him sighted in. When they heard the sound of my three shots, Peio looked at Bob and said, "Not anymore he doesn't."

Back at my boulder, I was scrambling to get back on my rifle, there was no reason to be quiet anymore and things would start to get interesting at the firepit. Back on the rifle, I looked through the scope and saw Peio talking to Bob.

"Why are you involved with this?" Bob asked Peio.

"Because in the first case, you have decided to target friends of mine simply to obtain something that isn't yours. Secondly, you, like your brother, have broken the accepted rule that there is no kidnapping allowed in our business," Peio responded.

"I haven't kidnapped anyone, so that rule has not been breached."

"Technically you are correct, but the reason you did not kidnap Ms. Grier is that I moved her out of reach before you could do so. That being the case, the intent was there. The Council would see it my way, I assure you," explained Peio.

"So that was you who took her. I wondered how it was organized so quick. Another thing, you mentioned my brother breaking the rules. Explain that."

"Do you remember many years ago when your organization in New York was attempting to arrange a deal with the Cosa Nostra? Your brother decided to increase his leverage, similar to the situation we find ourselves in now, and kidnapped the wife of one of the lieutenants in the Cosa Nostra?" Peio asked.

"I remember that well," replied Bob.

"Do you also remember that this man's wife, while being held by your brother, was severely mistreated and abused?"

"It was said that she was, I do not know that to be true."

"Perhaps you can tell me your version of what happened next?" Peio inquired.

"From what I understood, someone in the Cosa Nostra found out where the wife was being held, entered the warehouse where she was at, and singlehandedly killed four men who were guarding her, including my brother."

"Actually, it was five men who were killed that day," corrected Peio.

"And how would you know that, old man?" asked Bob.

"Simple actually, I was the one that killed them, including your shit-headed brother."

It must have been at this point that I pulled the trigger on my rifle. I had sighted in on the guy on Bob's left and put the crosshairs on the top of his left side shirt pocket. When the bullet hit him, he dropped like a puppet whose strings had been cut. Since I was shooting from a higher elevation off of his left shoulder, the bullet would have gone through his heart and lungs killing him instantly. While I was transitioning to the guy by the van, TJ had brought up his Glock in a two-handed grip, and shot the guy on Bob's right twice, once in the center of his chest, and once in his forehead. He dropped instantly to his knees before falling off onto his right shoulder. By this time, I had jacked in a second round, and had gotten the guy by the sliding door of the van in my crosshairs. He was reaching into the van for something when I shot him in the middle of the back. I must have hit his spine as he just laid down half in and half out of the van. I shot him again to make sure that he stayed down. We have a saying in the oilfield, usually relating to equipment, that 'one is none and two is one', it seemed applicable here as well.

Meanwhile, Peio had pulled an old Colt 1911 .45 out from under the blanket and was pointing it right at the middle of Bob's chest, who had frozen with his right hand behind him, reaching for the pistol in his waistband.

"Allow me to finish, Bob. You found out about the cash, taken from that drug house years ago, from the inside man which Jeremiah and Joseph utilized to gain access to the house. What the brothers did not know at the time was that on the day they robbed it, it was the designated bank house, and held roughly several million dollars in small, used, unmarked bills. When they hit the house and saw the cash, they rightly decided that the cash, not the drugs, were the big score. They would not have to sell the drugs to get money, as they now had ready cash.

"Bret was simply the driver. After the event he drove the brothers to a storage facility and dropped them off, he was supposed to be paid for his services the following day. As you know, the brothers were killed the following morning, and the money was never found. It has not been found to this day.

"To put things in perspective, you have committed two unforgiveable offenses in the eyes of the Council. First, you were actively planning on kidnapping, and then murdering, Ms. Grier. Secondly, you were attempting to obtain cash stolen from an operation authorized by the Council and keeping it solely for the benefit of the Craic Crew organization. Essentially you would have been stealing from the Council. Either of these offenses would have put a death warrant on not only your head, but the heads of every single member of the Craic Crew organization."

Peio continued, "But this is not going to happen. Four of your lieutenants are dead here and now. I assume that the remaining three members of the Craic Crew executive staff are in town waiting for you to arrive with the cash. We will deal with them shortly. That leaves only you as a witness to today's event. As you will not be leaving here alive, that should decimate the Craic Crew organization, while allowing the rest of the members, which you never told about this escapade, to remain alive. Do you have anything to say?" finished Peio.

Bob got a sick grin on his face and replied, "Aye, I'll give it to you, old man, you thought of everything except one thing. I have had a man in your town for several days now watching Bret's gym and that auto shop. He noticed a certain blonde woman, and a certain dark-haired woman, seemed to spend a lot of time at the gym, and were friendly with Bret. He decided to tail them one evening after they left the gym and followed to that farm on the road up to this place. Once Bret told me the location of the handover, I thought it a strange coincidence that it was on the same road that went by that farm. I hate coincidences, but I realized that these women must have some value to Bret. I had three of my guys follow us and stop at the entrance to the farm. They are to babysit whoever is there, until our business here is finished. If my boys do not hear from me within the next 15 minutes, they were to grab whoever is at this farm and hold them for leverage. How do you like that, old man?"

Apparently Peio didn't like it at all as he shot Bob three times square in the middle of the chest, using my explosive rounds, and dropped him straight to the ground like the sack of shit he was. I really should patent those rounds as they did a number on old Bob as well. The front of the Dodge Caravan, which was directly behind where Bob had been standing, was now covered in bits and pieces of the now deceased Bob.

Before Bob had even hit the ground, Peio was on his sat phone dialing Rachel and letting her know to expect company. Specifically, the three remaining members of the Craic Crew executive council.

I had no idea as to what had been going on at the firepit as I was busy stripping the dead Craic Crew shooter on my boulder of everything that could identify him and putting it in a bag which he had thoughtfully brought with him containing food, water and spare ammo. I then picked up the bag, along with his rifle, and walked down to the farmhouse. As I got closer Peio, I could see that he was frantically signaling me to hurry. When I got to him, he told me about the remaining bad guys paying a visit to the ranch. TJ and I ran to the back of the farmhouse, jumped in the Suburban and took off fast for home. Peio and Bret stayed to help the sheepherders sanitize the area and figure out what to do with the bodies and the vehicle. This had to be done quickly before anyone happened to show up at the farmhouse.

If we had known the outcome at the ranch, TJ and I would have driven back at a more leisurely pace. Pulling into the top of the driveway, where it breaks through the cut in the hill, into the courtyard, I hit the brakes and slid to a stop. Without looking at TJ I said, "You don't see that every day."

In front of us was a blue late model Malibu parked about 20 feet in front of the porch at a slight angle to the right. About 10 feet to the right of the front bumper was Dog, crouched down staring at the body of Red the Watcher. On the porch, the girls were chatting and drinking coffee. The front door was open, and I could see another body, half in and half out of the front door. We drove up behind the Malibu, got out and walked up the stairs to the porch while keeping a sharp eye on the hound. The girls were still wired and a little in shock, so coffee was probably not a good idea at the moment, but I think everyone was so relieved at the outcome that it really didn't matter at this point.

Rachel, being the clown she is, said, "You're a little late, boys!" Before getting the full story from her and Heather, I borrowed the sat phone, called Peio and told him that everything was cool at the ranch, but we'd need another clean-up crew. He said he would be there in half-an-hour.

Apparently, this is what happened at the ranch. Rachel had received Peio's call letting her know that there were still three bad guys in the wind and that she could expect a visit. Her and Heather immediately gunned up and waited. Sure enough, the blue Malibu showed up and stopped at the top end of the driveway where it breaks into the courtyard through the cut in the hill. Rachel was watching from the side of the front window in the dining room office and told Heather they had company. Rachel ripped off a piece of duct tape from the roll on the desk, went to the front door, opened it and waved to Red and his crew. When she went back inside, and before she closed the door, she put the tape over the latch so that it would not latch back into the strike plate when she closed the door. Heather asked her if she was crazy, but Rachel had a plan. The Malibu drove into the courtyard and parked where we now saw it. Rachel, back at the side of the dining room office window, saw Red and two of his cronies get out of the car, one headed toward the back of the house, going between the barn and the house, while the other spoke to Red, who was leaning against the front of the car, before coming up on the porch in front of the door.

"You can either open the door or I'll kick it in, I'm coming in regardless," he had yelled through the door.

Rachel, who was standing about 10 feet back from the door with the shotgun said, "You'll have to kick it in, I'm not going to open it for you."

Things happened quickly after that. The clown at the front tried to kick in the door, but as it was not latched, he lost his balance and fell into the foyer. Rachel waited until he had gotten to his knees, and started to raise his revolver, before she shot him twice in the chest. Absolutely nobody survives two loads of buckshot in the chest from 10 feet. She made quite a mess of this guy.

While this was going on at the front door, the guy who had gone around back kicked in the back door and started to come through. Heather had crouched down between the wall that separates the kitchen from the pantry and the freezer. She held the Glock G43 which TJ had given her in a nice 'thumbs forward' grip pointing toward the back door. Once the guy kicked in the door and silhouetted himself in the doorway, she pumped three 9mm rounds through his center of mass and cut his strings.

Now while all this was kicking off, the weirdest part of the whole ordeal took place. Red was leaning against the front of the Malibu with his arms across his chest expecting his guys to bring the girls out without any fuss. Once he saw his guy at the front stumble through the front door into the foyer, followed by two shotgun blasts, he jerked upright and was reaching for the pistol in the back of his waistband. What he had failed to notice was this black shadow creeping up on him from his left, where it had lain hidden under the porch. Once Rachel started the dance, Dog launched from the corner of the porch directly at Red. Red must have sensed impending doom as he looked over and saw Dog coming hard and tried to turn and face the threat. Red may have been the fastest man on the planet, but he had no chance against Dog. Dog took three bounds, went airborne and hit Red chest to chest. Dog had turned his head parallel to the ground, and when he hit Red, his lower jaw went around Red's neck under his right ear and his upper jaw went around his neck under his left ear. Now we'll never know for sure what killed Red. Was it the severing of his carotid arteries and jugular veins when Dog crushed his neck with his jaws, or was it the snapped neck when Dog shook him like a rag? I'd vote for the snapped neck simply due to the lack of blood which you'd expect from shredded carotid arteries while the heart was still pumping, but I've been wrong before. At the end of the day, the result was the same.

While Rachel and Heather were telling TJ and I the story of the Battle of El Rancho del Loco Gallos, Bret, Peio, and some of Peio's buddies showed up in a small convoy of three trucks. Once Peio heard the story, he laughed his ass off and gave the girls big hugs and kisses on the cheeks. I think this did a lot to calm them down. Peio then got his guys busy cleaning up the mess and explained that although the shootings, and the death by werewolf, were totally legal, we could not afford for law enforcement to start investigating and discovering the whole story. I gathered up all the weapons which had been used that day and took them to the barn for a cleaning. While I cleaned, lubricated and stowed the various firearms, TJ started fixing grilled cheese sandwiches, which surprised me, and fed the girls, Bret and himself. The girls were doing well, but it would probably take a few days before they got a grip on what had actually happened. Dog, surprisingly, had found a shady spot on the porch and laid down. With all the people around, this was a first. I don't think he wanted Rachel out of his sight. I came down from the barn, grabbed a sandwich and a beer, sat on the couch next to Rachel and waited for her to come down from the adrenaline high.

Peio invited us all up to his house for dinner at seven that evening, then took off with the clean-up crew and Bret to get rid of the bodies and the Malibu. Heather, TJ, Rachel and myself just lounged around the rest of the day until everyone showered up, not together, and got ready for dinner. I drove Rachel and myself up to Peio's, followed by TJ and Heather in his pickup. Unknown to the girls, TJ and I had both tooled back up while they were showering as it just seemed like a good idea to be armed at the moment. When we arrived, it seemed like everyone we knew was there. Nick and Jem, Mrs. Robertson, Bret and Tito were all present and accounted for. Peio must have been cooking since he got back that morning as there were two grills going with brats, burgers, hotdogs and steaks, as well as French fries, onion rings, salads and dips galore.

The beer, wine and the last bottle of Laphroaig, which I happened to find in the gun locker earlier, flowed freely and it was quite a fandango. After everyone had eaten, we all sat around on the back porch and just enjoyed the evening.

I managed to get Peio by himself for a few minutes and made sure that the four-wheeler I had used had been collected, then asked him how much Mrs. Robertson knew about what had occurred earlier in the day. He just smiled and said that she knew the gist of what happened, but nothing about the killings. She just knew that Bret had been in a bind, the guys responsible had shown up from back East, and that we had convinced them to go back where they came from.

After a while, Peio got up and proposed a toast. "Today has been a day to remember and a crossroad in all of our lives. They say that if a man has one true friend in life, that he is a rich man. I count all of you as true friends, so therefore I am a very wealthy man. To true friends, may we forever remain so." Raising his Scotch, he took a sip and we all followed suit with whatever we were drinking. He continued. "Ms. Grier is healthy and ready to return home, the question is, where is home? I have discussed the issue with Bret. I feel that Ms. Grier should come out to Colorado and be one of us, but as you know, Cadillac Springs does not have a library to employ her. I have explained to Bret that if Ms. Grier will join us, that I have just received a windfall of 3.2 million dollars that I would happily donate to a new library, if Ms. Grier would agree to run it. It is imperative that the rest of you harass Bret until he agrees with my wisdom."

TJ and I looked at each other. Was it simply a coincidence that Peio had just come into a windfall of exactly the amount that Jeremiah and Joseph had stolen? Doubtful.

Later on, making some excuse to the others, TJ and I got Peio off by himself and asked him about the windfall. Chuckling, he told us that he had lied to Bob before he shot him. True, the money had essentially disappeared after Bret dropped off Jeremiah and Joseph at the storage units. Unknown to anyone else, they had put it in a storage locker at the Philly bus station on Filbert Street and mailed the key to Peio. The hit on the drug house had been sanctioned by Peio as the group dealing out of the house needed some discipline for various business infractions they had committed, that is, skimming off profits. The fact that on the night of the heist, the house was being used as the 'bank', was never mentioned to Peio when he was sanctioning the reprimand, as a result the cash was never part of the plan. Once Jeremiah and Jacob were killed, the money essentially disappeared. Peio also told us that once he had laundered the money, he had invested it in several ventures which had paid off handsomely, and that the true value was closer to fifteen million in today's dollars. Peio didn't need the money and really wanted to forget the whole mess, so what better way to spend the money than to build a library for Alyshia to manage? This would kill several birds with one stone. It would get Alyshia and Bret back together, it would get Alyshia out of Philly and that environment, it would give Cadillac Springs a decent library, and it would give the girls another female member in this male dominated club.

How do you argue with that logic? I think Peio may have been getting civilized in his later years, and I think Mrs. Robertson may have something to do with it.

Later in the evening the ones capable of driving bid Peio goodnight, while the rest stayed at Peio's until the morning while they sobered up. Personally, I was looking forward to getting randy with Rachel as our fooling around had been detrimentally affected by the recent situation, and I felt I needed the practice. I expressed this desire to Rachel and reminded her that I had a Little Bo Peep rain check I needed to cash. Rachel, with a glint in her eye, told me that she was feeling a bit randy herself, and that the Little Bo Peep outfit was 'surplus to requirements'. Life was looking up again!

CHAPTER 27

DURING THE NEXT WEEK, EVERYONE seemed to settle back into their old routines. TJ and Rachel would go to work at the shop, Heather and Rachel got back into the boxing and yoga routine, Tito controlled the Latino gangs in the area, Bret and Nick ran the gym, and Peio seemed to be spending an inordinate amount of time with Mrs. Robertson, you would even see them in town having lunch. I did essentially nothing.

My old truck was still undergoing secret treatment at the shop, so the only thing constructive which I could do was prepare for the next hitch in Kurdistan. I checked my untraceable e-mail account, nothing there. I went out and bought the required toiletries for a month, and I packed my bags.

Twelve days after the 'big event', Rachel drove me to the airport in Glenwood Springs, and once again I headed off for Erbil. Once in my office I read the handover notes which Nolan had left me and found out that both rigs had tested their respective wells and were presently involved in 'plug & abandonment' operations. This meant that during this hitch I'd have to get both rigs moved to their new locations and spud two new wells. It should be an easy hitch.

Calling over to Colonel Sivan's office I made an appointment to discuss the security arrangements for both rig moves, for the afternoon. Arriving at the front gate I again presented my Kurdish work permit card, complete with photo, to the young guard with the Kalashnikov AKS-74U Krinkov. He once again studied the card, then opened the gate and let me walk to the front door and go inside. Just inside the front door was a desk with another similarly armed guard, although a bit older, who again took my work permit, looked at it, picked up his phone and called someone. After a short discussion in Kurdish, he pointed to the stairs behind him and up I went.

If that sounded like a familiar routine, it was, and it was welcome after my previous hitch and the whole Belarus Consulate fiasco. The routine indicated, to me at least, that the colonel and I were back to our old relationship and there were no hard feelings about my previous moonlighting for the Jankowski Group.

Knocking on Colonel Sivan's door, I was told to come in. I did and found Sivan reclined back in her office chair chuckling.

"It is good to see you again, Jeb. You have a confused look on your face, like you expected to be arrested when you came in my office. Do you have a guilty conscience?"

"With the illustrious Asayish, guilt may or may not be an issue when you are arrested," I replied with a grin.

"Not true, and you know it. What can I do for you today?"

"Two things. First, we need to discuss the security arrangements for the two upcoming rig moves. Second, you could go to dinner with me tonight and leave Colonel Nebez at home."

"I have already made the security arrangements based on the previous rig moves. You can review them at your convenience and adjust as necessary. As to your second request, I could accompany you to dinner, without my husband, but I guarantee you that your fear of being arrested would be realized before we finished the starters. I suggest we invite Nebez."

"Okay, I bow to your superior knowledge of such matters. How does seven o'clock at Shakespeare and Company sound?" I asked.

"Perfect," she purred. Female colonels in the Asayish purr when they feel like it, usually before they pounce on some unsuspecting victim, but occasionally when they are being invited to a top-notch restaurant for dinner.

I asked her to e-mail me the security plan, said goodbye, and headed back to my office. The dinner that evening was relaxing and fun, the two colonels are great dinner companions when they aren't busting your balls.

The remainder of the hitch went without a hitch. The rigs got moved without any issues, and the wells were spudded and drilling ahead before it was time for me to go home.

EPILOGUE

RACHEL PICKED ME UP AT the airport as usual, dressed in a jean miniskirt and a tube top. You would think that by now she would realize that after I had spent a month in Kurdistan, that this would qualify as fairly dangerous attire. After the required kiss, performed with much grabbing of butts, we got on the road and back to the ranch. When I asked what was for dinner, I was told, frozen pizza. Which is code, in case you have forgotten, for 'dinner can wait, let's get naked', so we did and ate pizza later, at a more appropriate time.

The next day I went to work with Rachel as she told me my 1956 Ford F-100 was finally finished, and that her and TJ wanted to unveil it. Getting to the shop I shook hands with TJ, real men do not bump fists, and then went to look at my truck which should have been in the second bay but wasn't. Rachel then blindfolded me, which outside the bedroom I never allow her to do, and guided me out to the paint booth. Once inside she asked if I was ready, then removed the blindfold.

There in front of me was the most beautiful truck I had ever seen. They had painted it a dark metallic green, so dark that in the shade it looked black, but in the sun, it shown dark green. They had also cut four lines of louvers into the hood, a line of fifteen louvers left and right of the centerline of the hood, and a line of seven just outboard of these lines. All four lines were centered on the hood. To accent the paint, they had added real, painted-on pinstriping in lime green, not so much as to be gaudy, but just enough. Also, the raised lip on each louver had a narrow, lime green lip, this was copied on the original vent louvers just forward of each door. They had also replaced just about everything else underneath. The differential was a Ford 9 inch by DiffWorks at 3.73:1. I still had my four-link rear suspension by Heidts Products, but my brakes had been canned in favor of Baer Extreme Plus, six-piston calipers with 14-inch cross drilled rotors on each corner, powered by a Corvette C6 master cylinder. The front and rear shocks were now coil-overs, the whole front suspension had been replaced with a Corvette C5 subframe and the steering was now performed by a Corvette rack and pinion system.

My brand new Cragar Black 'D' Window Steel wheels had been thrown out and replaced with Foose custom 19" x 10" fronts and 20" x 10" rears. The front wheels wore Pirelli 255/40/ZR19 rubber while the back wheels wore Pirelli 285/30/ZR20 rubber. Rachel did not get to the top of her game for no reason, she was lightyears ahead of me.

It was simply the prettiest, coolest truck I had ever seen. I really didn't know what to say so I reached over and gave Rachel a hug and a kiss. When I reached for TJ, he told me if I kissed him, he would shoot me. I asked them if I could take it home. They said I could, as long as I kept my foot out of it until I'd run the engine in. When I fired it up, I could tell that they had also put in custom headers and dual exhausts, it simply gurgled like a brook until you put your foot down, then it was a throbbing howl. I was in heaven. I told them that I'd see them at home, and that for doing this for me I would gladly barbeque this evening, and for them to drag Heather with them after the boxing session.

I drove my new toy over to the Safeway and bought barbeque makings, but when I went to put the bags in the back, I saw that they had also redone the wood bed with mahogany wood slates with stainless steel runners. I had to go back into Safeway to get some old cardboard boxes to put under the makings. No way I wanted to damage the wood.

I finally got home, slowly, and put my new truck to bed in the barn. I then went to the house and got the grill ready to light, and the burgers prepared and laid out with the brats. The buns were laid out on the island ready to warm up, and I chopped up onion and tomato for those who wanted it. I ripped the lettuce by hand before putting all the veggies back in the fridge. I had also bought three cases of Coors. If you remember we had forsaken beer while we dealt with the boys from Philly, but tonight was sort of a celebration of life and new pickup trucks, so beer was in order. I put four six-packs in the fridge to chill.

TJ showed up after work, which is the first time I'd seen his 1950 Chevy pickup since I'd come back from Kurdistan. He'd painted his truck as well. It was now a dark charcoal gray with black trim and yellow pinstriping. It looked good, but not as good as mine, in my humble opinion. He was still running that 5-liter Coyote motor, so he could definitely back up the looks. Jerk.

We sat on the porch sipping beer while waiting for the girls, when TJ brought up the question of whose truck was quicker. I told him that there was only one way to find out and that was head-to-head, in the quarter mile. He asked what the bet would be, and I said, simply the bragging rights as to the quickest pickup. I suggested that after I had run mine in, in about 2 weeks, that we announce that we were going to race, and make a party out of it. I'd sort out the venue, we'd invite our entire crew, then have a party back at the ranch afterwards. TJ grinned and said I was on.

The girls finally showed up, so I got the meat on the grill then handed the spatula to TJ as I took Heather up to the barn to show off my new truck. She made all the right noises required when some guy shows off his new ride, then said she was hungry and needed food. For girls, food is apparently more important than hotrod trucks. Figure that one out.

Getting back to the porch, TJ passed the spatula back to me as he still didn't know what it was for, and I proceeded to flip burgers and brats and take them inside as they were finished. Once everyone had eaten their fill, I grabbed a plate and made two brat buns and two cheeseburgers, grabbed a beer and joined everyone on the porch.

TJ had told them about the proposed race cum party, and the girls were instantly in planning mode and chattering like squirrels. It was nice to be back home, and nicer not having to worry about Belarusian diplomats or Philadelphian gangsters. Around nine, after everyone helped clean up the mess, TJ and Heather retired to the bunkhouse, while Rachel and I watched some TV before going upstairs to make up for some lost time.

The next day I stayed at home for two reasons. First, I had to find at least a slightly legal venue to hold the drag race and second, I needed to research and see what else I could do to my motor to ensure that I won.

I could not find an old airfield runway suitable. The only one around was the Flying Dog Ranch strip, but it was only just over 300 yards long. I suppose I could have found a suitable stretch of public road, but that had the potential of getting us in trouble with Jake the sheriff. I finally called an oilfield buddy of mine up in Rangely, who happened to be married into the family which were part owners of the Western Colorado Dragway in Grand Junction. I explained what I needed, and he said he'd get back to me in an hour.

On the second issue, ensuring I smoked TJ, I couldn't think of any mechanical advantage I could give myself which did not entail an engine rebuild that I did not have time for. His fuel injection and automatic transmission would give him an edge, so I'd just have to race smarter and ensure that I was properly tuned up for whatever altitude we were racing at.

My oilfield friend called back and told me that we could run at the strip in Grand Junction on any given Friday morning, Friday nights were dedicated to the Street Program, but we would have to 'rent' the strip safety people, equipment and so forth due to insurance concerns. I got the price for renting the safety people and equipment and agreed to do it. I set the date for a week from this Friday at eleven in the morning. I then asked what altitude the track was, and he told me 4996.7 feet officially. I'd need to reset the timing at the track as my ranch was at roughly 6600 feet. Now I needed to run the truck in properly before Friday.

Driving the new, improved 1956 F-100 into town, I stopped by the shop to tell Rachel and TJ the plan and have them tell everyone else. I also told them I couldn't do any lunch runs since I needed to run the truck in before Friday. That done, I drove out of town toward Glenwood Springs until I hit I-70. For the rest of that day, and Wednesday and Thursday, I drove back and forth from Glenwood Springs to Palisade, running at various speeds and various rpms, until I had a few hundred miles on the engine, roughly ten trips between the towns. Thursday night I installed a tachometer to the driver's side windshield pillar and set the redline at 5000 rpm. I then checked the spark plug gaps and the dwell. All I could do now was pray.

Meantime, the girls had prepared coolers of food, snacks and drinks, and it was a party atmosphere at the ranch. I couldn't see where TJ was doing anything to his truck, and he didn't seem worried in the least. Jerk.

I had to pull Rachel aside and ask her who had installed my Edelbrock 7166 carb and intake manifold. If TJ did the installation, it may be sabotaged. All is fair in drag racing. She pulled me close and whispered that I shouldn't worry, she'd installed it, set it up and it was good to go. Okay, I loved her for a variety of reasons, but you have to admit that not many girls will install and set up your four-barrel carburetor so that you can kick her employee's butt in the quarter mile.

Friday morning, we were all up at six to get on the road by six-thirty. Breakfast consisted of coffee and Pop Tarts. Hearing engines pulling into the courtyard I looked out the front door and there was Bret in his 1966 Impala SS with a really good-looking Caribbean looking lady. I hadn't had a chance to see Bret since I'd been home, but Rachel told me that Alyshia had come out to visit. Alyshia was a stunner. She wore her hair in a long and loose island hairstyle, which I found attractive, and was more a curvy type, like Heather, as opposed to a sort of well-developed racing snake like Rachel and her protégé Jem. Her glasses fit the librarian motif, the strapless, silky looking mid-thigh sundress and sandals did not. What a package!

Next came Tito in his 1968 Fleetwood, Nicholas and Jem in his 1970 Cadillac Coupe Deville, and finally Peio and Mrs. Robertson in his old Suburban. It looked like the party was on, so we all got on the road to Grand Junction. We convoyed through New Castle, Parachute and De Beque until we arrived in Grand Junction around nine o'clock. Cutting southeast on Highway 50 we drove until we hit Highway 141 and took it to the entrance of the dragstrip.

TJ and I pulled up to the Christmas Tree at the start line and shut down. Everyone else parked behind the start line and started getting out beach umbrellas, lounge chairs and coolers of everything required for a hot morning at the track. I got out my timing light, tools, and my notebook, then set my timing for 5000 feet and readjusted my carb. After doing this, I went and got a cup of coffee from Rachel, and some donuts from Nick and Jem. Since I had not met Alyshia yet, I strolled over to where her and Bret were hanging out in lounge chairs under a huge umbrella, drinking some sort of health drinks and chatting. When I came up to them, Bret and Alyshia both got to their feet and Bret properly introduced us. If Alyshia was smoking hot looking from the vantage point on my porch, she was on-fire up close. Bret was a lucky guy. It was well worth smoking the Craic Crew to get Alyshia out here. I asked her how she liked Cadillac Springs. She said it would take her awhile to get used to not being in a city, but it was growing on her. I then asked if she'd given any thought to starting a library in town? She replied that she was discussing that with Mr. Peio, but then got a big smile, and said she'd love to do it. I told her it was there for the taking, but keep in mind that she'd be in close proximity to a reprobate gym owner that we both knew well, which was a definite downside to the offer. Bret looked at Alyshia and said something like, 'even out here in the sticks you get assholes', which I thought was a bit rude.

Around that time, the safety crew rolled up and it was time to get down to business. They were professional and inspected just about every nut and bolt on the trucks. They said they'd be ready in about half-an-hour, once they got the Christmas Tree up and running. They didn't need to worry about the speed trap at the other end as this was not for time, just for the win.

Eventually we were told that the track was ready to go. Bret drove Rachel, Heather, Jem and Alyshia down to the finish line in his Impala to set up their cameras, while Peio, Tito and Mrs. Robertson sat back under their umbrellas to watch the festivities and provide adult supervision from the comfort of their lounge chairs at the start line. The track boss had us suit up in fire resistant coveralls and gloves, and had us put on full-face helmets sans visors. This was starting to get real. He then explained how the Christmas Tree worked before telling us to get in and start our engines.

TJ and I inched the trucks up through the stage lights until we were 7 inches from the start line, and both the top and the bottom of the blue circle were illuminated. As this was a standard tree, the three yellow lights illuminated top to bottom with a half-second delay between lights, with another half-second delay before the green light, or go-light, illuminated. On the first attempt to start, I jumped the green light and false started, which meant we had to do the whole staging thing again. The second attempt had TJ false starting. I think we both had a case of nerves as we both wanted those bragging rights. Getting staged up for the third time, we both had calmed down a bit, and when the yellow lights started 'dropping' we throttled up to launch rpm's and when the green light lit, we were off.

TJ had an automatic transmission and was from that Coonass school of drag racing, which dictated that you instantly cram the gas pedal to the floor and hold it there until you cross the finish line. I, on the other hand, being old school, with a manual transmission, rode the clutch for a fraction of a second to make sure that I didn't lose traction. My strategy then was to keep my foot to the floor and shift at 5000 rpm until I ran out of gears.

TJ broke traction right at the start, and the rear end of his truck slithered a bit to the left. Since I rode my clutch for an instant, I didn't break traction, and pulled away nicely. At 5000 rpm I slammed that Muncie gearbox into second and kept my foot down. The problem was, when I clutched to shift gears, TJ gained on me as he was well into 'foot-to-the-floor' Coonass mode and didn't need to clutch. I was still a few lengths ahead when I hit third gear, but I had lost some more ground during the shift. Hitting fourth, TJ was at my tailgate and howling up beside me.

As we crossed the finish line, his grill was just behind the level of my cab. I won by half a length.

TJ flipped me the bird as we rolled out in the cool down area after the speed trap. Crossing over at the end, I came back down his lane, and he came back down mine. The girls were jumping up and down, celebrating just like they did back in my high school days. It brought back fond memories. I got out of my truck and Rachel jumped in my arms and gave me a big smooch. Heather did the same thing to TJ, but I didn't know why. Didn't she realize that he was a loser at this point? TJ came over and shook my hand with a big grin on his face. He told me if the race would have gone another 50 yards, that he would have won. "True enough," I said, "but a quarter mile is 440 yards, not 490." I then admitted to him that if he hadn't broken traction at the start, he would have had me. But that was the difference between a mature, seasoned drag racer and a Coonass wannabe. He flipped me the bird again, definitely a sore loser.

After driving back to the finish line and packing up everyone and everything, we drove back to the starting line, parked and had a little party. I gave the safety crew a check for their services, and eventually we packed everything up and convoyed back to the ranch, where the real party started.

I parked the 1956 Ford in its place of honor in the barn, then walked down to the porch to get the grill fired up. The girls, Heather, Rachel and now Jem and Alyshia, had gone into the kitchen to get the meat ready for the grill as well as all the fixings. Mrs. Robertson took one look at what they were doing and kicked them out of the kitchen saying that they had no clue as to how to properly prepare brats and burgers. Apparently, we had been doing it wrong for years. Brats were supposed to be poked with a fork then soaked in a mixture of beer and diced onion for an hour before putting them on the fire. The ground beef for the burgers was supposed to have the correct amount of black pepper, salt and bread crumbs kneaded in to them prior to cooking. Who knew?

The boys were all parked off on the porch drinking beer and telling lies. I remembered that I had just made a faux pas, trotted up to the barn and grabbed a bottle out of the case of Laphroaig, which I had remembered to order earlier in the week. Taking it to the kitchen I poured a glass each for Mrs. Robertson, Tito and Peio, and handed them out. Mrs. Robertson, still busy in the kitchen, told me I was an angel. I told her to be sure to mention that to Rachel as often as possible.

The meat was finally deemed properly prepared by Mrs. Robertson, so I took it out to the grill and got busy cooking it. Eventually the crew lined up and I served everybody before serving myself and handing the spatula to TJ, who still had no idea what it was for.

It was quite an end to a summer of adventures. Peio, Tito and Mrs. Robertson were settled comfortably in the living room just chatting away while eating, and drinking my Laphroaig, while the rest of us were out on the front porch just catching up on things. Alyshia had the girls enthralled with stories of her Anguilla vacation, while Nick, TJ, Bret and myself just sat around drinking beer, ogling the girls, and comparing the relative attributes of each.

Around nine, everyone paid homage to me, the King of the Quarter Mile, while heckling TJ for coming in second and being the 'first loser'. Eventually everyone started making their way back to their respective homes, or wherever they were bunking that evening.

Rachel and I finished cleaning up the place and finally called it a night around ten thirty. You may be interested in knowing that I finally cashed in that Little Bo Peep rain check that evening.

CPSIA information can be obtained
at www.ICGtesting.com
Printed in the USA
LVHW091647271021
701710LV00005B/947

9 781914 965081